STARGATE

"Dial us home, Carter. Now."

Daniel stepped to the edge of the platform. "Jack, what's going on?"

"We're gating out of here, that's what." Jack rushed over to the DHD. "We'll head to the Alpha site."

"Wait a minute!" Daniel ran down the platform steps. Sam and Teal'c followed close behind. "Don't we want to figure out where 'here' is, first?"

"Not really, no." Jack jabbed a finger in the air. "Someone's playing games with us and I'm not in the mood."

Someone needed to calm their normally fearless leader fast.

Fortunately, Teal'c took the fall. "O'Neill, have you any memory of—?"

"Nada. Bupkiss." Jack's voice lowered.

"Me, either," said Daniel.

"The last thing I remember was..." Sam frowned. "Well, that's odd."

"Carter?"

"Sir, I remember who I am." She gestured at Jack, then Daniel and Teal'c. "I remember all of you, but—"

"Yeah, I'm having trouble, too," Daniel said. "My long-term memory's fine, but short-term's—"

"Gone," Jack whispered.

STARGATE SG·1™

THE DRIFT

DIANA DRU BOTSFORD

FANDEMONIUM BOOKS

An original publication of Fandemonium Ltd, produced under license from MGM Consumer Products.

Fandemonium Books, PO Box 795A, Surbiton, Surrey KT5 8YB, United Kingdom

Visit our website: www.stargatenovels.com

STARGATE SG·1™

METRO-GOLDWYN-MAYER Presents
RICHARD DEAN ANDERSON
in
STARGATE SG-1™
AMANDA TAPPING CHRISTOPHER JUDGE
and MICHAEL SHANKS as Daniel Jackson
Executive Producers ROBERT C. COOPER BRAD WRIGHT
MICHAEL GREENBURG RICHARD DEAN ANDERSON
Developed for Television by BRAD WRIGHT & JONATHAN GLASSNER

WWW.MGM.COM

ISBN: 978-1-905586-60-8 Printed in the USA

For Merlin,
Sleep well in Elysium, old friend.

To be in hell is to drift;
to be in heaven is to steer.
— George Bernard Shaw

Author's note:
This story takes place shortly after
season eight's "Avatar."

PRELUDE

PLANET DESIGNATION: UNKNOWN
STATUS: UNKNOWN
TIME: UNKNOWN... UNKNOWN... UNKNOWN...

HE STUMBLED across darkness, through a rippling pool, and out onto…

Where the hell was he?

Blazing white sunlight forced his eyes shut. That begged a larger question.

Oh, for crying out loud. Who the hell was he?

For the life of him, he couldn't remember his name.

He felt warmth. Clean air. Complete stillness. No sounds of animals or civilization, just lapping water right behind him. He opened his eyes. Took note of the grayish stone platform beneath his feet. He turned around, coming face-to-face with a vertical stone ring at least three times his height. The ring loomed over him, its center filled with a bluish watery puddle.

He found the massive thing familiar. Almost comforting in an odd sort of way.

As if he and the ring were old friends.

How he'd managed to go through it without getting wet didn't bother him, not as much as the not knowing… anything.

A ring filled with water?

That made no sense. None. Zip.

If this stone monstrosity was his pal, then why all the red V-shaped lights around its outer edge? He counted seven but, for all he knew, there might be more underneath the platform. Were the lights the ring's way of saying hello?

Chevrons. Okay, sure. Now he'd figured that out, what about the rest? Something niggled at him. Something about survival tactics. Learn as much about the environment before deciding on a course of action. It was the right thing to do, though he'd no clue how he'd learned that little chestnut.

He took a good, hard look around. Fern-covered hills stretched out in every direction. No buildings, no people, no nothing. The platform was on top of a hill with a widening set of eight steps leading down to the ground. A few feet beyond stood a pedestal with a canted circular top.

That pedestal… Was that his ticket home?

Edging closer to the wall of water, he considered returning the way he came. Maybe, the answers were back there. Wherever 'there' was. He took a step, raised an arm to go through.

A blast of heat pushed him away from the ring. When he stopped, the wind subsided. He tried again, only to be blocked by yet another warm gust.

He stepped back, and the air stilled once more.

Okay, something wanted him to stay put. He could do that. Squinting up at the bright blue sky, he briefly wished for a pair of sunglasses.

Sunglasses. There was something familiar about wearing sunglasses. Going through the ring and seeing…

"Nope. I got nothing." With a sigh, he sank down on the top step, his back to the shimmering water ring. If he could only remember.

Remember what?

A wisp of air ruffled against his neck. More a breeze than an outright gust. With it came memories of sounds. Gun shots. Screams. Then, flashes of sensation. Stepping through another wall of water as the ground rumbled. Lost friends.

Failure.

He ransacked his memories, determined to match sounds to feelings. A single gunshot. A woman's cry. A child's blood. Guilt so thick that his throat swelled shut.

He swallowed hard, pushing away shades of things he couldn't remember.

Wasn't sure he wanted to remember.

The breeze returned. This time cooler, almost comforting. His mind settled, allowing a memory to surface. No, not a memory. More like an urge, a pressing need. There was something important he needed to do. Somewhere important he needed to be. Important people he was supposed to…

Protect?

He shook his head — pretty sure that wasn't the case. Sweat dripped down his back. The frustration, the sun, the heat, it was all getting to him. Maybe he couldn't remember who he was, but he could certainly get more comfortable. Take off a few layers before he boiled to death.

He reached up to unzip his vest and jacket. He stopped. Not because he recalled wearing a vest and jacket at some point, but because now… Now he wore a fleece pullover. That was wrong, this much he knew.

Putting a hand to his head, he discovered a wool watch cap. He tore it off. Standard black-issue, no insignia. He glanced down at his get-up: a black tee, green fleece pullover, black fleece trousers. Heavy black boots, but with thicker, more rubbery soles than normal. Whatever 'normal' meant.

"In this heat?" He peered upwards. A sun far whiter and much larger than Earth's peered back.

Sunlight. Warmth. Earth…

Earth. He needed to protect Earth.

No. He'd done that already. At least a half dozen times, but from whom?

He clenched his fists, frustrated at the games his mind played. He should be able to remember. He should know. The breeze blew across his neck again. Cooler this time. Soothing.

Like a long-lost friend.

Something shifted. A small weight appeared in his left fist. He unfurled his fingers, revealing a rectangular block of dull metal in his palm. A hinge along one side allowed the top to open and shut. He pried it open, the recognizable clink stirring yet another memory just out of reach. He spun the wheel inside the block. A flame ignited.

A smile tugged at his mouth. There were good memories tied to this… This Zippo. Really good memories, but he couldn't reach them. Instead, he felt the heavy weight of expectation.

With plenty of self-doubt to go with it.

He snapped the lighter shut and glanced over at the pedestal again. This was ridiculous. Why couldn't he remember the way home? The pedestal was the key, but as much as he tried to squeeze the answer from his muddled mind, it wouldn't come.

And that royally pissed him off.

Behind him, a familiar *thwap* hit the vertical puddle, and then a whoosh. Boots scuffled on stone.

He clenched the Zippo in his fist and turned around. A familiar face peered at him from behind a pair of glasses.

"Sir, are you all right?" Another person. A blonde woman. He recognized her. Knew her. Wished he could say her name —

"O'Neill!" A third person. Tall. Dark. Someone whose strength he'd valued. Hell, admired was more like it.

A moment's dizziness overcame him and then…

The fog lifted.

He knew the people before him as well as he knew the back of his own hand. Daniel Jackson, Lt. Colonel Samantha Carter, and Teal'c stood beneath the shadow of the now dormant Stargate. Each of them gazed at him expectantly. All three wore the same green fleece pullovers, black pants, watch cap, and thick boots.

General Jack O'Neill remembered everything. Everything except how he'd ended up God knows where, unarmed, and with Skaara's lighter. He knew he'd stuffed it inside his locker back at the SGC.

The damn planet was driving him nuts.

With a curt nod to his second-in-command, he stormed toward the DHD. It was time to get the hell off this rock.

"Dial us home, Carter. Now."

CHAPTER ONE

Ten hours earlier...

EARTH—66th PARALLEL SOUTH
ENROUTE VIA USAF GLOBEMASTER C-17
18 AUG 04/0500 HRS MCMURDO STATION
17 AUG 04/1300 HRS STARGATE COMMAND

GENERAL'S choice had allowed Jack to pick a seat far aft, far away from the onboard gaggle of dozing civilians and military. Unable to sleep, he yanked out a handful of deceptively innocuous folders from his briefcase.

Pens and pencils.

Forms and folders.

Pulling out the various things he'd need to do his job, it became apparent just how much his life had changed since being promoted. A general's arsenal wasn't made up of P90s, 9mm revolvers, or tidy little packages of C-4.

Nope.

A general's arsenal was a briefcase stuffed with enough mind-numbing crap to make a Goa'uld wither in surrender.

That is, except for the casualty reports.

He shoved the briefcase under his jump seat and resigned himself to the work that went with the pay grade. Glancing at his watch, he did the math. If local time was sixteen hours ahead of the SGC, that made it 0500 hours. A little less than three hours to kill before McChord AFB's 728th Airlift Squadron landed this tub of a C-17 transport. Three hours to read through the latest round of losses thanks to Ba'al's super-soldiers, sign-off on a boatload of transfer requests and requisitions, and then try to join the others in taking a nap.

Perchance to dream?

Not likely.

Perchance to remember?

Apparently, that was even less likely. Memories could be such pains in the ass. Uncooperative, sneaky little bastards that stayed under wraps even when needed.

The aircraft jolted sideways and then settled back down. In addition to the gaggle of military personnel, a dozen scientists dozed off in seats lining the cabin walls. Waist-high supply pallets took up the cavernous interior's middle.

Jack peered out the small window. At an altitude of 45,000 feet, he didn't even bother to try and make out the Southern Ocean down below.

He closed his eyes, trying to make sense of the one thing he couldn't quite grasp. It wasn't a physical memory he sought, more like tapping into a feeling. One he wasn't keen on revisiting.

The C-17 shuddered again.

And again settled down.

Silently cursing the invisible wind pocket, and the hole in his memory, Jack resigned himself to busy work. Was he getting old? Was that why he couldn't remember?

Thor had been wrong. Plain and simple. Sure, he mostly recalled what had happened when the Ancient Repository stampeded through his brain, but there was a gap. A hole that his Asgard buddy hadn't accounted for when Jack was revived. A black hole even Carter couldn't help fill.

If he'd told her. Which he hadn't.

The truth was, he hadn't told anyone. Not even General Hammond, who was counting on him.

Big mistake.

He glanced at his folders and groaned. Of course, the casualty report was on top, listing far too many names under his command. Hell, one name was one too many.

Before forcing himself to open the damn file, Jack took a

moment to double-check on three people who happily weren't on that god-forsaken list. Three names that could have been at the top if things had gone differently the past few months…

Directly across, Carter slumped in her jump seat. Eyes squeezed shut, she had a pair of orange rubber earplugs wedged in against the whine of the C-17's turbines. Jack was willing to bet dollars to donuts that sleep didn't come easy for her these days. Not since her recent reunion with Fifth. That demon-spawn human replicator and his infamous hand-in-the-head trick was enough to keep anyone from catching forty winks.

She wouldn't talk about it, but then Jack wasn't big on the sharing front either so who was he to judge? That didn't mean he was blind. She smiled less. A lot less. Hopefully, time spent fiddling with the weapons platform would be a decent distraction.

Daniel sprawled out on a pallet between them, clearly in the land of Nod. A book was split open and plastered on his face. Jack winced, knowing he still owed Carter an apology for biting her head off when Daniel went missing during Tegalus's zealot-ridden civil war. It had taken a month to get Daniel back. A month that made Jack question yet again if he really could fill General Hammond's sizeable and shiny shoes.

The last on Jack's list of near-losses was Teal'c, feigning sleep on a jump seat to Carter's left. Or maybe he was kelno'reeming, if he even did that anymore now that Junior was out of the picture. Ramrod straight. Eyes barely closed. None the worse for wear after a near no-exit scenario from that alien virtual-reality gizmo chair.

Speaking of…

Jack had a training mission to prepare.

Which was a bit of a problem. Sure, he remembered sitting in the Ancient weapons chair. A moment's frustration at how the thing was too short in the leg-room department. The gummy feel of those gel packs. The chair back radiating enough heat to warm his six. The sound of gunfire. Laser shots. Carter shouting for him to do something, and then—

The plane pitched right. Not enough to wake anyone up, but Jack gave up on the tour down memory lane. It wasn't just that he couldn't remember how to use the damn chair. He didn't want to. He didn't want to think about losing control. Not knowing what needed to be done. Sitting on the sidelines while a rickety-old device grabbed his brain and did the job for him.

Enough. Once they landed in Antarctica, it would all come back to him.

Or not.

He flipped open the casualty report, determined to make every name an indelible mark in his head. In the greater balance of what mattered most, he wasn't sure which ranked higher — remembering how to use the one weapon which could protect the planet…

Or remembering the men and women who'd fallen in doing so.

PEGASUS ICE RUNWAY
ROSS ISLAND, ANTARCTICA
18 AUG 04/0750 HRS MCMURDO STATION

Daniel peered out the window as the C-17 descended into blackness. Down below, a narrow band of lights outlined the runway. The illuminated pathway twinkled in assurance like miniature red and blue lighthouses, a guarantee to pilots that yes, landing a heavily loaded plane on a 110-foot thick glaciated ice shelf was no different than landing on asphalt. Ice that could be months or centuries old.

A slight thud, a momentary jostle, and they landed. Daniel leaned right to counter the plane's forward momentum as it rolled across the snow-covered ice tarmac. Across the plane, Sam and Teal'c did likewise, their black-cap clad heads bent sideways in unison.

"Piece of cake," Jack said, his eyes stayed fixed on the open folder on his lap. He'd done paperwork all night, a very un-Jack-like behavior even with his recent promotion to general and SGC commander.

As the plane slowed down, Daniel grabbed his backpack from beneath his seat and stuffed in his hardbound copy of the *Antarctica Treaty.* "I'm guessing the pilots do this sort of thing all the time… Flying into Antarctica when it's dark."

"I meant the negotiations, not the landing. You'll do fine."

Daniel winced. "Thanks, but after Tegalus — "

"Back on the horse, Daniel." Jack lowered his voice. "We talked about this."

They had, repeatedly. And even though Daniel knew Tegalus had been on the brink of civil war — with or without SG-1's arrival through the gate inspiring the Caledonian Federation to take action — he still hated the idea that he had failed to get the two sides to find common ground. "Look, I don't think I'm — "

"Just give the diplomats a tour." Jack slapped the folder shut. "Ply them with your charm and wit, tell them to back off on their demands, and in an hour they'll be gone. Then you and Teal'c can play around the outpost to your heart's content, Carter will kick-start the chair back up with those naquadah generators, and I'll — "

"It's not going to be that easy."

"Just get it done."

"But — "

"Daniel, let it go."

The plane came to a halt at the end of the 10,000 foot long runway. "*Welcome to the bottom of the world, ladies and gentlemen,*" the pilot spoke over the intercom. "*It's a balmy minus forty-five outside. Enjoy your stay.*"

Whoops and hollers broke out amongst the Operation Deep Freeze scientists. While Sam was all grins, clearly thrilled by her upcoming work at the outpost, Teal'c barely mustered a raised eyebrow.

"Not exactly Chulak, is it?" Daniel asked.

"Indeed." Teal'c had hoped to visit his home while everyone else headed south, but Jack had squashed that request, insisting the big guy join them at the outpost.

What was Jack up to? On an almost daily basis, he'd gone out of his way to spend time with each of them. Ever since Teal'c's mishap with the virtual reality chair.

Actually, even before that.

Now that Daniel thought about it, not a day had gone by since the Tegalus fiasco where Jack didn't join them for a meal or stop by either Daniel's or Sam's lab to chat.

The tail ramp opened and a bone-chilling gust welcomed them to Antarctica. Daniel swung up the fur-lined hood of his black USAF extreme weather parka. The scientists followed suit, their bright red parkas marking them as civilians. Although Sam and Teal'c had done the same, Jack predictably opted to keep to the minimum — his black watch cap his only cover.

A tractor crawled up the exposed tail ramp, grabbing the pallet Daniel had slept on last night. He assumed the boxes and crates contained food, technical gear, and hopefully, coffee. Lots of coffee. Enough to fill a bathtub.

Daniel squeezed his notepad in beside his research materials and the treaty book. Once the diplomacy part was out of the way, the chance to study the Ancient outpost without immediate threats to Earth would be a gift. No team members in urgent need of rescue. No pressure to find Atlantis' gate address.

No alien civilizations to tear down.

Enough with the guilt trip. He zipped his pack shut.

"Daniel?" Sam spoke up from across the plane. "Everything all right?"

Thousands dead. Buildings collapsed. All because —

"Daniel?"

"Sam, I'm fine." Lie firmly in place, he stowed his backpack underneath his seat and his guilt along with it. "How long till we can get off?"

"They need to finish unloading first." Jack shoved folders into a beaten-up briefcase. Each was marked with the official SGC logo, one labeled CASUALTY REPORTS, the other

TRANSFER REQUESTS. His tight, almost pinched face made Daniel instantly regret the idea that there wouldn't be any pressure while at the outpost.

"How bad?" He pointed at the briefcase.

"Bad enough." Jack snapped the case closed. "You can lose the seatbelt, you know."

In other words, Jack didn't want to talk about it.

Once the scientists unloaded, SG-1 followed while Jack stayed on board to talk with the pilot. The frigid air bit right through Daniel's parka, insulated coveralls, fleece pants and pullover as well as his two layers of long johns. The only part of him that stayed warm was his feet, thanks to three layers of socks and a thick pair of black rubber boots.

Spotlights lit up the immediate area, sending long shadows across the ground. The landing crew directed passengers toward an awaiting terra-bus outfitted with massive wheels. Steam from the plane drifted through the lights. Daniel had to assume the C-17's engines were kept running to avoid freezing up.

Antarctica was the coldest, cleanest, driest continent on Earth, but where others viewed the continent as nature at its most extreme, Daniel saw a puzzle. An Ancient puzzle he intended to solve given enough time. The once temperate zone had been the advanced race's home millions of years ago, but if they'd left for the Pegasus galaxy, how was it that some humans — like Jack, Colonel Sheppard, and others — had genetic markers which allowed the use of Ancient technology? Homo sapiens had only been around for 200,000 years.

It was a mystery, made even more so by the knowledge that Atlantis had left behind an outpost meant to protect a planet far, far away from their eventual destination.

As the scientists boarded the bus, a red truck with three-foot high tires pulled up. Windows lined its back half.

"That's our ride," Sam said.

"Is this means of transportation heated, Colonel Carter?"

"Don't worry, Teal'c." Sam picked up her backpack. "It'll

warm up once the katabatic winds die down." She ran toward the truck with Teal'c close behind.

Weighed down with his book-ridden pack, Daniel followed more slowly, leaning into the wind as it pushed against him. Not for the first time, he wished there really was an Archaeology.com website with CDs on everything from Blackwell's *History of the Latin Language* to Buckert's recently translated *Savage Energies*. Sadly, there wasn't, and he'd need all the help he could get in deciphering some of the more ambiguous passages on the outpost's panels.

Halfway to the truck, the wind abruptly stopped. Daniel faltered at the sudden absence of an opposing force. His pack swung forward, threatening to take him along with it. Someone grabbed his arm, preventing him from falling flat on his face.

"Need a hand?" asked Jack.

"I'm good, thanks." He gestured toward the truck. "Think there's coffee waiting?"

"There better be or someone's getting court-martialed." Jack patted his shoulder. "Let's go."

They walked side-by-side, stopping when the bus carrying the other passengers rolled by. Between moving his body and the lack of wind, Daniel started to warm up.

"Have you talked to Balinsky lately?" Jack asked as the bus cleared the area. "He put in a request to transfer off SG-13."

"You really did stay up all night doing paperwork."

"A general's work is never done."

"Did Balinsky give a reason why?" Daniel barely knew the redheaded archaeologist. Though they both had ties to the SGC's archaeology department, he wasn't crazy about Balinsky's over-quick assumptions when it came to long-dead civilizations. He'd made the same mistake early on in his tenure with SG-1 and it had almost gotten them killed. Several times.

Jack shrugged. "You think Dixon's too hard on him? Dave can be like that."

Like Jack wasn't. Daniel had been put through the ringer

many a time, but still... He'd never wanted to quit. Well, not because of Jack, at least.

As they approached the truck, someone wrapped up in a dark green parka and black coveralls jumped down from the forward cab and snapped off a salute. An equally dark green balaclava covered their mouth, making it impossible to tell whether it was a man or a woman.

The airman took their packs, held out a hand toward Jack's briefcase, but he waved them off. "Just get us in this thing, will you?"

With a muffled "Yes, sir," they were led toward the truck's rear end.

"I think Balinsky's making a mistake if he transfers off a first contact team," Daniel told Jack as the airman opened the hatch.

"So do I," Jack said. "But if he's not happy..."

A blast of heat welcomed them from inside the compartment. Bench seats lined the two walls. Sam and Teal'c had taken up residence on the driver's side, each with a cup to their mouths. From the steam wafting upwards, Daniel assumed his wish for coffee was about to come true.

Jack climbed in. "Dixon doesn't need a malcontent on his team."

Daniel followed. Together they took the bench opposite their teammates. As the airman loaded bags onto the floor between the seats, Teal'c handed out insulated mugs.

Daniel took a sip and regretted it. "Hot tea, really?"

Teal'c merely smiled and returned to drinking.

Though the mugs were warm enough, Daniel kept his hands covered. Until that rear door was closed, he had no intention of taking his gloves off. "I wouldn't call Balinsky a mal— "

"SG-13 deserves the best," Jack said, turning around in his seat to face the window.

"Well... All the teams do."

"Yeah." Jack stared out into the pitch-black Antarctic morning, his tea untouched.

The masked airman jumped in and offered Daniel his backpack. Lodging the mug between his legs, Daniel took the heavy bag. The airman slammed the back door shut and knocked twice on the roof. The truck kicked into gear.

"Will there be suitable heat at the outpost?" Teal'c asked.

"When Jack and I came down a few months ago to work with the Atlantis team, they were still putting in heaters." Hoping to put Jack in a better mood, he added, "Maybe we should keep it a bit chilly till the diplomats leave, then — "

"I'm sorry, Dr. Jackson," came a muffled reply from the airman. He pulled off his balaclava, revealing the ruffled black hair and ever-worried looks of Paul Davis, the Pentagon's adjutant to the SGC. "There's been a change in plans for the diplomacy talks with Daniel and the ambassador."

"Major." Jack turned from the window. "What's going on?"

"We've been at this for months, General, but the diplomats sent to McMurdo haven't become any less difficult."

"One look at the outpost should calm them down." Daniel glanced sideways at Jack. "It has that effect on people."

"What's the problem with the diplomats?" Sam asked.

"They've insisted the talks be held at McMurdo, on neutral territory." Paul ran a hand through his ruffled hair. "If we don't agree to their terms, the UN will demand the immediate removal of the weapons chair from Antarctica."

"Oh, for crying out loud, just toss those diplomats in a chopper and drag their asses up to the outpost."

Major Paul Davis sank down by the rear door, hating the idea of saying no to General O'Neill. "I can't do that, sir."

The general raised an eyebrow. "And yet, that was the original plan. Care to explain?"

"You were out of reach, sir. The ambassadors made their refusal known while your transport was coming in for a landing." Paul unzipped his parka as the truck slowly moved over the frozen sound surrounding Ross Island — home to the

U.S. Antarctic Program's McMurdo Station as well as New Zealand's Scott Base. "If it's any consolation, sir, the trainees have already headed up to the outpost. General Hammond is there as well, running their preliminary briefing."

"That's just what I need to start the day," the general quipped. "Eager nuggets. They've got the genetic what's-it to operate the weapons chair?"

Paul nodded. "The IOA handpicked each and every one of them, sir."

"By the way, Major..."

"Yes, sir?"

The general grabbed the thermos from Teal'c. "Nice try changing the subject there."

"I wasn't trying to, sir." He also wasn't trying to feel like a first-year cadet, but whenever he spoke with General O'Neill, Paul felt like he was still at the academy.

Though there was no denying he enjoyed every minute of it. It was the reason why he continued to ignore the Pentagon's recent reminder that he was due for promotion to Lt. Colonel. Any chance to work with SG-1 and Generals Hammond and O'Neill was worth staying at the rank of Major.

The general unscrewed the thermos's cap. "Last I checked, McMurdo isn't neutral, it's American. Isn't that — ?"

"It's American run, sir," Colonel Carter said. "But McMurdo's still neutral soil, so is all of Ross Island — "

"Because it's considered part of Antarctica," Dr. Jackson added. "Which is — "

"Neutral according to the treaty," Teal'c finished.

"Give me a break. The outpost's in Antarctica, too." General O'Neill poured water into his mug, stared at it briefly, and then plucked out the teabag. "A millions of years-old hangout for ancient aliens has got to be as neutral as it gets."

"Not that alien, sir," Paul said. "You carry their genetics."

"Lucky me." General O'Neill flung his teabag into a small can by the truck's rear door.

Dr. Jackson shook his head. "I'll bet the diplomats don't see the outpost like we do."

"And just whose side are you on, Daniel? I thought you wanted to poke around the outpost."

"I do," Dr. Jackson said. "But I don't think we can just drag the diplomats up there."

"Talk is talk." The general sniffed his mug. "What the hell kind of tea is this?"

"Rooibos tea, O'Neill. Colonel Carter introduced me to the substance as an alternative to chamomile." Teal'c curled his lip.

"I arranged for the Rooibos, sir. Teal'c's tretonin doesn't mix well with coffee or hot chocolate." The colonel shared a smile with SG-1's resident Jaffa. Paul never ceased to admire the comradeship amongst the team.

While Dr. Jackson explained the African origins of Rooibos, Paul glanced out the window. McMurdo's lights glowed in the distance. A faint pink flush hugged the horizon just beyond, a weeklong prelude to what would be the continent's first sunrise in months.

"Geez Louise, it's hot in here." General O'Neill unzipped his parka. Teal'c, the colonel and Daniel followed suit.

"All right, Davis. We'll play along with these namby-pamby diplomats if they stop demanding we yank out the weapons chair."

"Or shut down the new F-302 base," Colonel Carter added. "With Dr. Jackson's help — "

"If we're going to work together," Dr. Jackson said, "You need to get used to calling me Daniel."

Paul gave him a grateful nod. "While General O'Neill trains new recruits to run the chair, we'll work with the diplomats to find common ground — "

"Earth is their common ground," Teal'c said.

"That's true, but these particular members of the Security Council only see a violation of the Antarctica Treaty."

"No militarization," Daniel said.

"Exactly. And the F-302 base on the other side of Observation Hill doesn't help our cause."

"We need 302s stationed down here to protect the outpost," Colonel Carter said. "Especially while the *Prometheus* finishes its engine refit, or Ba'al could attack—"

"We're not the ones you need to convince, Carter."

"Yes, sir."

An exchange of glances went back and forth between the general and colonel, the crunch of heavy tires on snow and ice punctuating the silence.

Paul looked out the window again. McMurdo's lights were closer, illuminating the snow-covered, Observation Hill which separated the station from the F-302 base. "Sir, have you and General Hammond discussed the possibility of giving the F-302 plans to the Chinese? Their representative asked again."

"Are you nuts?"

Paul stiffened, just like a cadet. "No, sir, but..."

"They want something, don't they?"

"Please, Daniel. When don't they?"

"O'Neill, has your government not already provided such plans to the Russians?"

"We give the Chinese the 302 plans and the next thing you know, they'll want the plans to the 303. That's not going to happen." General O'Neill stared at Paul. "The Swiss sent someone, too. What do they want?"

Paul sighed. "Switzerland's still harping on about the Stargate being located in neutral territory."

"Like theirs, I suppose."

"Yes, sir."

"Who's the third?" Colonel Carter asked.

"Argentina. And they just want Antarctica," Paul answered.

The general stowed the thermos on the compartment shelf. "Isn't this all a moot point if the weapons chair is dead as a doornail?"

"Not if the Mark II generators work," Colonel Carter said.

Paul allowed himself a small grin. At least he could report one piece of good news. "Dr. Lee ran preliminary generator tests yesterday. Green lights across the board."

"Bill's already done the first power tests?" Colonel Carter glared at General O'Neill. "Just one day earlier, sir. I could've met you here."

"And miss out on all the traveling fun? Daniel, help me out here."

"No thanks, Jack. I think you're doing a fine job."

Another round of silence, the general openly scowling at each of his former teammates. The companionable vibe had shifted to a strained one, making Paul feel like he'd stepped into an argument between his parents. He immediately regretted saying anything about the Mark II test.

Teal'c broke the stalemate. "You cannot keep us forever in your sights, O'Neill."

"Et tu, Brutus?" The general sighed. "Look, we're here now. Okay? Just... Get the negotiations done."

"I'm still not convinced — "

"Make peace with the diplomats and then take a chopper up to the outpost by lunchtime. It'll be like old times."

"You mean like when we stood around and watched you freeze like an ice block?"

"Different times," the general insisted. "You and T can poke around. I'll stomp all over the trainees. Carter will tinker with her toys and get Lee all flustered. Then, Hammond will pat us on the back and we'll go home."

"Sure, Jack." Daniel smirked. "Just like old times."

CHAPTER TWO

CHULAK

50 years ago…

HUANG Sun Tzu crawled behind a broad tree, just beyond the stone spiral pathway, which led to the Chappa'ai. His breath stilled as Apophis' Serpent Guards stormed past. The clank of their armor echoed across the sandy canyon nestled between the two forest ranges. He counted their measure. Ten. Twelve. Fifteen armored Jaffa. Each twice his size.

A passing warrior glanced in his direction. Between one heartbeat and another, Huang flattened himself against the tree, becoming one with its trunk.

Let your rapidity be that of the wind, your compactness that of the forest.

Or so his great ancestor had once said.

The Jaffa moved on, none the wiser, and Huang released his breath into the warm air of Chulak's morning. Subterfuge would be difficult, but not untenable.

Lord Yu would be pleased.

Ten more Jaffa marched by. The leaves then rustled, a sound only discernible by those trained in the ways of Lord Yu's Dragon Guard. Huang nodded in greeting as his companion knelt beside him. He kept his eyes on the enemy troops until a dusty finger was pressed against his forehead. He swiped it away. "Is this truly necessary?" he hissed.

A soft sigh. A whispered breeze against the pounding of yet more Jaffa storming past. Lao Dan Shi swept back the cloak of his matched disguise, the gray of their enemy. Gray cloaks, iron mesh armor and chest plates, shorn heads covered by thin steel skullcaps.

"Success is necessary, my brother," Shi whispered as another squadron marched past. His forefinger plunged into a small clay pot within his palm and withdrew more of the charcoal powder.

"*And yet, you must be subtle,*" urged a voice from within the satchel at Huang's feet. He withdrew the Goa'uld long-range visual communications device displaying Lord Yu's noble visage. The silver-skinned device was strung within a frame of wires and rods. It was the only way Huang and Shi could speak over the great stellar distances separating them from the great Jade Emperor.

One of the many shortcomings of being only human. Naquadah did not flow through Huang or Shi's veins for they were destined to be Dragon Guards. To command Lord Yu's Jaffa in his glory.

The thudding march of Apophis' Jaffa trailed off. Huang peered out from behind the tree and confirmed they were taking up position around the Chappa'ai.

A horn blew in the distance. Shi cocked his head, listening for the telltale sign of more Jaffa approaching. "We must hurry."

"*What you must do,*" Lord Yu whispered, "*is stop them with guile, not war.*"

Shi gripped his staff weapon. "Why wait, my lord — "

"*Silence!*"

Huang watched on in pity as his more fanatical brother muttered his obedience to their master.

"*Upon your arrival, kill Apophis' Jaffa. Then, report back.*" Lord Yu's visage winked out.

Huang returned the device to his satchel. Shi placed his staff weapon by its side and waved a charcoaled forefinger in his direction.

Though reluctant, Huang surrendered his forehead. "This tattoo, this sigil... It is not the *wénshēn* I had hoped to bear."

Shi traced a circle upon Huang's forehead. "Our rightful tattoos will soon be ours if we succeed — "

"If?" Huang pulled back. "You doubt our mission?"

Shi grasped Huang's shoulder. "I am Lord Yu's servant... and your crèche-brother. Born together — "

"We shall succeed together," Huang completed the mantra which had bonded them since birth. Clones of Lord Yu's first Dragon Guards; they had been conceived, grown, and born by way of a device as old as the System Lord. Though they were echoes of the past, the product of a technology as ancient as the Goa'uld they served, Huang believed his destiny could be more if Lord Yu would only give him the chance.

Shi pressed his finger once more upon Huang's brow. A serpentine stroke shortly followed by a final upward arc just below.

"There." Shi wiped his hand across his iron mesh leggings. "You now bear the mark of a Serpent Guard."

Huang grabbed the pot of crushed charcoal and applied a matching tattoo to Shi's forehead. He pushed aside his repulsion to the false *wénshēn*, knowing it a necessary evil.

Huang was a devoted servant, a Dragon Guard trainee, and the genetic inheritor of the great Tau'ri philosopher Sun Tzu. To have his forehead tattooed with anything less than his lord's golden crest was anathema to everything Huang had worked for since birth.

"Do not press so hard," Shi whispered. "I would not have Baozhai see my head so stained upon our return."

Huang rocked back on his heels. "You know it is forbidden for us to mate, even with a slave — "

"*Kree*, Jaffa!"

Huang put down the pot and glanced around the tree. Many warriors now guarded the Chappa'ai, their staff weapons at the ready. Three Serpent Guards stood beside the dialing device, their silver tattoos marking their high rank. The morning glow of Chulak's two suns glistened across their foreheads as they awaited the approaching squadron.

Ka-chunk. The telltale sound of a first address glyph being entered into the dialing device.

The horn sounded again. Closer this time, but the footsteps

accompanying were few. Five, maybe six at the most.

Too small a number to infiltrate. They'd be easily seen when they slipped behind the nearing Jaffa. Huang sank back against the tree. "We have a problem, brother."

Metal hit stone once again as another glyph was pressed. Shi presented him with a toothy grin. Taller, leaner, Shi was always the optimist. He had truly inherited the warmer nature of his genetic ancestor Lao Tzu. "Every problem is an opportunity in disguise."

Again, the horn blew. This time only a stone's throw away. Huang stuck out his head to witness the final team of Jaffa march past. Grasping his staff weapon in his right hand, his left took firm hold of his brother's arm. "Then we must grab hold of this opportunity to stop our lord's enemy."

Ka-chunk. A second, then third glyph was engaged.

As one, Huang and Shi strode to the line's rear and assumed positions within the rank. Two towering Jaffa led the group, the smoothness of their faces a clear sign of their youth. They could not be more than fifty years of age. The warrior on the left was dark-skinned, his shoulders broad as a tree. The other equally tall though his skin was pale as snow.

The group marched toward the Chappa'ai. No heads turned. No comments were made. The two escorts and three warriors passed the dialing device as a silver-tattooed Jaffa pressed three more glyphs. The dark-skinned youth flicked a finger at Huang and Shi, indicating they should take position to the Chappa'ai's right.

Huang strode past the dialing device, stealing a glance at the glyphs engaged on its pedestal.

It was the Tau'ri address! He was certain of it. Only Chulak's point of origin was missing. Feeling Shi's eyes upon him, Huang gave the briefest of nods. Shi's thumb hovered over his staff weapon's firing mechanism. Huang stopped him with a short jerk of his head.

Not yet, brother. Not yet.

They could not attract attention. Not unless the address worked.

"*Hi'ato*, Jaffa," warned the brown-skinned Serpent Guard. Walk on.

The two hurried to the platform, but not before he overheard the two escorts speak.

"Bra'tac must be made aware of their slovenliness." This from the paler Jaffa escort.

"See to it, Va'lar," the dark warrior pronounced. "Once our brothers have departed."

And us along with them.

A final ka-chunk to enter the point of origin, and a surge of power shook the ground. Huang tensed. A moment later, the Chappa'ai disgorged its force. The way to the Tau'ri was open. The liquid horizon settled across the ring of the Gods and a great cheer went up through the Jaffa ranks.

"*Tal Shak*," shouted the lead silver-tattooed Serpent Guard. "Go and secure the Tau'ri for Apophis' return!"

The chosen warriors approached the platform, hesitancy upon their brows. Upon closer inspection, Huang noticed all three looked very much alike. Tan skinned, muscular. Two carried jagged scars across their faces, the other's unmarred. For all Huang knew, they could be triplets, born together.

And together they would die.

Huang bent his knees minutely. To truly follow Lord Yu's directions, he knew that they must avoid force until through the other side. The staff weapon in his palm argued against his effort of patience.

One step. Two. The warriors climbed the platform steps. To his side, Shi had slid his hand down his staff weapon, his thumb yet again reaching for the trigger. Huang prayed his brother would be patient.

The warriors reached the Chappa'ai, turned around and thumped their fists against their chests in salute.

"For Apophis," they chanted. "Emperor of all Goa'uld!"

A great cheer went up amongst the ranks. The three warriors turned back around and stepped toward the Chappa'ai.

"Now," whispered Huang.

He leapt to the platform with Shi at his side. Two warriors had already entered the shimmering pool, but the third whirled toward them, his weapon raised.

Shi double-kicked the warrior's ribs, bringing forth a grunt. A final punch to the Jaffa's stomach pouch sent him sprawling, but not before Huang ripped the staff from his hands. "Hurry," he cried to Shi. They stepped toward the Chappa'ai.

A staff weapon blasted across their path.

"*Kree ta*!" yelled the dark-skinned Jaffa. Smoke steamed from his staff weapon as he strode toward them.

"We must go!" Huang raced to the Chappa'ai's watery horizon. Below the platform, the assembled Jaffa raised their staff weapons, but with only one more step, it would no longer matter. With Shi, he would be safely through the other side.

In the land of the Tau'ri.

"*Shol'vah*, stop!" Another blast from dark warrior. This time at their feet. Huang had never seen a Jaffa with such precise marksmanship.

Huang reached out to drag Shi through the Chappa'ai, but his brother spun toward the dark warrior. Shi raised the stolen staff weapon in his hand, thumbed the trigger, and—

Collapsed. His chest blackened.

"Go," Shi mumbled, blood spurting from his mouth.

Between heartbeats, the desire to destroy the dark Jaffa fought against the logic of Lord Yu's mission.

The moment passed. The need to complete his brother's wishes remained, and Huang dived into the Chappa'ai.

In the instant between his departure from Chulak and his

arrival in the land of the Tau'ri, Huang prepared himself. He knew two of Apophis' Jaffa would be there. Out in the open. Easy to kill.

One could not hide in a desert.

Lord Yu had told them much about where the Tau'ri had buried — and now must have unburied — their Chappa'ai. A land known as Giza. Much wind. Dry heat.

A brittle cold stung Huang's face. He flew from the Tau'ri's Chappa'ai clutching his staff weapon and satchel. Pulling up his knees, he hit the ground and rolled sideways. He'd only a fleeting glance of snow, ice, and being inside a monstrous cave before the Chappa'ai's horizon winked out.

The cave dropped into darkness. Footsteps shuffled across the icy ground. Huang stilled his breath, waiting.

An arc of blue fire shot past his feet. A zat'ni'katel. The Jaffa were still here! Another bolt erupted toward him. Before a third could find its aim, Huang jumped to his feet and swung forward his staff weapon.

He could not gain a clear shot. The Serpent Guards crouched behind a mound of ice to one side. Twin bolts of energy shot forth from either side of the mound. Huang searched the cave for cover and found none.

He would make cover where there was none. Tilting his staff weapon upwards, he blasted the ice-covered snow ceiling over the two Jaffa. His target hit true. The warriors collapsed in a spew of water, ice and rock.

Huang was alone.

It was time to return to his lord and master. He spun around the cave, searching for the dialing device.

There was none. He was stranded.

In the frozen land of the Tau'ri.

CHAPTER THREE

MCMURDO STATION
ROSS ISLAND, ANTARCTICA
18 AUG 04/0835 HRS MCMURDO STATION

A HALF hour later, the truck transporting Paul and the SGC team passed a whitewashed sign welcoming them to McMurdo. A few orange parka-clad scientists hiked by, their flashlights broadcasting on the snow ahead them. In the days to come, the station's winter staff of two hundred scientists and support personnel would more than quadruple when the sun finally appeared on the Eastern horizon.

The truck turned onto the side road leading to Building 155, the station's main center. A bank of spotlights illuminated the power, water, sewer and telephone lines, all running above ground to keep from freezing. Paul rattled off the names of various buildings for General O'Neill and the SG-1 team. Over a hundred buildings made up McMurdo, mostly built of well-insulated corrugated tin and raised on short stilts to keep the snow from building up.

The truck came to a halt besides the ramp leading up to Building 155. Parkas were slipped on and zipped. Wool hats tugged down. General O'Neill cracked open the back door and the harsh cold of Antarctica rushed into the compartment. He grabbed his briefcase and jumped down. Paul waited while the others each collected their belongings.

"It will be good to see General Hammond again," Teal'c said. "When do we depart for the outpost?"

Paul climbed down and shut the truck door. "A helicopter is waiting to take you now if you'd like."

"Yeah, about that..." General O'Neill pulled up his hood.

"Teal'c, stay and help the negotiations."

"Sir?" Paul asked in unison with Colonel Carter.

"I do not understand, O'Neill. How would I assist?"

"Just stand over them. Be intimidating. And watch Daniel's six."

"My six is fine, thank you." Daniel paused for a moment, tilting his head. "Although, it wouldn't hurt for the diplomats to meet Teal'c."

"Sir, I don't think this is a good idea," Paul countered. Negotiating the future of the weapons chair was critical to Earth's safety, and moving it was not an option. They still knew too little about how the platform operated to chance any kind of relocation that might cause permanent damage.

"Having Teal'c at those negotiations is my idea, Major," the general said, "so just go with it."

"Yes, sir." Paul tugged his balaclava down to combat the relentless wind. He needed to get everyone inside before they froze. He gestured toward the building. "We should get inside."

He led the way up a rocky pathway, past rows of shacks and buildings lit up by lampposts. Someone had plowed recently, exposing the bare volcanic rock underneath on which the station had been built. McMurdo sat on Hut Point Peninsula, some twenty miles away from Mt. Erebus, which was also located on Ross Island. Paul had been assured that the volcano was only mildly active. Considering how this day was going, a volcano erupting was the least of his worries.

Colonel Carter ran up to join him. "Major, I'd like to get to the outpost as soon as possible."

"Not a problem, Colonel." He pointed toward a brown pre-fab shack. "Captain Biggs can take you to the helicopter pad. It's right behind the main dormitories."

"Goggles?"

"Ready and waiting."

"Thank you, Paul." Even through the hood of her parka,

he could see the colonel's signature smile. "Sir, we should head over if you're ready?"

"I am. Daniel, you ready to kick butt with those diplomats?"

"Save the chair, save the outpost. World peace by lunchtime. I got it." Daniel turned back toward the road. "You know, we've never 'officially' been to McMurdo before."

"Don't worry, you'll get the introductory briefing." The general patted Daniel's shoulder. "It'll be fun."

"A fun briefing? That's somewhat of an oxymoron, isn't it?"

"Happy Camper training," Paul explained. "Air force personnel are exempt, but since you're civilians it's required. Even repeat visitors — "

"Don't spoil it for them, Major." The general tapped a gloved finger on Daniel's chest. "Make those folks see the light of day." He gestured toward the still dark sky. "Metaphorically speaking, of course."

"Jack, what if I screw up again? What if — "

"Get it done, Daniel!" General O'Neill spun toward the USAF support building and headed off with Colonel Carter in tow.

Surprised by Daniel's insecurity, Paul considered pressing him for details, but decided against it. If Generals Hammond and O'Neill believed he could help settle the outpost issue with the diplomats, Paul had to believe they were right.

He gestured toward Building 155's double doors. "Teal'c, Daniel, shall we?"

"Yeah, I'm freezing. Teal'c?" Daniel ran toward the entrance.

No answer came from the Jaffa. Paul glanced over his shoulder to discover why. Teal'c had turned to face the frozen McMurdo Sound that separated the station from the continent's mainland and the outpost. Paul wondered for a moment if Teal'c knew that, or if he was appreciating the green ribbon of light rippling over the horizon.

Knowing Teal'c, he was doing both.

"The Aurora Australis," Paul explained. "They're caused by photonic emissions in the Earth's upper atmosphere. Solar wind particles funnel down and accelerate along the Earth's magnetic field lines."

"And those gold-white lines?"

Inside the aurora, several striations undulated in counterpoint. The outer green band swayed left while the golden-edged white lines would bend right, seeping out of the ribbon's edge. The aurora would then solidify and repeat the process, all in a slow, meandering pattern.

"That's unusual," he admitted. "Gold bands usually are a reflection of how much energy's absorbed, but I've never seen polar lights behave like that before."

"So many years ago," Teal'c whispered. "I often wonder..."

Paul assumed Teal'c referred to when the SGC first discovered the Antarctic gate. "Seven years is a long time."

"Indeed." Teal'c shuddered, as if shaken from a reverie.

The aurora disappeared. Another gust blew across the ramp, cold enough this time to bite right through Paul's parka. He shivered. "We should get inside."

"I agree." Teal'c's dark eyes turned wistful under the glare of a neighboring spotlight. "Though it should feel like only a moment in my hundred-and-six years," he whispered, "my time with the Tau'ri has been most gratifying."

Taken aback by the Jaffa's openness, Paul could only nod in agreement.

"Major Davis?" Teal'c's voice returned to its normal deep tone. "What does this 'Happy Camper' training entail?"

Glancing up at the six-foot-three alien warrior, Paul gulped. "How do you feel about having a bucket on your head?"

MCMURDO HELIPAD
ROSS ISLAND, ANTARCTICA
18 AUG 04/0915 HRS MCMURDO STATION

"...never agreed to enlisted civilians, Carter. Hammond's making a huge mistake."

"Yes, sir." Sam let General O'Neill blow off steam as she

strapped into the Bell 212 helicopter's starboard seat. As it was, she barely heard him over the already running rotors.

Outside, the sky had changed from a pitch black to a rose-tinted dark gray. Still too dark to fly blind, but she had a definite plan to take care of that problem.

Flipping on the cabin lights, she retrieved her pre-check clipboard from the dashboard. Small red ticks marked off each item. Captain Biggs had generously prepped the chopper, but Sam knew the only safe pilot was an obsessive one.

"Cool! A real reason to visit the coldest place on the planet!" The general pointed out the front window. Down the hill from the helipad, the lights of McMurdo twinkled, but the 'cool' General O'Neill referred to — an Aurora Australis — hovered to the east. As they watched, the green wispy glow dissipated into the ionosphere.

While the general pulled on his helmet, Sam glanced off to their right at the helipad's windsock. The bright orange cone was a little less than half full. She checked the wind gauge. Fifteen knots and holding steady. Happily, the gusts they'd experienced upon arriving at McMurdo were gone. Flying would be a cinch as long as it stayed that way. She donned her helmet.

"Whose idea was this anyway, Carter? I can't believe we're just going to sit back and let them take a whirl in that blasted weapons chair."

"If we want the best, sir, don't we need to look past our own borders?" Placing the clipboard on her lap, she turned off the overheads. Her eyes adjusted quickly, thanks to the green-lit instrument board.

"How are these people going to understand the stakes?" The general unzipped his parka. "Some of their governments don't have the same attitudes about national security, they don't — "

"I don't think General Hammond had a choice, sir. The Atlantis Expedition left a big hole in personnel qualified to operate the Ancient weapons platform."

"Fine, we have to protect the planet. I get it." He slapped his harness shut. "But why can't they use that gene therapy thing and grab some SG teams? Slap 'em with the shot, and then let them live down here."

"The International Oversight Committee insisted on international involvement, sir, including both civilians and military." She toggled the gyro switch. So far, so good.

"Gotta love those IOA folks."

"Sir, you were at the Homeworld Security briefing. General Hammond discussed this with us at length."

"This whole share and share-alike… Why is it that every time we save the planet, we first have to deal with folks like the IOA, Kinsey, or the NID?"

"Well, Kinsey's gone."

"That's a happy thought."

"I don't see any other option, sir."

"I'm tired of all the — " The general tilted his head back against the headrest. "Forget I ever said anything."

"General?" Sam twisted in her harness to look at him.

He didn't return the glance. Instead, he stared out the fore window. "Life's a moving target, Carter, and I'm tired of raising my gun."

"Sir?"

He waved her off. "Finish your pre-flight, Colonel."

"Yes, sir." Sam turned back to the instrument board. Over the years they'd served together, General O'Neill occasionally made mention of retiring yet again, but he'd never meant it. He loved their work just as much as she did.

Then why did he sound so convincing this time? As she checked the directional control pedals, she made a mental note to set up a team night once they got back to Colorado Springs. Maybe that would help the general feel more connected.

Between taking over SG-1's command, coordinating with the science departments, and juggling work with a newfound effort to have an actual life, Sam knew she'd been remiss in the team bonding department. And while General O'Neill technically wasn't part of SG-1 anymore, a few pizzas and watching a bad science fiction movie with the others couldn't hurt.

She scanned the instruments one last time. "Hydraulic controls on. Throttle, fully open. Engine anti-ice set to on." She flipped on the rise switch.

"Take her out, Colonel. The sooner we get this over with, the sooner we get back to the SGC."

Sam lifted the collective control stick. The chopper inched upwards, nice and smooth, its spotlights bouncing off the ice-packed snow below. Once they rose a good fifty meters from the helipad, she nudged the cyclic control forward and the chopper headed out toward the outpost.

The F-302 base came into view as they flew over Observation Hill or 'Ob Hill' as Captain Biggs had called it. As the chopper neared the peak, she spotted the large wood cross commemorating Robert F. Scott's failed expedition. In the years since being rescued from the second gate, Sam had made it a point to learn as much as possible about the region's history. The Herculean efforts of Scott, Shackleton, Amundsen, and many others who braved Antarctica in the early 20th century had often inspired her during some of SG-1's more difficult missions.

The chopper cleared Observation Hill and flew over the F-302 base. The hill's rocky terrain did a good job of hiding the brown-paneled hangers and barracks from the casual eye. About fifteen miles down McMurdo's frozen shoreline sat Scott Base. As Sam caught a glimpse of the twin F-302s on the ice, she wondered just how much the New Zealanders knew about the interceptors.

"Is that safe?" asked General O'Neill.

"I'm sure the New Zealanders have been briefed, sir."

"That's not what I meant. Do we really want to have two billion-dollar birds sitting on ice?"

Someone waved to them from next to one of the F-302s. A pilot, most likely. "This time of year, the ice shelf's at least ten to fifteen feet deep."

"Yeah, but is it safe?"

"As safe as the runway we came in on, sir."

The chopper cleared the base and Sam flipped off the spots. Switching to infrared mode, she slid down her night vision goggles. Her brain took a second to adjust to the lack of depth perception.

"Those AN-PVS 15s work for you, Colonel."

"Don't really have a choice, sir." Sam adjusted her headings to follow the Ross Island coastline further south toward the outpost along the barrier between where the McMurdo and Ross Ice Shelves joined. "Captain Biggs seemed to think the C-17s might start using them for winter flights."

"Makes sense." A light tapping sound came from the general's direction. Though Sam couldn't shift her focus from the terrain ahead, she knew General O'Neill well enough to recognize fidgeting when it happened.

"ETA 'til outpost twenty-five minutes, sir."

"And I'm counting every second in anticipation — Whoa!"

A stiff wind shoved the chopper's nose to the right. Sam applied pressure to her left pedal to adjust the tail-rotor's pitch. The chopper straightened out and she settled back in.

She checked the gauge. "The wind's back down to ten knots, sir. We shouldn't have any more problems."

"Sweet." The general tapped his fingers against the console. "A civilian could do this training, you know. I've got more important things to do like approving Walter's latest parking space request or signing another round of Siler's requisitions."

"Running the SGC keeping you busy, sir?"

The general merely grunted.

Sam grinned. General O'Neill never got tired of downplaying his importance to the SGC in both a leadership position and as a strategist. Or in this case, being the most qualified person on the planet to operate the weapons chair, whether he thought so or not. She told him as much.

"I never should've let Sheppard go with Weir to Atlantis. The man liked Antarctica. We could've built him his own personal bunk at the outpost."

"Yes, sir." Another gust pushed against the chopper. She adjusted the rudder.

Sam envied John Sheppard and the others who'd gated to another galaxy. Not that she didn't love her job leading SG-1. She did! But the possibility of discovering Ancient technology far beyond anything anyone could imagine was tantalizing. Although, when she'd heard Rodney McKay had been assigned to the expedition, her envy had turned just a bit to pity.

The general picked up his finger drumming routine again, this time tapping against his leg in syncopation with the rotors. "God, I hope Daniel doesn't screw up."

"Why would he?"

The finger drumming stopped. "It's Daniel who needs to believe that, Carter. Not Hammond, Davis, you or me."

"Just out of curiosity, sir, how do you think Teal'c can help? I mean, other than his firsthand knowledge of the Goa'uld, he's not exactly — "

The general laughed. "Kind of like sending a grizzly to babysit a salmon stream, isn't it?"

She chuckled. "At least it gives Teal'c something to do."

"Yeah, well, I know how that goes." The finger tapping started up again.

Sam chewed her lip. Teal'c didn't need to be in Antarctica, and he didn't need to stay with Daniel. Whatever troubled the general, whatever motivated his need to keep SG-1 close at hand, clearly he wasn't going to talk about it.

Another gust nudged the chopper, this time coming from behind, pushing them in the right direction. Grateful for the boost, she nudged the cyclic control forward and headed toward the outpost. With any luck, they'd shave off a few minutes.

Although, knowing the general's mood, the trainees might not be so lucky.

MCMURDO STATION
ROSS ISLAND, ANTARCTICA
18 AUG 04/0940 HRS MCMURDO STATION

The rope tied to the waist of Teal'c's insulated coveralls tugged twice. "Just a few more steps to our right, Mr. Murray," came the muffled sound of his assigned companion.

"I disagree, Dr. Malan," he replied, his voice equally muffled by the white plastic bucket he wore to participate in this 'Happy Camper' training game required for McMurdo's civilian visitors. "Our goal is to reach the central pole. To that end, we must take ten steps forward and one, perhaps two to our left."

"Not if we want to win a set of bowling shoes!" Dr. Malan tugged the rope joining them again. He stopped. "Wait, how can you be so sure?"

Teal'c sighed. He could sense the pole ahead of them. Years of training by Master Bra'tac had taught him how to feel the presence of anything nearby. Convincing this young man to trust him would be difficult without offering an explanation.

While Teal'c understood the purpose of this training exercise — to remind civilians that they must use all their senses when in such a rugged environment — he also recognized the other element behind the simulation. "Did not the personnel director say we must learn to trust one another if we are to succeed?"

The taut rope slackened as Dr. Robert Malan's footsteps crunched in the snow. The biologist bumped into Teal'c's left side and stopped. "I really want to win. You understand, right? It's not just about the shoes — "

"If we lose, I shall personally acquire a set for you. Would that be a sufficient arrangement?"

"And you're sure? I mean..." More crunching of snow, the rope winding across Teal'c's back. "I could've sworn — "

"Grab hold of the rope and permit me to lead."

"Okay, dude. Go for it. You lead, I'll follow."

With one hand on the rope between them, Teal'c set off

to the pole. He took two steps forward and then another. He stopped, waiting for Dr. Malan to catch up. Yes, he could sense the pole ahead. Only a few more feet. "Seven more paces and we will reach our objective."

He took another step.

Dr. Malan followed. "Objective. Like a military thing? Oh, that's right. Dr. Edmunds said you were with the Air Force. Awesome. Well, forward march, airman."

Teal'c smiled beneath the confines of his bucket. The enthusiasm of youth never changed, no matter the civilization. The biologist reminded him very much of Rya'c, and perhaps even himself many years ago when serving as Serpent Guard within Apophis' ranks. So sure of himself. So sure that what is seen is what things are…

As he took another step forward, Teal'c considered the possible ways he might exact revenge on O'Neill for insisting he remain at McMurdo. Not holding back on their next ping-pong match was certainly one option. Replacing his beloved red Jell-O with green was yet another. In either case, Teal'c would most certainly find retribution.

"Are we there yet?" asked Dr. Malan.

Teal'c's gloved hand grazed the wooden pole. He stopped. "We have succeeded."

Removing the near stifling bucket from his head, Teal'c sucked in a refreshing bout of the cold, dry air. The miraculous Aurora Australis lights had been replaced on the horizon with a red wisp of pre-dawn glow.

Turning toward the other eight teams scattered across the snow-covered parking lot, he searched for Daniel Jackson. His friend had been partnered with the National Science Foundation's director for McMurdo. Lean, white-haired, and with a beard as long as the Tau'ri's Santa Claus, the exceptionally tall NSF man had said little during formal introductions, except to argue over the partnerships assigned by Hannah Presley. The station's personnel director had been gracious, but firm in her refusal to change the assignments. It was a talent that reminded Teal'c very much of Colonel Carter.

Plastic thwacked against wood. Teal'c spun back around to his own partner.

"Ouch!" Dr. Malan pulled off his bucket. He grinned widely beneath his sparse red beard. "Hey, we did it!"

"We have a winner!" Hannah Presley ran over to them, blowing a whistle. "Everyone inside — there's hot chocolate and a snack waiting in the cafeteria."

Buckets were raised and much laughter ensued as the teams disengaged their partnered tethers. That is, all but one team. Far over on the parking lot's other side, Daniel Jackson and Dr. Edmunds turned away from each other as they untied their rope. The NSF director threw his bucket to the ground. He mumbled something Teal'c could not hear and stormed off toward Building 155. Scooping up the neglected bucket, Daniel Jackson followed at a slower pace.

"Hey, thanks for the win," said Dr. Malan, rubbing snow off his short red beard. "If you're up for it, I can give you guys a tour of the main complex."

Teal'c bowed his head. "That would be most appreciated."

Dr. Edmunds stomped past the pole. "Back to work, Malan."

The biologist stared at the NSF director's retreating back. "What's his problem?"

"Not exactly the warmest welcome I've received," said Daniel Jackson as he joined them.

"Don't mind Edmunds," said Hannah Presley. "The bergy bits in the sound have a warmer nature than him."

"Bergy bits?" Teal'c asked.

"Miniature icebergs," explained Dr. Malan.

Buckets in hand, the four reached Building 155's back entrance just as the wind picked up yet again. Dr. Malan yanked open the heavy door. Most of the buildings in McMurdo were made for the cold weather with walk-in freezer doors to block out the elements. The only difference was that instead of walking into a freezer, this was more like walking out of one.

Inside, they removed their outerwear to dry. When Dr. Malan inquired as to why Teal'c's watch cap remained on his head, Daniel Jackson thankfully changed the subject by asking if there was any tea. They hurried toward the cafeteria and Hannah Presley promised to return shortly with a selection of Rooibos.

The cafeteria was at the end of a long hallway beside a bank of windows that rattled against the wind. Teal'c looked in at the large open-style dining area — far larger than the SGC's commissary. In the center were many food stations. Several dozen community tables lined the walls.

"Good thing we got inside when we did." Dr. Malan pointed out the window toward a wooden building further up the road. A row of flags flapped briskly. "Hey, how about that tour?"

"Don't waste your time with those two, Malan." They turned around to find Dr. Edmunds leaning against the wooden door leading into the cafeteria, arms crossed, his bearded chin thrust upwards.

The NSF director dropped his arms and strode up to Dr. Malan, separating the young man from both Teal'c and Daniel Jackson. "They may not look like military, they may not act like military, but they are military."

"As I explained earlier," said Daniel Jackson, "I'm a linguist and an archaeologist and — "

"Have absolutely no reason to be here." With that, Dr. Edmunds stomped off. The sound of his footsteps echoing through the corridor only served to punctuate the howling wind outside.

Dr. Malan apologized. "Edmunds's not a bad guy, he's just what my mom calls 'prideful.' Don't take it personally."

"Don't worry about us." Daniel Jackson awarded the young biologist a smile. "We're used to it."

Used to it, indeed. Teal'c observed the NSF director depart. Edmunds's arrogance was no different than what he'd had come to expect from Goa'uld System Lords.

The wind rattled the windows once more, a howling gust that lent agreement.

FERRAR GLACIER
18 AUG 04/0940 HRS MCMURDO STATION

Jack grabbed hold of his armrests as another gust jolted the chopper starboard. "Nice flying there, Ace."

"I can't explain it, sir." Carter jockeyed the collective, her arm vibrating against the strain. "Even Katabatic winds don't just pop up out of nowhere."

"Pop up, you say?"

She smiled faintly, but didn't reply. Too much wind, Jack supposed.

The first time he'd been choppered from McMurdo to the outpost, the trip had started out as a bit of a lark. The sun had been high overhead, the sky as blue as a robin's egg, and the snow-covered brown mountains surrounding Ferrar Glacier had gone on forever. Then, that errant drone chased Sheppard's helicopter halfway across McMurdo Sound.

He'd expected things to go differently this time, but so far? Not so much. The ride itself had been anything but smooth. One moment Carter had the chopper airborne nice and easy, honing in on the outpost. The next, they were fighting gusts that would put a hurricane to shame.

"You sure you can do this, Colonel?"

"Trying, sir."

"Well, try not to flatten us like a stack of pancakes," he said only half-jokingly. Every trip he'd traveled to this damn place always ended badly. Why should this be any different?

He checked the altimeter. "Fifteen hundred feet to go."

Carter switched on the head beams and yanked off her night-vision goggles. "The wind's shoving us down too — "

The chopper lurched left. Below, a circle of blinking red landing lights and a solitary spotlight marked the outpost helipad. The instrument panel's green lights reflected against her scrunched-up face.

"Easy, Carter."

"Eleven hundred feet, sir." She shifted her grip on the collective. "Piece of cake."

The chopper took a sudden drop, making him wish he'd never eaten that donut Biggs offered before take-off. "Make that an even thousand," Jack said, reading the altimeter. "Maybe this isn't such a hot idea."

Over the roar of the wind, he heard Carter's feet tap the pedal controls. "Have a little faith, sir."

"Hey, I'm all about faith, but — "

The chopper's nose pitched upward, throwing him back against his seat.

Carter wrestled them to a steady horizontal, the chopper shuddering against the strain. "I've flown in worse."

He eyed the altimeter once more. Seven hundred feet to go. "Maybe we should head back. Try again later, when the wind's died down."

The rotors groaned, another shudder seized the chopper, and then…

The shaking stopped.

"The wind's gone." Carter flashed him a grin.

He returned the smile. "Faith, my ass. Nice flying."

"Thank you, sir."

He leaned back. "Take us down, Colonel."

"Happily." Carter wiped her brow and brought the chopper down by the mammoth glass and steel dome housing the elevator that led down to the Ancient outpost.

Jack grabbed his briefcase and jumped out, half-tempted to kiss the ground. Except it wasn't ground. Beneath his feet was a whole lot of ice. At least two hundred feet of it.

"General O'Neill! Colonel Carter!" A heavily bundled figure waved at them from the tunnel leading inside.

Carter raised a hand over her brow and did a half-turn.

"They must have moved the dome since my last visit."

"To cover my fancy drill work," Jack explained, still mystified by how he'd macgyvered the ring transporter to bore through two hundred fricking feet of solid ice. He remembered holding a soldering gun. He remembered sparks. Hell, he even had a faint reminiscence of Teal'c keeping him company.

But how he got those rings to cut through ice like a knife through Swiss cheese? Completely clueless.

The figure receded inside the dome tunnel. Jack nudged Carter toward the dome. "I've had enough hypothermia for one lifetime. Let's go."

Carter hoisted her backpack and followed him inside. As soon as they ran under the 'White Rock Research Station' signage, the parka-clad figure hit a button. The outer door slid down and the man pulled back his hood.

General Hammond grinned at them both. "Welcome to the outpost." He strode toward the inner door and slapped the button to open it.

As the inner door retracted, Jack pushed back his hood. "General, it's good to see you."

"I told you, Jack..." He led them further into the dome, swiping another button to close the inner door. Ten feet inside, an elevator waited. "Call me George. We're both generals now."

"Old dog, new tricks, sir." Jack followed him into the elevator cage. "How's the Pentagon treating you?"

"It has its ups and downs." Hammond punched the button for the bottom level.

The door closed. Digital numbers flashed above the control panel as they descended—just like the elevator back at the SGC. Grateful for at least one constant, Jack's unzipped his parka as the air warmed up.

While Carter followed suit, Hammond kept his parka closed. Jack raised an eyebrow. "Too cold for you, sir?"

"Still a Texan at heart, I'm afraid. Even Colorado Springs was a bit chilly for my tastes."

"Are you enjoying Washington, sir?" asked Carter.

"I never thought I'd say this, but yes, I am." Hammond gestured at Jack's briefcase. "I see Walter's kept you busy."

"Not exactly the ammo I'm used to carrying," Jack admitted.

"Welcome to my world," Hammond said with a laugh. "I understand the diplomats insisted on meeting with Dr. Jackson back at McMurdo. That was a good idea, by the way."

"General?"

"Having Teal'c join in. Give those folks a taste of what's really out there."

Jack grimaced. "Sir, about that. Can't you drag them — ?"

"They'll do a fine job," Hammond insisted. "You worry about wrangling those eager trainees."

Hammond chatted with Carter as the elevator descended, but Jack barely paid attention. His mind was too busy, trying to figure out the best way to tell the general the truth.

How could he train a bunch of nuggets if he couldn't even remember himself?

Pull it together, O'Neill.

It wasn't like he'd had to train the Atlantis gang on how to use the chair. They'd figured that out all by their little genius selves.

The elevator hit bottom, the cage door slid open, and Carter excused herself. She dashed across the outer chamber in search of Dr. Lee. Jack watched her go.

That is, until he caught sight of the one gadget he hated even more than the chair.

Eight-feet high, barely two-feet wide and deep, the Ancient stasis unit he'd spent way too many months in stared back at him from across the room. How he'd willingly stepped into that metal coffin... Well, he'd deliberately shoved that memory in the same box as all the others.

Last time he'd been at the outpost, there'd been plenty of distractions to keep him from thinking about the damn thing. Daniel and Weir's enthusiasm. McKay's uppity Canadianisms.

Sheppard's ability to operate the chair as if it was a Gameboy.

"You ready, son?" Hammond stepped out of the elevator. Other than a dozen or so scientists futzing with gear at various workbenches, the chamber was fairly empty. A few airmen hung out by a bank of communications equipment at the far wall, drinking coffee, filling out paperwork. All run-of-the-mill.

Though he didn't feel 'ready,' Jack grinned. "You bet."

Sure, rummaging in the dark corners of a crowded box of memories was exactly what he wanted to do.

"The trainees are in the break room so you've got some time to work with the colonel and Dr. Lee. Take a spin in the chair and test those Mark IIs."

"Yes, sir."

Hammond frowned. "Is something wrong, Jack?"

"Nothing a good rummage sale won't fix, sir."

"Excuse me?"

"Just a little joke, General."

Hammond nodded, hopefully buying the lie. "I'll go let the trainees know you're here." He stepped nimbly around a cart being pushed by a scientist and headed toward the break room.

Alone and ignored in a room full of geeks, Jack sucked it up and made his way to the weapons platform chamber. He marched past his former resting place, refusing to give the metal box another thought. Once through the archway, he caught sight of the chair. Carter and Lee were bent over a monitor, unaware of his presence. The 'easy-chair from hell' — his pet name for the Ancient weapons chair — just sat there nice and dormant. Its trellised back was upright. The platform dark.

And yet somehow, he had it in him to make the thing light up like a Christmas tree. In that chair, he could shoot out enough weapons to take out an entire Goa'uld fleet.

Or so they'd told him.

Carter had said to have a little faith, but faith was a funny thing. It required all sorts of clichés like doubting doubters. Believing in the evidence of things not seen. Or, losing control to a higher source. Inside his own head, no less.

He strode toward the chair, knowing he had no choice but to rely on another old chestnut — fake it 'til you make it.

BUILDING 155—MCMURDO STATION
18 AUG 04/1015 HRS MCMURDO STATION

Daniel huddled with Teal'c and Robert Malan around the rec room's foot-high Plexiglas tank. A hand-drawn sign encouraged them to touch the tank's mostly albino inhabitants.

"Is that a starfish?" Daniel asked, surprised by its pale yellow coloring. It clung to a rock in the center of the tank while the other creatures stayed underwater.

"That's an Antarctic sea star." Malan gently touched one of the sea star's limbs. He pointed to a handful of spindly yellow slug-like creatures, each the size of a child's fist. "Those are anemones."

"Why are they so light-colored?" Daniel asked.

"Lack of sun, temperature. A whole bunch of reasons." Malan stroked the largest anemone's spine. Its tendrils retracted. "You need to come over to Crary Lab. We've got a much bigger touch-tank over there. Flatworms, isopods, crustaceans. All sorts of local marine invertebrates."

"I'm afraid that's not possible." Paul glanced at his watch. "We've only got about twenty minutes left."

"I've got an idea!" Malan joined Paul at the door. "How about after the meeting we show them the lab, the NSF Chalet, and maybe take them up to the weather station?"

While Paul did his best to let the redheaded biologist down easy, Daniel copied Malan's earlier action, grazing one of the anemone's multiple tendrils with his fingertip. Soft, almost rubbery, the tendril slipped from his touch.

Teal'c leaned in beside him. "Will not the diplomats be angered if we are late, Daniel Jackson?"

"We've got time."

"Would not that time be best used in preparation?"

"I suppose." Daniel touched the pale starfish. Its skin was softer than normal. More pliable.

"And yet — "

"I'm stalling, I know." Daniel grinned at his friend. "Just trying to gather my thoughts."

Teal'c tilted his head. "You have prepared for this discussion for the past week."

"Yeah..."

Teal'c copied his action, touching the starfish's back. "This is not Tegalus, Daniel Jackson."

"No... It's Antarctica," Daniel replied. "These are my own people, Teal'c, but to be honest, I'm not sure if that makes it any easier."

"But perhaps more difficult?" Two of the starfish's points curled upward as Teal'c stroked its back. "And like the people of Tegalus, these diplomats will do what they want unless otherwise convinced."

"Fat lot of good I did convincing the Caledonians and the Rand Protectorate."

"As you say, these diplomats are your own people." Teal'c retracted his finger from the tank. "Do you believe it your responsibility to make them understand the outpost's importance?"

"That's why I'm here, isn't it?" With a sigh, Daniel turned from the tank and took a look around the room. Stacks of newspapers, books, and board games covered the center table. On another table by the far wall, a chess set waited for players. Next to the chess set stood an all too familiar wooden board covered in a series of crisscrossed lines. Several dozen black and white stones bunched together in one corner of the board.

Daniel blinked in surprise. *Wéiqí* — the ancient Chinese game known by most today as 'Go' — wasn't that popular a game. He wondered who would be playing it at McMurdo.

It'd been barely a year since he'd been captured by Lord Yu and forced to play. While not the strangest experience of his lifetime, Daniel couldn't deny that his hours-long discussion with the Goa'uld had left its mark. Especially Yu's insistence that Daniel learn how to be both a warrior and a scholar.

Though he wouldn't admit it to anyone, he'd embraced that advice whole-heartedly ever since.

Teal'c followed his eye line. "You cannot always help those who do not wish to be helped, Daniel Jackson."

"No," Daniel whispered. "But I can still try."

"You know, Mr. Murray..." Malan replaced the tank's cover. "You don't need to wear a hat inside. It's like — "

Major Davis cleared his throat. "We really need to head toward the meeting room."

"Sure, sure. We're going that way, anyways." Malan led them down a wide hallway with office doors on either side. He pointed out the various rooms including the radio and television stations, the library, and the personnel office.

Daniel kept a smile plastered on to be polite. The tour stopped to admire a weather monitor. Malan dragged Teal'c in for a closer view while Paul held back, his face pinched and anxious.

Daniel didn't blame him. Gating to a Goa'uld enemy stronghold would be easier than what lay ahead. Despite Jack's parting order to 'get it done,' this wasn't going to be easy.

Jack's latest orders rankled. He'd changed since taking command of the SGC. Not enough for anyone else to notice, but Daniel did. How could he not? Jack seemed quieter. Not necessarily more removed, just subdued.

Before his promotion, Jack had definitely been more animated. Sure, he'd argue loudly. He'd groan and complain. But he'd also listen. Jack would take in everyone's thoughts before making a final decision. Sometimes those decisions weren't the best, but more often than not, Jack had bent when Daniel needed him to.

The man still listened, but sometimes he behaved as if he'd already made up his mind before any arguments could be made.

Of course, there were issues Jack was privy to as a general that Daniel could barely guess at.

When the tour stopped in front of a closed door with a small window in its top half, Paul thanked Malan for the tour — a not-so-subtle cue that the young biologist needed to leave.

Malan pumped Teal'c's hand. "Don't be afraid to join us tonight in the bowling alley. It'll be fun!"

"I shall consider your invitation." Teal'c tipped his head, oblivious to the scientist's hero-crush.

"Dr. Malan…" Paul glanced at his watch.

"Oh, right. Gotta go!"

As Malan hurried off, Daniel shared a smile with Paul. "Bowling for fun — "

"Still putting that promotion package together, Davis?" a voice called out behind them.

Daniel turned toward the newcomer. A man dressed in an F-302 jumpsuit strode toward them. When he stopped in front of Paul, Daniel read his name patch: Kenneth Ferguson, Lt. Colonel. Ferguson was lean, with an aquiline nose and eyes that seemed to take in everything without missing a beat. His buzz-cut blond hair was just a breath above being shaved clear off.

Paul introduced Ferguson. "The Colonel and I went through the academy together."

Ferguson smirked. "And yet you're still a wee little major. That's got to be boring. What's the matter? Can't your CO write up a decent recommendation?"

Paul stiffened. "Actually, Colonel, the board review happened several months ago. I'm good to go."

"Congratulations," Teal'c said.

"That's great," Daniel said, ignoring the colonel's petty comments. "When does the promotion happen?"

"Yeah, Davis," Ferguson chimed in. "When's the ceremony?"

"I haven't said 'yes' yet." Paul glanced through the door's window.

Ferguson slapped him on the back. "Of course not. You've

been in the service more than sixteen years. Why would you ever want to be promoted?"

"I'm happy with the way things are."

"Sure you are," Ferguson said. "Tell you what, Colonel Thanks-but-no, when you decide to get off your ass and go through with the promotion, call me. I'll be sitting in the front row." He tossed off a wave and strode toward the galley.

"You okay?" Daniel didn't really understand military ranks and promotions, but he got the pecking order. If Paul was turning down a promotion, there had to be a good reason.

"Yeah, I'm fine." He turned back toward the door. "Before we go in, let me brief you on these diplomats."

Surprised at Paul's sudden change of topic, Daniel glanced at Teal'c who raised an eyebrow in response. Inside, three ambassadors hovered around a coffee service by the far wall. Two men and a woman.

"The tall man with the mustache is Markus Duebel, Switzerland," Paul said. "He's been with their diplomatic corps for over twenty years, but from what I've put together, he's been booted out of just about every place the Swiss sent him."

"Great. A grumpy career diplomat," Daniel observed. Duebel had a reserved air to him. He poured cream into his cup, added sugar, and then stirred it in, every movement economized. Even the man's facial movements were minimal. Duebel didn't smile or frown while talking with the other man in the room. He simply was. His steel gray hair added to his stern aura.

"All three of them are basically bottom of the barrel ambassadors. Kicked out, fired, re-hired. I'm guessing the UN didn't believe they needed to send their best." Paul pointed at the shorter man gesticulating wildly at Duebel. "That's Jorge Diego Suarez, Argentina. You know their deal."

"They believe they own Antarctica," Teal'c said.

"Not all Argentines think that way," Paul explained.

"Mostly just the upper-class." Daniel decided Suarez probably belonged in that category. Unlike the other two who had donned simple cold-weather fleece pullovers, the Argentine diplomat wore an expensive cable-knit sweater. His black hair and beard were neatly trimmed, not a hair out of place.

And from the way his hands waved, he enjoyed a good argument. Too bad Jack wasn't around. There wasn't anyone better at shutting down someone like that in a heartbeat.

The third diplomat turned toward the door. She was Asian, not more than five-foot-three. Short-cropped black hair and bangs framed a face tattooed with what seemed a permanent scowl. She sat down at the table in the center of the room and sipped her coffee while the two men argued.

"That's Quing Zhu," said Paul.

"She desires something of value," Teal'c observed.

Daniel pulled back from the door. "Not that I'm surprised considering how little we've lived up to our end of our promise to share technologies from the program, but how can you tell?"

"She remains separate from the other two," Teal'c said. "Watch. She is impatient."

As if on cue, Zhu glanced toward the wall clock and frowned.

"Maybe that's just her nature," Daniel said. "Guys, whether we like it or not, China's a member of the Security Council. If President Hayes trusted them enough about the Stargate — "

"After last year's diplomatic fiasco over Lord Yu," Paul said, "I'm not so sure the president trusts anyone."

Teal'c's frown only punctuated Paul's point. Though Daniel had missed SG-1's run-in with the Chinese government last year — mostly because he was Lord Yu's prisoner at the time — he'd learned during his debriefing all about how the Chinese had unwittingly allowed Yu's spy to infiltrate the SGC.

A spy that China wouldn't allow the Pentagon to interview.

"So those are the players." Paul dropped a hand to the doorknob. "Teal'c, you're just here to observe, but — "

"I have pledged my allegiance to this world, Major Davis. I will remain silent."

Daniel grinned at his friend's avowal, wishing he felt as

confident. "I think what he's trying to say is — "

"I am ready." Teal'c lifted his chin. "This is merely a battle of a different sort."

"A battle of words," Paul said with a nod.

"It's not a battle," Daniel insisted. "We have to help these UN diplomats understand why the weapons chair — though technically in breach of the treaty — needs to stay put."

"Daniel Jackson, is not world peace the primary reason for the United Nations?"

"Of course." Grabbing the doorknob, Daniel silently prayed these negotiations would go far smoother than his last attempt.

"Then is it not also true that if the chair's removal causes it to malfunction, any hopes of such peace will be destroyed if the Goa'uld could attack again?"

Stunned by the simple truth in Teal'c's words, Daniel did the only thing he could.

He opened the door.

CHAPTER FOUR

EARTH

50 years earlier...

"*YOU ARE certain*?"

"Lord Yu, the glyphs were correct. This is the land of the Tau'ri." The cave's bitter chill nicked at Huang's face, the frigid air bit at his lungs. He had retrieved both cloaks from the dead Jaffa, but it was not enough. He needed to return home.

"There is no dialing device," he spoke into the communications device, his teeth chattering. "All that remains is ice and snow. Giza is no longer — "

"*Impossible*!" Lord Yu's fist smashed down out of view, but Huang heard a table splinter from the impact.

Gripping the frame, Huang raised the communications device above his head. "My lord, do you not see the ice upon this cave?" He panned the device across the snow-covered walls. "If this was once a land of sand and warmth, it is no more."

He lowered the device. "My lord, I must ask for rescue. Cannot an Al'kesh — ?"

"*No. You must find the Tau'ri.*"

Fear seized Huang's heart. "No one could survive in a place such as this. Not even the Tau'ri."

"*Do not presume to know about the Tau'ri.*" Lord Yu's eyes took on a distance gaze. "*They are a formidable people. How else could they cast out Ra*?"

Lord Yu returned his gaze to Huang. Haunted eyes peered out from the silver sheen of the communications device. "*Something is wrong. You must go forth. Discover who is responsible.*"

"My lord, I implore you. Without Shi..." He swallowed hard

at the thought of his dead brother. "Without tools to — "

"*Shi's death is unfortunate, but he can be replaced. As for tools... Have you not the weapon of those Jaffa you killed?*"

"I do, but — "

"*You have their clothes to reinforce your own. You have your wits. Your training. What more could you need?*"

Huang bowed his head. "A squadron of our Jaffa would make this more obtainable, my lord."

Lord Yu grunted. "*Under your command, I presume?*"

"Yes, my lord."

"*And I suppose you seek the* wénshēn *so as First Prime you could command such a legion?*"

Huang dared not look his master in the eye. "I do, my lord."

"*You are a fool!*" The Goa'uld's voice boomed throughout the cave. "*You live to feel pure molten gold poured upon your skin so that you may carry my sigil. I seek the knife which will cast a far graver wound.*"

Huang recoiled in horror at the idea that he only lived to covet the *wénshēn*. "Forgive me, my lord. I meant only that — "

"*Only the dead can be forgiven,*" said Lord Yu with an imperious wave of his hand. "*Is that what you wish? To die?*"

"No, my lord."

"*Then, go forth. Contact me once you have seen what remains.*" Lord Yu's palm covered the display.

The communications device winked off.

Huang did as he was commanded, refusing himself the pity a lesser man might carry. If he was to be First Prime one day, if he was to prove himself worthy to Lord Yu, he could do no less.

First, he stripped the armor off both Jaffa. Removing their tightly-woven black shirts proved simple and once he'd slipped them on, one over the other, his torso eased its shaking from the cold. He began to remove their chainmail leggings, but decided against it. Both pairs were too large, and adding metal leggings would only make it more difficult to move. He instead removed his own leggings, wrapped one of the cloaks around his lower limbs, and then slipped the leggings back on.

And though the two dead Jaffa had been his enemies, he chose to restore their armor to their bodies. They had been mighty warriors and were due that respect. Though Huang was not Jaffa, he knew the legend of Kheb was core to their belief. If these two souls were to meet their paradise, they should do so in honor, dressed as befitted all warriors of any rank or race.

Now warmer, he stowed the communications device in his satchel and searched the cave for some sign of a way out. In the direction of the Chappa'ai there was only a wall of packed snow and ice, but a faint amount of light came from somewhere. He only needed to find its source. He strode to the far other end and looked upward. There. A small crevasse at the top of a steep incline. If he was not mistaken, sunlight poured in from the sky above.

Using two weapon staffs as poles, he egressed the sloping wall. The crevasse was too small, but he quickly widened the opening with his hands. More sunlight poured through.

He glanced one last time at the cave below and trembled, but not from the cold. A thousand years had passed since Lord Yu had left Earth. It was very possible that Huang — and the Jaffa he had killed — were the only living beings that would ever step foot through that Chappa'ai again.

The thought sobered him as much as Lord Yu's command to discover what had become of Giza and the land of the Tau'ri. He crawled through the opening, his feet seeking purchase as he went. Finally, he freed himself from the snow-bound cave and rose up to greet the changed land.

Bright sunshine reached his face. Snow fell upon his brow.

Stumbling further from the cave, he gazed down upon a world far different than his master had ever described. Desert flatlands were not what lay before him. Instead, he witnessed a frozen wasteland. Glacial cliffs. Soaring mountains. A rugged landscape impossible for any being to survive.

And yet...

In the distance, a great plume of smoke belched into the sky. Perhaps, a sign of life.

Setting that as his direction, Huang set forth to serve his master's bidding.

CHAPTER FIVE

ANCIENT OUTPOST
FERRAR GLACIER, ANTARCTICA
18 AUG 04/1020 HRS MCMURDO STATION

"HEY, BILL." Sam nodded toward Dr. Lee as she entered the weapons platform chamber. Though General O'Neill was still in the outpost's main area, she'd need to hurry if she wanted everything ready for the chair's next test with a live subject. Namely, the general.

"Be with you in bit," Lee said from a monitor stationed by the rear wall. "I'm on a conference call with Dr. Rick Dale, an old friend of mine over at the Mount Erebus Volcano Observatory."

The Erebus Observatory was located on Ross Island, some twenty-seven miles away from McMurdo. Last Sam checked, the volcano hardly spat out anything past its inner caldera.

"I'm just gonna..." She pointed toward the dual computer display monitoring the Weapons Platform.

Lee hit a key and turned around. The word 'mute' flashed on his screen. "Prelims went off without a hitch."

"Thanks for doing that. He can't see the chair, can he?"

"Who? Oh, you mean Rick?" He turned back the screen. "Nope, I narrowed the camera's view. Don't worry, Colonel."

He tapped the keyboard again and the mute function disappeared. As Lee continued to chat with his friend, Sam slid onto a stool by the monitors and chafed her hands together to warm her fingers. The chamber was kept at a cool thirty degrees to insure the ice-covered cavern remained intact. A bit cold for bare hands, but wearing gloves while inputting the program she had planned just wasn't going to get the work done fast enough.

If everything went as planned, the Mark II would definitely power the chair. She'd designed the power system, run the simulations, and had even double-checked the math — which was no easy feat when having to convert from Base-10 to Base-8 so it could interface with the chair.

While she'd told General O'Neill that a little faith went a long way that belief was firmly rooted in science. Most scientists couldn't blend a religious belief and a scientific mind, but Sam had no trouble combining the two. Especially after all that she'd seen throughout the Milky Way. Just as she'd had faith the chopper would handle a bit of wind because of the laws of aerodynamics, she also believed those immutable laws were an extraordinary miracle.

She entered a few keystrokes, calling up a system report on Dr. Lee's preliminary test. The backup Mark II had kicked in for a few microseconds, but she had just the remedy to keep that from becoming a problem. Popping in her flash drive, she bypassed the system, and copied over its files.

"Colonel Carter," Lee said loudly. "What's he doing?"

Sam looked up from the monitor. General O'Neill was poking at the control gel packs on Ancient weapons chair's armrests. His brow furrowed, his shock of silver hair still ruffled from his helicopter helmet, the general seemed lost in thought. Troubled, actually.

Lee looked over at the general and then back to Sam. "Should I sign off?"

"Give us a few minutes, and then yes, it's probably a good idea to get back to work." Without waiting for a reply, she hurried over to the general's side. "We're ready, sir."

He frowned. "Yeah. About that, Carter..."

"It won't take long," she assured him. "We just need a live guinea pig in the chair for a few moments."

"A guinea pig, you say?" He turned toward her, his expression softened.

Sam mustered up as much enthusiasm as she could.

"Nothing wrong with being a guinea pig, sir." She flashed him a smile, hoping it would pull the general out of whatever troubled him.

It didn't work. General O'Neill turned his attention back to the chair, his eyes hooded. Somber.

"What was it like, Carter?"

"Operating the chair? Sir, you'd know better than me, I don't have the genetics."

He shook his head. "I don't mean the chair. I meant back when that entity thing took over your body and stuffed you in that computer mainframe in the M.A.L.P. room."

"Oh," Sam replied. "That."

"Yeah, that."

"To be honest, sir, all I remember was feeling like I had no control." She shuddered, realizing how similar the sensation had been to Fifth's attack, a thousand horrific images seared into her brain.

"You must've had some kind of control," the general said. "Otherwise, you couldn't shout at us through every frigging monitor on the base."

"I suppose that's true." She closed her eyes, trying to shut the lid on any thoughts of Fifth. She knew it wouldn't hold for long. Too many nights waking up in a cold sweat were proof-positive that Fifth had left a mark.

"Carter?"

"Right. Being in the mainframe was like..." She remembered the disorientation. The feeling as if she'd never get out. Was that how General O'Neill felt when he sat in the Ancient chair? "It was like being in a dark room without any door, but — "

"There's always a but, isn't there?"

She smiled. "Yes, sir, there is."

"Care to share?"

"I still knew who I was. I still had that knowledge." She shrugged. "After that, it was just a case of using that knowledge as a weapon."

"Now you sound like Daniel." His lips flattened in a thin line, General O'Neill turned to stare at the chair.

"Sir, when you were in the chair, you obviously were still in control, otherwise — "

"How could I knock out Anubis' fleet?" The general straightened his shoulders. "That's a good point."

"You're still in control, sir." She gestured toward the chair. "It's just a weapon."

"A weapon that has to crawl around my head to do its job." General O'Neill sighed. "Problem is, I'm not quite sure I recall how to make it work. I mean, I remember…"

He fell silent. Though Sam wasn't surprised to hear he couldn't recall his last use of the chair, she was surprised to see how much it seemed to bother him. He'd read her report of what happened during the mission to battle Anubis. She was sure he'd read Daniel's and Teal'c's, too. Maybe, he just needed a good analogy to put his mind at ease.

"That's the easy part, sir. Just concentrate. Think of the chair as a trigger on a rifle. Focus on your target."

"Whoa. Hold on." He jabbed a finger at the chair. "Tell me those drones won't be connected while I'm sitting in that. Or any of those nuggets, either. Trust me, Carter, it's not fun being chased by one of those things."

"We've bypassed the drones, General," Lee called out from behind the monitors.

General O'Neill eyed Lee with skepticism. "And how long have you been eavesdropping?"

"Me?" Lee's face reddened. "I… uh… I was on a conference — "

"Just tell me this thing isn't going to blow up." The general marched around to the front of the chair. Any visual sign of his earlier trepidation was gone, tucked away in a room so locked down that even Sam didn't have the key.

Keys!

"Sir, don't sit down yet." She hurried back over to the control system and checked. The file transfer was complete. A few clicks, a password prompt, and she typed in an alphanumeric string. A low hum initiated from the primary Mark II. The secondary stayed dormant, its yellow standby light blinking in confirmation.

"Does it work?" Lee joined her by the control screen.

"So far, so good."

"Does what work?"

Sam scribbled the passphrase on to a pad by the monitor and handled it to Lee. "I've created an automatic switch so the second Mark II can take over if the first falters. Converting the chair's input take from the enormous power of vacuum energy to the naquadah's more direct stream was like trying to re-jigger a piece of equipment from using A/C power to D/C, so I— "

"Ah!" General O'Neill stopped her. "I'm sorry I asked. Are we ready to light this thing up?"

"Yes, sir. Just remember— "

"Finger on the trigger, Carter. I get it." The general scrubbed a hand over his face. "Okay, no time like the present."

He sat down in the chair and nothing happened.

Sam switched the display over to the monitoring computer. Power was steady. By all rights, it should work. She peered around the display at the general. He had his arms crossed, his eyes squeezed shut. "Sir, you need to concentrate."

"What do you think I'm doing, whistling Dixie? Oh, wait a second." The general splayed his hands along the gel packs.

The chair came to life, its translucent panels illuminating a soft blue glow. The platform's equally milky panels mirrored the color and luminescence. As the back reclined, the chair rotated around, revealing a hauntingly neutral face on the general. A face that reminded Sam of just how close they'd come to losing him months ago when the Repository threatened to wipe his mind permanently.

Opening his eyes, General O'Neill glanced in her direction. He waggled his eyebrows. "I got it to work, huh?"

"I had every faith you would, General."

"So now what?"

"We'll run a few more tests. Make sure everything's in order before General Hammond brings the trainees in."

"Lucky me."

Sam headed back toward the monitors. "You see, sir? Piece of cake. With the right genetics, anybody can do it."

"Anybody," said the general, his voice wooden. Distant.

"Sir?"

"I'm fine, Carter." He squeezed his eyes shut again. "Anybody can do this."

BUILDING 155—MCMURDO STATION
18 AUG 04/1045 HRS MCMURDO STATION

Teal'c gulped down yet another cup of Rooibos, thankful for the container of red leaf tea Hannah Presley had brought him. Though it was not a cure-all for his current circumstances, he found the soothing drink a suitable contrast to the heated exchange between Daniel Jackson, Major Davis, and the diplomats.

The negotiations were little more than verbal sparring. One ambassador would jab. Daniel Jackson or Major Davis would parry. Time passed with little achieved, the ambassadors unwilling to compromise on any ground. It was obvious why all three of the diplomats had been sent to Antarctica.

They were petty fools and cowards.

Major Davis sagged back against his chair. "Our standing orders are to find weapons that will protect Earth against the Goa'uld."

"Weapons which have radically altered the balance of power on this planet," Ambassador Zhu said, stabbing a finger on the table. "That balance must be — "

"An order which the UN Security Council supported," Daniel Jackson continued, ignoring the woman. "If it wasn't for the Ancients weapons platform, Anubis wouldn't have been just a threat, he would have — "

Ambassador Zhu harrumphed. "Anubis is gone. There is no need for the weapons platform to remain here in Antarctica in violation of the treaty."

"Madame Ambassador, we need more time to study the chair before taking any chances it — "

"No more waiting. Certainly your scientists have had enough time now to determine the best means of removal." Ambassador Duebel smoothed down the sides of his mustache, a mannerism of public grooming Teal'c found pretentious. "Per Article One, no weapons of any kind — "

"But, sir — "

"No!" Ambassador Juarez waved a finger at Major Davis. "The weapons platform's presence violates the very spirit of the treaty. The Americans are fools to believe otherwise."

Teal'c clenched his jaw in disgust.

Beside him, Daniel Jackson sighed. "You really believe that? After everything we've done to protect you?" He pulled off his glasses and pinched the bridge of his nose. "That chair is the only reason — "

"You keep bringing up the same argument," Ambassador Juarez roared. "This only proves my point. Americans abuse Earth's resources as if — "

"Enough!" Teal'c leapt up and faced the enemies of his friends. The three ambassadors froze in their chairs.

Daniel Jackson glanced in his direction, began to shake his head, and then stopped. "I think Teal'c would like to add something to our discussion."

Teal'c gazed steadily upon the ambassadors, allowing his stature to create a moment's pause. Would it also allow him to impress upon them what was at stake?

Finally, Ambassador Duebel shrugged. "Though Mssr Teal'c has no say in these matters, I am willing to hear his perspective. Objections?"

"It matters little," Ambassador Zhu said with a tilt of her head, "but we will allow him the courtesy as a guest."

"This is a waste of time," Ambassador Juarez murmured.

Teal'c turned toward the Argentine Ambassador. "Then I will be brief."

Ambassador Juarez opened his mouth to speak.

Teal'c stepped closer. "I have served this world for more than seven years. I will have my say, Ambassador."

The man's face went white and he shut his mouth.

Satisfied, Teal'c returned to his chair. "I wish to speak to your accusations that the Americans are fools — "

"That is none of your concern — "

"You are wrong, Ambassador Zhu. It is the concern of every being in this galaxy. Your territorial disputes mean nothing to me nor to the Goa'uld."

Once sure the Chinese ambassador would hold her tongue, Teal'c pressed on. "These Americans you denounce as fools, it is they who have sacrificed hundreds of lives in defense of this world. Sacrifices that have included many men and women I named friends. To call them fools dishonors their memory."

"Forget us Americans for a moment," said Major Davis. "What about the Russians? They've sent several teams through the gate. They know firsthand — "

"The Russians have become American puppets," said Ambassador Juarez.

"Puppets," Ambassador Zhu added, "who are rewarded in a manner you refuse to share with others."

Teal'c observed the exchange of glances between Major Davis and Daniel Jackson. He knew what rewards the Chinese ambassador spoke of. Rewards she had yet to openly ask for. If O'Neill believed them unworthy of the F-302 fighter jets, Teal'c trusted his friend's judgment. O'Neill was not Apophis or some other Goa'uld demanding blind trust. His trust had been earned.

And yet, if the Americans gave the Chinese the plans to the F-302s, would they not have one more ally?

"Puppets and fools," muttered Ambassador Juarez. "The

Russians and Americans deserve each other."

"And so you would dishonor their deaths as well?"

All three ambassadors suddenly found the table in front of them to be of great interest.

Daniel Jackson leaned toward him and whispered, "I think the ambassadors get your point, Teal'c."

"I do not think so. Indeed, in their attempts to discredit the Ancient weapons platform, they not only dishonor those who have given their lives to protect this world, but its inhabitants as well."

Ambassador Duebel crossed his arms. "Do not presume to understand what Earth requires, sir."

"It is you who does not understand. Many countries have sent representatives to train with General O'Neill in the use of this technology, including your own. They do this to defend Earth. All of Earth. Should you not honor these people by seeing what it is they do before dismissing their efforts by dismantling the weapons platform?"

The ambassadors remained silent. Ambassador Duebel picked at his pant leg, while Ambassador Juarez stared at a wall, the lines on his face deepened by his scowl. Major Davis had found something worth removing from his sleeve while Daniel Jackson used the moment to clean his glasses.

Ambassador Zhu arose from her chair, awarded Teal'c a glare, and then went to the far window where refreshments had been set up. Outside, the sunless day cast a colorless pall over the base.

"We have somehow digressed from the subject at hand," Ambassador Zhu said as she retook her seat, a glass of water in hand. "The chair must be moved, and further, China remains emphatic that our people should know the details of the Stargate Program. Allow us to decide what is right and what is wrong."

"To use your own words, Madame Ambassador," said Daniel Jackson, "we've somehow digressed from the point of this meeting. These negotiations — "

"Remove the weapons chair from Antarctica or there will be no negotiations." She turned away in her seat, a clear sign of dismissal.

The Chinese ambassador played at a game, nothing more, Teal'c reminded himself. He reached into his pocket and took hold of his tretonin as a distraction. The cool glass and metal vial served to remind him of the greater picture. For the Jaffa to find the freedom from the Goa'uld he enjoyed, they needed these Tau'ri to cooperate.

"Ba'al would support your demands to dismantle the chair," he finally said. "As would Moloc. Amaterasu." He kept his voice low. Deliberate. "Perhaps even Lord Yu."

Ambassador Juarez whirled toward him. "*Quiénes son?*"

Teal'c leaned forward, his face neutral. "I speak of other System Lords who would happily see the Tau'ri destroyed. They wait, patiently, believing themselves far superior to your planet's abilities."

"How well you have been indoctrinated by the Americans," said Ambassador Zhu. "More ghosts under the bed to scare us?"

Major Davis interrupted. "If the Chinese really think the chair should be removed, why send one of their own for training?"

The two other ambassadors gaped at Ambassador Zhu.

"Is this true?" asked Ambassador Duebel.

The Chinese diplomat merely shrugged. "She is there only to placate my government and the IOA."

"A political appointee who just happens to have the ATA gene?" Major Davis asked.

Zhu bowed her head. "An unnecessary exercise."

It was then Teal'c saw an advantage and took it. "The Chinese do not strike me as a people who waste time on the unnecessary."

"I must agree with our alien visitor." Ambassador Duebel rose. "In fact, I wonder if China has a specific place they wish this weapon moved."

"Is this true, Madame?" Ambassador Juarez's chair toppled

backward as he jumped up. "Your country holds rank on the IOA. Did you intend to have the weapon platform for yourself?"

Ambassador Zhu's chin lifted in cold defiance. "I resent what you imply."

Ambassador Duebel once again smoothed his mustache. "We imply nothing, though there is merit in reconsidering our positions based on this newest information."

"I agree," Ambassador Juarez said.

Ambassador Duebel faced Major Davis. "Could a tour of the Ancient outpost be arranged?"

"Absolutely," said Major Davis, a relieved smile on his face. "When would you like to go?"

Ambassador Duebel shifted his gaze to Ambassador Zhu. "Now, if that's possible."

"Just give me a few minutes to arrange a chopper." The major headed toward the door, but then stopped. He turned back. "How many should I say will be going?"

"I will go." Ambassador Juarez joined Major Davis at the door.

Ambassador Duebel favored Teal'c with a smile. It was open. Honest. Possibly even apologetic.

"We shall all go."

ANCIENT OUTPOST
FERRAR GLACIER, ANTARCTICA
18 AUG 04/1050 HRS MCMURDO STATION

Jack studied the faces of the IOA trainees. The 'anybodies' Carter had referred to earlier. They stood in various forms of attention against the wall opposite the weapons platform. Oval origin patches on their red-fleeced pullovers marked them as Europeans, Russians, and Americans. Ten military, two civilians, the trainees ranged from a sixty-something retired U.S. Army vet to a Chinese girl barely out of her teenage years. A dozen genetic freaks in all, each one with the genetics to kick-start the Ancient tech.

Anybodies. Just like him.

A couple of them coughed, a few scuffled their feet. A last check of his clipboard, a forced smile, and he called the roster, hoping to God he'd remember who was who.

"Okay," he said as cheerfully as he could, "who's first?"

Ten hands shot up. No surprise, all the military folks had volunteered. The two civilians just stared at the weapons platform, a matched pair of terrified grins plastered on. One was an Italian, a guy by the name of Michael Castellano, with a ponytail long enough to use for rock-climbing. Then there was the Chinese girl who looked too young to be there. Lanky limbs, long hair pulled back. Too fresh-faced. The girl reminded him of Cassie when she was sixteen.

General Hammond strode into the room. As Jack met his gaze with a nod, the general joined Carter and Lee behind the chair. The brainiacs kept futzing with the Mark II, but so far, so good.

Jack returned his attention to the trainees. He waved at a young man with dark-hair and a serious buzz cut. "You first."

"Thank you, sir," he said with a French accent.

"Name?" Grabbing his clipboard from the platform, Jack gestured for the nugget to take the hot seat.

"Sub-Officer Andre Charpentier." He slid into the chair.

"Sub?" Jack asked. "As in submarine?"

"*Oui*. I serve aboard the *Améthyste*, a nuclear-powered submarine." He reached for the armrest controls. "The rank is not unlike a sergeant in your nation's — "

Jack stopped him before he could palm the controls' gel packs. "Listen, Carpenter — "

"It is Charpentier." He stretched out the last few syllables as if he was talking to an infant.

"Yeah, whatever. I'm not sure how things operate — "

"General..." This from Hammond.

Whoops. Jack kicked his normal self to the back of the bus and tried again. "Sgt. Charpentier," he said, emphasizing those elusive last syllables. "Go ahead. Put your palms on the controls, nice and — ”

The chair activated, tilting back as he followed his instructions. “Like so?”

“Sweet.” Flashing Charpentier an encouraging grin, Jack turned on a small boom box Carter had set up for him behind the chair. A perfect mix of P90 reports, zat fire, and a few staff weapon eruptions to boot. The noise bounced off the walls in a melodious cacophony of battle.

Yep, he missed that sound.

Charpentier bolted from the chair. “I cannot!”

“What?” He shouted over the sound effects. “I haven't even told you what to do yet.”

Charpentier stepped down from the platform, flinging a hand at the boom box. “How do you expect us to concentrate with that infernal noise?”

“Okay! Okay!” He punched the sound off. Carter gave him a bemused grin and then returned to tinkering with her gadgets.

Jack faced the trainees. “Hear me out, folks. If and when you're called on to operate this chair, the enemy will attack without hesitation. You will have backup. You will have people protecting your six — ”

“Our what?” asked one of the German trainees. Jack was pretty sure his name was something Merkel. Peter or Paul or one of those saintly names.

“He means your rear-end.” This from Ryan Hall, the gray-haired army vet. Hall was a bit too smug for Jack's liking, but what choice did he have?

Jack took a peek at his watch. Eleven hundred hours. Lunch couldn't happen soon enough.

“We're ready for the next trainee, sir.”

Thank God for Carter.

“Okay, folks.” He clapped his hands together. “Let's try this again. Who's next?”

A sea of raised hands answered his call. They were an enthusiastic bunch, that was for sure.

He pointed at the Eastern European gal. "Okay, you. Name?"

Thin, blonde, and with pretty much the saddest eyes Jack had ever seen, the trainee stepped forward. "Private Dora Vukovich, sir."

Jack checked the list. "You're from — "

"The Republic of Serbia." Vukovich raised her chin.

"Climb on in." He gestured at the chair. "Let's see what you've got."

Vukovich sank into the chair, rested her hands on the gel-controls, and the lights flashed on. As the chair tilted backwards, she closed her eyes. "I am ready, General O'Neill."

"Good job, Vukovich. I'm going to turn the boom box back on, okay?" When she gave him a quick nod, he flipped on the sound effects.

The chair remained active. So far, so good. Time to see what she's really made of.

Jack stepped in front of the chair and waved his hand in the space over her head. "Now… Think about Earth."

Vukovich's eyes snapped open. "I do not understand."

"Just imagine you're in space, looking down on the planet."

Bingo. Earth came to life in all its holographic glory. A shiny blue marble with a honking big land mass centered near the southern pole.

"That is not Earth!" a trainee called out behind him. "Have you never seen a globe or even a satellite photograph?"

Jack shut off the boom box and whirled around. It had been a girl's voice. With a Chinese accent. He jabbed a finger at the culprit. "Pipe down because you're next. Name?"

"Weiyan Shi," the girl managed to squeak out.

"Civilian?"

The girl bobbed her head nervously.

"Okay, Shi. I'm guessing you were too busy to pay attention in General Hammond's briefing." Jack scowled at the trainee.

Merkel raised his hand. "The Ancients representation of Earth is from long ago. From when the continents were as one."

"At least someone took notes." Maybe too many notes. Jack tucked that observation aside and flipped the battle symphony back on. He turned toward Vukovich. The hologram of Earth still hung in the air, nice and solid. "You're doing fine, Vukovich. Now imagine there's some other someone up in space with you. Some big bad goon — "

"No. I will correct the display." The girl squeezed her eyes shut.

"That's not the point." Jack glanced up at the global display. The midsection bulged outward. "What the hell are you doing?"

"I will prove the civilian wrong. Not just anyone can serve in the Serbian army! I am not an idiot." Vukovich's face reddened as she kept up the strain of whatever-the-hell she was doing.

The platform began to vibrate. Nothing huge, but enough to put Jack's teeth on edge. On the head's up display, the sphere became an egg, then a cube. The land mass stretched upward with what could have been a lopsided version of Europe — including the old Soviet Union — spread across the top half. The whole thing looked like a fun house version of Earth.

Carter stared at the display too, her brow furrowed. "Sir, you might want to get her to stop."

"Yeah, look, Vukovich. That's enough."

"*Ništa*. No." She gripped the chair's arms.

The platform's vibrations intensified. And then, something fell on Jack's head.

Ice dust… From the outpost's ceiling.

Someone yelped. Jack quickly glanced toward the trainees. One of the trellised panels had fallen on the Chinese gal.

He turned back around and yanked Vukovich from the chair. "I said cut it out!"

The rattling stopped immediately. The image collapsed, the chair turned off. Vukovich ran from the room. A collective gasp raced across the trainees as Jack watched her go, completely confused.

When no one moved to pull the panel off Shi, he jumped

down off the chair platform and helped her out. "You'll be fine," he assured her.

"No, no, no," the girl mumbled. She yanked up her left sleeve and then her right. She ran her hands up and down her bare arms not once, not twice, but three times. It was as if she was looking for injuries that just weren't there.

If the girl was a hypochondriac, she wouldn't last more than a day.

"Shake it off, Shi," Jack barked at her deliberately. If the Chinese were going to send a civilian, he had no other choice but to give her a crash course in hanging tough. "A few bumps and bruises never hurt — "

"Take a thirty-minute recess, people," General Hammond announced to the room. "If you'll follow me, I believe lunch is available in the break room."

Stunned, Jack could only watch Hammond stomp past, frowning. The general shook his head in that don't-argue-with-me way of his.

What the hell?

Shi tugged down her sleeves and followed Hammond out through the archway. The other trainees trailed close behind.

Jack looked over at Carter and Lee. "What the hell just happened?"

"We're on it, sir!" Carter pulled a stool up to the computer and pounded at the keyboards.

How the hell were these nuggets going to fight the Goa'uld if they couldn't handle a little technological hiccup? Suddenly, he wasn't hungry anymore. Not for lunch, that's for sure.

He headed off toward main chamber. Maybe there was cake. Which would be a good thing. It would take a helluva big piece to knock down the bitter taste in his mouth.

There were times George was near convinced God put him on Earth for one reason and one reason alone — to keep Jack O'Neill in line.

The man had to see the bigger picture. Otherwise, the trainee program was doomed before it had gotten off the ground. While everyone else finished lunch, George followed Jack back toward the chair room. Just as they passed the Ancient stasis unit, he pulled Jack aside.

And got an earful. The trainees were unfocused. They were too young. Too old. The civilian additions were worthless. All the while, Jack fiddled with the stasis unit's molding as if he was trying to pry the thing apart. Thankfully, the blue-gray metal and silhouetted rivets wouldn't budge, but Jack continued to yank at its edges. The activity kept him in one place so George allowed him the outlet.

The man was no fool. Clearly something else was bothering him. After a few rounds of the man's whispered frustrations, however, George knew he had to shut Jack down. "You need to take a step back, son. There's more here than meets the eye."

"You could've fooled me, General."

"Everyone wants the same thing, to protect Earth."

"Maybe the military trainees, but civilians, sir? Really?"

George sighed. "Be patient. They'll fall into line."

"General, I'd follow you to the ends of the Earth. Heck, I'd follow you to the end of any planet, but if the Pentagon picked these people, it makes me wonder what the hell they were thinking when they promoted me."

"You know very well that the Pentagon had no say in the selection of these trainees. The IOA did the base genetic testing. Furthermore, none of these volunteers are even aware of the whole program. They don't know about the Stargate and — "

"Everything all right, sirs?" Dr. Lee had poked his head out of the weapons room.

"Just hunky-dory." Jack stepped closer to the stasis controls, his back to the scientist.

Ignoring Jack's ill temper, George faced Lee. "We're a bit busy here, Doctor. Is there something you need?"

"Ah… No, sir." Lee blinked a few times, like a rabbit caught in the crosshairs. "Colonel Carter's running one last test on the Mark IIs. I was going to see about getting another shipped down from the SGC for backup. If that's okay with you, General O'Neill?"

Jack's face darkened, but he kept his tone civil. "Yep, sure. Whatever Carter wants."

"Right, thanks."

When Lee was out of earshot, George returned to dealing with his troubled charge.

Jack stared into the stasis unit, his hands braced against each side. "I can barely remember getting into this thing."

"Can't or won't?"

A shadow passed over Jack's face and he dropped his hands.

"Look, I understand your reservations, but the IOA believes including other nations will help Homeworld Security's cause, not hurt it."

Jack spun toward him. "Sir, I request permission to be reassigned."

"You don't mean that."

"I'm thinking the Alpha site." Jack smirked, a clear tell that he was blowing smoke at himself as much as anyone else. "Heck, I'll even go babysit one of those science outposts Carter helped set up. Anything's better than here because if the president keeps letting the IOA tell us what to do, there won't be a here much longer!"

George straightened up to his full height. Maybe he wasn't as tall as Jack, but he sure as hell had the stars to back him up. "General O'Neill, you are not alone in securing Earth's survival."

"I know that, sir." Jack returned his gaze to the stasis unit. "It just feels that way sometimes."

"Imagine how it'll feel when you're in a Pentagon office with nothing more than a couple of pens for weapons."

Jack whipped his head around so fast that it was a surprise it didn't fall off.

"You're surprised?" George smiled at his protégé. "I still plan on retiring in the not-too-distant future. Someone needs to take over."

"Begging your pardon, sir. I respect your job. Your title. Your efforts."

"But?" George crossed his arms, waiting for the inevitable.

"Well, sir. It's bad enough being on the sidelines — "

"Why would I want you in the nosebleed section?"

"Sir," Jack lowered his voice, "while I like to say I took the job as head of the SGC because of the pay bump, the truth is... I took it so the other guy wouldn't."

"General Philips, you mean?"

Jack scowled. "Philips is a moron."

"And now? Admit it, you like the position. At least some of the time."

"I like it when my people get home safely. That was easier to do when I was out in the field, watching their sixes — "

"It's a fine thing, being a hero who'd die for their country."

"I don't mean it like that, sir."

George waved his apology aside. "It's one thing to die for your country, but right now this planet needs heroes who would much rather live for it."

"General O'Neill?" It was the Castellano boy. He rushed up, his long ponytail flopping behind him.

"Yeah?" Jack said wearily.

"We're ready, sir. Just say the word." The young Italian attempted a salute. It was sloppy, his hand practically flopping outward as he finished. Between the grin and the salute, George liked the young man instantly. His heart was most definitely in the right place.

Jack frowned. "Just say the word?"

Castellano brought himself to attention. "We really want to help protect the planet. We just need you to show us how."

Jack's frown softened. "Sounds like a plan, Castellano."

Cautiously relieved, George put a hand on the lad's shoulder. "Why don't you gather the others and bring them in? General O'Neill will be there shortly."

With a grin, Castellano threw another salute and dashed

off toward the main chamber toward the awaiting trainees.

Jack raised a hand to the back of his neck. "Oh, geez..."

"Look, I know this isn't easy."

"You can say that again."

"You're a general now. Your job isn't about tactics anymore. It's about strategy." He jerked a thumb at the trainees who had begun to head back into the chair room.

"And having a strategy that involves drop-kicking them isn't going to fly," Jack murmured. "I get it."

"Just pretend they're from another planet," George advised. "Give them the same respect, the same leeway."

"I suppose..."

"Those men and women want to learn how to defend this planet. And I think they have as much right to as you do."

"Yes, General."

"So go and train them."

Jack flung off a mock salute not much better than Castellano's.

George found himself laughing. It felt good, considering the last few hours' tension. "And Jack?"

"Sir?"

"Try to call me George. We're equal rank now."

"Au contraire, mon general! I'm just a measly little brigadier. You've got two more stars on those shoulders, sir. I've a long way to go 'till I've earned them."

"You're damn right," George answered with a smile. "Now teach those folks how to do their part."

With a nod, Jack headed back into the chamber.

"General Hammond, is this a good time?"

George turned toward Daniel Jackson, newly arrived along with Teal'c and the three quarrelsome ambassadors. Hopefully, seeing the weapons platform in use would convince them to back off their demands to dismantle the chair. Removing the chair from Antarctica was too big a risk right now. They didn't know enough yet about the technology to guarantee it could be reassembled and work as needed.

George had read the SGC's most recent casualty reports. The Goa'uld were still out there and still wreaking havoc. Without Earth's best line of defense, those reports would only get worse.

Though Jack made an effort to be as courteous as possible, he stuck to his guns and called on Weiyan Shi next. She climbed into the chair and the panels lit up instantly.

So far, so good.

Before he could even ask, she called up the display of Earth.

"Nice work." Determined to make Hammond happy, Jack smiled broadly.

The girl silently followed his orders. The further into the session they got, the more Jack began to believe that a civilian — at least this civilian — might not be un-trainable. The girl had definite potential.

Maybe Hammond was right. If he thought of these nuggets as aliens, cut them some slack, then maybe — just maybe — they could make some honest-to-God headway.

"Why have you not turned on the sounds?"

"You want them on?"

"I do not wish to be treated differently." Shi kept her focus on the globe floating overhead.

Huh. Jack could appreciate that. He reached over to the boom box to turn it on.

"Actually, sir..." Carter joined him by the base of the chair platform. "Before adding battle sounds, it might be worth seeing if she can tap into some of the other displays stored in the platform's memory banks."

"I will try." Shi settled further back into the chair.

A small commotion at the room's entrance caught Jack's eye. Daniel and Teal'c. With them was some older Chinese woman. One of the ambassadors, most likely. She shoved her way up front past the trainees. All scowls and fists. He raised a hand palm-up at his former teammates, the universal sign for 'what gives'?

Daniel shrugged apologetically. Teal'c dipped his head in greeting. Jack decided that either meant negotiations went off without a hitch or things were SNAFU. Knowing the SGC's luck as of late, his bet was on the latter.

Carter climbed up on the platform. She peered down at the girl, giving her one of those big grins that could make a Goa'uld think twice. "What's your name?"

"Weiyan Shi. Please, call me Weiyan."

Carter smiled. "Okay, Weiyan. You've seen pictures of the solar system. Can you try and call one up in your mind?"

Weiyan squeezed her eyes shut. In a heartbeat, the hovering Earth morphed into a three-dimensional image of planets, moons and a bright glowing sun smack dab in the middle. Jupiter came around for a pass, an all too familiar sight. Jack had seen the planet firsthand, thanks to his little expedition with Teal'c when Apophis had rigged their X-302 for a one-way ticket to nowhere.

He counted the planets off in his head. Nine total. No, wait. A tenth slid by. Then another. "Carter, is that our solar system?"

Carter stepped off the platform. "It's possible."

"With eleven planets?"

She leaned in and whispered, "Sir, the *Prometheus* has found several new planets out beyond the Kuiper asteroid belt. We just haven't made it public knowledge yet."

"Uh, guys?" Daniel joined them by the base of the platform. "Is that what I think it is?"

"Yep. Didn't you get the memo?" Jack crossed his arms, going for nonchalance. It wasn't often he was a heartbeat ahead of Daniel when it came to the science stuff. Might as well enjoy it while he could.

A quick glance back at a grinning Hammond made his euphoria all the sweeter. Okay, maybe training these nuggets wasn't so bad. It certainly beat dealing with paperwork back at the base.

Which anybody could do.

"Did it work?" Weiyan opened her eyes. She gazed up at the display with the barest glimmer of a smile. Almost as if she'd never done it before — the smiling part, that is.

As far as the map was concerned, Jack was pretty damn sure that had never happened before, either. Certainly not him or Sheppard for that matter.

"General O'Neill, you are wasting precious resources."

Jack turned toward the voice. It was the pushy Chinese ambassador. He opened his mouth, wanting nothing more than to tell her to take a flying leap, but Hammond shook his head.

Oh, yeah. Diplomacy. Act like a general. Right.

He forced a grin he wasn't feeling. "Seems to me she's doing an outstanding job, Ma'am."

"I am not a ma'am," she said through gritted teeth. "As the appointed ambassador from China, I order you — "

"*Tíng zhǐ*! Do not interfere!" Half-risen from the chair, Weiyan gripped the arms. If anything, the backlit panels glowed hotter. The color deeper, bluer.

"Remove her," the ambassador demanded. "Do it or I will!"

A hushed gasp ran through the trainees. They backed away from the chair.

"No. This is where I belong." Weiyan held onto the chair. "*Bie li wo*."

The two fell into a whiplash of Chinese, but Jack held back, unsure of what to do or what to say. Their voices grew louder, the trainees backed away further.

The rumbling started up again. Nothing huge, but Jack recognized it from this morning's aborted session. He hesitated, unsure what Hammond would want him to do with this incipient Chinese civil war.

The tremor kept up. Jack glanced at Hammond for help. The general put a hand on the woman's shoulder. "Madame Ambassador, would you please come with me?"

She crossed her arms. "I will not."

The arguing between the two women grew louder. The

rumbling kept up, too, like a freight train chugging through a station. Behind Weiyan, the chair's back panel lights pulsed.

"What the hell's going on, Jack?" Daniel whispered.

"You tell me. You're the linguist!"

"They're talking so fast, I can't."

"Weiyan, get out of the chair!" Jack gestured at Teal'c to remove the ambassador.

Teal'c slid in front of the near-crazed woman, blocking her access to Jack, Carter, Daniel, and more importantly, the chair where Weiyan...

Sobbed?

The rumbling intensified. Ice dropped from the ceiling. A rock-sized piece barely missed Carter. "Dr. Lee! Enable the safety program!"

"I can't find the pass key!"

Carter started off toward the monitors, but stopped short when another chunk of rock fell in front of her.

"The girl's a fool," the woman ranted. "A disgrace — "

"No!" Weiyan shot up from the chair. "I am not some little girl." She pounded a fist on the near gel pack.

A burst of light, an awful cracking sound of the floor splitting in two, and Jack found himself falling. Carter, Teal'c, Daniel... Their bodies tumbled against him as he spiraled downward.

A flash of red. Weiyan was falling, too.

A horrible roar filled Jack's ears. His arms flailed, seeking purchase, but he kept falling.

Until he hit bottom. Then, the last sound he heard was his head smacking something hard.

With a sigh, he sunk into the black.

CHAPTER SIX

EARTH

50 years earlier...

HUANG trekked across the great frozen valley, away from the Chappa'ai, away from his passage home. Though many hours had passed, sunlight was eternal in the frozen land of the Tau'ri. A fact never mentioned by his master Lord Yu, but no matter. The young Dragon Guard headed toward the great plume of smoke in the distance, determined to fulfill his Lord's bidding. He would find the Tau'ri. He would learn what had become of the land of his ancestors. He would not fail.

Left, then right. A step forward. Left, then right. Another step followed.

He used the two weapon staffs retrieved from Apophis' dead Jaffa as walking poles. Each stride forward was advanced first by a jab into the snow to insure it would hold his weight. He was no fool. As a child, he'd played often in the snow-covered land surrounding Lord Yu's fortress. What might seem like a dense patch could in truth be barely more than a gossamer of snow blanketing an endless crevasse underneath. The thick snow beneath his feet could be his enemy.

And yet...

He paused a moment to gaze out at the barren snowscape, the craggy rocks, the ancient blue-white glacial monuments which spoke to the eternal beauty of nature. The blues were bluer. The quality of light strikingly different from anything he had seen before. The sun above cast a softer, whiter shimmer above snow banks.

Huang's heart ached with the absence of his crèche-brother. If only Shi had survived to see the honesty in this landscape.

If only he was here to feel the cold, crisp nature of the wind.

If only the kresh'ta who had killed Shi was here now. Huang would rip the symbiote from the murderous Jaffa's pouch and watch him die in agony.

Left, then right. Another step forward. Huang knew he must stop soon and rest. It had been many hours since he'd left the Chappa'ai. He glanced once more toward the smoke emanating from the distant mountain beyond the valley and across a great flat expanse of land. The journey there would take many days.

More days than the sustenance he carried would allow.

He must keep his strength. Eat when he was hungry. Rest when he could. He stopped once more and crouched down, placing the staffs beside him. He unslung his satchel from his shoulder and pulled forth one of the two-score meatrolls wrapped in oiled parchment. Breaking off a small piece, he sighed. Only days ago, the slave Baozhai had packed these rations.

One more thing he would need to attend to upon his return home. Baozhai must be informed of Shi's death. Even if their affair was forbidden, Huang felt he must honor Shi by telling the girl of his brother's brave efforts and unfortunate demise.

When Lord Yu allowed him to return home, Huang would receive his *wénshēn*, take up his right as First Prime, and then do battle in Shi's name to ensure that honor lived on in all Dragon Guards to come.

Huang stuffed the other half of the meatroll back into the satchel, knowing he must stretch his food supplies. A shrill birdcall grabbed his attention. He looked up in time to see the bird's white underbelly and black-tipped wings soar downward toward the flat ice at the valley's end. Its wingspan was enormous, perhaps twice the length of a full-grown man.

And possible food to aid his journey.

"*What is your progress*?" asked Lord Yu from within the communications device.

"Arduous, my lord," Huang replied, removing the wired ball

and frame from his satchel.

"*Show me.*"

"Yes, my lord." Huang arose from his crouching position and held the communications rig aloft. He slowly turned around so that the System Lord might see a full panorama of the daunting landscape. He ended facing the smoke which rising from the distant mountain. "That is my destination, Lord. Certainly the Tau'ri — "

"*Impossible. Giza had no mountains, only flat desert.*"

"My lord?" Huang lowered the communications rig to eye-level. "Can mountains such as these grow in the thousand years since your time amongst the Tau'ri?"

"*As I said, impossible.*" The System Lord stroked his emperor's tuft, his face pensive. "*Tell me, you have been there for several days now. When last did the sun set?*"

"It has not, my lord."

Lord Yu harrumphed. "*Then you are not in Giza. If the Tau'ri's year is still the same length, it is summer where you have arrived.*"

"But my lord... The ice! The snow!"

"*You are at the southern pole. I am certain of it.*"

Huang took a step back in surprise. "But the Chappa'ai — "

It was a step he would forever regret.

He plummeted into a crevasse he had not seen. Powdered snow spilled across his face as gravity pulled him downward. When he jerked his arms outward to stop his descent, he lost his grip on the communications ball. The more he reached through the engulfing snow for the ball, the more snow toppled down. His eyes and skin stung from the burning cold. Though he held mouth shut, the snow filled his nostrils. He flailed against the avalanche of snow, sinking further and further down.

Some tired part of him, far off in the distant reaches of his mind, told him to stop moving. He did so, his descent immediately halting. Light still reached him though he'd sunk beneath the surface. That meant he wasn't too far below.

It meant he could still survive. Still escape.

But to what end? He had failed. Failed his master. Failed Shi.

Even if he could crawl back up to the surface, without the communications ball, he could never return home. Lord Yu's guards would fire without pause upon any unannounced arrivals through the Chappa'ai. So would the Serpent Guards of Chulak.

There was no planet to turn to, no means to return home.

Huang floated in the snow, allowing its insulation to warm his misery.

He had failed his other crèche-brothers, too. Qin Shi. Kong Qiu.

Kong Qiu.

The words of Qiu's great ancestor Confucius echoed across Huang's memory. A learning line from his boyhood tutor.

Failure is not falling down, but refusing to get up.

Slowly, ever carefully, Huang drew in his left arm. The snow didn't pull him down further.

He brought his right knee up to his chest. The snow remained calm. Pushing his leg downward, he pushed himself up. The snow gave him no argument. In small measures, he inched his way toward the light…

And broke through to the air above. One final push and he crawled from what could have been his snowy grave. Sliding on his belly, he moved back toward his earlier footprints, several arms' length away. It was only then that he allowed himself to sit up, gasping in great gulps of air.

His satchel was gone, and with it any source of food. While the snow would provide him with water aplenty, he would need to eat to survive. He looked for his staff weapons. One had disappeared, but the other was safely where he'd placed it earlier. He retrieved the staff and glanced overhead. The bird from earlier was gone, but where there was one, certainly more would come.

With the staff in his grip, he rose to meet the southern pole of the Tau'ri. Yes, he had failed his master and his family, but he now knew he could survive.

He would survive. He must. For to do otherwise would give his life no purpose.

And his brother's death no meaning.

He would learn the truth of the Tau'ri. And then, he would find a way home, his duty to his lord and master complete. Then, and only then, would he ask Lord Yu's aid in crushing the Jaffa who had killed Lao Shi.

It was only a matter of when and where.

CHAPTER SEVEN

ANCIENT OUTPOST, ANTARCTICA
18 AUG 04/1435 HRS MCMURDO STATION

TWO-HUNDRED feet beneath the Ferrar Glacier, the once calm, almost serene outpost had become mayhem. Airmen rushed across fallen ice and snow. Scientists struggled to retrieve toppled-over equipment. Between sobs and shouts, diplomats and trainees huddled in the main chamber.

Through the entire ruckus, George held vigil over a ten-foot wide hole in the floor beside the still activated weapons chair. Somewhere hidden below the milky-white force field covering the ragged tear in the floor were his people: Jack, SG-1, and the Chinese trainee.

Someone stuck a cup of coffee in his hand. "Thank you."

Dr. Lee shuffled up beside him. "Have you tried calling out to them?"

"Repeatedly." George took a sip of the welcome coffee. Black, two sugars. Someone knew him all too well.

Lee stuck his foot out toward the hole. "It's possible the force field muffles sound waves."

"I wouldn't do that, if— "

A faint electrical charge shot out from the force field, attacking Lee's boot. The scientist stumbled back a few paces.

"Doesn't carry much of a punch, does it?" Still, George had tried to break through multiple times with nary a dent. "Are you all right?"

"I think so." Keeping his distance, Lee peered at the hole. "The edges are mostly yellowish sandstone sandwiched between layers of dark gray volcanic basalt."

"Drillable?"

"If the force field hasn't spread under the floor beyond the hole, sure. It's too thick to see much of anything."

"Let's bring in a drilling team," George suggested. "Contact McMurdo."

"I'm not sure drilling's a good idea, General." Lee pulled his glasses off and wiped them on his fleece pullover. "With this much geological instability, it could bring the whole outpost down on us."

"And we'd lose the weapons chair," George realized. He drained his cup in disgust. "What happens next, Doctor?"

"Next, General?" Squinting, Lee returned his glasses to their rightful position.

"That's right, Doctor. Next." George threw his shoulders back and stared the scientist down to make his point. He knew Lee was in shock. They all were, but now wasn't the time for standing around and contemplating their navels. "That fall probably knocked our people unconscious, otherwise General O'Neill would be yelling bloody murder. Get that force field down and our people retrieved. Am I clear?"

As if to reinforce his point, a low rumble started beneath them. The trellised panels rattled. A few moments later, the shaking subsided.

"Aftershocks," Lee mumbled. Holding on to one of the pillars arranged around the platformed chair, he knelt down until his face was only inches from the force field. "I think one of the scientists might have some gear I could use."

"Then go get that gear and bring it in here, pronto," George ordered. "The sooner you get started, the sooner we'll have our people back."

PLANET DESIGNATION: UNKNOWN
STATUS: UNKNOWN
TIME: UNKNOWN... UNKNOWN... UNKNOWN...

There's a moment when nothing exists while stepping through an active Stargate. It's that microsecond between heartbeats. A sliver of nonexistence where all sensations disappear. There's no sound, no scent, no taste or touch, and certainly nothing to see.

Until stepping out the other side.

Daniel stood on a stone platform no different than countless other platforms on countless other trips. The loamy scent of rich soil tickled his nostrils. Rolling hills covered in jewel-green ferns spread out as far as the eye could see. Bright sunlight warmed his face.

Sunlight. Warmth.

As opposed to?

That didn't make sense. As a student of ancient cultures, he would use that instant of gate-travel to wipe away presupposed expectations. While first impressions could be wrong so could making comparisons. He'd learned that the hard way. He always needed a moment to push aside his last location so he could judge a new planet fairly.

It was no different this time. Except, when he mentally tried to push away that last moment before stepping through, nothing came to mind.

Perspiration dripped down his back. Upon hearing the event horizon collapse behind him, he decided to unzip his operation jacket. His hand came in contact with a fleece pullover. A glimpse of Sam and Teal'c showed them wearing the same thing: green fleece pullovers and black wool pants.

So was Jack, who'd somehow arrived ahead of them, wearing the same get-up and seeming very pissed. Especially since no one had a GDO.

"Dial us home, Carter. Now."

Daniel stepped to the edge of the platform. "Jack, what's going on?"

"We're gating out of here, that's what." Jack rushed over to the DHD. "We'll head to the Alpha site."

"Wait a minute!" Daniel ran down the platform steps. Sam and Teal'c followed close behind. "Don't we want to figure out where 'here' is, first?"

"Not really, no." Jack jabbed a finger in the air. "Someone's playing games with us and I'm not in the mood."

Someone needed to calm their normally fearless leader fast.

Fortunately, Teal'c took the fall. "O'Neill, have you any memory of — ?"

"Nada. Bupkiss." Jack's voice lowered.

"Me, either," said Daniel.

"The last thing I remember was…" Sam frowned. "Well, that's odd."

"Carter?"

"Sir, I remember who I am." She gestured at Jack, then Daniel and then Teal'c. "I remember all of you, but — "

"Yeah, I'm having trouble, too," Daniel said. "My long-term memory's fine, but short-term's — "

"Gone," Jack whispered. His eyes darkened, causing Daniel to wonder what had happened before the rest of them had arrived.

Sam gestured toward the DHD. "Uh, Daniel? I can't find the point-of-origin symbol."

Daniel slid between Jack and the DHD and studied the DHD's round control panel. Everything seemed normal; two concentric rings of nineteen glyphs apiece surrounded the central red half-sphere control globe. On closer examination, he found a new glyph-key. Twin lines twisted around each other like a double helix. He pointed it out to Sam.

"You're sure?" she asked. "I've never seen that before. Teal'c?"

SG-1's resident Jaffa bent over the DHD and examined the glyph. "Your estimation is as good as mine."

Behind them, Jack exhaled loudly. "It's a 'guess,' T. As in 'your guess is as good as.'"

Teal'c straightened up from the pedestal. "I have often found Colonel Carter and Daniel Jackson's hypotheses to be far superior to mere guesses. Should we not trust them now?"

"You'll get no argument from me." With a flourish, Jack gestured toward the DHD. "Dial it up, Colonel."

"Yes, sir." She pressed the first key, its telltale kachink followed soon by the gate's top chevron lighting up.

"You see that?" Jack smacked at Daniel's arm. "Six more symbols, one big kawoosh, a quick hop to the Alpha site, and we'll be home for supper."

Kachink. Five more symbols to go.

"I still think we're making a mistake." Daniel turned his gaze toward the valley below and the hill just beyond.

Kachink. Three down, four to go.

He couldn't see any buildings. No other identifiable markings. But that hill…

Kachink. Another chevron lit up.

"There's something familiar about this place," he announced.

"No, there really isn't." Jack yanked off his pullover revealing a black long-sleeved t-shirt underneath.

Kachink.

Daniel followed suit, pushing his sleeves up to reveal the same shirt, only white. "That's odd."

Jack looked down at his shirt and then at Daniel's. "Not half as odd as…"

"What?"

"Nothing," Jack answered with a scowl. He turned back toward the DHD. "Hurry it up, Carter. Our attire isn't exactly in line with the local climate."

"O'Neill, should we not determine what brought us here before returning to the SGC?"

"Later, T." Jack shoved his hands into his pockets. "SG-1 can come back with weapons, GDOs, the whole works."

Kachink.

Daniel couldn't help but notice Jack's left hand balled up in his pocket, as if he had something in it. He checked his own pockets. Nothing. Not even a bit of lint.

"Last one, sir." Sam tapped the new point-of-origin key, and pressed down on the control globe. As the red sphere lit up, Daniel tensed. No matter how many times he'd been through the gate that moment of anticipation never failed.

Until now.

There was no active wormhole.

"What the hell?" Jack threw down his pullover.

"The DHD should work," Sam reported. "The correct glyphs light up. The control globe's engaged."

Jack's face went taut. "Fix it."

"Sir, I don't have any tools."

"I don't care!"

As Sam flinched, Daniel heard a distant rumble. Like a waterfall. No one else mentioned it so he returned to the matter-at-hand. "Calm down, Jack. We'll figure it out. We always do."

"Look, Carter, I'm sorry." Jack rubbed the back of his neck, a gesture Daniel had seen him repeat several times since they'd arrived.

Jack caught Daniel's glance and dropped his hand to his side. "Just, figure it out."

The rumble grew louder. Daniel could feel it in his boots. "Anyone hear that?" He turned his gaze upwards, but saw nothing. Just blue sky and a bright sun.

"We're about to be hit by an ambush, aren't we?" Jack glanced up as well. "I'm thinking Ba'al or one of his cronies got bored. That has to be what that thing was about earlier."

Thing? Daniel raised an eyebrow. "What did you see, Jack?"

"Leave it alone, Daniel."

More rumbling. Pebbles around the base of the DHD began to scatter.

Teal'c scanned the horizon. "The skies are clear, O'Neill."

"Sir, I recommend dialing the gate manually," Sam said.

"Right. Good!" For the first time since their arrival, Jack actually smiled.

The rumbling stopped.

Jack gestured toward Teal'c and then the gate. "Do it."

Teal'c climbed onto the gate platform. Taking hold of the inner ring, he pulled downward for a manual dial. As the ring slid through the outer rim, Daniel considered their circumstances. Beyond not being able to remember how they got there, two other things bothered him. First off, it was sunny, which somehow seemed wrong. Second, Jack kept fidgeting with his pocket, almost as if he was…

"What's that?" Daniel pointed at Jack's pocket.

"Nothing." Jack stuck his hands behind his back. "You realize we have no weapons."

Daniel shrugged, letting Jack's misdirection slide for the moment. "We've been in worse spots."

"Not in these get-ups." Jack headed toward the gate platform where Teal'c stood, staring up at the Stargate. "What's the hold-up?"

"Observe." Teal'c gestured toward the inner ring as it spun through the various symbols. "It will not lock."

"That's not possible." Sam ran up the platform and grabbed hold of the inner ring, stopping its forward momentum.

Daniel joined Jack at the platform's base. He peered up at the Stargate. All seven chevrons were still lit up. "Try turning it the other way."

With a slight bow of his head, Teal'c grasped hold of the ring and tried to push upwards. It wouldn't budge.

The ground trembled again.

"All right," Daniel said. "This is bad."

"That's an understatement." Jack ran up the steps and positioned himself behind the gate. With Teal'c on the other side, the two pushed against the inner ring, but to no avail.

Daniel climbed up and joined the others in pushing and pulling at the inner ring. In the distance, the tremors continued — a low constant rumble.

"This is going nowhere." Jack wiped his brow. "Somehow, we've busted the thing."

"It could be worse," Daniel said.

"Oh, really?" Jack said with more than a bit of sarcasm.

"We could be surrounded by enemy troops," Teal'c offered.

"The day's not over yet." Jack pointed over at the DHD. "What would happen if we popped the top off? That doesn't need anything other than brute strength. Or Teal'c."

"Sir, I'm not sure that's a good idea," Sam said. "If we break the control crystal, it might prevent any wormhole from forming — outgoing or incoming."

The platform started shaking. Daniel grabbed onto the gate. "We should find a safer place. Someone will report us missing."

Jack raised an eyebrow. "Like who?"

The rumbling calmed and Daniel let go. "General Hammond — "

"Hammond's in D.C." Jack crossed his arms. "Is there anything else you're forgetting?"

"That wasn't forgetting. That was habit. You've been General all of — " Daniel tried to push aside the fog covering his recent memories. He remembered Jack's first speech as general. Sam's promotion to Lt. Colonel. The Atlantis expedition leaving for the Pegasus Galaxy.

The rumbling returned, strong enough to shake the platform. The chevrons' glass and metal parts rattled against the Stargate's stone surface.

"My God, I can't remember."

"Tell me about it," Jack shouted. "I couldn't even remember who I was when I got here."

That piece of news alarmed Daniel, but he didn't have time to ask Jack more. The tremors had intensified to an almost deafening rumble.

The platform surged sideways. Daniel stumbled to his knees. As he scrambled to his feet, Sam ran down the stairs toward the DHD. Jack raced to the platform's edge.

"Carter, stop!"

An explosion of dirt sprayed up around the DHD. Jack dived off and knocked Sam out of the way as the ground surrounding the pedestal thrust upwards. The DHD toppled to its side.

A loud crack reverberated across the platform. Daniel watched in paralyzed horror as a fracture snaked open along the steps leading up to the gate.

Teal'c grabbed his arm and together, they jumped off the platform. Above the din of the tremors, a grinding noise started up. The gate began to sway back and forth.

"Run!" Following Jack's lead, they raced down the hill. Daniel stumbled to keep up, tripping over micro-fissures erupting across the fern-covered terrain.

Dirt spewed up in front him. He stumbled backward. Another spout of earth exploded to his right and he lost his balance. Teal'c grabbed his shirt collar, yanking him back on to his feet.

Jack led the way as they raced down the hill. The overgrown ferns scratched at Daniel's face, but he kept on running.

Finally, they reached the bottom of the hill, the tremors diminished. Another hundred yards and the quake stopped.

Jack raised a fist, signaling them to halt. "Everyone all right?"

Daniel opened his mouth to answer, but never got the chance. A thunderous boom erupted behind them. He spun toward the sound only to see the hill they'd just descended torn in two. For a moment, the gate swayed back and forth, perched precariously close to one edge of the forming crevasse. Another tremor hit. The tear in the ground widened, and the gate toppled into the chasm below.

The hill collapsed and the Stargate was buried.

Teal'c felt no small measure of ease when the world ceased to shake. True, the Stargate was inaccessible, but he had long come to believe that SG-1 could and would always succeed in finding a means of escape.

To believe otherwise would serve no purpose. He recognized this as he climbed to his feet. O'Neill stood up as well. Though he whispered a soft groan, the man showed no signs of injury. Colonel Carter crouched beside Daniel Jackson. She ripped a strip of cloth from her shirt and wiped his face clean of blood. Upon closer examination, Teal'c was gratified to find his friend had only suffered minor cuts.

"Everyone all right?" O'Neill asked.

"Dandy," said Daniel Jackson as he attempted to wipe dirt from his face.

"I am also well." Teal'c permitted himself a brief smile at the young man's adoption of O'Neill's phrase.

"Carter?" O'Neill knelt down.

Colonel Carter nodded. "Fine, sir. Just a bit shook up."

O'Neill rose and raised a hand to his brow, blocking the sunlight. "Let's figure out what we have and then what we need to get out of here."

"We'll need a Stargate, for one thing," said Daniel Jackson.

"You let me worry about that."

Colonel Carter glanced at the field of rubble from which they'd escaped. "Daniel's right, sir. We have no way of knowing how stable the ground above the gate will be and without the right tools to dig it out— "

"I said, let me worry about that." O'Neill spun on his heels and strode off in the opposite direction.

Teal'c scanned their very much-altered surroundings. Beyond the collapsed hill, a large grass-covered plain stretched out for several miles. Though his vision was not as it once had been while carrying a symbiote, he believed he could see an expanse of trees at the plain's far end. Without closer inspection, he could not be certain.

To either side and behind them rose more hills, each no more than a hundred yards from their current position. O'Neill had reached the base of the hill to their rear and sat down. He bent and retied his shoelace.

Daniel Jackson stood up. "You don't suppose he's thinking of what happened on Edora, do you?"

"I do not," Teal'c said. "The circumstances are sufficiently different."

Colonel Carter also rose. "For one thing, he had us on the other side working to bring him home."

Teal'c grimaced at the memory. More than four years ago,

a meteor shower on Edora had buried the Stargate, stranding O'Neill beyond their reach. It had taken three months of little to no sleep for then Major Carter to devise a means to pierce through the hardened naquadah above the Edoran gate's horizon. Teal'c had volunteered to go through and tunnel the remaining way to the surface. It was only when little oxygen remained that O'Neill had found him. In a certain sense, the rescue had been mutual.

Indeed, most of SG-1's missions had been resolved by group efforts. This is why it disturbed Teal'c to see O'Neill withdraw at a time when they needed him most. Action was required and though O'Neill no longer led SG-1, he remained their de facto leader.

With a curt nod to Daniel Jackson and Colonel Carter, Teal'c jogged over to O'Neill's location. The effort left him a bit more winded than it should have, but then the past hour had certainly taken its toll on all of them.

He slowed as he neared O'Neill, allowing his brother-in-arms a moment to collect himself. "Should we not search for a solution to our predicament?"

"And what predicament would that be?" O'Neill asked, pulling a small metal object from his pants' pocket. With a flick of his wrist, the cap flipped back.

Teal'c raised an eyebrow upon seeing the lighter. He had searched his pockets shortly after their arrival and found nothing. "I do not believe any of us found similar items in our possession."

O'Neill thumbed the wheel. When a flame sparked up from the lighter's metal cage, a brief smile appeared on his face. Perhaps an indication that O'Neill had returned to good humor.

The smile faded. "You know what? I'm not buying this so-called predicament we've gotten ourselves into."

"And yet the Stargate is buried."

"Hell, T, we couldn't get it to work even when it wasn't." O'Neill snapped the lighter shut.

"Then what do you propose?"

"That we find a way off this rock." O'Neill stood up and steadily met his gaze.

"Do you believe that to be possible?" Teal'c asked, inwardly pleased by his brother's renewed optimism.

O'Neill glanced once more at his lighter and then returned it to his pocket. "It's not like we have a choice, but yes, I do. Something's not adding up here, and I've got a hunch I know what this is about. If I'm right, I'm gonna be pissed."

"A hunch. Somewhat like Colonel Carter or Daniel Jackson's estimations?"

"Possibly, but I don't think we're in any danger. Let's move out."

Though none of them had watches with which to measure time, O'Neill sent each member of SG-1 in a different direction with orders to return within what 'felt like' thirty minutes. Teal'c volunteered to survey the plains beyond the flattened hill.

As he cautiously made his way past the scattered remains of broken rock and debris, he searched for any sign that the Stargate might be easily unburied. The possibility of retrieval became less and less likely as he walked by boulders as large as O'Neill's truck scattered across the area. Though he regretted admitting it, even he would not be strong enough to move them out of the way.

He walked beyond the destruction, stepping over smaller rocks that littered the landscape. Many of them seemed smoother, as if worn away by the action of water. Perhaps Colonel Carter could explain how the hill's collapse could cause such a phenomenon.

Upon reaching safer terrain, Teal'c picked up his pace. He jogged across more even ground and long-bladed grasses, heading toward the tree line at the field's end. As he reached the woods' outer edge, a glint of silver flashed from between the deeply fissured tree trunks that populated the woods. Teal'c dropped to his knees. A Jaffa's armor reflecting against the sparse sunlight may have been the cause. Another flash prompted him to creep inwards, remaining low to avoid detection.

He heard no sound of birds or wildlife. There were no footsteps save his own soft tread. Often, low hanging branches studded with red conical-shaped flowers impeded his momentum. He knew he should turn back, having far exceeded O'Neill's thirty-minute window, but what he could discern from the flashes might be critical to SG-1's survival. He proceeded forward until he came to the edge of a cliff and looked out.

In the canyon below, a multi-spired citadel sprawled for many miles. At its center stood a single oblong tower, built of metal and glass, undoubtedly a good half-mile high. Sunlight glistened off its windows. Though Teal'c was too far away to be certain, he believed he saw movement along the citadel's outer stone wall, a ten-foot high ring of white stone polished to such a sheen that the neighboring lake shimmered against its sides. He counted six terraces around the city's outer buildings, each formed of colored glass panels cross-braced with steel beams.

Be they friend or foe, whoever had accomplished such an engineering feat would certainly have the means to assist SG-1. Teal'c hurried back to his friends, hopeful that O'Neill's hunch was right and that such assistance would come freely and not at a price too high to pay.

"A penny for your thoughts, Carter."

Sam suppressed a grin. Whatever had troubled General O'Neill earlier seemed to have flown out the proverbial window. He was practically jovial, squatting down beside her, chewing innocuously on a blade of grass.

They'd taken up position behind a bush some fifty yards back from an archway carved into the wall surrounding the city Teal'c had discovered. From what she could see so far, the people living there had to be extremely advanced. There was no other way to explain the slender, graceful buildings or the cableless cars sliding up their sides. What she wouldn't do for a —

"Carter?"

Sam rocked back on her heels and sighed. "To be honest, sir, I just wish I had some of my equipment." She glanced up at the sun. It hadn't really changed altitude since they'd arrived on the planet. "A spectrometer would be nice. The light's — "

"A P90 might be useful." He plucked another blade of grass.

"Sir, you probably shouldn't sample the local vegetation. We've no way of knowing if it's poisonous or not."

"Oh, I don't think we're in any trouble from that quarter." He waved the blade toward the archway. "We've got company."

Two men dressed in belted beige-colored tunics, off-white trousers and matching shirts took up guard on either side of the arch. "It's tough to see this far off, but I think they're wearing side-arms, sir."

"You think we should waltz up to them and ask for help?"

Sam shrugged. "I don't see any other choice."

"Certainly our appearances do not seem threatening," Teal'c said, crouched on her other side.

Behind her, Daniel handed his watch cap to Teal'c. "It wouldn't hurt to be a bit less conspicuous."

"So what's your plan?" the general asked as Teal'c positioned the hat over his gold serpent tattoo.

Sam faced the general, surprised. "My plan, sir?"

"At the moment, Colonel," he pointed at her, "you're SG-1's commanding officer. I'm just a lowly general in your keeping."

"Yes, sir." She squared her shoulders. "Well, since this is a first contact — "

Daniel tapped her on the shoulder. "Your resident archaeologist-slash-linguist should take lead."

The general snorted. "Why am I not surprised?"

"Daniel's right, sir. We've no way of knowing if they're friendlies or not, and he's better at playing ambassador than — "

"I get it, Carter. You don't need to explain." The general glanced back at Daniel. "At least, not yet."

Thankful for General O'Neill's support, Sam studied the city guards. They were armed, SG-1 wasn't, and unless she wanted to wait until dark and sneak in, there really wasn't anything they could do to change the situation. Realizing she was putting off the inevitable, she gestured forward with two fingers. "Daniel, you're up. Teal'c, take our six. General O'Neill?"

"Yes, ma'am?" The general tossed aside his blade of grass.

"You're with me."

At Daniel's suggestion, they rose slowly from their position behind the bushes, arms raised.

The guards didn't move.

"Hello!" Daniel strolled ahead. "We're from Earth. And to be honest, we could use your help."

Eyes forward, arms resting at their sides, the guards remained motionless. Sam held her breath as they closed the distance to ten yards. She smiled to show they were friendly.

Daniel held up his hand, signaling an all-stop. With a nod from Sam, the general and Teal'c came to a halt. Daniel continued on, walking up to the guard on the left. "My name is Daniel. This is Samantha Carter, Teal'c, and Colonel O'Neill."

The general coughed none too subtly into his hand.

"Sorry," Daniel said. "I mean General… General O'Neill."

Neither guard moved a muscle.

"Why do they not respond?" Teal'c asked.

Daniel narrowed his brow. "Maybe they're trained that way. As long as we don't present a threat, they'll ignore us."

Sam stepped up to the other guard. "We'd like to talk to your leaders, if— "

"Forget it." The general strode up and snapped his fingers in the guard's face twice. No response. The man didn't blink. "These guys would put Buckingham Palace's guards to shame."

Teal'c cocked his head. "Buckingham Palace?"

"It's in England," Daniel explained. "The Queen's guard isn't allowed to react to the tourists unless there are extraordinary circumstances."

The general waved a hand in front of the guard. "I guess we're not that extraordinary."

"Indeed." Teal'c leaned into the archway. "There are many people within the city. Perhaps they will consider us more — "

"Extraordinary?" Sam gestured for the general and Teal'c to close ranks. "Guards may be one thing, but there's no way to know how the city's inhabitants will react. I recommend proceeding with caution."

Daniel took the lead again and they passed through the archway. They came out onto a wide avenue running parallel with a series of meter-high granite obelisks. Rows of purple flowers — reminiscent of lilacs — lined each side of the street. Though there wasn't anyone in the immediate area, a glance upwards revealed locals walking across various bridges leading in and out of the central tower. Some were dressed in pale flowing robes. Others wore outfits similar to the guards by the arch.

Sam inspected the tower's base. Unlike the broad top levels, the narrow bottom was made of brownish stone. One end appeared to be open with a pulsating light emanating from inside. She clenched and unclenched her hands, wishing yet again for the proper equipment.

"Here's someone," Daniel said.

A white-haired woman dressed in long robes headed their way. Sam guessed she was in her late sixties. She carried a metal case, about the size of a shoebox, and as she neared, Sam noticed floral garlands wrapped around her wrists. The woman strode with a grace that belied her apparent age, her robes flapping behind her.

Daniel hurried over. "Hello, I'm Doctor — "

The woman walked on by, ignoring all of them.

"I guess you're not her type," the general jerked his head in Teal'c's direction. "Here come two more. Be nice, Daniel."

A man and woman, both dressed in the same military garb, marched toward them. As they neared, Sam stepped off to stand by one of the obelisks, careful to not step on the flowers lining the walkway. They really did remind her of lilacs though they didn't carry the same heavy scent.

"Excuse me. Hello?" Daniel called out to the approaching couple. "We've come through the Stargate."

They kept walking, not batting so much as an eyelid.

As they passed Teal'c, he offered, "Perhaps their language is dissimilar, Daniel Jackson."

"Good point." Daniel shoved his glasses further up the bridge of his nose. "Chappa'ai?"

Nothing. They breezed past him like he was nothing more than an ant on the sidewalk.

"*Anulus? Circacona*?" He dropped his hands. "*Porta*?"

"Enough with the playing nice." General O'Neill darted out in front of the couple and raised his hands. "Listen, folks — "

The man strode right through the general without so much as a ripple.

He continued on, the woman at his side. The general whirled toward Sam, the white scar on his eyebrow stretched tight. "What just happened?"

"I don't know, sir." Though it would explain why the flowers didn't put out any scent. She bent down to pick one.

Her hand passed through it. "Maybe it's some kind of hologram technology?"

Daniel walked over to another obelisk and waved his hand. It went directly through. He headed around to the other side.

"Perhaps ghosts?" Teal'c added.

"Ghosts, my ass." General O'Neill pointed toward the departing couple. "They've got something to do with this. The lost memories, the gate. The whole shebang."

"Maybe…" Daniel mumbled from behind the obelisk. "Guys, I think I found something."

Sam hurried over to join him. Rectangular rows of block-like glyphs covered the obelisk's back end.

"I have seen this language before," Teal'c observed.

"You should have," Daniel said. "It's Ancient."

General O'Neill took a step back from the obelisk. "Ancient as in 'old' or Ancient as in — "

"The Ancients." Daniel pointed to a lower section of the text etched into the granite. "It's an older dialect. Similar to the language we found on Heliopolis."

"Ernest Littlefield's planet." Sam glanced back up at the traffic on the bridges outside the central tower. Ghostly foot traffic, she reminded herself. "Can you translate it?"

"Huh." Daniel's head jerked up. "That's interesting."

"What?" the general demanded. "Daniel, so help me god. If you tell me I have to stick my head in another brain-sucking machine to get us out of here, I'll quit. I'll resign my — "

"I didn't mean that sort of interesting. Although, really? You'd quit?"

"Daniel…" The general growled.

"Just kidding. Sort of." He pointed toward the bowed top of the stone where the Ancient glyphs were twice the size as the lower text. "According to this, the planet or the city, I'm not sure which, is named Pedion Elysium."

"Like Elysium Fields?"

Surprised, Sam raised an eyebrow in his direction.

"I do read, you know. *Henry V.* Act four. Scene one."

"William Shakespeare," Teal'c said. "'What infinite heart's-ease must kings neglect that private men enjoy.'"

"Yeah, that's the one." The general's grin disappeared.

"You can remember Shakespeare, but not how we got here?" Daniel asked.

General O'Neill crossed his arms. "Can you?"

"No. But — "

"Then don't mock, Daniel. It doesn't suit you."

Pushing aside the idea that General O'Neill and Teal'c both read Shakespeare, Sam examined the stone's lettering more closely. "What does this Elysium have to with the Ancients?"

"Actually, it makes sense." Daniel waved toward the flowers at the base of the obelisk. "The lilacs. The woman with garlands on her wrists. In Greek mythology, Elysian Fields. Or Elysium if you use the Latin derivative like — "

"Daniel," the general warned. "Cut to the chase."

"Right." Daniel ran a hand through his hair. "Elysium was considered the hero's final resting place. The Greek poet Pindar referred to Elysium as an island." His eyes went wide. "Now that I think of it, Pindar's account mentions a Kronos."

"We killed that slimy snakehead off years ago."

"I don't think it's the same, Jack. In this case, Kronos could be connected to the Hellenistic embodiment of time."

"Time. As in?"

Daniel gestured to a lower passage. "In this case, more like..." His fingers traced along a line of text. "More like slipping free of time. This place, Pedion Elysium..." He whirled toward the general. "'A final resting place!' I think this might have been one of the last colonies of the Ancients before they ascended."

"You mean like Vis Uban?" Sam asked. "How does that explain how we got here?"

"Or why the people appear as ghosts," Teal'c added, "unaware of our presence."

"Jack, don't you get it?" Daniel excitedly raised his hands toward the walkways above. "If this is — was — one of the last pre-ascension colonies of the Ancients, your Ancient genetics might have something to do with how we got here."

"And that's supposed to make me happy, how?" Pissed, Jack turned toward the central tower. What Daniel said made sense. It confirmed his suspicions. Underlined his resentment at having that damned ATA gene.

Sure, being able to save Earth's butt had its benefit. But this time, thanks to his grandparents' great-grandparents' heritage, they were somehow stuck on a god-forsaken planet with a bunch of walking Ancient holo-ghost-whatevers. The whole thing made him want to lie down, just turn his brain off, and take a nap.

"Help! Somebody? Please!"

The cry for help came from the other side of the wall. It sounded like a woman, but he couldn't be certain. Without another thought, Jack broke into a run with SG-1 hot on his heels. They reached the arch and he jerked up his fist, signaling the team to halt. He peered through the arch and saw a small-built woman with a long black ponytail. She ran parallel with the outside wall, away from their position.

Whoever she was, her get-up was pretty much like his, except her pullover was red, not green. Could be a friend. Could be a foe. He had no way of knowing. He pulled his head back and gestured toward Carter and Teal'c to take the far left. With a nod back to Daniel to follow, he slid out the right side and hugged the outer wall.

"*Yo ren ting jian wo ma*?"

What the hell?

The woman turned around and froze when she caught sight of Jack and the others.

High forehead. A narrow, but square jaw. She wasn't so much a woman as a barely out of teenaged youth.

He wasn't sure how, but he knew this girl.

"You!" He stormed toward her. "You know what's going on here, don't you?"

"Jack!" Footsteps behind him announced his conscience coming to tell him to back off.

This time he refused to listen.

"No, Daniel." He grabbed the girl's elbow. "The gate's gone so how did you get here?"

"I don't know!" The girl started to do the very thing Jack hated more than anything.

She started to sob.

He counted to three, letting his temper simmer down.

"I think you do know," he finally told her. "I don't know how, but I've seen you before. And, I think you know who we are, too."

"Sir..."

"Not now, Carter," he said, gritting his teeth. "I want the truth, damn it. I'm tired of this bullshit."

"I told you," the girl yelled, breaking free from his grip, "I don't know!"

The ground started shaking again.

"O'Neill — "

"Yeah, I feel it." But he really didn't care. Not anymore. He seized both her arms and held on. "Who the hell are you and how the hell did you get here?"

The rumbling intensified beneath his feet. Walls cracked. He thought he heard glass shatter.

The girl jutted out her chin. "I. Don't. Know!"

A boom shot out, echoing across the canyon. The wall to Jack's right shattered into a spray of rock, spewing toward them with ferocious velocity. As he yanked the girl out of the way, a second boom shook the ground, tossing him off his feet. With a hand over the girl's head, he kissed the dirt and hoped for the best.

In less than a heartbeat, the tremors stopped. He waited another moment just to be sure.

"It's over, Jack." A hand on his arm. Daniel. "You better take a look."

Jack released the girl and climbed to his feet. Daniel was pointing back toward the city or, rather, where the city had once been.

The canyon was empty. Rippled waves of heat rolled across a barren wasteland populated only by yellowed grass, dirt and dust. No, Jack realized, that wasn't quite true. Squinting against the hot sunlight, he made out a small brownish building, no more than a story high. Maybe a half a click off.

"Was that not the central tower's location?" Teal'c asked.

"You see it, too?" A glance at Carter gave Jack the nod he needed to confirm he wasn't certifiably nuts.

Movement next to the building caught his eyes. The outline of a person. Maybe a man. Too far off to tell. Whoever it was, he — or she — waved their arms. A bit of cloth flapped in the breeze. A flag of some sorts. Or a robe.

That damned breeze.

A sudden chill seized Jack's bones and he tried remember.

No. No trying.

He strode up to the girl. "You're that trainee from the outpost, Weiyan — "

"Weiyan Shi," the girl said. "Why are we not in Antarctica?"

CHAPTER EIGHT

ANTARCTICA
50 years earlier...

HUANG crept toward his prey, resisting the urge for self-ridicule. As First Prime of Lord Yu, he would have sought greater enemies on the field of battle. The Jaffa armies of Sokar, Apophis, even Ra would have trembled as he led the Dragon Guards against them.

Instead, his life had been reduced to exile within the frozen wasteland of the Tau'ri's southern pole. Worse, his head and heart warred over whether it was just to kill the creature before him. The odd black-and-white bird waddling before him walked more like an old man than a bird in search of flight. Its orange-lined black beak crooned piteously as if calling out in loss. To kill such a creature felt wrong.

But necessary. Hunger gnawed at Huang's belly as he watched the bird cease its cries. It stopped walking, preening the dense white feathers on its chest. Two days had passed since losing his satchel. Two days with no food and little sleep. A blizzard had hit only hours after losing his gear, forcing him to find refuge in an ice cave. For hours he'd laid within the rippled blue ice, wrapped only in his cloaks. On occasion, his eyes would play tricks on him, casting golden-white tendrils of light across the cave's floor. He would squeeze his eyes shut against the mirage, his mind rolling over the great failure that had led to his plight. Staving off self-pity, he strived to find hope, or at least the chance of it in the future.

Upon the storm's end, he had ventured out again to follow the great glacial cliff along the frozen sea. He felt for all the world as if he stood alone on the Tau'ri's planet. He was not fool enough to believe Lord Yu would send rescue. For all his master knew, he was dead. If Huang did not find true shelter from the cold soon, that would surely be his fate. Several of his toes had begun to blacken with festers swelling near the tips where his nails had worked loose.

But first, he must eat. Even if it meant killing the man-like bird to do so. Less than ten paces from what would become his next meal, Huang thumbed the staff weapon's trigger. The firing head opened, releasing a short crackle of energy as it charged.

The bird's head swung up. A single caw erupted and black eyes darted in Huang's direction. Its oblong wings flapped though no flight occurred.

A single shot blasted off its head.

Using his staff weapon, Huang hobbled over to the dead bird. Blood oozed from its severed head. He pulled out his belt-knife and sliced the creature's breast open, revealing a thick layer of fat. The pungent stench curdled in his nose, smelling more like fish than fowl.

Breathing only through his mouth to fight off the stink, he sliced down further, revealing tender red meat underneath. He carved away the fat, filleted the breasts and withdrew them from the carcass. Flipping the bird over, he took a half-step back and blasted its feathers with the staff weapon. Over the ensuing embers, he roasted the meat on his knife's point.

He bit into the barely seared meat and immediately spat it out, overwhelmed by the rank taste. Shoving down the bile that threatened to rise, he forced himself to eat the entire thing.

As he consumed the putrid meal, disgust crossed his mind. A reflection of how purposeless his life had become.

Here sits the once-future First Prime of Lord Yu, relegated to eating whatever vile sustenance I can find.

A glimmer of golden light flashed to his far right. At first he believed it only a trick of his eyes, teary as they were from the smell. When the light flared again, he rose up from his meal and turned toward its source.

Nothing. The light had disappeared. In the far distance, many days' walk from his position, smoke bellowed from a high mountain. With reluctance, he admitted to himself that the smoke did not come from the same location he'd seen days ago. The earlier storm must have forced him off-course.

Even so, where there was smoke, there would be Tau'ri. Huang heaved a heavy sigh. He knew not what he would do upon meeting them, but if Lord Yu cared so greatly for these people, Huang had to believe they would welcome his presence.

The golden-white light flashed again, emanating from beyond the next bend in the glacial cliff. Ignoring the pain in his feet, Huang ran until he reached a tattered red flag attached to a pole wedged into a stone cairn.

The light was still there, hovering a mere hand's length above the wedged-together pile of rocks. Huang cautiously approached. The cairn was no more than a few paces wide though its top stones were higher than his head. Too small to be the burial place of any Tau'ri, he knew not what the cairn contained.

He picked up one of the rocks, its surface smooth. Weatherworn, he realized. Glancing up at the light, Huang noticed long white tendrils extending from its center.

"Thank you," he said, though the very idea of speaking to a light felt foolish. "Are you a friend of the Tau'ri?"

The light ascended from the cairn, its tendrils folding in along its central column. Huang stumbled back in fear that he'd upset the strange being.

"Are you foe?" he dared asked.

The light flared bright gold, and then, disappeared.

Huang returned his attention to the cairn. Grabbing stone after stone, he pulled down one wall and then another. Several bundles nestled between the stones, covered by what appeared to be gray woolen blankets. They would help keep him warm on his journey. Lifting up a blanket, he discovered that it was fashioned as a pairs of pants. Relief washed through him. The added clothing would aid his climb up the mountain to the Tau'ri. He gathered up the woolen clothes.

A glint of metal beneath them caught his attention. Pulling back more of the woolen items, he found small, colorfully wrapped packages. Some shaped like blocks, covered in what seemed thin metal paper with strange letters printed on top. Others were cylindrical, bright red containers with black lids. More writing appeared on their sides as well. Pulling out the containers, he discovered even more packets. Of the items present, the largest pile was of long, thin bars, each swathed in more layers of the metal paper.

He unwrapped one, discovering inside a dark brown solid substance, squarely scored. Though the bar was very cold, the metal paper must have insulated it well enough to escape freezing. He broke off a piece. Sniffed it. A musky aroma with a sweet edge. He bit into it.

It was food!

In excitement, he ripped open more packages. There was hard bread, a fatty meat, and lumps of white crystals tasting very sweet.

Biting off another piece of the brown bar, he searched for the billowing smoke from the mountaintop. It was gone!

Fear gripped his stomach. Had the light destroyed the Tau'ri? Was that why it had encouraged him to pillage such a vital resource?

Huang swallowed hard, the Dragon Guard trainee within reasserting itself. Lord Yu must be warned. If the light was at war with the Tau'ri, only the great System Lord would know how to combat such a force.

Grabbing as much of the supplies as he could carry, Huang retreated to the cave in which he had taken refuge. There he donned the woolen clothes. Fed, warmed, and alert, he picked up his staff weapon and headed forth to retrace his steps to the Chappa'ai. He would find the dialing device, certain it must be buried somewhere within the cavern's ice-covered floor.

From there, he would travel to one of his master's protected worlds and send work back to Lord Yu. In doing so, perhaps the Goa'uld would see the success in his endeavor, and not his failure.

As he strode past his earlier hunting place, snow began to fall.

CHAPTER NINE

PLANET DESIGNATION: UNKNOWN
STATUS: UNKNOWN
TIME: UNKNOWN

"WHY ARE we not in Antarctica?"

"Good question." Jack broke off staring at the girl long enough to get the lay of the land. A warm wind blew against his face. Dust and dirt swirled across drab, lifeless plains, the only color provided by SG-1's green pullovers, and the red one worn by the girl.

A kid. Barely out of her teens. Yet somehow, she had something to do with whatever in the hell was going on.

One piece of the puzzle down, too many more to go.

Movement way off in the distance caught his eye. Someone was definitely waving from the one surviving piece of a city that had disappeared into thin air. Jack was pretty sure the building had been the base of the city's central tower.

There was something familiar about whoever it was, something about the long, flowing white robe they wore, too. Jack squinted, feeling like he should take action. Like he should know what to do.

What he wouldn't give for a P90.

"O'Neill," Teal'c said, pointing toward the far off building. "Should we not approach?"

"We should do something," Daniel said. "Whoever it is, maybe they can help us get home."

"Yes, please," Weiyan whispered. "I want to go home."

Jack looked back at his team. Daniel had draped a protective arm around Weiyan. The girl was practically shaking in her boots. Carter flashed one of her A+ smiles of reassurance.

She should really bottle that smile up. She'd make a mint.

"Plans, sir?" Carter turned toward Jack, the smile gone.

All of them turned expectant gazes toward him, waiting for him to make the first move. Say the right thing. Make a decision.

A wave of fatigue hit him. He stuck a hand in his pocket, wrapping his fingers around the Zippo. Another familiar thing, though he hadn't a clue how it got there.

It wasn't as if he didn't miss what the lighter represented. He did. Skaara's death had been tough to take, but staying ahead of the Goa'uld this past year had been too big a distraction.

Hell, just staying alive had been a distraction.

"Jack?"

"Yeah, Daniel?" The words came out barely more than a croak. His throat was dry, tight.

"General, shouldn't we — "

"Just... Just give me a moment, Carter." The wind felt wrong somehow. It tugged at his clothes, coming from too many directions. Hell, the entire situation was wrong.

The ground rumbled faintly beneath Jack's feet and he knew.

He knew it was up to him to remember. Remember how they got there. For all their sakes.

He looked again at what he was pretty sure was a man standing by the building. Turning back toward the disheveled surroundings, he felt everyone watching him, waiting. The weight of their expectations pressed down hard and a private flare of reproach welled up in response. There'd be time enough to deal with self-pity later.

A soft rumble started up again. Low, almost a growl. Another piece of a puzzle he couldn't fit into place.

Shrugging off his uneasiness, he said, "All right, SG-1. Let's go make nice with the native." He turned back toward the building.

The man was gone.

MCMURDO STATION
ROSS ISLAND, ANTARCTICA
18 AUG 04/1530 HRS MCMURDO STATION

Paul Davis had just hoisted another injured civilian into the awaiting Bell 212 when the floodlights across the central compound kicked back on. A good thing, too, since the chopper was parked so close to Cray Lab that one of its blades nearly touched a neighboring electric pole. Sliding the side hatch shut, he waved at the chopper pilot and gave the go.

The chopper lifted off the ground, inched forward away from the pole, and then headed toward Pegasus Air Field where the civilian would be evacuated on a C-17 to New Zealand. Paul watched as the blue neon lights along the chopper's tail and blades illuminated the last dull gray night of Antarctica winter.

The sun would rise tomorrow. A whole hour and thirty-nine minutes of sunshine. As much as the floodlights helped in finding survivors, Paul knew the sunlight would bring disadvantages along with advantages.

It'd be easier to find the dead.

"We found another!"

Station personnel ran past, heading toward a collapsed smaller lab down the hill. With a sigh, Paul took off after them. He immediately kicked himself when his cold breath stung his face. A fur-lined parka wasn't enough in the sub-zero temperatures, not when minus twenty degrees Fahrenheit was the norm. He should have pulled on a pair of coveralls. Tugging his balaclava back down over his face, he found himself grateful for at least some protection.

He arrived at the collapsed building as an injured civilian was being put on a gurney. The man's face and red beard were covered in blood. Knowing instantly who it was, Paul's heart dropped. He stepped up to the gurney and looked down into the pained face of Dr. Malan.

"Major Davis..." Malan coughed, spitting up more blood. "Where's Mr. Murray? Is he all right?"

Squeezing the young scientist's hand, Paul lied. "He's around here somewhere. Don't worry about him."

"He's gonna miss bowling. He's gonna miss meeting..." Malan dropped his head to the gurney and closed his eyes.

One of the volunteers put a finger on Malan's neck and checked his pulse. "He's alive, barely."

Paul released Malan's hand and stepped back. "Where will you take him?"

"Byrd Station's a good 1400 kilometers away," the volunteer said as he strapped Malan to the gurney. "But it beats going back to New Zealand. He's got internal injuries so we better get him up to the airfield quick. Excuse us, Major."

Paul said a silent prayer as they carried the gurney toward another waiting chopper. The chances of Malan surviving the trip to Williams and then on to Byrd weren't good.

"Major Davis!" A parka-clad woman ran up to him, her face buried inside her hood.

"Here!" Paul stomped his feet against the cold as she approached. A black patch on her chest labeled 'Operation Deep Freeze' let Paul know she was part of the science community. "There's a call for you on the long-range radio. A General Hammond."

"Which way?" Of the hundred or so buildings that made up McMurdo, more than half had collapsed in the quake.

"The NSF chalet. Edmunds's office." She pointed up the hill toward the Swiss-style wood building.

"The chalet didn't suffer any damage?"

"Just don't use the front entrance," she shouted as the chopper bearing Malan headed off. "The doors are wedged shut from the seismic activity."

"Thanks." Paul hurried up the hill, allowing himself a brief head shake. Seismic activity? More like a pancake flattener.

Once inside the chalet, he rushed down the hall to Edmunds's office, picking his way over fallen ceiling tiles, reams of papers strewn everywhere, and several broken bulletin boards. Finally, he found the NSF Director's office. The door was half off its hinges.

"I don't give a damn about the military's special projects," Edmunds bellowed into the radio, his back to the door. "You people are here to support the NSF. Now get down here and — "

"*And I don't give a damn whether you care or not.*" The radio's crackle did little to hide General Hammond's Texan twang. Or his obvious impatience. "*The President has authorized* — "

Edmunds switched off the radio. "Ha, like I care."

"Sir..." Paul cleared his throat and stepped inside. Edmunds eyed him without any warmth. The NSF Chief of Operations for McMurdo was much loved by the civilian population for his anti-military stance.

Edmunds pushed back his chair and stood up. All six-and-a-half feet of him. Paul recognized it for the intimidation effort that it was so he kept his face neutral.

"I suppose you want to talk to that asinine jarhead?"

"Yes, sir." Paul didn't bother pointing out that Edmunds's use of a derogatory term for the Marines wasn't exactly relevant apropos a USAF general.

Edmunds stepped out from behind his desk. "Then do it, but hurry things up. We need to keep the channel clear."

"Thank you."

"I'm not stupid, Major."

"No one ever said you were, Doctor."

"Earthquakes rarely hit this part of the world and when they do, they're small in scale." Edmunds waggled his finger. "You military folks are up to something."

"Sir — "

"I wasn't here back in March," Edmunds said, "but I've heard enough from the winter staff to know something happened. Something big. Strange lights in the sky, F-302s shooting off from behind Observation Hill like it was the end of the world. And let's not forget all the new Air Force personnel coming through here ever since — "

"Need to know, sir."

Edmunds glowered, his mood coalescing into barely contained fury. "You're going to tell me I don't need to know, when we've just lost seventeen people?"

Paul slid past him and picked up the mic. "Sir, I'll need the room."

"Five minutes, Major." He strode toward the door.

Paul waved the mic as a reminder. "Sir, the sooner I talk to the general, the sooner I can rejoin the others and assist in the search and rescue of your personnel."

"Make sure that you do." Edmunds stomped off.

Paul sucked in a breath and counted to five. He blew out and thumbed the microphone's talk button.

"This is Major Paul Davis for General Hammond. Over."

ANCIENT OUTPOST, ANTARCTICA
18 AUG 04/1610 HRS MCMURDO STATION

"*...the entire continent's been struck, sir. I'm hearing reports of anything from a 7.1 to a 7.4 scale earthquake.*"

As George listened to Major Davis' report, he glanced up at the outer chamber's concave ceiling. Striated stone blended with what looked like frozen waterfalls. Best he could tell, the Ancients had built the place to last. The roof hadn't cracked or suffered any other damage.

He thumbed the radio mic. "How many causalities, Major?"

"*At McMurdo? Seventeen plus another ten or so injured. We were lucky, General. Only two hundred winter here besides our F-302 pilots.*"

"And the pilots are fine?" George held his breath, hoping for the best.

"*All present and accounted for, General. We lucked out, but I received a report a short while ago that a wing led by Captain White completed an easterly flyby, and... Sir, New Zealand's Scott Base flattened. No survivors.*"

George took in the bad news, steadying himself against the

pallet of crates where the radio had been set up. Davis detailed the status of McMurdo and signed off to go assist with recovery efforts. As George put down the radio mic, someone stepped up beside him, a cup of coffee in hand. He took the proffered cup and sipped greedily.

Hell, by this point he should have just asked for the whole coffee pot.

"General Hammond?"

Dr. Lee stood at the pallet's edge, blinking rapidly behind his glasses. Beside the stocky scientist was a face George hadn't seen in several years.

"It's good to have you here." George smiled grimly at Lieutenant Graham Simmons. "The coffee's much appreciated."

The young man returned the smile. "It's good to see you, too, General."

"I sort of wanted some coffee, too," Lee said, indicating George's half-empty cup.

"There's more over by the elevator." George waved his cup toward the cage conveyor where someone had been smart enough to set up a coffee and food station. While the trainees had been relegated to the break room, the diplomats hovered in the main chamber by the coffee, anxiously waiting for an available chopper to airvac them back to McMurdo.

Lee glanced over at the diplomats and shrugged. "Uh... Maybe later. I wanted to give you a preliminary report."

George put down the coffee. "Go ahead, Doctor."

"Actually, some of this will be easier if I just show you."

Lee shambled off toward the weapons platform chamber.

George followed with Simmons at his side. As they passed the de-activated Ancient stasis unit, he pushed down ten tons of regret. He'd been powerless to save Jack the last time an Ancient contraption had got ahold of him. This time, George would move Heaven and Earth if need be.

Inside the chamber, Lee grabbed two military-issue green parkas hanging off a trellised panel. He handed one to George.

"You'll want to put this on. We've switched off the heaters in the chair room."

The room was already barely above freezing. George offered his parka to Simmons. He'd need it more, dressed only in a standard uniform.

Simmons waved him off. "I'm fine, sir."

Lee zipped up his parka. "We were hoping the colder temperature might convince the chair to shut off."

"Convince?" George shrugged on his parka, but kept it open. "Dr. Lee, are you trying to tell me the chair, this weapons platform — ? Is it sentient? Is the chair the reason we can't get to our people?"

"Honestly, we've no way of knowing." Lee circumnavigated the pillars bordering the hole. Someone had installed a walkway plank over the force field leading from the weapons platform to a bank of three monitors on the chair's left. A low-level hum emanated from the Mark II generators.

George glanced at the force field, hoping for even a flicker that might let him see down below.

"Do you think they're all right, General?" asked Simmons, joining him by the hole's edge.

"I certainly hope so, son." George pulled himself away and joined Lee by the monitors. "Why haven't you turned off the generators?"

"We considered doing that, but I was worried we might damage the chair if we shut the generators off without shutting down Colonel Carter's power filter program."

"Forget the chair and forget the program, Doctor Lee, just shut those damn things off!"

Lee bent down and switched off the generators. The hum disappeared instantly, but the chair remained lit up.

And the force field didn't so much as flicker.

"Yeah. I didn't think that would do much good." Lee returned to the monitors. "I'm pretty sure the generators didn't activate whatever device set things off. I'd bet it has something to do with the chair."

"Is that possible?" asked Lt. Simmons. Of his own volition, he'd taken up sentry duty by the hole.

"We think the trainee's genetics — "

"Weiyan Shi."

Lee pulled his glasses off and frowned. "Sir, as strong as General O'Neill's ATA genetics are, I've seen two stronger cases. Major Sheppard, who's now on Atlantis — "

"We hope." He pushed aside his concern for the fate of the Atlantis team. "Who's the other case?"

Lee stuck his glasses back on. "Weiyan Shi. She's stronger than Sheppard's and General O'Neill's combined. I'm willing to bet she's the one who got the chair to activate this Drift device."

"Drift device?"

"As in Continental Drift. We think it's running right beneath the force field." On Lee's central monitor, he called up a map of the planet. "Colonel Carter's report on the Proclurash Taonas mission — "

"The planet where they retrieved the ZPM to power the weapons chair in the first place?"

"That's the one," Lee said. "The Taonas chair showed them a map of Earth from millions of years ago which looked like this." He tapped a key and the center screen displayed a planet with a single land mass.

Hitting another key, he animated the image. The land mass broke up into more recognizable pieces which slid apart into a facsimile of Earth today. "Immense seismic activity caused Continental Drift and it's what we're experiencing right now."

"Earthquakes happen all the time," George said. "All over the world."

"Normal earthquakes. The key word here is 'immense.' In the last hour, I've located an off-the-charts form of energy, right here in the outpost. Fifteen feet below this floor."

The doctor tapped another key. A new image came up. A graph with a bunch of squiggly lines peaking high above a red line toward the top. "Whatever's been activated, it's emitting enormous levels of solar-photonic energy downward, right into the basalt layers — "

"Basalt. You mean like the dolerite around the hole?"

"That's one type, yes." Lee placed a sample of the grey rock on the table beside the monitors. "Deeper down in the earth's crust, basalt magma is formed by decompression melting of the mantle." He raised a small hammer over the sample. "The photonic energy emitted is applying tremendous pressures. Strong enough that if the force field is shut off while the device is still running — "

Lee smashed the hammer down, splitting the rock into three uneven pieces.

"The force field is protecting the outpost?" Simmons asked.

George frowned. "The very force field we're trying to shut down is the reason the outpost hasn't collapsed."

"Exactly," Lee said, "but the rest of the region wasn't as lucky, and further tectonic activity pushing against the basalt could eventually tear apart the plate. Scott Base collapsed because it sat closer to the plate's fault line than McMurdo."

"Sir, we should evacuate McMurdo." Simmons knelt beside the hole and peered down.

Lee joined the lieutenant. He stared at the hole and said, "General, evacuating McMurdo will only prolong things."

George steeled himself, recognizing the preamble to something much worse. "Go on," he said softly.

"We're pretty convinced the device gets its photonic energy from some sort of solar energy retrieval system."

"If you haven't noticed, Doctor, Antarctica hasn't seen the sun in months."

"That's true." Lee shoved his hands into his pockets. "The lack of sunlight's probably why the tremors stopped for now. The device only had a residual charge leftover. The thing is… Twenty hours from now, the first real sunrise is due. When that happens, the quakes will start up again, and well, it's likely the seismic pressure will extend outward, resulting in quakes and tsunamis across the world."

Simmons turned away from the hole and faced Lee. "All because the ground is being bombarded with photonic energy?"

It was then George realized that he'd heard the term before. "Didn't the System Lord Yu retrieve some Ancient technology using photonic energy?"

Lee picked up a stray pebble from the floor and dropped it into the hole. Predictably, the pebble bounced back. "The Goa'uld used it for shields — "

"And cloning," George said, still unhappy with the manner in which that particular SG-1 mission had ended. Though the key objective of rescuing Dr. Jackson from the Goa'uld had succeeded, Jack's decision to let Yu live hadn't gone over well with the President. "What are our options?"

Lee turned away from the hole. "We need to find a way to alter the force field so we can gain access to that device and shut it down."

"Let's put one of the trainees back in the chair," George suggested.

Lee shook his head. "Based on how this whole mess started, I'd like to explore some other options first. There might be a way to redirect the field, bend it so we can get to the device. I just haven't figured out how yet."

George found himself wishing — not for the first time — that Colonel Carter was up here and not down below. She'd have this entire mess figured out in an instance.

Wishes and horses, he reminded himself. "All right, Doctor. Pull together whatever resources you can to shut that thing down. We've got less than twenty hours."

Daniel had been so surprised by the man's disappearance that he accidentally breathed in some of the dust stirred up by the quakes. He began to cough uncontrollably.

Jack started to pound his back, but Daniel waved him off.

"We've seen this before," Sam said. "On the Nox's home world."

"The Asgard have some sort of cloaking device, too," Jack added.

Daniel swallowed a few times, finally calming down his cough. "I don't think it's the Asgard, Jack."

"Because? From what Thor's told us in the past, the Asgard used to be buddies with the Ancients."

"This just doesn't seem like the Asgard's style."

"It's possible we're dealing with an entirely different race." Sam turned away from the building and cocked her head as if listening for any more tremors. "Maybe they stumbled onto some kind of Ancient technology and don't know how to use it."

"Hence the tremors," Teal'c offered.

Sam shrugged. "Without any equipment to measure seismic activity, it's impossible to tell if that quake was real or — "

"Something we were made to imagine." Daniel sighed. A gust of hot wind stirred up the yellowed prairie grass, creating mirage-like waves that stretched out as far as he could see.

"Besides the sun, heat, and lack of snow and ice," Sam said, "this place has a lot in common with Antarctica. Pristine terrains, windy air, both examples of nature in its extreme."

"But how did everything change so dramatically?" Daniel asked. No matter which direction he turned, there was nothing to see. The city, the hills, even the trees were gone. The only thing left standing was the low building about a half-mile off, its dark brown stone facade swallowing the harsh sunlight — almost like a black hole.

A whimper caught his attention.

Weiyan had sunk to the ground. She'd tucked her head between her drawn-up knees and wrapped her arms around them. Her shoulders barely shook, but Daniel didn't need to be a mind reader to know how terrifying this must be. He knelt down beside her, placing a hand on her back.

"I didn't do anything." Her legs muffled her voice. "I have

tried to be good. I have tried — ”

“It’s okay. We’ll get out of here.” He glanced up at Jack and then added, “Somehow.”

“Don’t look at me.” Jack shrugged. “I’ve got nothing.”

But Daniel did. He stood up. “I think we do.”

“Daniel…” Jack narrowed his eyes. “Are you carrying weapons I don’t know about?”

“No.”

“Water?”

“Well, no.” Daniel swallowed again, wishing that wasn’t the case.

“Food?”

“No, but — ”

“Just stop.” Jack raised a finger warningly. “We have nothing.”

“Pedion Elysium.”

“’Pedy-my’ beg your pardon?”

“Pedion Elysium. It’s a name, Jack!” Daniel raised his arms to indicate their surroundings. “If we have a name — ”

Sam shook her head. “I’m sorry, Daniel, but I don’t see how it’s relevant.”

“It’s not like we can gate home,” Jack added, “and get your books to figure it out.”

Daniel dropped his head. They were right. The name was useless without knowing its context. It’s meaning. “There’s a reason we found that obelisk.”

“Yeah, well, without water, food, or weapons,” Jack said, “the fact is we’re screwed unless our mystery host comes back.”

“It is not my fault,” Weiyan mumbled.

“It’s okay,” Daniel assured her. “No one said you did anything wrong.”

“Speak for yourself.” General O’Neill jabbed a finger at Weiyan. “You — ” He strode toward her, the anger in his face visible, almost tangible.

“You were in the chair when the floor was ripped out from under us. What did you do?”

A slight tremor started up, the sound like the faint roar of an engine running off in the distance.

She jumped up and away from Jack. "I tried to do what you asked. I tried to be a good trainee."

Daniel returned a hand to Weiyan's shoulder for support. Being on an alien planet was one thing. Dealing with Jack O'Neill could be enough to send her over the edge.

"Technically," Sam offered, "Weiyan was half out of the chair, sir. It's possible she triggered some sort of safety protocol. We don't know enough about the outpost's technology to be sure."

"Indeed," Teal'c added. "It might only have been a matter of time before such a thing occurred."

Jack raked a hand through his hair. "Why now? We've had dozens in that chair and nothing happened."

"And why the memory lapse?" Sam asked. "We didn't remember being in Antarctica before we got here until — "

"She showed up." Jack jerked a thumb toward a subdued Weiyan.

At least she'd stopped panicking. She'd taken up watching the four of them talk. Daniel supposed it must be pretty much like watching a game of tennis.

A thought occurred as he focused on the horizon again. Shortly after his return from ascension, he'd read a report from one of SG-1's missions that might have something to do with their situation. "Jack, when we were transported here — "

"Don't ask me." He waved a hand at their surroundings. "I've never seen this place."

"Yes, but did the process feel familiar at all?"

"Familiar as in how?"

"Like the time you and Colonel Maybourne went through that portal?"

"The Furlings' technology," Teal'c said.

"Maybourne's little paradise?" Jack grimaced. "Nope. This was different."

"Different how?"

"Well, for one thing, I didn't forget who I was."

"Good point." Daniel did a three-sixty, taking in the desert landscape once more. "Well, one thing's for sure... Whatever technology got us here could be even more useful than the Stargate."

"Stargate?" Weiyan asked.

"Daniel." The general sliced a hand across his neck. "Clearance levels. Need to know. Hello?"

"Oh." Daniel spun toward him, his mouth gaped open. "It's a little late for that."

"Yeah. I suppose it is." Jack exchanged a glance with Sam. "Look, Miss — "

"Weiyan, please." She gave a slight bow, her earlier fear of General O'Neill apparently subsiding. Just like the tremors. Daniel strained his ears for a moment, but didn't hear anything. Hopefully, they'd seen the last of any seismic activity.

"Are we on another planet?" Weiyan asked. "One built by those who created the weapons chair?"

Daniel thought back on that city with its extraordinary architecture and its people. People who'd walked right through them. "Sam, what was that? A hologram?"

"I really don't know, Daniel. They'd need an enormous power source to create something that complex."

He gestured toward the now non-existent city's one remaining relic. "What if it's housed in that building? Shouldn't we take a closer look?"

"He's got a point, Carter." Jack shoved his hands in his pockets. And yanked them out again as if they'd been burnt.

Neither Sam nor Teal'c noticed — their attention was turned toward Weiyan — but Daniel had. "You all right?"

"Yep, terrific." Jack thrust his hands behind his back. "Let's go take a look at that building."

Daniel pushed up his sleeves. It wasn't getting any cooler. "If nothing else, we could get out of the sun. Maybe we'll find more answers inside. Maybe there's more to this Pedion Elysium — "

Jack snorted. "Would you stop with the Elysium thing? It's not going to help."

Sam grabbed Daniel's arm. "We don't know what's real and what isn't. That building could come down on top of us if there's another quake. The last thing we need to do right now is make assumptions."

"Colonel Carter is correct." Teal'c knelt down and scooped up a handful of the pale brown soil. "As General O'Neill indicated, we have no resources with which to determine our location."

Sam sighed. "Or, any way to get home."

"Indeed." Teal'c flung the dirt down and stood up.

And yet… Daniel mouthed the words Pedion Elysium to himself. There was something there. Something just out of reach. If only —

"O'Neill!" Teal'c pointed toward the distant building.

A golden-white curtain shimmered into life just above the building. The curtain broke into three, no, four ribbons of undulating light. Streaks of a darker gold emanated downward, all pointed toward a glowing white object forming in front of the building.

"Holy crap," Jack said.

"It's like the Aurora Australis," Sam said. "Only, instead of green or red, it's more like a golden-white."

"In the daytime?" Jack pointed at the undulating gold-white ribbons.

"It's possible photonic emissions from the upper atmosphere are combining with solar wind particles, sir."

The white-outlined form began to glow.

Jack stepped up beside Daniel. "Anyone you know?"

He had a point. "You think it's an Ancient?" Daniel asked.

The emerging coruscated white strands reminded him of his once-mentor Oma Desala. Of Shifu. And of someone else. Another Ancient. Another Ascended Being he should remember, but couldn't. A face so obscured it made all of Daniel's other recollections of his time as an Ascended Being amongst the Ancients seem like easy memories.

"Jack, this could be our ticket home."

"Yeah, possibly," Jack said.

"Daniel Jackson," Teal'c said, coming up to stand on Daniel's other side. "If the Ancients remain removed from human affairs as you once explained, how can you be certain they will assist us now?"

The glowing strands elongated, reaching up toward the ribbons of golden white light overhead. The two energy sources intertwined, creating a blindingly bright light show.

"Nice parlor trick," Jack said.

"The Ancients don't play tricks," Daniel said.

"Tell that to old oily-faced. Don't forget, Anubis is ascended, too. Or at least, he's some half-assed version."

"Anubis is dead." A twinge in Daniel's shoulder reminded him of when Jack shot him a few months ago when the half-ascended Goa'uld hijacked his body. "There's no way that's Anubis."

He edged closer.

"Who is Anubis?" Weiyan asked.

A thunderous crack erupted overhead with all the power of a sonic boom. Daniel looked up as green lightning tore through the ribboned lights and shot upwards and smashed against the sky. After a moment, a black tear appeared at its epicenter. A ragged edge of nothing.

The wind picked up. Weiyan crouched low. Jack, Teal'c and Sam leaned forward. Daniel found himself doing the same to keep from being blown backward. Above the building, the gold and white strands bent toward the gaping hole in the sky. The maw widened, the stream of lights swallowed into its jaws.

And then, it disappeared.

CHAPTER TEN

ANTARCTICA
48 years earlier...

"FOUR HUNDRED and twenty-two." Huang dipped his forefinger in the ash pot. It was the only words he permitted himself upon rising from each slumber. The only words he allowed to mark the passage of time. He pressed his finger against the wooden panel beside the stove and swept downward, the short slash joining the many of others of his exile.

Four hundred and twenty-two days. A useless, but necessary task since discovering the Tau'ri hut upon the frozen shores. At times it seemed the sun would never reappear. Other times, it seemed to never set. He silently reprimanded himself. He should be grateful to have found the Tau'ri's long-forgotten domicile.

When he'd originally set out to return to the Chappa'ai so that he might warn his master of the being of light, a blizzard had so blinded his passage that he had become lost. It was only after many hours of wandering that he stumbled upon the abandoned wooden hut and discovered its contents. Within he found crates of food, furniture, and a fully equipped kitchen. Along the back wall hung frozen carcasses of blubbery, flippered creatures.

Most importantly, he'd found black and white papers bearing images of men. Tau'ri men. Some pictures had the men on skis, others showed them standing beside massive dogs bearing collars.

Where the men had gone was unknown. Huang could only assume that the being of light had taken them.

Turning away from the blackened marks upon the wall, he

lit one of the many oil lamps he'd found around the square hut and hobbled over to one of the hut's few windows. His toes had healed many days ago, but walking was still a challenge.

He gazed at his reflection in the window through weary eyes. Cracked lips. A straggling beard that warmed his face and throat. Though it was not a First Prime's proper appearance, it was a truth he had come to accept with one exception.

Raising the ashen finger to his forehead, he drew the *wénshēn* of Lord Yu between his brows. Another daily ritual. Another means of seeking solace amongst the failure of his lot.

He peered out the window toward the shoreline. Many days ago, long sunsets had splashed wild colors across the sky, followed by an endless barrage of darkness and a night sky full of stars. The night's black had now turned to a red-tinged blue, the scattered clouds almost purple. Barely a sliver of the sun was above the far horizon, but it was a start. Soon daylight would come again and he would have to make a decision. A decision that gave him great unease.

Satisfied with the soot-stained tattoo, he returned to the stove. The last of his fresh meat simmered within the pot. He had learned through trial and error of the need to hang the mournful-eyed creatures for several days before cooking them. The brains he could cook upon taking down the legless beasts, but the meat tasted more of fat than meat if not aged.

To remain or to go? That was the decision he must reach before the ice thinned again. If he stayed, he would need to hunt soon, a difficult challenge as he'd lost his staff weapon months ago, while attempting to cross the thin ice that separated the hut from the glacier that held the Chappa'ai.

Four hundred and twenty-two days.

Huang sank onto a wooden chair by the stove, soaking in what heat he could to disperse the hut's cold air. Had too much time passed to warn Lord Yu? Would his master consider him dead?

A pounding at the door. He bolted to his feet, staring in

horror. Had the being of light come back?

Voices shouted from outside. Men's voices, in a language he did not know. Huang grabbed the lamp. If necessary, he would use it as a weapon.

The door burst open and three men stumbled in, all dressed in great orange coats, their hoods lined with black fur.

Huang raised the lamp menacingly. "Stay back!" he yelled in Goa'uld, his tongue thick from lack of use.

The men pulled back their hoods. All three wore beards though the tallest of the three kept his short around his long face. In unison their hands raised in surrender, the tall man speaking to him again in the mysterious language.

"*Bie guan wo*!" Huang warned them to stay back again, this time in the tongue of his Tau'ri ancestors.

The tall man's eyes widened and he smiled. "*Wo de shang di, ni shi zhong guo ren*!"

You're Chinese!

CHAPTER ELEVEN

ANCIENT OUTPOST, ANTARCTICA
18 AUG 04/1830 HRS MCMURDO STATION

THE FLOOR buckled as George scrambled for cover. He dove for the computer table. As he slipped underneath, another jolt pushed upwards. His head smacked against the metal underside and then he dropped like a ton of rocks. To his right, computer monitors crashed to the ground, their screens shattering upon impact.

Wall panels rattled. Ice from the ceiling pelted the ground. A scream from the outer chamber pierced the tremor, but unless George wanted to get himself killed, there was nothing he could do until the tremor ended. The airmen and marines assigned to the outpost would protect the civilians and diplomats until this was over.

If it was ever over. The last time George had been in an earthquake was during basic training at Vandenberg. The Air Force base had shook for a moment or two, but this latest tremor just kept on coming with no end in sight.

Round after round of ice and snow dumped onto the force field covering the hole in the ground. Each time another round hit, the energy field glowed and sparked.

Behind all that snow, he got a glimpse of Dr. Lee. Head tucked in, the scientist belly-hugged the Mark IIs as if his life depended on it. George scrambled from under the table to help — the damage those naquadah generators could cause would make the earthquake seem like a picnic.

He'd made it half way toward Lee when the quake stopped. A light dusting of ice and snow fell on his face and he wiped it off. Lee still clutched the Mark IIs.

Threading his way through the broken equipment scattered across the ground, George knelt beside the scientist and laid a hand on his back. "It's over, son."

"You're sure?" came the muffled reply.

"You're the scientist. You tell me."

Lee lifted his head, his glasses fogged up. No doubt he must have been breathing pretty hard. His face was as white as the now snow-covered force field.

"General Hammond!" Ambassador Duebel stormed through the archway, his clothes dusty and torn.

Behind Duebel were the other two diplomats — Juarez and Zhu. The Chinese ambassador sported a wide bandage across the left side of her face, thanks to a chunk of rock that had gone flying when the floor first caved in.

George cursed silently. Someone needed to keep these people out of the room. Where had Simmons had disappeared to? He'd lost sight of the lieutenant when the latest quake hit.

As the diplomats drew near, George deliberately ignored them. Instead, he pulled Lee up from the ground and patted his shoulder. After a few words of encouragement, the scientist hurried out, shouting for replacement equipment and a clean-up detail. Lee may not be military, but he understood the need for order.

And the need for haste. George privately hoped Jack and the others had weathered the trembler intact, but there was no way to know. Though the snow had melted off the force field, it was still intact and murky as mud.

Ambassador Zhu crept up to the hole before he could stop her. She knelt, reaching out a hand toward the force field.

"I wouldn't do that if I was you," he warned.

She snapped back her hand.

Duebel side-stepped, blocking George's view of the Chinese ambassador. "We demand to know your plan."

George stopped just short of scowling. "Plan?"

"Yes, General Hammond." Spit flew from Juarez's mouth.

The Argentine ambassador wiped a hand across his face and then stabbed a finger at the force field. "Your brilliant military's plan to destroy the outpost before it destroys us."

George counted to three and then responded as blandly as he could. "Ambassadors, I'm not going to sit here and quibble over what the military is and isn't responsible for... Not now. Not when our focus should be on shutting down that device and then mounting a rescue effort."

"Forget your rescue efforts!" Juarez flung a hand toward the force field. "Esperanza Base was destroyed! Fifty-five people, including ten families and two school teachers, all gone!"

George was taken aback. The Argentine Base was over 2,400 miles away, located at the very tip of the Peninsula on Antarctica's far other side.

Fifty-five people. No wonder Juarez was beside himself. George gave his condolences. "We're doing everything we can, short of— "

"Really, General," said Duebel, "you're doing nothing of the sort." He toed the broken monitor at his feet. "Scientific study isn't enough. Please do not misunderstand, I fully recognize the lengths General to which O'Neill and his team have gone in order to protect this world in the past, but there's more at stake now. First, Scott Base and now Esperanza. Something needs to be done."

"What of China's stations?" Ambassador Zhu called out. "Have there been any reports?"

"Not yet, no." Juarez' eyes narrowed. "At least, not of your official bases."

Zhu returned to gazing at the force field, ignoring the obvious dig at what everyone involved with the Antarctic region already knew. George had heard reports that the Chinese were building several stations up on Dome Argus, but what they wanted up on the highest point of the Antarctic Plateau wasn't his current priority.

Stopping the quakes and retrieving his people was what

mattered. If they could access the floor down below by altering that force field, it was entirely possible to take care of both problems in one fell swoop.

Dr. Lee reentered, leading a pack of airmen carrying replacement monitors. Simmons brought up the rear. He rejoined Ambassador Zhu by the hole and gave her a polite nod.

She rewarded him with the faintest of frowns.

"You must destroy the outpost," Duebel stated, "before more earthquakes tear apart the entire continent."

"I wish it were that simple, Ambassador." George shook his head. "We're dealing with technology we've barely begun to understand. We need more time."

"This isn't about the earthquakes," Juarez shouted, his face bright red with anger. "You're more concerned with rescuing your people than the several thousand spread across this continent. With one phone call, I could contact the UN Secretary-General and the IOA Chair. They would demand your president — "

"Leave him be," Zhu announced.

"Excuse me?" Juarez whirled toward the Chinese Ambassador, his mouth agape.

"Quing..." Duebel strode over to Zhu's side. "I know the young woman trapped below is — "

"You know nothing." Zhu rose from her position by the hole's edge. She turned toward George and though he expected to see a measure of the anger exhibited by the other two ambassadors, he instead saw what could only be described as genuine concern.

"I want you to destroy the outpost," Juarez repeated. "That is the only way to stop the earthquakes."

Zhu took a menacing step toward him. "And I want you to cease speaking an endless loop of gibberish."

"Who do you think you are?" Juarez sputtered.

"China's ambassador to this region." Zhu raised her chin in defiance. "We must allow General Hammond and his people the opportunity to — "

"Be careful which side you align with," warned Duebel.

Zhu shrugged. "At the moment, I am aligned with the truth. These people have had far longer to study this technology than we. Yes, there have been losses, and yes," she faced George, a pinched smile on her face, "there have been promises left unfulfilled, but we must recognize the greater picture or..."

Bowing her head, the ambassador turned away.

Duebel and Juarez spun on their heels and stormed out. By the hole's edge, Zhu gave Simmons an acknowledging nod. Grateful for the reprieve, George thanked her for the support.

"Do not thank me just yet."

Flailing white tendrils strained against the gaping rip above the building. As Sam watched the phenomenon, she raced through possible explanations, examining and tossing aside each idea as it cropped up. A black hole? No, she'd feel its gravitational force. Some sort of reverse effect on the aurora? That didn't make any sense, either. And why the more gold-colored aurora? Gold usually meant a higher energy charge, but again, why?

The black maw widened further, pulling at the cluster of tendrils. The tendrils shrunk, a final flash of white illuminated the sky, and the phenomenon disappeared.

A gasp. Sam glanced to her left. Weiyan's mouth hung open in a perfect O.

"What the hell was that?" General O'Neill asked.

The ground rumbled again. Nothing threatening — at least, not yet — but it was enough to scatter a few errant pebbles.

"Carter?"

"Sir, I really can't say." She wiped the sweat from her forehead. The sun had come back out in full force. "Not without a way to measure what we're seeing."

She'd kill for a scanner, a spectrometer, heck, even a pair of binoculars.

"Take a guess."

"What we're seeing just isn't possible, sir."

"And yet, there it is. So?"

Sam shrugged. "Without having a way to quantify what kind of energy — "

"In other words..." He pressed his lips together.

"I really don't know." She frowned, hating to let him and the others down.

"It's all right, Carter," he said, giving her an assuring tap on the shoulder. "Nice to know even you can get stumped by the impossible."

"What do we do now?" Weiyan asked. "I want to go home."

The earlier rumbling died off and Sam's stomach unclenched in relief. One geophysical problem was bad enough.

"We can't stay like this much longer, Jack."

"I agree with Daniel Jackson," said Teal'c. "Even I cannot sustain myself in this heat for more than a few hours."

Daniel wiped his brow. "We have no supplies, no — "

"But we do have a shelter." General O'Neill raised two fingers and pointed toward the building. "And I'll bet anything that's the key to this whole *mishegas*."

"Wait a minute," Daniel said. "Shouldn't we — ?"

"What? Sit here and wait for that thing to come back?"

Daniel frowned. "I don't think it was a 'thing,' Jack."

Teal'c mimicked Daniel's frown, only more pronounced. "Do you still believe it was an ascended being?"

"I don't know."

The general shrugged. "Sure looked ascended-y to me. Let's move out." He headed off at a slow lope toward the building with Teal'c at his side, and Daniel close behind.

Sam turned around to make sure Weiyan was ready to follow. She gave the girl an encouraging smile. "Don't worry, it's not much more than a half a mile — "

An ear-splitting crack reverberated to Sam's right. As Weiyan jerked her hands up to cover her face, Sam whipped back around toward the men. The building rippled, but at first she thought it was a trick of the heat. A mirage.

The rumbling intensified and she realized the ripples were pushing outward, toward the general and the others. Another boom shook the ground.

The building began to crack in two under the pressure of the massive turbulence. Several hundred feet off to the left and right of the building, hills erupted from the ground. Fountains of dirt sprayed from all sides. Sam watched in horror as all three men stumbled backward.

"Sir!"

Daniel fell. General O'Neill and Teal'c grabbed hold of his elbows and lifted him up, never missing a step as they ran like hell toward Sam and Weiyan.

Weiyan.

She'd curled up into a ball, her arms over her head.

Two hundred feet away, another hill savagely erupted.

"Get her up," the general shouted over the rumbling.

Sam dragged Weiyan to her feet. "We need to run. Fast!"

Weiyan's eyes rounded in fear. "I will try."

She didn't move.

"Go! Go!" shouted General O'Neill, darting ahead with Daniel and Teal'c close behind.

"Please, Weiyan." Sam took hold of her hand. "This whole area's unstable. We need to put as much distance — "

The general doubled-back. "We have to go, Colonel!"

An ear-splitting blast exploded behind them. Sam scooped the girl over her shoulder, fireman-style, and ran as fast and as far away from the eruption as possible.

"Wait!" Daniel pointed back the way they'd come.

The tremors had stopped. Panting from the exertion, she turned toward the building.

It was gone. The newly erupted hills surrounding the area were still there, but the ground had settled down. The air had become suddenly still.

The tundra-like grasses from earlier were gone except for a

few tufts on the newborn hills. Where the building had once been was now a flat plain of pale, lifeless dirt.

"That's impossible." Sam set Weiyan down. "Land just can't change. Not this fast."

"We must retrace our steps, O'Neill. We must find our original point of entry onto this world."

"I'm all for that, T." General O'Neill spread out his arms and turned around full circle, "But unless your spidey-senses have a clue about which direction to go, we're screwed."

"That's the one part of this whole puzzle that's still foggy," Daniel said. "I remember the Ancient outpost. I remember falling through the floor. Then next thing I knew — "

"We were here," the general said. "Coming out of the Stargate. Thing is, I don't remember stepping through one to begin with, let alone why." He turned toward Weiyan. "Or how you got here, for that matter."

A low rumble started up. Sam hoped it was just an aftershock, not another full on quake.

"I had told you that I don't know." Weiyan had backed away from the general, shaking her head vehemently.

The vibration intensified. Not by much, but enough to jostle the dirt at their feet.

Sam tensed, ready to run. Her vision darkened. She put a hand up over her eyes, convinced it was fatigue.

"Colonel Carter."

Sam dropped her hand. Teal'c pointed toward the horizon. The sun had dropped dramatically, hanging low over where the building had once stood.

"General!" Sam directed his attention toward the setting sun.

"Yeah, I see it." His voice had gone flat, his eyes never leaving Weiyan.

The ground continued to rumble. Low, like a wounded animal growling its warning to keep away.

But that wasn't possible. The planet wasn't alive.

Or was it?

General O'Neill ignored the escalating tremors, or he didn't care. As he stepped closer to Weiyan, Sam watched him clench his fists, straining to keep his anger in check.

"You did something to the chair," he said.

"I don't know…" Weiyan's hands shot up, covering her face.

"That's bullshit."

"Jack, leave her alone." Daniel grabbed the general's arm.

The ground kept shaking.

"Sir, we should get ready to — "

"You were there, Daniel! She deliberately slammed down on one of the gel packs." General O'Neill wrenched his arm free. "You heard her. The only way we're getting out of here is the way we came. Either she tells us what she did or we're screw — "

Another boom echoed across the plains, or canyon, or… Sam couldn't even decide what to call it anymore. The geography kept changing.

Planets don't change that fast.

"Who are you?" the general demanded.

The ground shifted beneath them. Sam staggered forward, but Teal'c stopped her fall. The rumbling deepened. It was nearer. Stronger than before.

"General…" She rechecked the horizon. Swirling dust covered the sun, leaving only a red-tinged corona visible.

"O'Neill!"

Fifty meters to their left, the ground cracked open. A splitting maw widening with each passing moment.

"Jack?"

The fissure lengthened, heading in their direction.

"Run!"

Teal'c remembered running. Hills thrusting upwards. Dirt and rocks flying through the air. A sudden pain against his left temple, and then…

Nothing.

He stirred into awareness, greeted only by darkness. Within

the black, a sense of heat without sun. Peace. Ease.

The pain was gone.

No. That was impossible. He must wake up. His friends would require his assistance. They were stuck—

He tried to open his eyes, but could not. It was as if a great weight held him in place, refusing to allow him to awaken. He struggled against the unseen restraint.

A golden-white ribbon of light danced across his vision, hovering just beyond his reach. "Why do you hold me here?" he demanded.

The ribboned light flowed nearer. "Wait. Learn," a voice said in the dark. "All will be well."

The voice had spoken in Goa'uld. Of this, he was most certain. Cold fury welled up within him. If a Goa'uld was responsible—

Calm washed over him. A silent assurance his former oppressors were not responsible, and yet… He must know the truth. "If all is well, why do you hold us here?"

The light dimmed its brightness, becoming only a single rope-like strand. "If you cannot find the truth right where you are, where else do you expect to find it?"

"You speak in riddles."

"There are no riddles. Only events to unfold."

Teal'c imagined himself raising an eyebrow in response. "Which events do you speak of?"

The ribboned light winked out.

Clink. Snap.

Metal against metal. A familiar sound. Teal'c strained to find its source, but the darkness would not release him.

Clink.

A feather's touch circled his emblem and he found himself free to open his eyes. At first, the sunlight was too strong. His lids fluttered as they adjusted to the brightness.

Snap.

"Come on, big guy." O'Neill's voice urged. "Rise and shine."

Teal'c opened his eyes to find his friend and Weiyan Shi

kneeling beside him. The trainee's hand lay gently on his forehead. Behind O'Neill stood Daniel Jackson and Colonel Carter, their relieved smiles most gratifying.

O'Neill waved his lighter at Teal'c. "About time you came back to the living."

"We thought we lost you for a moment there," said Daniel Jackson.

Teal'c raised a hand to his left temple.

"Easy, Teal'c," warned Colonel Carter. "We may be in some kind of illusion, but still... You took quite a blow."

He felt no cut or abrasion where the rock had hit. There was no pain. "I am well."

"Can you sit up?" Weiyan Shi glanced over at O'Neill who gave an approving nod. A hesitant grin spread over the young woman's face. "You were very brave," she said to O'Neill. "Teal'c might have died if—" Her voice broke.

"Nah," O'Neill drawled. "Can't knock this guy down for long." He grinned. "Trust me, I've tried."

Teal'c raised an eyebrow at O'Neill.

"What?" his Tau'ri brother asked.

"You have made peace."

"And you made us worried sick. Well, not me, but Daniel and Carter were going nuts." O'Neill sternly glanced up at the remainder of SG-1 who rewarded him with matching smiles.

Weiyan Shi grabbed hold of Teal'c's arm and though she was far smaller, she had the strength to assist him as he stood up. He privately berated himself. He shouldn't feel so weary. With a brief nod of thanks, he found his balance and then proceeded to recount what had happened while unconscious.

O'Neill frowned upon his sharing the being's words. "'All will be well,' my ass. We're like rats in somebody's maze."

The ground began to tremble.

"Sir," warned Colonel Carter.

"Rats, Carter! Anyone hungry? Maybe they'll send us some cheese."

"If you don't calm down," admonished Daniel Jackson, "you'll start off another earthquake."

"How is that possible?" Teal'c asked.

"None of this is possible," Colonel Carter said, "but we can't deny the cause." She pointed to O'Neill and then Weiyan Shi. "Or the effect."

O'Neill squeezed his eyes shut and sighed heavily. His face dropped to a blank visage, one Teal'c had seen many times in battle when concentration was paramount.

A moment later, the tremors stopped.

Worried for his friend, Teal'c asked, "Are you well, O'Neill?"

"I'll be fine." He opened his eyes, raised his hands in mock surrender, and managed a small, unconvincing smile.

"You have to stay calm, Jack," advised Daniel Jackson. "Otherwise, we'll — "

"I get it. It's all an illusion. No need for a repeat, all right?" O'Neill dropped his arms to his sides.

"Sir, if we're going to do something — "

"Do?" O'Neill sighed heavily. "Do what? Walk around in circles while some 'thing' plays with our heads? Whatever the hell it meant, finding 'the truth,' was a load of crap. Pure, unadulterated crap." He strode off several dozen paces and halted, his back to them.

Weiyan Shi made to follow, but Teal'c stopped her.

She shook her head. "Is he always so angry?"

"This is one of his better days," Daniel Jackson murmured.

Teal'c knew his friend merely joked about O'Neill's temperament. The two were as close as brothers — brothers who bickered like children, even though they would die if required. It was important Weiyan Shi understood this as well. "Given time, General O'Neill will come to terms with our situation. You will see."

Permitting his friend a moment's respite, Teal'c turned his attention to their newly arranged surroundings.

"It's different, isn't it?" asked Colonel Carter. "For one thing, that building's gone."

"If it was truly ever here." Teal'c looked out over their changed environment. The once flat, undistinguishable plains had been reformed into a valley with several hills marking its border. In the direction O'Neill had moved off, the steepest hill loomed. Its forward face was sheared off, revealing dark gray vertical striations within the rock's face.

There was a familiarity to the terrain, a sense that he been here before, although... As 'here' did not really exist, he found the matter all the more disturbing.

He said as much to his companions.

Daniel Jackson agreed. "You said that being wanted us to learn. Did it say what?"

"It did not." Teal'c searched his memory. "Though I must wonder why the being believes it necessary to continue changing our environment."

Weiyan Shi looked over her shoulder and Teal'c followed her gaze. She was watching O'Neill. He, in turn, was gazing upward toward the hill's top. In his right hand, he flipped his lighter open and shut. It concerned Teal'c that his friend felt the need to distance himself. That was not his normal behavior. Nonetheless, he understood O'Neill's need for a moment's meditation. If he did not control his emotions, the ground could rip open once more.

O'Neill must have felt eyes upon him because he turned back and frowned. "I'm going for a hike."

"Is that wise, O'Neill?"

"Sir, one of us should go with you," Colonel Carter said.

"I'm just going to stretch my legs. Get a better look at our surroundings." O'Neill pointed at the hill's jagged peak. He then gestured toward Weiyan Shi. "Keep an eye on our guest."

With that, O'Neill headed toward the hill's far side where there was a gentler slope. He began to climb.

Weiyan Shi glanced back at Teal'c. No matter what O'Neill

believed, Teal'c was certain the young woman had no part in their current circumstances. "Do you have a question?" he asked her.

She inched forward. "You said this looks familiar."

"Well, kind of," Daniel Jackson responded, "but none of this is real. It just looks — "

"Yet I have not been here before," Weiyan Shi insisted. "The previous variation..." She gestured toward the hill behind them and then at those around the valley. "That was familiar. It looked very much like the Taklamakan Desert."

"Western China." Daniel Jackson paused, peering out at the valley. "Weiyan, just how close was the similarity?"

"Very," she whispered, wrapping her arms around herself. "My mother would take me there when I was very young. We would go to the desert's most northwest region. There was nothing there." She swallowed visibly. "I was very little. Six, maybe seven. I would complain. There was nothing to see or do, but she would insist we visit the place where she met my father."

"Did you not know your father?" Teal'c asked.

Weiyan Shi shook her head. "He left my mother soon after she became pregnant, although..." She swallowed nervously. "We met once, after my genetic testing so that I might serve China. He said that he would soon be going very far away. To visit his ancestral home."

"It is a great honor to witness one's ancestral home," Teal'c replied, privately troubled that a father would forever abandon their child. "One day, when the Goa'uld are truly gone, I will visit Dakara to see the birthplace of the Jaffa."

"But you will return? To rejoin your friends and family?"

He gazed down into her troubled face. "Of this I have no doubt."

"You make it sound like we'll escape," she said.

Teal'c considered the being's words of wisdom. Whether they were caught in the trap of some alien enemy or a planet of their imaginations, he knew the only truth that mattered.

"Have faith, Weiyan Shi. SG-1 has never failed."

Climbing up the steep hill overlooking the shifted terrain should've knocked Jack out. Or at least, it should've made him thirsty. Or hungry.

It didn't do squat.

As he sat down, swinging his legs out over the edge, he recognized that his main objective for the climb had pretty much failed, too. He was still pissed. Still ready to knock someone — or something — out for dicking around with them.

He felt utterly, completely, pathetically useless.

If they were rats in a maze, he was the king of the rats.

"Come on, O'Neill," he muttered to himself. "It's not like a P90 would be much use against..."

Against whatever was toying with them.

With a sigh, he leaned back and pulled the Zippo from his pocket. His Zippo. Now that was a whole other piece to this insane puzzle. When Teal'c had been knocked unconscious, Jack had taken the chrome-plated lighter out. He'd almost told Carter about its mysterious appearance when his gut told him not to — they'd think he'd gone nuts.

He turned the lighter over in his hand. The casing looked the same. Scratched up, a dent on the top. With a flip of his wrist, the cap swung back, making that oh-so-satisfying clink.

He dropped it to his lap. Who was he kidding? The thing was a useless piece of junk. It wasn't like a Zippo would help them escape. It was useless.

He knew the feeling and he didn't like it. There were gaps in his memory. Gaps waiting for answers that were in short supply.

He scanned the valley floor. If he had to guess, he'd say that from the sun's position, the local time appeared to be mid-afternoon. Waves of heat rippled against the far horizon, creating a mirage of water surrounding the immediate area.

There really wasn't much to see. Mostly barren dirt and a few rocky hills along the perimeter. The area where the building had stood showed no signs of anything, not even a pebble out of place. To the right, a pile of rubble broke up the otherwise smooth ground. Which was odd, but probably didn't mean anything.

In fact, if he had to point to a landmark, the big sloping hill at around ten o'clock stood out like a sore thumb.

And it looked damned familiar.

Carter, T, Daniel — heck, even Weiyan at some point or another — had found something familiar in the changing landscapes. For him, not so much. Until now.

It bugged him, not knowing where they were or how they'd got there, but what really bothered him was his own reaction to the situation. He needed to get a grip. He needed to stop acting like a green nugget barely out of training.

He picked the Zippo back up, hefting its weight in his hand. What he really needed was a long, hard look at himself. A painful reassessment of just who he was and how he could still make a difference. Contribute. Make things better.

And not just in their current situation. Hammond had told him his job wasn't about tactics anymore, but strategy. Fair enough, but without tactics, any strategy on how to get out of this mess would be an utter waste of time.

Hence the feeling of uselessness.

Jack flipped open the Zippo again and thumbed the wheel. The flame sparked up. Surprised, he almost dropped the lighter over the edge. He blew out the flame and yanked out the inner tube. The bottom was dry as a bone. He sniffed the cotton, which would usually be soaked in fluid to light the wick. Nothing.

Somebody was toying with them. Big time. More importantly, why with the lighter? It didn't mean anything to anyone except him. Not since Skaara had died, ascended, taken off for the big dead-and-gone Ancients Club.

He couldn't deny that everything they'd seen 'smelled' of the Ancients — ascended beings or whatever-the-hell they liked to call themselves. The Ancient writing. A city definitely decorated by whoever set up the Antarctic outpost.

Why in God's name would any of those high-and-mighties be involved with these shenanigans?

He slammed the inner tube back into the casing. He glanced down at the others at the bottom of the hill. Daniel was scribbling in the sand. Typical Daniel, always asking questions. Always trying to figure things out.

Always strategizing.

Jack climbed to his feet. He should be down there, helping. Maybe he was useless in the grand scheme of things, but that didn't mean he couldn't make it easier for the others. He gazed at the valley floor one more time, taking note of the pile of rubble.

Maybe it would help Daniel. Maybe it wouldn't.

But at least it beat doing nothing.

Daniel sank down between Sam and Weiyan. "How long has Jack been gone?"

Teal'c sat down as well, crossing his legs. "No more than fifteen minutes."

"So we wait." Daniel noticed Weiyan was tracing a circle in the sand. "What's that?"

"I will spell out our names in Chinese." Along the circle's circumference, she drew arrows pointing outward from each of the four quarters. "Many years from now, perhaps someone will find a record of our existence here."

Sam frowned. "With the way this landscape keeps changing, I'd be surprised if your drawings last very long."

"But if something does remain, could it hurt our situation?" Weiyan drew another set of arrows around the circle, this time pointing inward. "Perhaps the next time everything changes, this will not."

"A guide of sorts." Teal'c said.

Weiyan mumbled something.

"I beg your pardon?" Sam asked.

She dashed a sleeve across her eyes. "'A man who does not

know where he's been cannot know where he's going.'"

"Sun Tzu," Daniel commented.

The girl dipped her head.

"Weiyan..." Sam stepped toward her. "What happened in the chair? Why did you lose control?"

Weiyan's face paled. "It's not my fault."

"No one's blaming you." Sam put a hand on her arm. "We just need to understand what happened. It might help us get home."

A recognizable vibration started up under Daniel's feet. It was faint, but definitely there.

"Weiyan Shi, you must calm yourself," Teal'c said softly.

The rumbling stopped.

"Maybe the general's right," Sam said.

Daniel poked a finger in the sandy dirt. "About what?"

She shrugged. "Maybe we are just rats in some imaginary maze."

"I don't know, Sam. It feels pretty real to me, although..." He glanced over his shoulder at the hill Jack had climbed. It was still there. Looking down at Weiyan's drawing, he noted that the circle and arrows were still there, too. The tremor, slight as it had been, hadn't erased the drawing.

That's when it struck him. "Maybe we can't remember how we got here." He shimmied back to give himself a wide space. "But we can remember what's happened since we did!"

"Of what do you speak, Daniel Jackson?"

"Pedion Elysium." When Sam and Teal'c both stared at him blankly, he traced a square in the dirt. The Goa'uld symbol for 'ped.' Beside it, he traced another symbol.

"That's a glyph from the Stargate's DHD," Sam said.

Teal'c leaned over and studied the symbol Daniel had written. "Do you believe Pedion Elysium to be a gate address?"

Daniel sat back on his heels and glanced at him. "It's possible, isn't it? I mean, we were able to translate Proclurash Taonas into a gate address by matching syllables to glyphs.

Why wouldn't that reasoning work for other gate addresses?"

"Proclurash Taonas was only six syllables, Daniel." Sam pointed at the glyph in the sand. "Ped-i-on E-Ly-si-um." She raised one finger and then another. "That's seven."

"There are seven glyphs in a full address," Teal'c said.

"Well, sure," she said, crouching down beside Daniel, "but, Proclurash Taonas was an Ancient outpost, and from everything you've told us, Daniel, their language was similar to Latin."

Daniel drew an 'I' below the 'ped.' "It is, or was, but Pedion Elysium is from Greek mythology."

"Like Atlantis."

"Exactly. Since the glyphs on the DHD are based on Goa'uld symbols for constellations," he drew a feather beside the 'I,' "and the Greeks borrowed some of the ancient Egyptian language to form their own... Teal'c, is this right?"

"Almost," the Jaffa said, bending down to trace a second feather beside the first. He then sat back, a bit unsteadily in Daniel's opinion.

"You all right?"

Teal'c frowned. "I am well, Daniel Jackson." He pointed toward the feather in the sand. "This is the symbol of Ma'at, a minor Goa'uld who once arbitrated disagreements among the System Lords.

"Cronus had her destroyed when she misjudged an argument between him and Ra. It was many years ago." Teal'c gestured toward the double feather in the dirt. "The symbol of two feathers represents her scales of justice."

"Libra!" Daniel exclaimed. "In Greek mythology, the constellation of Libra was depicted as the scales of justice." Beside the feathers, he drew another glyph.

Sam shook her head. "Daniel, this is interesting, but I don't see how figuring out the coordinates for this place — "

"A place that is not even real," Weiyan added.

Daniel's glasses had slid down his nose. He pushed them back up, annoyed at the distraction. "If someone or something is holding us here, there's a reason they wanted us to see that city, the obelisk, and — "

"The name." Sam raised her hands. "Okay, I get it. So two down, five to go. What about that one?" She pointed to the 'ON.'

Sounding out the syllable, Teal'c leaned forward and drew a jagged line beside it. "In Goa'uld, the word means water."

"That's easy." Daniel traced another glyph besides Teal'c's drawing.

"Aquarius, the water pourer. In ancient Greek mythology, Aquarius was responsible for the Great Flood myth."

"China had its own floods," Weiyan said softly. "My father spent much of our reunion reciting the legend of the great Emperor Yu and how he saved our people from extinction."

"Well, actually..."

"Daniel," Sam warned. "Stay on track."

"Indeed," Teal'c added.

"Sorry — sorry." Daniel hurriedly wrote the remaining Goa'uld symbols beside each remaining syllable. A flowering reed for the 'E,' a prostrating feline animal for the 'LY,' a long line with two ovals in its center for the 'SI,' and a bird — somewhat similar to Earth's owl — for the 'UM.'

He uncrossed his legs and shifted to kneeling in front of the symbols. "Some of this is going to be tough." He paused for a moment, and then, next to the flowering reed drew another glyph.

"How do you get the constellation Hydra from that?" Sam asked.

"The Goa'uld symbol represents a reed." He heard footsteps behind him, recognizing the long, easy gait as Jack's.

Daniel pointed at the glyph. "Reeds grow in water and since Hydra was a mythological water serpent in Greek mythology — "

"There's something over by where the building used to be." Jack stopped next to him. "Daniel, whatcha doing?"

Daniel explained his idea.

"Bit of a stretch, don't you think?"

"Do you have any better ideas?" He looked up at Jack, noticing that the lines on his face seemed more pronounced.

Jack cocked his head and studied the symbols in the dirt. "Maybe. Maybe not, but keep going."

"Not if you're going to argue about it."

O'Neill flattened his lips, but then his face relaxed. "I'm fine, Daniel, just... Work it out." He pointed toward the Goa'uld symbol for 'LY. "Is that a lion?"

"Of course, a lion!" Daniel drew another glyph beside the Goa'uld symbol.

"Leo."

Sam gestured toward the long line with the two ovals in its center, the Goa'uld symbol for 'SI.' "What about that one?"

"I honestly don't know," Daniel admitted. "It's similar to the middle Egyptian hieroglyphic for the letter 'S,' but — "

"Terra," Jack said, his voice distant. Flat.

Daniel glanced up again. Jack stared down at the sixth symbol, but his eyes had glazed over, as if he —

"Jack?!" Daniel leapt to his feet.

"Are you well, O'Neill?"

Jack continued to stare at the ground, his gaze blank, his features slack. It was if he was possessed. If Daniel didn't know better, he'd swear Jack had reverted to his time as a vessel for the Ancient's knowledge.

A shudder ran across Jack's face. "Planeta Terra," he said.

"The planet Earth? How — "

Jack knelt down in the sand, one hand stretched out toward the symbols. He stuck a finger in the sand and drew a symbol.

The symbol for Earth.

"Planeta Terra."

Jack felt his knees press into the ground. He felt the dirt scratch his index finger as he drew the Earth symbol. He even sensed his mouth open and shut, repeating the words, "Planeta Terra."

But he had no damn idea why.

"Jack?" Daniel's voice. Far off. On the other side of a tunnel.

He was like a man on a runaway train. Out of control, no way to get off. No way to know where it went next. In a sense, the entire experience since falling through the Ancient outpost into — who knew where — was one giant exercise in control, and the lack thereof. He had to control his temper, but now? He had to let go of what? His head? Let some slimy alien jump in and play with his brains?

His finger lifted from the Earth symbol, dropped down to scratch another glyph beneath — right beside what looked like a really bad rendition of the owl on those potato chip bags, except without the glasses. He drew the last glyph.

"Aquila," his mouth said.

"Of course," Daniel's distant voice replied. "The eagle that belonged to Zeus, the Greek god."

"Sir, you did it." Carter's voice now. "A definite gate address."

Whoever controlled Jack's actions allowed him to study the seven glyphs.

"General O'Neill!" A hand shook his elbow. "Oh, please wake up."

"I don't know if that's a good idea, Weiyan." Daniel again, being Daniel. Worrying.

Somebody better worry. Jack couldn't feel his legs. His entire body became stiff, unmovable.

"Something's wrong," the Chinese girl cried out. Jack hated the Chinese. Well, not all of them. Just those scum suckers who'd made his life a living hell during Black Ops missions in the eighties, and then when SG-1 had to rescue Daniel from Yu.

That had not been fun.

"We need to help him."

The hand shook his arm. Smaller, weaker, but it did the job. Jack could feel himself keel over, slowly — as if gravity pulled him sideways — until his face smacked against the dirt. It hurt like hell, but he felt it!

"The building has returned," Teal'c announced.

Feeling like himself again, Jack stood up. Weiyan kept hold of his arm. "It's okay, thanks," he told her, gently prying her fingers off his arm. He suddenly felt like an ass for being such a bastard to this kid.

"I am glad you are awake again," Weiyan said with a smile.

He returned the gesture. "Yeah, that was a hoot. What's going on, kids?"

Teal'c pointed in the opposite direction to the hill Jack had climbed earlier. That butt-ugly squat building was back. Closer this time, maybe three hundred feet away. Standing next to it was most positively, absolutely, a person.

"Stay here," he ordered. "I'm going to go have a talk with our host."

"Hold on, Jack. This gate address? It's familiar."

"So?" He glanced down at Daniel. "Last time I checked — right before I became the second coming of *The Exorcist* — there wasn't any gate."

"I think we've been here before. Okay, not *here*-here, because this isn't really a place, but some other time. On a mission."

"And yet, you have no idea what it means."

Daniel scowled as only Daniel could do — rude yet Jack recognized that he meant well underneath it all.

"Don't you think there's a reason we worked this out?" Daniel asked.

Jack squinted, barely able to make out the alien standing beside the building. He thought of him — or her — as an alien, because really? What else could it be, popping in and out like that? The alien wore a bleached-white cape, the cloth flapping against a breeze that had kicked up. A bit of dust swirled on the valley floor around the building. The alien didn't budge, but it did seem to be —

"Is it waving at us?"

"It appears so," Teal'c confirmed.

Jack stepped around the graffiti he'd help scribble in the dirt. "Well, whoever it is, they have some explaining to do."

"Hold on," Daniel said. "I think we should go with you. In case you have a — "

"What? A relapse? A good, long look at what senility has in store?" He stabbed a finger at the glyphs scrawled out in the dirt. "Stay here and figure out what that address is about."

Daniel frowned, but Jack ignored it. He nodded curtly at Carter, Teal'c and the trainee kid and headed off toward the building. He resisted the urge to run, knowing he needed to keep his adrenaline in check. Keep his temper under a tight lid. So instead, he focused on putting one foot in front of the other, shoving his frustrations as far down as they would go.

The ground trembled. Slightly, but most definitely there.

One foot, then the other. No anger, no frustration.

Just the truth, please, with a side of 'get us the hell out of here.'

The ground kept on shaking, but he kept on going. He switched from watching his feet to looking up at the building. The alien had stopped waving. In fact, it wasn't even there anymore.

"Damn it." Jack doubled his pace. If he could outrun the alien, creature, or whatever it was that held them in this god-forsaken place, then maybe, just maybe —

With a loud crack, the ground split open barely ten feet ahead of him.

He stopped. Calmed himself down. Deep breaths. Relax.

Get a grip, O'Neill.

Another tremor hit and the crack widened. Was it trying to block his way?

It was an illusion. He knew that. He took another step forward.

The illusion widened. Hell, the illusion became a damn deep chasm. He stepped to the left, intending to go around, but the ground rumbled again. Within seconds, the crack widened, stretching off in each direction as far as he could see.

He stopped just short of its edge and peered down into a bottomless, jagged tear in the ground. He kicked a pebble over the edge and it dropped. He listened for the sound of it hitting bottom.

The sound never came.

At least the tremors stopped. That's something.

"General!"

Jack whipped around. Carter and the rest were rushing toward him. "I thought I told everyone to stay back."

"Whoa!" Daniel got there first, halting a few feet back from the chasm's edge. "I think someone's trying to tell you something."

Teal'c came up on his other side, with Weiyan right behind him. "Whomever that someone is, Daniel Jackson, they are no longer present."

Carter leaned over the edge and Jack restrained himself from pulling her back. "Sir, I hate to ask, but..."

He shook his head. "I swear on my single pair of stars that I wasn't pissed."

"Pissed?" Weiyan asked. She hovered behind Teal'c. Jack couldn't blame her. He'd hide behind the big guy, too, if he had any sense. This entire experience was getting too damned —

The ground shook again.

"Come on..." Now the thing was reading his thoughts!

"Everyone, get back," Carter yelled over the rumble.

Jack didn't argue. He reversed course, away from the craggy pit of nothing. That is, until he noticed that the crack was shrinking.

Moments later, the gap sealed up, the ground no different than before.

Weiyan slipped out from behind Teal'c. "How is that possible?"

She took a step forward. Nothing happened. She took another step and the ground rumbled.

Jack joined SG-1 in rushing forward to stop her.

The tremor stopped.

Jack glanced as his team. "Take another step."

They did. Nothing happened. Urging Weiyan on, Jack led the others in taking several more steps. They walked right over where the ground had cracked open earlier.

A few more paces and Jack held up his fist, the signal for everyone to stop.

This was getting ridiculous.

"All right, fine!" he yelled toward the abandoned building. "I get it!"

"Oh, no. No, no, no," Weiyan called out from behind him.

"It's all right." He kept his eyes peeled, hoping the alien would make another appearance. "Piece of cake. We'll all go together."

"No, you don't understand," the girl sobbed.

Jack turned around to find Weiyan jerking down on her zippered fleece. "What the hell?"

She'd yanked up her pullover. Underneath, her entire lower stomach was covered in blood.

The ground rumbled.

CHAPTER TWELVE

BEIJING, CHINA
1968 MAY 25

HUANG huddled beneath the central stairwell of the Ministry of Foreign Affairs, clutching the ancient scroll in his hand. Doors banged open and shut. Screams ripped through the air. Gunshots rang out across the many marbled floors.

The Red Guard had stormed the building, determined to fulfill China's Cultural Revolution by any means possible. Out with the old and in with the new. Their hatred of old customs, culture, habits and ideas had made the diplomatic corps a likely target. If Huang's bunkmate had not warned him that morning of the Red Guards' plans to kill diplomats who clung to those ideals, he would not have had the opportunity to rescue his precious find.

Footsteps pounded on the stairs above. Huang retreated further back into the shadows and sat down with his back against the wall. He stuffed the scroll carefully into his faded blue proletarian's overalls. In anguish, he listened as great sculptures were toppled, paintings were slashed, and tapestries ripped in two. The Red Guards chanted their mantra rejecting the old ways again and again.

The China of Lord Yu was gone. Crushed in a revolt of perilous power mongering, swathed in false promises to the masses. Violence wrecked the streets. Troops of Red Guards killed and maimed anyone who did not fit the ideals of their leader, Chairman Mao. A man who claimed to want great peace and prosperity for his people.

But who acted no better than Lord Yu's enemies. At times, Huang wondered if indeed Mao Zedong and his ferocious Red

Guards were not Anubis or Apophis in disguise.

Huang drew in his legs and rested his head upon a knee. He had made a grave mistake coming to China, allowing his rescuers to do what they believed to be the right thing. When Sir Edmund Hillary discovered him in Antarctica, Huang hadn't the strength to out-run the Tau'ri. Hillary belonged to a land called New Zealand and along with his countrymen, he had come to reclaim the frozen land. To build bases of operations that would be known as Scott and McMurdo.

In broken Chinese, Hillary had insisted Huang return to what he believed to be his homeland of China. Huang had tried to tell Hillary the truth of his origins. He tried to convince him of the threat to the Tau'ri, of the being of light, but the explorer had only laughed and escorted him to a primitive craft called an airplane. Huang resigned himself to his situation in the hopes that upon returning to the land of his ancestors, he might find the means one day to return through the Chappa'ai and share both news of China and the being of light.

Ten years later, no opportunity had arisen. Huang learned to speak modern Chinese, was given a position as a gardener, and told to be thankful that he had food in his belly and clothes on his back.

Far off in another part of the building, gunshots rang out. Believing himself safe for the moment, Huang withdrew the stolen scroll from his overalls. Upon hearing that all ancient artworks were to be destroyed by the Red Guards, he had taken the scroll from the wall outside the office of the Vice Minister of European Affairs.

He unrolled the scroll carefully. A few black painted pictograms covered the top half of the eight-foot long red cloth. The bottom half showed a man standing by a golden river, its banks swollen. The waters appeared ready to break from their boundaries, but the man appeared calm. Serene.

He bore an imperial tuft upon his chin. Dressed in a red mianfu, the horsehair tail of Lord Yu's green hat was longer than Huang remembered. Nonetheless, the scroll gave Huang solace. Assurance that his master and lord's eternal nature might someday allow Huang to return. To be forgiven. To once more take up his mantle as Dragon Guard or perhaps even First Prime.

A door slammed open at the top of the five-story stairwell. Voices murmured. Three, perhaps four men. They began their descent, speaking in calm, hushed tones amidst the chaos.

Huang quickly rolled up the scroll, secreting it once again in his overalls. Creeping forward, he peered up the stairs. Black shoes and blue pant legs climbed downward. He glanced across the stairwell to the exit. The door led out into the rear gardens overlooking a barricaded street. He'd used it often as a means to enter the building when in need of the facilities.

Huang slid along the wall to the door, flattening himself against the cool stone.

Let your rapidity be that of the wind, your compactness that of the forest.

With a silent prayer, Huang opened the door. He slipped outside, carefully closing the door behind him.

Blooming flowers, budding trees, and great bushes lined the long white building of the Foreign Affairs Ministry. Huang had spent much of his time working in these gardens, along with a half-dozen others. Today, however, the gardens were empty, the other workers hiding in their homes in fear.

Behind him, the door began to open, the men's voices loud with laughter. Huang picked up his gardening pail with its pruning shears and scurried to the closest tree he could find. He pulled out the shears and set to work, stowing his anxiety behind the most placid face he could muster. A worker's face.

"Halt!" A Red Guard yanked the shears out of Huang's hands.

Forcing himself to remain calm, he turned toward the guard. Young, with a terrible haircut, baggy blue pants and a green shirt, the man was little more than an over-aged boy, at least fifteen years younger than Huang. Perhaps twenty, maybe twenty-five. Red squares lined each side of his collar.

"Wait, comrade," said another man behind him. Older, fuller of face and body, the man wore a blue-collared tunic. He had a vigorous manner about him, his eyes darting across the garden, seemingly assessing everything in mere moments.

He gestured for the guard to back away. Narrowing his eyes, he approached Huang. "You are a gardener? A worker for the Foreign Ministry?"

Huang nodded, afraid to say anything that might encourage the Red Guard to attack him with the shears.

The man scowled. "Gardening is a leisure of capitalistic classism. A look backwards, not forwards."

Huang wanted nothing more than to proclaim his truth. To tell his origins. That by his very nature as a clone of the great Sun Tzu, he was a 'look backwards' to what was great, or rather, what had been great about China.

Knowing he must survive, Huang held his tongue. He glanced up into the tree he had been working on. It was a cherry tree.

He returned his gaze to the man and offered a hesitant smile. "I look toward the future, sir. This tree shall bear fruit. Sustenance for those in need."

The man bowed his head in respect. "An admirable and necessary work. One that we will not keep you from, comrade."

The man gestured to the guard to return his shears. Huang nodded his thanks and the man walked off, his companions in tow.

Huang allowed himself a silent, but deep sigh of relief.

It was short-lived.

"One more moment," the man said, striding back to the tree. "Do you know who I am?"

"I— "

The man raised his hand once more, an almost imperial gesture. "I am your Chairman. The work you do here is good, and I will remember your words. Gardening for sustenance is something China's people should achieve."

"Yes, Chairman."

"Can you read?"

"I can write my name, but reading?" Huang pressed his lips together. He had tried to learn the modern symbols of China's language. So far, the task had been difficult.

"I have not the time, Chairman."

"If you haven't read, then you are not familiar with the old ideologies. I approve." The Chairman pointed at the Red Guard who took Huang's shears earlier. "Bring him inside."

"Chairman?"

"As a worker, he will— What is your name?"

"Huang."

"As a worker, Huang represents the people. He will make a fine diplomat."

Huang staggered backward. "But, Chairman, I know little—"

"You know enough. Learn to read, but read sparingly. Care only for the people, and you will do well."

"What office should I take him to?" asked the guard.

"Assign him to the new Vice Minister of the Americas."

"Americas?" asked Huang.

The Chairman beamed. "Have you never heard of the United States?"

CHAPTER THIRTEEN

ANCIENT OUTPOST, ANTARCTICA
18 AUG 04/1910 HRS MCMURDO STATION

ANOTHER quake slammed through the outpost. George yanked Ambassador Zhu away from the hole as a new wave of snow and ice plummeted from the ceiling. Shielding Zhu with his body, he took the brunt of it, ice and snow pelting his back. The vibrations intensified. He quickly scanned the room to make sure Lee and Simmons were safe. Lee had grabbed on to the Mark IIs while the lieutenant stayed by the hole, hanging on to a nearby column.

"Simmons, get back from there," he yelled over the thunderous roar, but the lieutenant didn't budge. He kept looking down in that damn hole.

Another jolt. George fell sideways, his head smacking against the floor. As he struggled into a kneeling position, he could only hope the force field protected Jack and SG-1 down below. At this rate, the outpost would be torn to pieces.

And the planet, too, if they didn't shut the damn thing off.

The tremor stopped, only to be replaced by loud hissing and popping sounds emanating from the force field. George glanced over at Zhu. She seemed none the worse for wear. Dr. Lee had risen to his feet, double-checking the straps on the Mark IIs.

"General, I can see them!" Simmons pointed down at the hole.

George scrambled to his feet and raced over to the force field. It was as clear as glass. Down below, a motionless Jack laid next to Weiyan Shi on top of a glowing circular platform the size of a Hummer. Backlit trellised panels glowed underneath. Sprawled around the outer edges were Colonel Carter, Teal'c and Dr. Jackson, forming a semi-circle around the other two.

Or more specifically, around Weiyan. She'd fallen exactly center.

A control crystal protruded from her lower stomach. Or rather, the remains of one. Larger than a DHD controller, the red crystal was charred black.

"There should be more blood," Dr. Lee observed.

Zhu's ashen face made George wince. Normally, he'd ask Lee to be less clinical, and more sensitive to the fact that civilians were about, but he needed the scientist to focus on getting them out, not playing diplomat.

He'd have to do that himself.

Zhu sucked in a sharp breath. "Is she…? Are they…?"

Weiyan's hand slid across her stomach, coming to rest just beside the burned out crystal.

"There!" Simmons pointed toward Colonel Carter. Her left arm raised a few inches and then dropped back down. As if she was trying to pull something.

"How is that possible?" Zhu asked, bending down beside the hole. "Why are they all unconscious?"

"I'm not sure." Lee rubbed his beard. "I mean, I have a theory, but — "

"Spit it out, Doctor."

"It could be a side effect of the photonic energy emitting from the device, or — "

George raised a hand to stop the doctor's preamble. "You'd said the device derives its energy from the sun. Why would it keep them unconscious?"

"Hold on, let me show you." Lee ran over to his computer table. He lifted up a toolkit and grabbed a pad of yellow paper. "See now, why couldn't I find this earlier?"

"Perhaps the pad had disappeared," Simmons whispered.

George gave the lieutenant a stern look. "Doctor, please."

"Sorry!" Lee rejoined them, pulling a pen out of his coat pocket. He drew a fair facsimile of the platform below.

"Photons are pure energy. They register as both particle and waves." He drew a series of waves emanating out from the center. "If General O'Neill and the others were knocked unconscious from their fall, they might be susceptible to Mu-waves. Electromagnetic oscillations that can affect neuron activity in their brains, forcing them to stay unconscious."

"Can these Mu-waves hurt them?" George asked.

Lee shrugged. "I don't really know that much about the physiological affect, but I'd bet they're having some pretty wild dreams."

"What about Weiyan?" Simmons asked. "Why isn't she bleeding?"

George looked back down at the six-sided crystal sticking out of her stomach. A horrific sight to say the least. "Does that crystal have something to do with it?"

Lee shook his head. "If the crystal was lit up, then yes, maybe. But it's broken which could be why the device is behaving this way."

George watched Samantha Carter's hand tighten into a ball. "How much time do we have, Doctor?"

Lee ran over to his computer and tapped a few keys. "The sun rises in less than eighteen hours."

"I need to contact Major Davis." George glanced out the archway leading to the main area. Two airmen were carrying a civilian on a stretcher toward the elevator. Against the far wall, another airman was speaking on the radio, requesting a med-evac chopper.

"Sir?" Simmons hurried to his side. "I took the liberty of contacting the major before the latest tremor. He's still busy helping with recovery efforts at McMurdo."

"I almost envy him," George replied. At least someone was doing something constructive. He turned back toward the chair and it occurred to him that maybe there was something to be done here, too. "It's time for a new approach, Doctor."

"Sir?"

He turned to Simmons. "How many trainees are still here?

"At least five." The lieutenant gestured toward the archway

leading to the outer chamber. "Should I — ?"

"Whoa, General. Wait a minute." Lee's head shot up. "Putting an untrained person with the ATA gene into that chair is what got us into this mess."

"And it might be the only way out at this point. If we don't take the risk, we could lose much more than General O'Neill and SG-1."

"We could lose the world." Lee slid out from behind his computer. "I'll go find out which trainees are still here." As Lee hurried out, George dropped his gaze to the comatose General O'Neill. If the stakes weren't so high, he'd be amused by his protégé's uncharacteristically still form. Jack was a ball of energy, never not-moving. Even during briefings, he'd fidget with a pen, a coffee cup, or even a button on his BDUs.

The president had once referred to Jack as a living spin-top, never happy unless in motion. George snorted, remembering the man's recent promotion ceremony. President Hayes had pinned the stars on himself. He'd said it was like trying to shoot a moving target.

But now, Jack lay motionless. If the frown lines on his face weren't deeper than normal, George would've believed him dead.

He prayed it wouldn't come down to that.

Footsteps announced Dr. Lee's return. To George's dismay, only two trainees followed him in. Ryan Hall, the retired army vet, and Sgt. Miguel Helado, the young Argentine whose arrogance was enough to convince George they were doomed before the soldier even got in the chair.

He strode up to the two trainees and stuck out his hand. "I cannot thank you enough for being willing to help."

Hall gripped his hand and pumped it hard. "Happy to, General. Just tell us what to do."

George turned to Helado to do likewise. "You too, son. It's appreciated."

The Argentine didn't take his hand. "I do this to save my own country, sir, not yours."

Though taken aback, George held his tongue.

Lee coughed. "He's right in a way, General. If we don't get the device turned off soon, Argentina and Australia will— "

"Thank you, Doctor." He gestured toward the chair. "Let's get this underway, all right?"

"First try shutting the device down." Lee escorted Helado around the hole to the back of the chair. "If that doesn't work, try moving the force field downward, away from the top of the device so we can deactivate it ourselves."

Helado's face turned white as he walked across the wooden board leading to the chair and sat down. The seatback lit up. "Now what?"

Lee returned to his monitors. "Concentrate on the device. Try to shut it off."

Helado closed his eyes and the chair back reclined into the active position. His face scrunched up, he sucked in a breath…

Nothing happened.

"Concentrate on the force field," Simmons offered. "You want to bend it downwards, away from the control crystal."

Helado's eyes popped open. He glanced left and then right. "What was that?"

Lee shrugged. "I didn't feel anything."

Hall rubbed his arms. "I felt it, too."

"Like a wind. A breeze, yes?" Helado shivered.

"General," Zhu said, her voice impatient.

George skirted around the hole until he was as close to the chair as possible. "Sgt. Helado, if you could just focus?"

"*Sí*. Of course." Helado's eyes closed again.

The platform rattled. The back's illuminated panels flickered. The floor shook, not as intensely as before, but bad enough to topple over a decorative panel by the archway.

"Watch out!" Simmons yelled.

Helado jumped from the chair just before a chunk of ice fell on its seat. More ice and snow tumbled down from the ceiling as Helado ran across the wooden plank and took cover by the Mark IIs with Lee.

"Get back!" George yelled.

A shudder ran across the floor. Zhu and Hall crouched a few feet away from the hole, their arms covering their heads. Simmons was back at his default position, holding on to a column by the hole. Ice and snow smashed into the force field, immediately disintegrating into a burst of rising steam.

"Evacuate the room!" George shouted over the din.

Hall and Helado dashed out, but Zhu crouched lower, staying put. "I am not leaving!"

A final shake and the tremors stopped.

George exhaled, his breath turning to wispy fog in the cold room. Glancing back down at his unconscious people, he could only hope that whatever had them in its grip was also keeping them warm enough to escape hypothermia. Lying still like that for so long couldn't be good.

Simmons seemed no worse for wear. Not a hair out of place. "Earthquakes and sub-zero temperatures seem to agree with you, Lieutenant."

"Yes, sir." Simmons managed a faint grin. "I was raised in a very warm climate, but I like the cold. Would you like me to see if any coffee survived that last round?"

"You read my mind. Thanks."

As the young man hurried from the room, Zhu wiped a hand across her eyes. "We have failed. Weiyan will die and — "

"Not true," George said. "We just haven't succeeded yet."

"That's the real irony in all this," Lee said. "If Colonel Carter was here, she'd have the device shut down in no time."

George glanced at Samantha Carter's still form. Her hands no longer twitched, though her brow was creased. Whatever was going on in the colonel's brilliant head, it was clear she, too, was struggling to figure it all out.

"What happens now?" Ambassador Zhu asked, more to the force field than to anyone else.

The scuffle of footsteps announced someone else had entered the room. "I have spoken with the UN Secretary-General and he has agreed."

George whirled toward the voice.

Ambassador Duebel glared back at him. "Destroy the outpost now or I will arrange to have it done myself."

Once Sam managed to get Weiyan to lie down, she probed the girl's abdomen. She used her palm to scrape back the blood pooling around Weiyan's belly button, around her hips, up high around her ribcage. There had to be a good pint, at least.

"This makes no sense," she reported to the others. "There's no incision, no cuts, not even a bruise."

"I don't feel anything." Weiyan laid a hand onto her bare stomach. "It doesn't hurt, but," sucking in a breath, she lifted her hand, the fingers coated in the viscous stuff. "No, no. I cannot bleed like this. Not now."

The girl was panting, clearly terrified.

"You've got to breathe slower," Sam told her gently.

"I will try."

"It's going to be okay." She took off her pullover. The fleece was made to wick away moisture in cold weather, she couldn't ask for better material to blot up the blood.

"Any chance at an explanation?" The general knelt down beside them, his eyes narrowed in concern. "I thought we'd decided this was all imaginary."

"I can't explain it, sir." The fleece soaked full of blood, and yet, still more seeped out around Weiyan's navel.

The general handed over his pullover. "Teal'c's earlier knock to the head didn't leave any wounds, so what gives? None of this is real."

Weiyan's breathing had calmed down from massive hyperventilation to ragged whimpers. Daniel crouched beside her.

"We know there are some similarities between here and the real world. Weiyan's..."

"Go ahead," Weiyan sobbed. "Say it. I lost my temper."

"It happens." Daniel squeezed her elbow. "Just ask Jack."

"Watch yourself," General O'Neill half-warned, half joked.

"Is anyone thirsty?" Sam asked. "Or even hungry?"

"No, which is strange enough, but if we're gonna talk about imaginary versus real, we should probably talk about this." The general pulled out his Zippo.

"Skaara's lighter," Daniel said. "I thought you packed it away in that cigar box of yours after — "

"After we pulled your ass out of Lord Yu's little fortress last year? Yeah, I did." The general flipped the lighter open and thumbed the wheel. The flame sputtered to life. "Cute trick, huh? No lighter fluid." He snapped the lid shut.

"O'Neill, if you did not carry the lighter with you to Antarctica — "

"Good question, T." He stuffed it back in his pocket. "Part of me thinks we're dealing with Skaara, or another of Daniel's ascended buddies."

Daniel shook his head. "They don't interfere. Not like this."

"You can't be sure, Daniel." Sam wiped up the last of the blood on Weiyan's stomach. The bleeding had stopped. "You can't even remember why you left them."

"Or why they kicked your sorry ass out."

"You're right," Daniel said. "I don't know, but this just doesn't seem like something they'd do."

Sam pulled down Weiyan's shirt to cover her stomach. "I just don't see how any of this is possible. We're here, but we're not — "

"Yes, but when Weiyan got angry while in the chair," Daniel said, "a quake happened."

"Subsequent earthquakes have directly tied into General O'Neill's and Weiyan's emotions," Teal'c added.

"True," Sam said. "But if this is all imaginary, then where are we really? For all we know, we're still at the outpost."

"And if no one there can get to us," Daniel said, "Weiyan could be injured. It could have happened when we fell."

"No!" Weiyan bolted up from the ground. "I don't feel any pain. I am well, I tell you." She clenched her fists. "I am well. Please," her voice lowered, "do not let me die."

"No one's dying." General O'Neill gathered Weiyan in his arms and held her as she cried.

Sam glanced up at him, surprised though warmed by his gesture. Then, a chill ran up her spine. A reminder of the impossibility of their situation. She hated to be the one to break his moment's kindness, but it had to be done. "Sir — "

"Leave it alone, Carter." He gave Weiyan a brief bear hug and then stepped back. "We're getting out of here. Trust me." He tugged down on his shirt. "We've got a good record of getting out of far worse things that this, don't we, people?"

"General O'Neill is correct," Teal'c said. "We have indeed escaped from far more challenging situations."

"Even holographic ones," Daniel added. "Look at what happened with the Gamekeeper."

The general scowled. "Do we have to?"

"That was different, sir." Sam shook her head. "We experienced yours and Daniel's memories over and over again, but we weren't hurt."

"So... This isn't a hologram?"

"I don't think so, sir." Sam pointed toward the building at the far end of the basin. "Otherwise, would that structure be here through every permutation?"

"And why the city?" Daniel asked. "Or, more importantly, why give us clues like that obelisk? Or Jack having a sudden bout of speaking Ancient?"

General O'Neill turned toward Daniel, "You're convinced that Peda-lite Elysium — "

"Pedion."

"Whatever." General O'Neill waved his hands. "You really think that's a gate address?"

"Sir, you were the one to fill in the last few syllables." She met his grim gaze with one of her own. Twice before, Sam had watched the Ancient Repository take over his brain and had always felt unsettled when it happened, as if the general would slip away and never come back.

Frowning, he turned toward the building across the valley floor. "I still feel like we're rats in somebody's maze."

"Or children with a puzzle," Teal'c commented.

"I am bleeding again!" Weiyan pressed a hand against her stomach.

Sam pushed Weiyan's hand out of the way and pulled up her pullover. A blotch of blood oozed from her otherwise healthy skin. "How do you feel?"

"Sleepy." Weiyan glanced at the general and then sniffled back a sob. "I will try to be brave."

Sam grasped her hand. "Good, that'll help, but if we don't stop the bleeding soon, you could lose too much." She made to pull her hand free, but —

Weiyan grabbed hold with her other hand. "I must confess."

"I don't understand."

"I am — I am a hemophiliac."

Sam gasped. "That's impossible. How did you get on the trainee program if — ?"

"I cannot tell you why I was accepted, Colonel Carter. Only that my bleeding," she touched her stomach, "is serious!"

Sam exchanged a look with General O'Neill. If Weiyan lost much more blood she would die, and all the assurances in the world wouldn't make a difference. "Sir," Sam said, "we need to figure a way out of here. Soon."

He nodded. "I'm going to take Daniel and scope out the area. See if we can figure out a way off this rock."

"You can't do that, sir. Whatever's controlling this environment wants us to stay together."

"I am willing to journey with you, General." Weiyan placed a hand on her forehead.

"Yeah." General O'Neill shuffled his feet. "I don't think that's such a hot idea. Teal'c?" He jerked his chin toward the ground.

"You must conserve your strength." Placing an arm on her elbow, Teal'c eased Weiyan down to the ground. "When we do find a means of escape, we will undoubtedly need your help."

"Teal'c's right." Sam scooped up the general's pullover and used it to wipe Weiyan's stomach. "The bleeding's stopped again. What I don't understand is why this started all of a sudden. There's no wound."

Weiyan dropped her gaze. "Earlier I noticed my stomach was damp, but thought it only sweat."

Teal'c lowered himself to the ground beside her. "Whoever has placed us here is most cruel."

General O'Neill grunted. "Just once I'd like us to meet a technologically advanced race bent on being nice."

"Don't forget the Tollan, sir." As soon as Sam mentioned their former allies, she regretted it. Thanks to the Goa'uld, they were all dead.

Shoving the thought aside, Sam patted Weiyan's shoulder. "Stay put. You'll bleed less." She nodded at Teal'c who had taken up residence beside the young girl.

"I will assist her if needed."

Satisfied, Sam joined General O'Neill and Daniel a few feet away.

"That guy keeps popping in and out," the general said. "What the hell is that about?"

"We don't even know if it is a guy," Daniel said.

"Guy. Girl. What does it matter?"

"The general's right, Daniel." Sam shaded her eyes to scan the building in the distance. The sun's lack of movement alone was a clear indicator that they weren't in a natural environment. "The one thing we do know is that whoever it is, they want us to go forward together."

"Maybe." The general shifted his stance forty-five degrees to the right of the building. "But what about sideways?"

"What good will that do?" Daniel asked.

The general nodded toward the building's far right. "I saw some rubble earlier. While on top of that hill."

"Rubble." Sam raised an eyebrow, unsure where the general was going with this.

"That's right, Colonel, rubble." He draped an arm around Daniel. "And we all know how archaeologists love rubble."

Daniel glanced at her and then General O'Neill. "And you think where there's rubble, there might be something else to explain — ?"

"How the hell to get out of here? Yes, Daniel. What do you think, Carter?"

Sam exhaled, relieved to try something and even more, relieved to see the general back in a constructive frame of mind. "I'm game. Daniel?"

"I'm always up for rubble," Daniel said. "What about Weiyan? Should we take her with us?"

Sam thought about that for a moment. "I'll stay behind."

"Negative, Colonel. We might need you."

"Sir, if you're right, and if heading on a diagonal from the building doesn't cause another seismic event, we could try this in phases. You two go first. If you find anything you deem worth securing a new position for, signal us. I'll cross, then Teal'c can bring Weiyan."

"Works for me." General O'Neill clapped his hands together. "Let's move out." He raised two fingers in the air and then pointed toward their destination.

With a parting lift of an eyebrow, Daniel followed.

The two men trudged forward, or rather, sideways. Sam couldn't help but wonder what had spurred General O'Neill into action and dare she admit it, a better mood.

Twenty feet. Thirty feet. She held her breath, steeling herself for another tremor.

Fifty feet. General O'Neill turned around and waved.

Relieved, Sam waved back.

"Rats in a maze, Daniel."

"Jack, I don't think that's what this is all about." Topsoil spilled from Daniel's fingers. So far, he'd recovered a few marble shards, several large splinters of polished wood, and a three-foot wide granite pedestal — the same stone that had held the obelisk.

If they were inside some kind of holographic projection, someone was going to a lot of trouble to spare no detail.

"You're right about one thing," Daniel said. "Rubble pretty much describes what we have here." Without any tools, he had to dig with his hands. It was slow, tedious work. He used his fingertips as a brush, sweeping back one area, and then the next. Sure, he could just plunge in and hope for the best, but if he broke something — a bit of stone, or something that could be a clue — he'd regret it.

"I'd kill for a pair of sunglasses," Jack muttered, standing a few feet away.

"You could help me sift through this."

"You're the archaeologist, not me."

Daniel lifted his head, the relentless sunlight near blinding him. "Do you want to find a way out of here or not?"

"Someone needs to stand guard."

"Against what? Another earthquake?" Daniel jabbed a finger toward another small mound of dirt, bits of marble, and granite. "Tell me the big bad general isn't afraid to get his hands dirty."

"Big bad, my ass." Jack sank down beside the other mound and grabbed a handful of dirt.

"Careful," Daniel warned. "Go slowly. We don't want to miss anything." He demonstrated how to sift through the dirt.

"Hey, if it gets us out of here, I'll pick this apart speck by speck." Jack got the hang of it pretty quick — which should have surprised Daniel, but it didn't. When motivated, Jack had a knack for picking up skills if the need arose.

After watching him excavate for a few moments, Daniel returned to his own efforts. Eventually, the loose dirt he'd brushed aside gave way to more firmly packed soil.

And a definite chunk of granite.

"Found something." He carefully swept away the soil packed around a three-inch wide, foot-long vertical piece of smooth granite. "This looks like a piece of the obelisk!"

Flipping it over, he noticed blocky indentations along the back. He brushed away the embedded dirt and there they were, the letters P and E. The first two Ancient letters for the word Pedion.

"That's good, right?" Jack took the granite chunk from his hands.

"Maybe. I'm not sure what we can do with it, though. We already know the planet's name. We need the rest of the obelisk if we're going to make any sense out of this."

"If you found that, we'll find the rest and you'll figure it out," Jack muttered. He returned to his work with the topsoil.

Something had been eating at Jack earlier. That much was clear to Daniel. Feigning nonchalance, he cleared away more dirt from the immediate area. "So, what's going on with you, anyway?"

"Digging like a kid in a sandbox. Wanting to ring the neck of whoever decided to treat us like lab rats."

"We're not rats."

"Oh, sure, you say that now." Jack shrugged. "But hey, we're trapped somewhere and need to get out. Same old, same old."

"That's not what I mean." Daniel deliberately kept his focus on digging. "You've been acting wonky since we left the SGC for Antarctica, and now— "

"Wonky?"

"Yes, wonky… Ah!" Daniel found another chunk of granite. The letters D and E. He placed it next to the first piece.

"Sweet." Jack handed over a matching piece of granite, this

time a good four inches wide and twice as long. The Ancient block-style letters for L, Y and S.

Daniel laid the granite down beside the others. He looked toward Jack, hoping to pick up their conversation where it'd left off, but Jack had returned to digging silently, a clear sign that he wasn't interested in talking. With a sigh, Daniel carried on sifting dirt.

Finally, Jack spoke. "Since when did 'wonky' become part of your vocabulary?"

"Don't change the subject. Something's eating you."

"Actually, I think that is the subject." Jack waggled a dirt-covered finger toward him. "You've changed these last few years."

"I've changed?"

"Yeah, you have." Jack attacked a new mound, no longer being careful. "Since coming back from Oma-land. For one thing," he tossed a handful of dirt aside, "you're snarkier."

"And that's bad, how?"

"I'm not saying it's bad, just..." Jack shrugged. "Be careful. You'll get yourself in trouble."

Daniel snorted. "This from the king of snark." And that's when it hit him. "You're changing the subject again."

"What do you want me to say? I'm getting tired of — "

"This is about what happened on Tegalus, isn't it?"

Jack single-mindedly tore into a new mound. "I can distinctly remember telling you on the plane that — "

"You think it's my fault the Caledonians launched the missile strike. That's what's bothering you."

"Trust me, Daniel, those jerks had it coming." Jack flashed him a tight grin. "As far as I'm concerned, you can get caught up in all the civil wars you want. Just do me a favor and get together with Teal'c. Maybe the two of you could schedule your mishaps a little further apart." He plunged his hands back into the dirt. "Bring Carter while you're at it."

Tegalus. Teal'c's near-death experience in the virtual chair. Sam's capture and torture by the Replicator Fifth...

Daniel rocked back on his heels. "You don't blame me," he realized aloud. "You blame yourself. You think you could — "

"Found another piece." Jack tossed over a fist-sized rock.

With a shake of his head, Daniel uncovered the letter I. He laid the granite piece down beside the others. "We've been at this for, what?"

"Twenty minutes, I guess." Jack waved his wrist in the air. "No watch. Which is really annoying, by the way."

Daniel shook his head. "I don't mean the digging. I mean the Stargate Program. We've been at this a really long time. The losses, the near misses — "

"It's all part of the job."

"Maybe being a general's your problem. You've drifted away from who you — "

"Daniel..." Jack's voice took on that warning tone, the one that said 'stop pushing.' He shoved both hands into the hole he'd pulled the last stone from. His shoulders jerked a few times until he fell back on his rear, another large chunk of granite in his hands.

Daniel wiped the thick dirt off Jack's latest find, discovering the final letters U and M. The Ancients' version of an M always surprised him, looking more like a blocky Y.

"There are benefits to being a general, you know." Jack wiped his hands on his pants. "Best parking space in the lot. Well, next to the NORAD commander, that is. Plus, I get to eat great commissary food, sit back — "

"Not here, Jack. You can't sit things out while we're trying to figure out how to get off this world."

"You don't think I know that?"

Daniel laid the last piece down beside the others. "What I think doesn't matter."

"Stop trying to play shrink. You're not very good at it." Jack jerked his chin toward the obelisk fragments. "I don't think we're going to find anymore chunks of this stuff."

"This doesn't make sense. On the original obelisk, there

was writing here." Daniel pointed to an empty area below the middle letters. "Where did it go?"

"Does it say Pedion Elysium?"

"You've had the Ancients' knowledge downloaded into your head, you were forced to learn the language yourself to get out of that time loop, and you still can't read Ancient?" He traced the first few letters and sounded out the pronunciation slowly for Jack to follow along.

"Stop!" Jack put his hands over his ears. "There's only so much information this brain can handle at once, and Ancient just isn't high on my list of priorities."

Daniel fought the urge to roll his eyes. "Yes, then. It says Pedion Elysium."

"Which clearly someone, or something, wants us to see. The question is, why?"

"You think the being that talked to Teal'c — this alien — is playing a game with us?"

"Yeah, and this," Jack waved a hand at the granite pieces, "is a clue to that game."

"Maybe it isn't a game." Daniel stared at the words. He'd managed to work out a gate address — thanks to Jack's odd little Ancient Repository relapse — but so far, he couldn't figure out why that address was important. "Could the alien be trying to tell us something? Something we need to know, but for whatever reason, the being has to be sneaky about telling us?"

"Sneaky?" Jack snorted. "That's a snarky word if ever I heard one."

"Maybe it is, but unless you can tap into any last shreds of the Ancient Repository like you did earlier — "

"Did not."

"Did so." Daniel deliberately glared at Jack. "This is important. We need to know the significance of this name or — "

"We'll go on being rats in a maze."

Teal'c stretched his legs out. Fatigue washed over him, a moment's weariness he allowed in hopes that like a wave it would crest and become no more. He sought inward for his strength, believing he had only to grasp —

A hand pressed against his knee. "You all right?"

Teal'c opened his eyes and forced himself to smile at Colonel Carter. "I am simply performing a moment's kelno'reem."

"Kelnor-what?" asked the young girl sitting beside him.

"Kelno'reem. A meditative practice to steady the mind."

"I thought you didn't do that anymore." Colonel Carter's eyes narrowed in suspicion. "At least, not since your symbiote was removed."

Teal'c knew he should speak the truth to his friend, but as there was nothing she or anyone else could do, he said nothing.

Fortunately, Colonel Carter had more pressing issues to attend to. Weiyan Shi no longer bled, but she could no longer stand, either. She had paled considerably. A sheen of sweat covered her forehead and her lips were pale. Teal'c exchanged worried looks with his teammate, aware that each hour that passed diminished the chances of her survival.

"I wish to go home," Weiyan Shi whispered. She reached out her hand to him.

Under other circumstances, Teal'c would not lie, but this young woman — barely more than a child — required comfort. As if she was his own, he took her hand, pressed it firmly in assurance. "Even now O'Neill and Daniel Jackson seek a means of escape."

"That's right," Colonel Carter said. "We do this all the time. Get into trouble, figure it out, jump back through the Stargate, and — "

"But General O'Neill said that without a Stargate, we have no means of escape."

Teal'c squeezed the girl's hand. "You do not know General O'Neill as we do. He often jokes in impossible situations."

"It's a deflection thing," said Colonel Carter. "The general's just trying to keep things light so everyone can focus."

Weiyan Shi coughed. "He has not joked very much in my presence."

"He just needs to get to know you." Colonel Carter lifted a hand above her brow and looked further into the valley.

Gently releasing Weiyan Shi's hand, Teal'c followed her line of sight toward the location of Daniel Jackson's and O'Neill's dig. The two men appeared to be pulling items from the ground. "Perhaps they have found something of value."

"I wish we had radios," Colonel Carter said wistfully.

As did Teal'c. Nonetheless, they needed to know if any progress had been made. "I will attend to Weiyan Shi while you confer with the others."

"And risk having the ground crack open again?" asked Colonel Carter. "I don't know, Teal'c. We'd agreed to wait for a signal from the general."

"As O'Neill and Daniel Jackson were able to proceed, perhaps the being which keeps us here will allow you to do the same."

"All right. I'll talk to the guys and if they've found anything, I'll signal you to join us." With one last reassuring smile for Weiyan Shi, Colonel Carter headed toward the others. Teal'c watched as she carefully repeated their steps, moving on a diagonal to the building's right. Assured that she would not come to any harm, he looked back at Weiyan Shi. The girl had curled up on her side, her eyes closed. Her chest rose and fell in a somewhat steady rhythm.

Teal'c closed his own eyes again. Striving for a moment's balance, he inhaled deeply. He could not perform a deep level of kelno'reem now that his symbiote had been removed. That said, he could still assert some level of control over the rhythm of his heart, the temperature of his body, and even the tumultuous nature of his mind when necessary.

He exhaled forcefully, expelling worn breath out through his nostrils. He inhaled once more, allowing the warm air of their surroundings to fill his lungs. He looked inward, imagining the air mixing with his blood.

"You fool the others," Weiyan Shi said by his side, "but I can see that you aren't well."

Teal'c bowed his head. "Admittedly."

"You aren't human, are you?" Weiyan Shi pushed up to a seated position. "You speak English like the Americans, but you use different words, as if— " She sucked in a short breath.

"Are you in pain, Weiyan Shi?"

Pressing her lips together, the girl nodded curtly.

"Should I retrieve Colonel Carter?" He began to rise.

Weiyan Shi grabbed his leg. "Please, stay with me. I'll be all right. I'm just tired. Like you." She tugged at his pant leg. "I'll try to feel better, ok?"

"You use the word 'try' very often."

"Isn't that important? We should always try to do what is asked of us." This last she recited as if from a child's nursery rhyme.

Crossing his legs, Teal'c pointed this out.

"My mother taught me to always try. You sound like my father. Or at least, the one time I spoke with him. He didn't believe in trying. He said one must simply do what needs to be done." Weiyan Shi lay down, resting her head upon her clasped hands.

"Your father sounds like he is a wise man."

"Was," she mumbled. Her eyes closed.

Teal'c followed suit. He dropped his chin toward his chest, breathed in, and—

"Will General O'Neill be angry if I ask where you're from?"

He peered once more at this curious young woman and considered her question. In the end, the responsibility for her knowledge was her own, and given their current circumstances, it would be unjust not to give her at least some sense of the truth.

"I am from Chulak."

Her eyes widened. "Chulak. Is that far from here?"

"As we have no means of knowing where 'here' is, I can only say that it is far from Earth."

She coughed again, the sound worrisome. "You're the first alien I've ever met."

"My ancestors were of Earth."

"Does that mean we're related?"

"I do not know." Teal'c had never considered that possibility. If the Jaffa had indeed evolved from the Tau'ri, those who walked upon Earth now could be his distant kin. Was it possible that this was yet another reason for his affinity to O'Neill, Daniel Jackson and Samantha Carter? The idea gave him comfort.

A sudden boom across the sky cast aside his musings. The sound was familiar, though certainly out of place. He bolted to his feet, listening. Dizziness threatened to overcome him, but he pushed it aside.

"It wasn't me," Weiyan Shi said. "I am not angry. General O'Neill must have lost his — "

Teal'c shot up a fist to signal silence. Though short-lived, the sound reverberated across the valley, the vibrations rippling through the air long after the initial boom had dissipated. He strained to hear confirmation of what he feared.

He did not have long to wait. A high-pitched whine, that of a ship slowing as it entered the upper atmosphere, emanated from the skies above. Moments later, a Goa'uld mothership appeared from behind the clouds and began its descent.

"How is this possible?"

"What is it?" Weiyan Shi cried out.

"An enemy you should have no wish to meet. Can you run?" He grabbed her arm and lifted her up. The effort was difficult, but adrenaline now coursed through him, casting aside his fatigue. Another glimpse at the ship confirmed that it drew closer, no more than a half-mile away.

"I — I will try." Weiyan Shi stepped forward, stumbled, and fell to the ground.

"No, Weiyan Shi. We will not try." He swept her up into his arms. "We will do."

He ran to join the others.

"Orders, sir?"

Jack watched the Goa'uld mothership descend at break-neck

speed, headed right toward them. At its current trajectory, it would set down smack between them and the building. Too close for comfort.

"O'Neill!" Teal'c ran toward them, Weiyan slung over his shoulder. He set her down beside Carter. "We must take cover!"

Too hard to believe.

"Jack! Shouldn't we do something?" Daniel jumped up from their little — and now insignificant — pile of granite letters.

Too impossible.

"General, we must hide!" pleaded Weiyan.

"From what?" He yanked the Zippo out of his pocket. Flipped the lid back. Thumbed the wheel. The flame came to life. Nice and neat.

Sunlight bounced off the incoming mothership's black metallic hull. Its pyramidal edges looked sharp enough to cut anything in two as it entered the lower atmosphere.

Jack waved a hand over the lighter's flame. Nothing. Nada. Not even the littlest bit of heat. "Yeah, that tears it." He snapped the lighter shut and exchanged a glance with Daniel.

"You do not believe it is real," Teal'c observed.

Jack stuck the lighter back in his pocket. "I think that's been pretty well established. How much longer do you think we have before that thing lands?"

"Ten, perhaps fifteen minutes."

"Carter, am I crazy?"

She raised her eyes upwards and frowned. "No, sir. I don't think you are, but — "

"Yes! You are all crazy!" shouted Weiyan.

Jack whirled toward the girl, ready to calm her down. When he saw her digging a hole in the ground, he realized it would take more than just a few words.

Cupping her hands, Weiyan was scooping back armfuls of dirt. Her hair had half-tumbled from its ponytail, hanging around her face in a disheveled mess. The sandy soil covered her blood-soaked shirt as she frantically dug like her life depended on it.

Weiyan was right, in a sense. Their lives did depend on what happened next, but not necessarily in the way she believed.

"Whatcha doing?" he asked as calmly as he could.

"What you will not. We must dig a hole. Hide. Protect ourselves."

"Weiyan Shi." Teal'c bent down beside her and grabbed her wrists. "What you see is not real."

Weiyan yanked her arms loose. "You cannot be certain. What if they harm us? We will be killed."

A shadow passed over them. The ship was coming in for landing. Jack had to fight every instinct that screamed out to help the girl dig that hole.

"We must hurry or we will die!" Weiyan kept on digging. She worked fast, creating a hole at least two feet deep.

"Jack, you're sure — ?"

"I'm sure, Daniel," he roared over the mothership's entry rockets. "Sure as I've ever been. But somebody needs to stop that girl before she hurts herself."

Weiyan jumped in and curled up in a ball. Satisfied that she couldn't get into any more trouble, Jack returned his focus to the incoming ship. Not for the first time, he wished he had his scope.

Daniel glanced over his shoulder at Weiyan and then back at Jack. "I don't get it."

Jack snorted. "Welcome to the party."

"That's not what I mean. Why aren't we experiencing another earthquake? She's panicked. You've got to be feeling at least a bit anxious. Although, you've become awfully calm about all this."

"Don't let the bravado fool you. Seeing that ship is akin to a dog hearing a whistle."

The ship touched down in front of the building. Jack noticed there were no portholes like those he'd seen on Cronus's and Apophis's motherships. He held his breath as the ground rumbled from the impact, the sound too similar to the earlier quakes for his taste. The pyramid's primary hull retracted upwards, revealing a multi-tiered base with lit panels underneath.

"That ship's taken some serious damage," said Carter.

Scorch marks streaked across the side facing them, but the thing Jack noticed the most was the lack of an outer frame. It was like the pyramid had lost half its mass.

"There's something off about the ship, T. Something's missing."

"That is not a *ha'tak* class ship, O'Neill. It is far older."

Jack studied the ship's pyramid shape again. Then it hit him. The thing was a dead ringer for Ra's ship. A shudder went through him. "God, tell me that isn't Ra. With all the crazy-assed backwards things we've experienced, that'd be — "

"I do not believe it is, O'Neill." Teal'c pointed toward the ship's apex. "The sigil is missing. I have seen it many times as Apophis' First Prime in battle against Ra's fleet."

"Then who the hell is it?"

"I cannot say."

A horrific grinding noise erupted from the pyramid's side. Squinting against the sunlight, Jack could make out a series of gantries opening up along the pyramid's base. As the doors slid upwards, swarms of armored Jaffa poured out of the ship.

There had to be at least a thousand of them, broken into four battalions, each group stomping off in a different direction. If his gut was wrong, and these bastards were real, there was a good chance this would become SG-1's last stand.

The Jaffa would make toast of them in minutes.

He shoved aside the maudlin thought. That pity-fest had ended hours ago.

A battalion headed directly toward them, led by a Jaffa wearing a red cloak instead of the typical dark gray. His silver tattoo glinted in the sunlight, but he was still too far away for Jack to make out his forehead marking.

Carter tensed beside him. "What if you're wrong, sir?"

"If I'm right, those Jaffa are just phantoms. Figments."

Daniel leaned forward to get a better view. "We should be

able to figure out whose phantoms they are pretty soon."

"O'Neill," said Teal'c. "If they are phantoms, should we not approach them for a closer look?"

"Let's first see how this phantom parade plays out."

The lead Jaffa stormed toward them, backed up by enough metallic stomping from his horde to make Jack's trigger finger itch. Without a rifle, all he could do was stand and watch.

And pray like a priest he was right.

Another fifty feet to go. The Jaffa didn't miss a beat as they neared. Further evidence for Jack that they weren't real. They weren't there.

Carter widened her stance, balling her fists as if it would do any good.

It wouldn't, but he sure liked knowing she had his back.

Twenty feet to go.

Teal'c stepped up to his other side with a fierce snarl of a smile. He always did like a good fight.

Ten. The lead Jaffa and his cronies kept marching toward them, their matching tattoos clear as day.

"That's Lord Yu's sigil!" Daniel said.

The Jaffa kept on marching.

Right through SG-1.

CHAPTER FOURTEEN

EMBASSY OF THE PEOPLE'S REPUBLIC OF CHINA
WASHINGTON, D.C.
2003 FEBRUARY 14

HUANG sat down behind his desk, stifling yet another yawn. It was past ten p.m. Why Ambassador Chen had insisted he remain in the office was unclear, but China's UN Security Council representative was nothing if not a persistent man. Chen's phone message implied grave importance. A matter unable to wait until morning.

As second-in-command to China's senior ambassador, Huang's office afforded him a magnificent view of America's capitol city. A blanket of snow had fallen, covering automobiles in great banks of white. While the majestic snow-covered mountains and trees of his long lost home were missing, the mounds reminded him of his time in Antarctica.

Without the clawing desperation to survive or the terrible isolation.

Or the endless reminder of his failure to Lord Yu.

Huang glanced about his office with its indulgent mahogany furniture, modern conveniences, and photos of his time among the Tau'ri. By their terms, he should consider himself successful. By his terms, nothing was further from the truth.

His gaze fell on a crudely painted pot containing a cherry tree sapling. A gift from a local elementary school. Pulling the pot closer, Huang reflected upon the irony that it was a cherry tree that had catapulted him from gardener to his current position. A position that had allowed him to thrive, but had yet to give him the access he sought to Antarctica, so that he might journey home.

Decades had passed. Time had marched on. And yet, he still craved the opportunity to return to Lord Yu and seek forgiveness.

He dipped a finger in the pot, scooping up some soil. Earth, he reminded himself, finding it odd that the American's name for their planet was the same as the dirt upon which they stood. As he contemplated the ironies of Earth's many languages, he lifted his finger and pressed the soil upon his forehead. A downward stroke, two horizontal slashes —

The door barged open. "We must speak."

Huang hurriedly wiped the *wénshēn* from his forehead as Chen entered the office. The ambassador's face was haggard with worry, his suit jacket unbuttoned, and his tie-knot loosened.

As he closed the door behind him, Huang took note of two folders under his arm. A red one, clearly belonging to the embassy, and a dark blue one as well. In his free hand, he carried a foot-long metal box.

"How may I be of service?" Huang rose from his chair.

"First, you must sign this." Chen plopped the red folder down on Huang's desk. Embossed across the top in modern Chinese type were the words TOP SECRET.

Huang opened the folder and scanned the single piece of paper inside. He had eventually learned the modern Chinese letters, the writing far simpler than ancient Chinese, or even Goa'uld for that matter. The paper contained a simple oath, a promise of non-disclosure and a vow to remain silent. If signed, Huang's security clearance would be heightened to the utmost level.

"It is my honor to serve, Ambassador." Huang quickly signed the document and returned the folder.

"Always so formal." Chen cocked his head. "There are times I wonder if you were born in the right century." Placing the metal box on the desk's edge, he sank into the opposing chair. "It is no wonder your wife divorced you."

"I was not worthy." Huang bowed his head. Taking a wife had been a momentary weakness, a forbidden act that had led to the birth of a child, yet another of his failures to follow Lord Yu's commands. He had left before the birth, selling the scroll depicting his master to the New York Museum of Art. He had sent the subsequent profits to his ex-wife to assist in raising their daughter.

A daughter he could not bring himself to meet.

"While your worth to family may be in question," Chen tossed the blue folder in front of Huang, "your tireless dedication to China holds value. I must share what I learned today with someone I trust."

The blue folder's cover carried several American emblems. That of the U.S. President, another of the United States Air Force, but it was the image at the bottom that caught his attention. Huang's fingertips grazed the logo in disbelief, for it surely looked like one of the Chappa'ai's symbols. Superimposed upon the image was an inverted English 'V'. At the top was embossed the letters SGC.

He repeated the letters aloud to Chen who waved a hand at the folder. "Stargate Command. Open the folder."

Huang did so, his eyes immediately glued to the top page. A photograph of the Chappa'ai stared back at him.

Stunned, he sat back in his chair. "Please explain."

Chen did so. A secret meeting had been held that day at the American's Pentagon. Along with the ambassadors from France and England, he had been informed of the discovery of the "Stargate" in 1928, buried in the sands of Giza, Egypt. Eight years ago, a Dr. Daniel Jackson had deciphered its meaning and the device had been activated. For the past six years, American military personnel and scientists had traveled through the Stargate to hundreds of planets. Thousands more had been charted.

Huang struggled to keep his face implacable. Flipping the page, he looked up at Chen and asked, "Have the Americans come in contact with — ?"

"Yes!" Chen's eyes widened. "Millions of humans live across the galaxy, taken from Earth centuries ago by a fierce enemy known as the Goa'uld." He pronounced the name incorrectly, eliminating the "a" so that it sounded more like the English word for ghoul with a "d" on the end.

Huang resisted the temptation to correct him. "What is known of this enemy?"

"They are parasites. Incubating in what are called Jaffa warriors. They take hosts as needed so they may rule over many worlds." Chen reached over to the folder and turned the page, revealing a photograph of several System Lords including Cronus, Nirtti, and...

"This one calls himself Lord Yu!" Chen stabbed a finger at the likeness of Huang's master. "This thing, this alien, claims to have ruled China for many centuries."

Reeling in astonishment, Huang raised the photograph for a closer look. His lord sat on a modern leather and chrome chair. A Tau'ri chair. The timestamp at the bottom left indicated the photograph had been taken in July of 1999. Only four years ago.

"Where was this taken?" he asked Chen.

Chen waved a hand at the photograph. "In Colorado. At Stargate Command during negotiations surrounding a non-aggression treaty. A treaty the Americans dared agree to without informing China or any other country. It is outrageous, to say the least, but there are further concerns pressing."

Lord Yu had been here. Here on Earth!

"We met another race of beings today," Chen said.

Huang dropped the photograph, a lump forming in his throat. Was it possible that the being of light had made its existence known as well?

"We met an Asgard. A small human-like being who instantaneously transported himself into the briefing room." Chen shook his head in disbelief. "Thor, Supreme Commander of the Asgard fleet, and a devoted friend of the Americans, it would seem. Clearly, they possess significant technologies, although," he pushed the metal box toward Huang, "we may have some of those technologies in our possession if we can determine their use."

Huang opened the box. Inside was a pair of fist-sized Goa'uld communication devices.

Undoubtedly, the communication devices would be disabled. For the first time in many decades, he regretted not having the naquadah in his blood to operate them. To contact Lord Yu and beg his mercy.

The silver skin shimmered.

Was it possible? If they were they still active, the right voice command might be enough to reach his master. Huang raised an eyebrow to cover his shock. "Do you know what they do?"

"I do not." Chen frowned.

"How — ? Where did you get these?"

"Do you remember a few months back when the Russians claimed they lost a missile submarine due to a meteor crashing into the Pacific some seventy-five kilometers away?"

"The *Rostov*?" Huang asked. "Did we not determine that to be a cover story? The ship was taking on supplies in the harbor at Vladivostok at the time."

"Apparently, a Goa'uld 'mothership' crashed into the Pacific Ocean. A ship belonging to a Goa'uld named Anubis."

Huang sat up straight upon hearing the name of Lord Yu's long dead enemy. How was this possible? As a crèche-child, he had learned by heart the tale of Lord Yu's battle a thousand years ago. A tale in which his master has vanquished the most evil of System Lords for having attempted to destroy Ancient China by flooding the Yellow River.

"We found these on the ocean floor during what we'd hoped to be a salvage operation." Chen hefted one of the communication devices in his hand. "It would seem the Russians knew about the Stargate Program for several years. In return, they've received untold benefits in the form of alien technology, including plans to the F-302, an advanced interceptor plane."

The ball's shimmer dissipated.

"The Russians knew?" Huang put a hand to his mouth to cover his disappointment.

Chen tossed the ball back into the box. "Turn the page."

Huang did so. Two photographs lay side-by-side. One of a team of green-clad American soldiers shooting at a glider, the other of a crude box-like duplicate, its wingtips exhibiting none of the grace of the Goa'uld aircraft.

"That is the F-302," Chen said with barely suppressed anger. "American military hardware inspired by knowledge gathered through the Stargate Program and capable of both aerial combat and space flight." He slammed his hand down on the desk. "Russia has the plans, but China? No. All we have been offered is the opportunity to send observers in exchange for keeping this enormity from public knowledge."

"Observers?" Huang swallowed. "I would volunteer for such a posting."

"You?" Chen shot him a glance. "Nonsense. I need you here as my second. This is a task for younger people. As Security Council members, however, we will receive weekly reports from the SGC."

"And our observers?"

"Of course," Chen said with a knowing smile.

Huang flipped to the next page. Another photograph of the Chappa'ai — the Stargate, he corrected himself. Deactivated in the picture, it sat at the far end of a large concrete-walled room, surrounded by U.S. military personnel armed with rifles. From Chen's information, Huang could only assume the photograph was taken at Stargate Command in Colorado.

Surely, there must be a way to infiltrate this operation. To activate the Stargate and return home. What he needed was information, the more the better. As his ancestor Sun Tzu once said, 'Knowledge is power.'

Huang would gather all the knowledge he could before planning his next move. From the corner of his eye, he glanced at the case containing the communication devices. A silvery ripple shot across the untouched ball's surface.

It was most definitely active.

His mind raced. Could he remember the right phrase? Could he truly and finally contact Lord Yu?

"Who runs this operation?" he asked with forced casualness.

"General Hammond," Chen replied, "and a Colonel Jack O'Neill. My impression from Senator Kinsey is that this colonel is something of a fool, though a brave one at that."

Huang closed the folder, the beginnings of plan taking shape in his mind. A fool, no matter how brave, would be a minor inconvenience.

One easily thwarted given the right subterfuge.

"May I study these for a while?" he asked Chen.

"As long as you do not leave the facility, of course." Chen strode toward the door. "I will be interested in your report." The ambassador dipped his head and departed.

Huang waited an hour, to be sure the embassy had shut down for the evening and that he was alone. His breath held, he pulled the box to him, opened it and spoke the words.

Soon after, Lord Yu's visage arose from within the ball's depths. Huang dipped his head in obedience.

"*You live.*"

"I do, my lord." Huang sucked in a tremulous breath and raised his eyes to meet his master. Behind Lord Yu, the twisted limbs of a miniature cherry tree blossomed on the far wall. At its base sat his prized jade statue, a woman cradling a baby.

"*Have you lived according to my tenets*?"

"I — I have," Huang lied. He told himself that once back in Lord Yu's service, he would tell the truth of his digression. He would admit to fathering a child.

But not today. Instead, he shared his experiences amongst the Tau'ri with his master, ending his tale with information about the Stargate Program. "I am prepared to return to your service, my lord."

"*No, not yet.*" Lord Yu stroked his imperial tuft. "*Much has happened during your absence, Huang Sun Tzu. You must perform for me one more task. One more enemy to ensnare.*"

"Anything, my lord. Who is this enemy?"

"*SG-1.*"

CHAPTER FIFTEEN

ANCIENT OUTPOST, ANTARCTICA
18 AUG 04/1945 HRS MCMURDO STATION

"WHAT DO you require, General Hammond? A direct call from the UN Secretary-General?"

"Not while there are other options." George blocked Duebel from stepping any closer to the hole and the platform beyond. "I'm sorry, Ambassador, but I take my orders from the President, not the United Nations."

Duebel stabbed a finger at the Ancient chair. "That thing has cost too many lives."

"It's also saved lives."

"I don't care about the past. It's the present that matters. Or should I say the future? Your own scientists have indicated that once the sun rises, the seismic activity emitted from that device could tear the continent apart."

"I am fully aware of the losses — "

"How many more must die before you accept your responsibility? Or is this about your precious SG-1?"

George sucked in a breath to calm himself down. "Mister Ambassador, given time we could still shut the force field down. The sun doesn't rise for..." He turned to Dr. Lee who had returned to monitoring the device on his computer.

"Seventeen hours," Lee said. "More or less."

"More or less?" Duebel shook his head. "You know the immediate destruction of this outpost is the right thing to do. Ambassador Zhu, do you not concur?"

Duebel turned toward Zhu. She sat at her self-appointed post by the hole, her legs tucked under. Her eyes never left the force field or her countrywoman underneath. Almost too intently, unless—

"Quing?" Duebel strode to Zhu's side and knelt down. "Your voice is needed." He grasped her shoulders.

"What would you have me do?" she whispered.

"Trust us, Madame Ambassador," George entreated. "Allow us the time to — "

"Trust. Like your government entrusted mine?" Zhu raised her head and glared right at him. "Two years have passed since you disclosed the Stargate Program to China. Two years in which we've watched you trust Russia with plans to your interceptors and naquadah generators, but not us. Never us."

Duebel's eyes widened. "Quing! This is not the time."

"This is precisely the right time." Zhu curled her lips in obvious disdain. "Intelligence points to the United States now providing Russia with plans to something called the X-303. An interplanetary defense spaceship code-named *Prometheus*."

Zhu returned her gaze to the force field. "Do not speak to me of trust, General. You haven't earned the right. Instead, prove it. Find a way to save this planet."

Duebel placed a comforting hand on her shoulder. As Zhu shrugged it off, the Swiss ambassador whispered harshly to her. George couldn't hear what Duebel said, so he turned away to afford them some privacy. As he did, Simmons, and a Security Forces airman with an M-16 slung across his back, hurried in.

The lieutenant pointed at a cup of coffee in the SF's hands and then at George. "Black, sir. We couldn't find any sugar, but there's enough left for one pot."

"Thank you, airman." George accepted the offered cup. "See if there's enough for the ambassadors, including Juarez — wherever he took off to."

"Yes, sir." The airman strode out.

George sipped his coffee. It was bitter, pretty much a good description of his day so far.

He glanced back at the two ambassadors still deep in private discussion. "'We have to distrust each other. It's our only defense against betrayal.'"

"Sir?"

George gave Simmons a wan smile. "It's an old saying, Lieutenant. Almost as old as I feel."

Simmons leaned in and whispered, "Sir, you should know. Ambassador Zhu — "

"Is Weiyan Shi's mother." He gulped down the rest of the coffee. "I'm not surprised, but I should have guessed sooner."

"General, you can't blame yourself for what's happened."

"Can't I?" George turned toward the Ancient chair. Its cold metal frame and alien architecture stared back at him, a reminder that for every step forward they'd taken with the Stargate Program, the cost had been enormous.

Shifting his view to the force field, he had to ask himself whether he opposed Duebel's demands to destroy the outpost because there was still time to find an answer before the sun rose, or was the truth simpler? Was it because he couldn't take any more losses?

A mild tremor shook the outpost, sending a light fall of snow down onto the force field and the surrounding floor. Some of it fell on Duebel.

"What are you waiting for, General? Another station to be flattened?" The ambassador brushed the snow from his gray hair and rose from Zhu's side, his face dark with rage. "Destroy the outpost and, while you're at, I want those interceptors that Quing mentioned removed as well. They should not be in Antarctica."

"Those F-302s are critical to Earth's last line of defense."

"They're U.S. military and entirely against the treaty." He wagged a finger at George. "Stop stalling."

"That's not the case, Ambassador.

"Mount Erebus has erupted!" Juarez ran into the chamber, waving a piece of paper. He bent over, panting wildly.

Duebel snatched the report from Juarez and scanned it. "The volcano has had a significant eruption." He handed it off to Zhu. "That's only twenty-three miles from McMurdo!"

"Ah, Mister Ambassador?" Lee scurried over from his monitors. "Erebus has persistent eruptions all the time. There's even occasional minor lava flows out to its inner crater, but never the outer caldera. An old college buddy of mine works up at the LEH, the Lower Erebus Hut, that's why— "

"Your friend is dead, Doctor." Zhu lowered the paper. "A rescue helicopter was sent to retrieve the Erebus team, but they found the hut demolished. A five kilometer-wide lava flow erupted from the crater and is burning a path all the way down to the Ross Sea."

"I don't believe it," Lee insisted. "We would've heard something. I would have…"

The scientist fumbled with his glasses. They dropped. George bent to pick them up, his hand grazing the brutally cold stone floor. He glanced over at Zhu, still sitting down. How she was able to handle the frigid temperature was beyond him.

Although, if one of his grandchildren were locked beneath an alien force field, George would suffer through anything to ensure their rescue. Which made his next decision all the more difficult.

He handed the glasses back to Dr. Lee. "I'm sorry for your loss, Bill. If you— "

"Rick said Erebus would never amount to anything," Lee mumbled. "He kept begging for more funds. He wanted to explore more, but the NSF wouldn't let him." He dropped his chin down. "It just doesn't make scientific sense."

"That's all this is to you," Juarez said, his voice dripping with spite. "A scientific anomaly to be studied."

"That's enough, Ambassador," George warned. "You've made your point."

"No, General. This is only the beginning." Juarez's chin jutted out in clear defiance. "Destroy this monstrosity," he waved toward the force field and then the chair, "or I will contact your president myself."

"I suppose an eruption could happen," Lee continued to

mumble. "Plate tectonics are a tricky thing… Although, something like a reversal of the magnetic poles could cause added stress, maybe the photonic energy's directed toward — "

"Get him out of here," Juarez demanded. "If I see another scientist in my lifetime, it will be too soon."

Lee apparently didn't hear the ambassador because he kept on rambling on. "Maybe it's not magnetic. If the computers work — "

"Bill." George laid a hand on the scientist's back, hoping he might bring the man's focus back to the here and now.

Lee's eyes rimmed with tears. "I'm sorry, General. Rick was at my wedding, you know?" He swallowed. "This is hard."

"I know it is, son." He nudged the scientist toward the archway to the outer chamber. "Contact Major Davis. Have him get over to the F-302 base at Observation Hill. Pronto. I want the Byrd Station Navy SEALS ordinance team brought here to the outpost ASAP. Ready to detonate."

Lee's eyes widened. "General, we can't!"

"I don't see any other option. Not unless you have a way to turn that thing off."

"Not yet, no. If we had someone with a stronger strain of the ATA gene, that might help, but with all the trainees evacuated…" Lee hung his head. "I'm sorry, General. I — "

"I'm sorry too, Bill."

Rubbing his eyes, Lee hurried toward the archway.

"And Doctor?"

Lee stopped and turned around.

"How many hours until the sun comes up again?"

"Less than seventeen now." Lee cocked his head. "Sir?"

"You've got sixteen hours to turn that 'yet' of yours into a reality. Make the call and then get back to work."

A brief smile flickered across Lee's face. George hoped it was enough to keep him focused on finding a solution before it was too late.

"General?" Lt. Simmons backed off from his position by the

hole and slipped in front of Duebel and Juarez. The two ambassadors moved off to join Zhu.

"How are our people, Lieutenant?" asked George.

"Still unconscious, sir, but General O'Neill's smiling, if that means anything."

"Why am I not surprised?" George pulled up the hood on his parka. The chamber had become damn near the temperature of an iceberg. "Is there anything else, Lieutenant? I'll need to call the president and obtain clearance before going through with — "

"Sir…" Simmons looked over at Ambassador Zhu. "Dr. Lee said that if we had someone with ATA genetics as strong as Weiyan's, they could use the chair to deactivate the device."

"Like mother, like daughter?" George eyed the Chinese ambassador. While she hadn't admitted to the relationship, certainly saving her child would be worth the revelation. "Once more you're a step ahead of me, Lieutenant. Why you haven't put in for a promotion yet is beyond me."

Simmons ducked his head. "I wouldn't want to leave the Stargate Program, sir."

"You sound like Major Davis." George drew in a deep breath, preparing himself for what would undoubtedly be an uncomfortable discussion with Ambassador Zhu. "Why don't you go see how Dr. Lee is faring? Tell him your idea."

"Right away, sir."

"And make sure Major Davis has those birds headed toward Byrd within the next half hour."

Simmons ran through the archway and out into the nearly abandoned main chamber.

George walked over to the ambassadors. Duebel and Juarez greeted him with silent nods, but Zhu remained focused on the force field, or more specifically, on what lay beneath.

"Sirs, would you kindly give me a moment alone with Ambassador Zhu?"

"What for?" Juarez's eyes narrowed with suspicion.

Duebel grabbed the Argentine ambassador's elbow. "Leave it alone, Jorge. He's agreed to our demands." He half-dragged Juarez out of the chamber.

George knelt down beside Zhu. "Madame Ambassador, why didn't you tell us Weiyan was your daughter?"

"Trust has many enemies and few friends."

"Trust us enough to help save your daughter," George said, refusing to rise to her bait. "Perhaps a turn in the chair."

Zhu laughed. A bitter, empty sound that echoed through the now empty chamber. "I don't have the ATA gene, General. Weiyan inherited that — and other traits — from her father."

George sank back on his heels. "And he's undoubtedly in China, thousands of miles away."

"Oh, further than that, in a manner of speaking," Zhu said bitterly. "Weiyan's father is in a psychiatric institution. Completely catatonic and completely insane."

Daniel instinctively ducked as an Al'kesh buzzed overhead.

Beside him, Jack stood his ground. "Would someone please explain how Lord Yu and his minions suddenly became citizens of this ghost town?"

"If we knew the answer, we wouldn't be — "

"They're not real." Sam crouched down beside Weiyan's self-made foxhole. "It's safe. Really."

"I guess old habits die hard," Daniel admitted. These weren't real enemy troops. These were phantoms. Ghosts.

But why?

He scanned the valley. The Jaffa battalion who'd marched right through SG-1 earlier had taken up position a good hundred yards back behind Sam. Another battalion came to rest by the opposite end, standing in front of a massive grass-covered hill. The two remaining groups continued toward the rear of the valley, toward the bottom of the cliff Jack had climbed earlier.

In total, there had to be at least five thousand of Yu's Jaffa, but again, why?

Teal'c pointed upwards. "More!"

Two more Al'kesh buzzed by, coming in for a landing.

"Someone — "

"Or something," Jack corrected him.

"Is trying to communicate with us."

"Ya think?" Jack whirled toward the battalion behind Sam and frowned. "I'd have preferred a postcard or an email."

"Jack, don't you see?" Daniel held out his hands toward the landing ships. "Somehow this all has to do with Lord Yu and the Ancients, which means the Ascended — "

"Daniel, you were ascended once, remember?"

"Yeah, but — "

"Ah!" Jack raised a finger. "You told us on Abydos, when you were all nice and glowy, that Ascended folks don't interfere. So what do you call this?"

"I don't remember saying that, but if Yu — "

"The last time I checked, Yu isn't an Ancient. He's a Goa'uld." Jack turned back toward the trio of Al'kesh now parked in the middle of the valley. "And I should've killed his slimy, snake-headed butt when I had the chance."

Daniel hated the Goa'uld as much as anyone, but during his imprisonment with Lord Yu, he'd discovered the System Lord still had emotional ties to his ancient reign on Earth, or more specifically to China. "Yu's not like the other Goa'uld."

"A Goa'uld is a Goa'uld. Carter, stay with…" Jack jerked his head toward Weiyan. "Daniel, Teal'c, you're with me. Let's go find out what this dog-and-pony show is all about."

Along with Jack and Teal'c, Daniel headed toward the closest Al'kesh. As they neared, people began to unload. Some dressed in blues, other in greens, reds and grays. Pretty much every one of them was dressed the same — all in ancient Chinese-style robes bound at the waist with swathes of darker cloth.

Civilians, he mused, until a giant of a Jaffa escorted a group of three women close enough for him to see the fear on their faces. And the white bandages on their feet. Their feet had been broken and bound in the ancient Chinese style meant to keep women from running away.

A style not used in China for quite some time. Daniel thought back on his time as Yu's captive a year ago and couldn't remember seeing any of the women's feet bound in that way.

Not that he'd seen more than two or three and only during his time in the lower levels of the fortress. No woman ever made an appearance in Yu's throne room. He wasn't even sure Yu had a Goa'uld queen. His Dragon Guard certainly didn't need them, being cloned by Ancient technology.

"Yu's slaves?" Jack asked.

"They can't see you," Daniel said. To prove his point, he walked right through the Jaffa guard. "This is… Odd."

"Odd doesn't quite sum it up." Jack waved an arm through one of the women.

Teal'c raised a hand, fingers spread wide, and swept it through the Jaffa guard. "If these are holographic projections, should there not be some visual — "

"After effect?" Jack headed toward the Al'kesh's ramp.

"Like a light trail or something?" asked Daniel.

"Or something is right. " Jack peered up the gantry. "Teal'c, come on."

As Teal'c turned to follow, Daniel noticed him grimace as if he was in pain. Then he shook his head slightly, put back his shoulders, and strode toward the ramp.

"You're wasting your time!"

"Since when has that stopped me?" He approached the ramp, stepped up —

And fell flat on his face.

Biting his tongue, Daniel turned away.

"Go ahead, say it," Jack grumbled. "Say 'I told you so.'"

"Those weren't exactly the words I had in mind."

"Head's up," Jack warned as a single cargo ship flew across the small valley and headed toward the grass-covered hill.

"What's going on there?"

Daniel pointed toward the large mass of people heading toward the hill. "Maybe if we get closer. Where's — ?"

"I am here." Teal'c walked closer. Actually, stumbled was more like it.

Daniel took a worried glanced at Teal'c and the sweat beading on his forehead. His skin had turned a gray brown.

Jack shook his head, a silent command to stay silent. There were times to listen to Jack and there were times to ignore him. Daniel chose the latter.

"Teal'c, are you feeling all right?"

Teal'c proudly lifted his chin. "I am well, Daniel Jackson."

"Back at ya," Jack said with a smirk. His way of saying, score one — tied on the 'I told you so' front.

Daniel ignored him. "You don't look so good. Maybe you should rest, head back to Sam and Weiyan."

"I will rest when we are free of this dilemma."

Another warning glare from Jack, and Daniel let it go. But not without promising himself to keep an eye on Teal'c.

The cargo ship set down on the hilltop. As its bay doors open, the crowd of soldiers and civilians dropped to their knees in prostration.

"How come they're not making more noise?" Jack asked.

"Perhaps they are, O'Neill, and we simply cannot hear them."

A figure emerged, but the hill was too far off to see anything other than a blur. Daniel assumed it was Lord Yu. As if on cue, the crowd rose, turned around, and headed back to their ships.

A rippling wave streaked across the valley and the ships disappeared. As did the people.

"What the hell?" Jack whirled around. He pointed toward the building that continued to exist through every vision.

Or nightmare.

A solitary Jaffa strode toward them. He didn't slow down as he neared, obviously unaware of their presence. He was Asian, young, and shorter than Yu's other Jaffa—no more than five-foot-nine. There was a quiet confidence about him as he walked. An inner strength.

An all too familiar strength. As the Jaffa drew closer, Daniel was unsurprised by his gray woolen cloak, cinched off to the side with a jade broach. Cropped black hair, green-flecked black eyes, and a square jaw. The sun glinted off the gold tattoo on his high forehead.

Jack jerked a thumb toward the Jaffa as he walked past, unaware of his audience. "Isn't that...?"

"Oshu," Teal'c stated flatly. "Lord Yu's current First Prime and lead Dragon Guard. He is not Jaffa. None of Yu's Dragon Guard carries symbiotes. They are clones."

"Sonuvabitch." Jack face darkened with rage as he watched Oshu draw closer. "Hallucination, ghost or whatever, that bastard's grand-clone gave us enough trouble last year that I'd like to ring all their necks."

"You mean Ambassador Huang," Daniel said. "Didn't the Chinese — "

The First Prime stopped beside them, seemingly unaware of their presence. He stared off toward the mysterious building.

"Guys, I'm not sure that's Oshu." Daniel approached the Dragon Guard for a better look. "He looks like him, but — "

"And again, I ask... There's a but?"

Ignoring Jack, Daniel stepped up to the Dragon Guard. A jagged white scar stretched across the man's chin. "Whoever this is, it isn't Oshu. That scar's old."

The air rippled again and the First Prime disappeared.

"And I repeat," Jack glowered, "what the hell?"

Before Daniel could answer, a multi-color wash of light rippled across the valley like a shockwave. It crashed against the cliff at the far end, surged up the craggy, exposed rock, and then dissipated as it breached the summit.

A Stargate materialized on the cliff-top.

Jack took a few steps toward the cliff and then stopped. He turned back toward Daniel. "Too good to be true, I assume."

A kawoosh erupted from the gate. As its event horizon settled down into a reflective puddle, more Jaffa exited, carrying large cargo containers. They descended the hillside.

Another wave of light streaked across the valley.

"Is this making anyone else dizzy?" Jack asked.

"It is disorientating, O'Neill." Teal'c took a step forward, or rather, he tried. Halfway through his stride, he stumbled backwards. "Something prevents my forward movement."

Jack stretched out his palm. It flattened against the air, as if he was miming touching a wall. "Well, that's… Cute."

As Daniel raised his hand to try the same thing, high-curved stone walls sprung up around them. Walls that he could see right through. Phantom carpenter-slaves joined a roof to the sides. He turned back toward the ever-present building. On top a newly built addition to its left, two Jaffa spread copper sheets over a turret-shaped frame.

"They're building Lord Yu a fortress," he whispered in awe.

"That's nice, Daniel," said Jack, "but we've been on Yu's home world, and this ain't it. No trees, no mountains, no snow."

"I don't know," Daniel admitted. "Clearly, this is — "

A warm breeze blew across the back of his head. "Did anyone else feel that?"

"You felt it, too?" Jack raised a hand to his neck.

"As did I," Teal'c said. "Though why is unclear."

Because it is so clear it takes a long time to realize it.

Daniel shivered, remembering Oma Desala's words. "Guys, I'm pretty convinced there's an ascended being here, somewhere."

Jack's eyes widened. "They're responsible for all this?"

"I don't know, Jack. None of this is making any sense."

Teal'c gestured toward the translucent building's interior. "Yu's Dragon Guard."

Four men strode down a perpendicular hallway lined with Jaffa. The guards dressed in Jaffa armor, but their cloaks were different colors. The First Prime still wore his gray one, while another wore a red, another blue, and the fourth wore green.

Daniel could see enough of their faces through the transparent walls to recognize the similarities to the four men he'd met last year. The guard with the red cloak had longer hair and the green-cloaked guard didn't have a beard, but otherwise, they were identical.

As they turned right and headed toward the end of the complex, time-lapsed images unveiled the completion of Yu's fortress. Tapestries and scrolls appeared on the walls. Furniture materialized. Lit braziers erupted to life. The Dragon Guards stopped at the hall's far end. Though it had to be at least fifty yards away, Daniel made out the high stone doors leading into the old building. They pushed on the doors, but nothing happened. They began to pound on the doors.

Daniel watched them, feeling as if Oma was in turn watching him. Why? To see what he'd do? There was something iconic about the images. Four Dragons. The Ancient building.

The four men broke into two groups, each pulling at a door. The doors started to crack open, slowly. As if they hadn't been used for centuries. Perhaps even millennia.

Lord Yu's words crashed down on Daniel. He remembered. He remembered it all. How the Goa'uld's original Dragon Guards died, and more importantly, where they'd died.

Blue light streamed out of the doors' ever-widening gap.

"My God, Jack. This is Kunlun. Pedion Elysium is Kunlun!"

"Kun who?"

"The planet Yu lived on before moving to his current planet. This is P3Y-702. The same place Yu captured me from last year!"

Daniel surged forward, pounding the invisible wall with his fists. He knew what would happen. He knew how this would end… And it would end badly. "We have to stop them!"

Jack pulled him back. "Daniel, you're the one who pointed out that none of this is real, remember?"

Daniel wrenched himself free. "Then why show this to us? Why would Oma do that?"

"You really believe this is Oma?"

"Who else could it be, Jack? Maybe she thinks we can help change the past somehow, maybe — "

With a thunderous boom, a brilliant light blasted from the doors. An eerie glow radiated outward, swathing the Dragon Guards in its blue pall.

"We're too late." Daniel forced himself to keep watching, even though he knew what would happen next.

Within moments, the four guards collapsed.

"Are they…?"

"Yes, Jack." Daniel turned away, sickened. "They're dead."

"Were dead. This happened a long time ago."

"Yeah." Daniel sighed. "I guess I finally understand first-hand what Oma meant." He glanced at Teal'c. "You tried to tell me, too."

Teal'c raised an eyebrow. "To what do you refer?"

"You mean her whole candlelight-is-fire bit?" Jack asked.

"No." Daniel rubbed his eyes. "More like, no matter what I do — whether it's Tegalus, or here, or anywhere — I can't fix others' mistakes."

"Welcome to the club." Jack squeezed his shoulder. "I'd offer you a t-shirt, but we're fresh out."

CHAPTER SIXTEEN

BEIJING, CHINA
2003 JULY 1, 6:30 AM

"I WILL be no more than an hour," Huang said as he climbed out of the escort car. Buttoning his black wool blazer, he peered through the restaurant window. Very few patrons were inside which suited him perfectly. Next door, the far more crowded American fast food establishment brimmed with Chinese citizens. This breakfast meeting was too important for grease and gummy pancakes. Authentic cuisine was needed.

It would be as much a parting meal for him as for his expected company.

He was greeted within the restaurant by a stooped old man dressed in the appropriate blue workman's shirt and pants. Selecting a rear table, Huang sat down facing the window so he might see his guest upon arrival. The server offered him a menu, but Huang waved him off.

"Your traditional breakfast," Huang ordered.

"Will your guest want cornflakes?"

He scrutinized the server. Surely, the man was old enough to know better. "When did cornflakes become a tradition in China?"

With a bob of his head, the server shuffled off into the kitchen. Huang checked his watch. In ninety minutes, his flight would leave for Colorado Springs in the United States. The benefits of being a diplomat meant he had no need to wait amongst the unruly people with whom he must share the flight.

The old man returned with a tray of covered ceramic dishes and wooden bowls. As he placed them neatly in the middle of the table, Huang reviewed his plans.

Thanks to one special capsule in Ambassador Chen's evening

tea, Huang was now lead ambassador to Beijing's UN diplomatic corp. That capsule had waited long to serve its purpose. Chen had shared a new update from the Security Council's report of the latest goings-on of Stargate Command. One of SG-1's team members had been apprehended by Lord Yu only hours ago. A Dr. Daniel Jackson — the man who had unlocked the Chappa'ai's mysteries.

Lord Yu had told him to look for a sign to commence his plan. Now, everything would progress as planned.

The US President had notified the Security Council of his intent to send in a rescue team. Huang had brought the news to Chen with his morning coffee. Chen had laughed off Lord Yu's facade, scoffing at the Goa'uld's efforts to pretend to be Chinese. That is, until Chen downed his cup and complained of chest pains. The embassy doctor had determined Chen suffered a heart attack. Who was Huang to disagree?

Upon Chen's hospitalization, Huang had called the US President, demanding SG-1 place their plans on hold until he could confer with them face-to-face. Hence his reason for flying to their base of operations. The President had drawled so heavily on the phone that Huang could barely understand half the US leader's apologies and assurances. All that mattered was that the SG-1 would wait until his arrival.

Hungry, and admittedly anxious, he reached out to uncover one of the small dishes. The right side of his blazer banged against the table. Quickly sticking a hand inside his pocket, he assured himself that the small lead box containing the two communications devices recovered from the Pacific Ocean were intact. They would serve as his bait and his means to an end. Huang would finally go home.

All he had to do was deliver SG-1 into Yu's hands.

A chime on the restaurant's doors sounded. Huang glanced up in time to see a young teenage girl close the door behind her. Her long black hair covered half of her face, but he still could see the resemblance to both her mother…

And himself.

"Weiyan!" He waved his daughter over.

As she neared, he thanked his inner courage for this meeting. Though Lord Yu would consider his offspring *bù zhǔn xǔ*—forbidden—Huang could not deny her existence in his heart.

"Father." Weiyan sat down across from him. "I am honored."

"Are you hungry?" He gestured toward the many dishes ordered. "Even a young woman like yourself must eat when opportunity arises."

"I will try, Father."

"One must simply do what needs to be done, child. Eat."

She laid a napkin in her lap. "This seems more like a vast dinner than a simple breakfast."

"A traditional Chinese breakfast can keep the body strong throughout the day." His eyes moistened with joy at her demure nature. Quing had done well in raising their child.

"Mother has never served such a meal. We usually eat cornflakes or boiled eggs."

He uncovered the dishes, naming each as they were unveiled. "First, a bowl of *congee*. It is a rice porridge."

He offered her a small plate of pickles. "Those can be added if you prefer." Next, he removed the lid to a broad ceramic bowl. "This is *yóutiáo* steamed in soya." Swimming in the milky liquid were deep fried sticks of dough. Finally, he removed a plate cover where beneath were puffy sheets of steamed bread accompanied by another small bowl of milky soy in which to dip the bread. He took up one of the bread strips and dunked it in the soya. "Like so, yes?"

Though she remained silent, her green-flecked eyes widened upon gazing at their meal.

"Is it too much?"

"No. No, Father." She took up a spoon and dipped it in the *yóutiáo*. "It's only… After so many years, I don't understand why you have contacted me."

Huang put down his half-eaten bread. "I am sorry for not contacting you earlier though my reasons were just."

"I shamed you," she whispered. "If I'd been born a male — "

"No." He grabbed her hand. "Never. The shame belongs to me, but please, do not ask for an explanation. I cannot give you my reasons. They must be held within me to protect you as well as your mother."

Weiyan withdrew her hand. "Then why now? What has changed?"

"I am leaving." Even as Huang said the words, a silent thrill ran through him, warring with this burning desire to know his child.

Weiyan put down the spoon, her food untasted. "Can I go with you?"

"It is too dangerous."

"Dangerous?" She sat back against her chair. "I do not wish you to die, Father. Not when we have just met."

"Death is not to be feared, child." He studied her face closely, trying to decide just how much of the truth he should share. "Have you not read the teachings of Sun Tzu?"

"*The Art of War*? Once." She shrugged. "All children must read his writings, but they don't really mean much. Not in today's world. Mother has me studying the sciences. She hopes I will pursue a degree in astro — "

"Once is not enough," Huang chided his daughter. "You spoke of fearing death. When you think of me, remember Sun Tzu. 'Until death itself comes, no calamity need be feared.'"

"I will remember." Weiyan again picked up her spoon and pushed the dumplings around. "Perhaps I should read Sun Tzu's work again. If it gives me solace during my treatments — "

"Treatments?" Huang's head jerked up.

His dishonor weighed heavily on his mind as Weiyan explained her blood illness. While he could not admit to her the cause, he knew that her hemophilia stemmed from the fact that as a clone, he should never have created offspring.

Though he had failed as a Dragon Guard trainee, that would soon be rectified, but Weiyan would carry his failure to obey Lord Yu's laws for the rest of her life. There was little he could do to make restitution for his trespass.

He reached into his chest pocket and pulled out a checkbook. While most of the funds from the ancient scroll had already been sent to Quing, there was still several hundred thousand Yuan left in his bank account.

"What are you doing?" she asked.

He wrote her a check for the entire balance. "Where I am going, money has no purpose." He ripped the check from the billet and handed it to her.

She did not take it. "I do not want money. I want my father."

Huang placed the check on the table with a sigh. "Your full name is Weiyan Shi. Have you ever wondered from where the second part of your name derives?"

She dropped her head. "Mother would not say."

That was because even Quing did not know the truth of that name. "Many years ago, I had a brother named Lao Dan Shi."

"What happened to my uncle?"

Huang swallowed back the bitter memory of Lao Dan's death. "That does not matter. Instead, let me share with you a saying that his..." He stopped himself from saying 'ancestor,' for Lao Dan had been a direct descendent of Lao Tzu, crafter of the great Tao. To explain the relationship would reveal too much.

Instead, Huang picked up the check and pushed it into Weiyan's hands. "A favorite quote of my brother's is worth remembering. 'He whose desires are few gets them; he whose desires are many goes astray.'

"Take the check, Weiyan. Perhaps it will help ease your struggles with this illness."

She folded the check and slipped it into her purse. "Where are you going? Home to the Taklimakan Desert where Mother met you?"

Picking up his chopsticks, Huang whispered, "Further away, if I succeed."

CHAPTER SEVENTEEN

F-302 AIR BASE
OBSERVATION HILL, ANTARCTICA
18 AUG 04/2010 HRS MCMURDO STATION

PAUL JUMPED off the transport's wide snow belts and onto the hard-packed snow. He flipped on his flashlight. The earlier gray haze had sunk again into a near pitch-black night. "Get back to McMurdo and find Colonel Ferguson," he told the driver, an army corpsman barely out of his teens.

"But Major Davis, what about — ?"

"No time to argue. Just do it."

Rebuffed, the corpsman bobbed his head and kicked the transport back into gear.

The sudden change from the overheated truck's box-like cab into the frigid cold tightened Paul's weary arms and legs. A lack of thermal layers underneath was to blame, but there'd been no time once General Hammond's orders came through. When Paul couldn't find Ken Ferguson to convey those orders, he'd commandeered the first available military vehicle and hightailed over to Observation Hill to get the 302s in the air and over to Byrd Station.

Hammond wanted the Navy SEALS ordinance team laying charges up at the outpost on the double. As much as Paul wanted to believe that there was still time to shut down the continental drift device, he understood why the president had approved the general's backup plan.

Paul cast his flashlight across the empty base. The quake had hit hard. He took in the collapsed sentry booth, the busted windows on the pilot barracks, and the two overturned jeeps beyond the sentry booth. The hangar had been squashed flat, so where were the F-302s?

A door slammed shut over at the barracks to his right.

"Major Davis!"

Two green-clad men raced toward him, each waving a standard-issue flashlight. They came to attention in front of him and snapped off quick salutes. Paul found himself envious of their USAF-issue leathered mitts as he rubbed his thinner fleece gloves together.

"Major Davis? I'm Captain White. This here is Captain Allen," said the taller of the two men, or at least, he supposed they were both men. It was hard to tell with their faces wrapped in balaclavas, the dark green face socks leaving only goggles to peer back at him.

As Paul returned the salute, a sudden gust of wind shot up from his left. "Where are the birds? Can they even fly in these kinds of wind conditions?"

"Flying in stiff wind's not the problem, sir," said Captain Allen. A woman's voice. Strong, confident. A lot like Colonel Carter.

"Then what is the problem, Captain?"

"This way, sir." Swinging her flashlight out toward the airstrip, she jogged off.

With White beside him, Paul hurried to keep up. "Any word from Colonel Ferguson yet? I sent an airman to find him and pass along our plans."

"No, sir," said White. "Standard radios haven't worked so well since the first quake, but knowing the Colonel, he'll be here soon."

"Great," Paul lied. They came to a stop at the edge of an ice field. "Where are the 302s?"

"You're looking at them." Allen raised her flashlight. A fifty-foot-wide cluster of broken ice thrust upward from what had been the airstrip. Jutting out from either end were matching wingtips. The F-302s' wingtips.

"Sea ice, sir." White added his flashlight's beam to the disaster. "When the earthquake hit, the resulting pressure shot out across McMurdo Ice Shelf and built up an ice ridge. The entire ice shelf probably looks like this now."

Paul cast his flashlight along the closer of the two birds. While the wingtips were free, most of the cockpit, the nose and tail were buried in what, under other circumstances, would be a startlingly beautiful landscape. Jagged blocks of exposed ice — some as big as a house — shined pale blue under the flashlights' glare, the color reminiscent of toothpaste gel.

Dropping his flashlight beam toward the base of the blocks, Paul asked, "Where are the wheels?"

"There." White illuminated a partially exposed strut. "And there." He swung the light left, revealing a partial wheel, the other buried within the ice.

"Can you dig them out?" Paul checked his watch. It was almost twenty-one hundred hours. A little more than fifteen hours were left 'til the sun peaked the horizon and turned the Ancient defense outpost into an offensive weapon against all of Antarctica and possibly beyond.

"Depends on how — "

The ground began to tremble. Ice cracked and popped. As the interceptors' wings vibrated, Paul held his breath, hoping it would only be a small aftershock.

He got his wish. A few seconds later, the ground settled down. The ice went on cracking for a few more moments, and then stopped.

Knowing next time they might not be so lucky, he pressed White for a timetable.

"We can use hacksaws to cut away the ice, sir, but I'm not sure we could clear enough to make a difference."

"Let's say you can. How long, Captain?"

White tugged at his balaclava. "The 302s can do up to Mach 6, but — "

"The UN Security Council won't like it, I know." Even under these circumstances, he knew there was no way they'd waive the restriction. "Sub mach speed, then. How long?"

"Under Mach 1? Byrd's about 1400 kilometers away, a little over 850 miles."

"Three to four hours, sir." Allen said, shutting off her flashlight.

Another, more distant round of rumbling started up and Paul braced himself. The sound grew closer and with it came a pair of headlights lighting up the entire expanse of the icebound runway.

It was another truck, pulling up to the frozen shoreline. As it came to a stop, Paul asked, "Any way you can shave off time without breaking UN protocols?"

"We could bring them to Marble Point," Allen offered. "That's only ten minutes away from the outpost. There are two tractor-trucks stationed there, sir."

"What the hell's going on?" demanded a new voice.

It was Ferguson. Hood flapping behind him, he stormed up to Paul. "Since when do you give the orders around here, Major?"

"Take it easy, Ken — "

"That's Colonel Ferguson, airman."

Paul stiffened, but held his ground. "Fine, Colonel. My apologies." He quickly outlined General Hammond's orders. "We just need to figure out a way to break the tires free."

"Why send a lieutenant when you can send a major?" Ken shook his head. "So now you're Hammond's messenger boy."

"Colonel." Paul dropped his voice so the pilots wouldn't hear him. "Whatever your beef with me is, sir, it'll have to wait. You know the stakes."

"Getting the 302s out is only half the problem. We need a runway." Ken waved a hand toward the ice. "As you can see, that's not gonna happen."

"We need those planes, Colonel."

"Yeah, well, you need a lot of things including getting your head examined, but that can wait, too." Ken yanked his hood up. "These birds can't just jump up in the air, Major."

"Jump… That's it!"

"Excuse me? What the hell are you thinking?"

"I am thinking, Ken. That's the point," Paul said, irritated with his one-time friend.

Ken sputtered off a string of profanities and threats, but Paul ignored him. He returned to studying the 302s, skimming his flashlight along the pressure ridge for possible gaps that would allow the pilots entry into the cockpits.

The beam from his flashlight landed on a crevasse halfway across the ridge. "Is the ice safe to walk on?" he asked Captain White.

"Uh, yes, sir. There's at least two hundred feet of ice underneath."

"Good." Paul walked out onto the ice, pointing his flashlight along the ridge, hoping to find another crevasse. He spotted one, less than a yard away from the other. Stepping closer, he aimed his flashlight into the six-foot high crack in the ice block.

Through the crack, he saw a 302's canopy. An idea was brewing in the back of his mind, but it would take a lot of faith on the part of the pilots, and Ken, to make it happen.

Paul swung his flashlight beam back toward shore. "Colonel Ferguson, at General Hammond's discretion, I must request that your pilots gain entry to these cockpits ASAP."

"I told you," Ken said. "We can't get these birds up without a runway."

"We won't need it," Paul replied. He ran back ashore.

"I don't get it. How the hell are we gonna follow through on Hammond's orders?"

"Ken, you're a topnotch air jock, but you have to trust me." Paul stopped in front of the F-302 wing commander. "We don't need a runway."

Being a colonel might have its advantages, but having the imagination needed for what had to be done next? That took the kind of eye-opening experience of someone who'd lived and breathed the Stargate Program since its inception. Paul had that kind of experience and right now, he wouldn't trade it for all the promotions in the world.

He turned toward the pilots, hoping they'd follow his lead. "You're going to jump, literally. Ground to space, and then back down right above Byrd Station."

"How do you figure, sir?" asked Allen. "We don't have a runway."

"Forget the runway," Paul said with a smile. "You'll take the 302s up through a ground-to-orbit hyperspace window."

"You're nuts," Ferguson said. "What the hell does a desk-jockey like you know about hyperspace windows?"

"Trust me, Ken. A lot more than there's time to explain."

Sam sat beside Weiyan's foxhole, watching the images rush by with mixed emotions. While her head knew the Jaffa, the ships, even the transparent buildings were only that, images, every fiber in her being wanted to bolt toward General O'Neill, Daniel and Teal'c. She wanted to help, not do babysitting duty. The men tried hammering on the invisible walls that penned them in. Whatever held them was more than just a visual display.

Force fields, she decided. But what was the power source?

"We must save them." Weiyan climbed from the hole. She stumbled to her knees.

"Take it easy." Sam pushed her down to a sitting position. The girl had calmed down, but she was still breathing pretty hard. "I don't think they're in any danger."

She crouched beside Weiyan and glanced down at her fleece pullover. It was dry. Clean. As if there'd never been any blood. With a nod from Weiyan, Sam lifted the lower half of the pullover. Nothing. Her abdomen was bare. "How do you feel?"

"Tired — Oh, no!" A reflection of blue light lit up Weiyan's face.

"What?" Sam's head whipped toward the building. A swath of blue streamed through its half-opened doors. The color was reminiscent of the Stargate's kawoosh, and for a brief moment Sam wondered if the energy source was derived from the same quantum energy that powered the gate.

The light spread further outward, enveloping the four Dragon Guards by the doors. They clutched their throats as if they couldn't breathe.

Though she wanted to believe her team wasn't in danger, she jumped up and bolted toward them. She got no more than three feet from Weiyan when her head slammed into another of the transparent walls.

Ignoring the pain, Sam called out. "Sir!"

No answer. Her teammates didn't hear her. Daniel pounded the air in front of him, frantic until Teal'c and the general grabbed hold of him and he dropped his fists.

The light intensified. From her vantage point, Sam could see the guards slapping their chests. A final burst of light shot outward, and the guards dropped to the ground.

The air rippled and the downed guards disappeared. The doors swung shut, but not before she got a glimpse of the light's source. Inside, a central core of blue light gyrated and throbbed. Below the energy form was a glowing circular platform the size of a big jeep. Backlit trellised panels shored up the sides underneath.

The doors slammed shut.

"That has to be the power source."

"Power to what?" Weiyan asked.

"Whatever brought us here. Whatever's generating all this." Sam raised her hands to indicate the valley. "It's possible that some elaborate device — "

"Created by the Ancients you mentioned?"

"Or someone else." She tried to smile for Weiyan's sake. It wasn't easy with her team still trapped out of reach. "For someone who nearly bled to death, you ask a lot of questions."

Weiyan wrapped her arms around her torso. "My mother refers to my questions as a bad habit."

Sam was taken aback. "Hey, if it wasn't for curiosity, humans would still be stuck in caves."

Weiyan dropped her chin to chest.

Sam turned her attention back to the team. General O'Neill was talking to Daniel, patting him on the back while Teal'c seemed to be scanning the opposing hill. He pointed toward the top where a new set of images unfolded in a staggered fashion, like those old animated flipbooks. Four graves were dug by Jaffa. More Jaffa appeared, lowering four bodies shrouded in black cloth into the ground. Sam had to assume the bodies were those of the Dragon Guards.

She blinked and another scenario replaced it. This one was of a group of Jaffa constructing a statue out of red clay, several stories in height. They'd built up the back half, which seemed to resemble a dog sitting on its hind legs. Another image flashed. Everything but the statue's head had been formed. Three nasty blades stuck out of its red clay spine.

"This is getting familiar," she said as much to herself as to Weiyan. "We found one of those statues on P3Y-702. On a hill, just like that one. But that's not possible."

Who was she kidding? None of this was possible. They were being manipulated. The question was, by whom and why?

The view changed again, the statue completed. Its teeth, bulging jaw, and eye ridges stared down into the valley in ferocious protection of the graves at its base. A solitary figure stood beside the statue, dressed in the green hat and recognizable red over-vest of Lord Yu.

The air rippled and the System Lord disappeared, but the statue remained.

"A *Zhenmushou*?" asked Weiyan. "It is an ancient Chinese tradition, a funerary beast meant to protect the dead."

Another image shimmered into life, right in front of the building. It was Lord Yu, again. As he stepped away from the building, a ring transporter activated and swept him away.

"Let's just hope the dead don't include the general, Daniel

and Teal'c." She cautiously raised a palm out in front of her and re-approached the force field. It felt solid enough. Smooth.

She slid her hand horizontally. "It's not hot or cold. It's just — "

"There?" Weiyan asked. "To see the sun and moon is no sign of sharp sight."

"That's beautiful." Sam dropped her hand down from the force field. "Maybe even more beautiful than this situation deserves."

"The words of Sun Tzu are often that way, even though they are words of war." Weiyan sighed. "I am grateful my father encouraged my reading of his work. Imagine how stunned he would be now to see such a large *Zhenmushou*!"

Sam looked over her shoulder at Weiyan. Her eyes shined with amazement, transfixed by the clay statue on the hill.

"Carter!" shouted General O'Neill.

"Finally!" Sam looked back toward her team, relieved the walls had vanished. The three raced toward her. In fact, everything had vanished with the exception of the statue and its freshly dug graves.

"It's Kunlun, Sam!" Daniel dropped down beside Weiyan. "Lord Yu's former home-world, P3Y-702." He grabbed a handful of the dirt and hefted it in his hand. "The events we saw? Just like Yu described when — "

"When he captured your sorry ass and almost got the rest of us killed," the general said, frowning.

Teal'c crouched beside Daniel. That's when Sam noticed the gray tinge to his skin.

"Teal'c, you all right?"

"I am well, Colonel Carter, a moment's rest will suffice." Teal'c sat down heavily. Sam knew he was overdue for a tretonin injection, but without a means of escape from their current dilemma, there wasn't anything that could be done. He probably didn't wish to alarm them.

"A bit of a break will do us all good." General O'Neill plunked down on Teal'c's other side. "Any guesses on why we're getting the *History Channel* edition of Lord Yu's life on this hellhole of a planet?"

Sam pointed toward the building. "I think the answer's inside there, sir."

"All right, Carter. You're with me. Let's go check that building out. You three stay here."

Immediately, vibrations started up beneath her feet. "Sir?"

The vibrations turned to a loud rumble. Dirt and stones scattered across the ground.

"Let's do it, Colonel." He started to march off toward the building.

Within seconds, the ground ripped open between the general and his target. A chasm formed at least twenty-feet long and endlessly deep.

"This is getting old." He took a step back and the ground sealed shut. He threw up his hands.

"I don't remember a building like that when we were actually on P3Y-702." Sam reported what little she'd seen of the device inside.

"I do," Daniel said. "Those doors were hidden behind some of the other ruins. I tried prying them open just before the ring transporter grabbed me. There were Chinese pictograms on some of the walls describing Kunlun and how it was built by — "

"Emperor Yu Huang Shang-Ti," Weiyan offered. "There are many legends surrounding Kunlun. I have even heard it said that the emperor's paradise was really a planet. An evil planet that destroyed the Emperor's first Dragon Guards."

Sam winced at the awe in Weiyan's voice. Looking back over the valley, she wondered yet again how much of Earth's ancient history was myth and how much was fact. Since the Stargate Program's inception, the line dividing the two had thinned dramatically.

"Weiyan," said Daniel behind her, "Chinese mythology places Kunlun on a mountain, not another planet."

The air rippled. Sam tilted her head, curious to see what images would be displayed next.

Lord Yu's ships shimmered into existence again, positioned only a few feet away. Behind them, the fortress walls also reappeared. This time, however, the images weren't static. The Jaffa led slaves up into the Al'kesh while members of the original four battalions marched back up the mothership's gantry, carrying large crates.

"Sir, those Jaffa. I'll bet they're carrying the Ancient photon emitter Yu has installed on his present home world."

"Oh, goody." General O'Neill groaned. "Another walk down memory lane."

"Don't you see, Jack?" Daniel waved a hand at the closing gantries. "We're watching events play out the way they did a thousand years ago, exactly as Yu told us."

"Then how come she knows so much?" the general asked, jerking his head toward Weiyan.

"My father told me," Weiyan's voice trembled. "He said Kunlun was not a myth, but I didn't believe him. He told me everything… all of it…" She flung a hand out toward the building. "All of it has happened just as he said!"

"And just who-in-the-hell is your father?"

Her eyes lifted toward Sam, wide in desperation. "I thought his tales were make-believe. I thought he told me fairytales so he could pretend I was the little girl he had never known." Weiyan buried her head in her hands.

The mothership's hull slid downwards, covering its multitiered base underneath. Sam recognized the signs of pre-liftoff.

"Carter, we need answers." General O'Neill jerked a thumb toward Weiyan. "Now, please."

Sam dropped down besides the girl. "Weiyan, is your father a member of the IOA?"

"No. Please do not ask me more. I swore I would not say."

"Do you want to get out of here or not?" General O'Neill said with remarkable restraint.

"I do!" Weiyan mumbled. "I just… I never thought…" Tears welled in her eyes, but Sam held back any demonstration of pity. The girl knew something. Something that could help them figure a way out of here.

"Weiyan Shi." Teal'c placed a hand on her shoulder. "You must share how you obtained this information."

Sam lifted the girl's chin, forcing Weiyan to not look away. "If your father's not IOA, is he military? Or an ambassador, maybe?"

"Was." Weiyan's eyes slid toward General O'Neill. "His name is Huang. Ambassador Huang."

With a cracking boom, Yu's ships blasted off.

Teal'c was so shaken by Weiyan Shi's revelation that the departure of Lord Yu's ships meant nothing. His teammates were equally stunned. O'Neill's clenched jaw only served to accentuate his attempt to suppress his undoubted anger.

"I have done nothing wrong!"

The girl dashed tears from her eyes.

Her eyes. Teal'c leaned in for a closer view.

Weiyan Shi's mouth quivered as he did so. "Forgive me, Teal'c. I did not know — "

"There is nothing to forgive," Teal'c assured her. "You are not guilty of your father's crimes."

The young woman did indeed have the intense black eyes marked with odd specks of green exhibited by both Yu's First Prime Oshu and the spy Ambassador Huang. A spy who had nearly cost SG-1 their lives when he'd impeded their efforts to save Daniel Jackson a year ago.

Her features, however, were different. Her nose smaller. Her face more oval.

"Weiyan," said Daniel Jackson. "If everything you've told us is true — "

"Oh, for crying out loud, Daniel!" O'Neill grabbed Weiyan Shi's shoulders and yanked her to her feet. "He put you up to this, didn't he? Is Huang here somewhere, getting his rocks off, watching us run around like rats in a — "

The ground trembled. Teal'c recognized the sign. O'Neill must control his temper.

Teal'c struggled to his feet, the task made all the more difficult by a weariness he could not ignore. None of the others seemed fatigued. Colonel Carter and Daniel Jackson had jumped to their feet with great alacrity.

"Where's your father, Weiyan?" O'Neill shook her, his face dark with rage.

"Jack!" Daniel pushed O'Neill back from the girl. "Calm down!"

"Shut up, Daniel. She knows something."

A great tremor erupted across the valley floor, throwing Teal'c to the ground once more.

Colonel Carter ran to his side. "You okay?"

"O'Neill must stop." Teal'c pushed himself up to his knees. "His emotions — "

A final shudder, Yu's fortress collapsed to rubble, and the quake faded to a distant rumble. All that remained was the hill bearing the great statute, the building in question, and the Stargate perched upon the cliff.

Teal'c looked to O'Neill. His eyes were closed. His chest heaved heavily, his nostrils flared. Teal'c dared hoped his brother could contain himself.

Weiyan Shi had already succeeded in doing so. She had wrapped her arms about herself, inhaling long, slow breaths.

"That's right," Daniel Jackson said. "Keep calm, both of you. Jack, your abrasive general card won't work here and you know it."

Weiyan Shi sank down beside Teal'c. She squeezed his hand. "Are you all right?"

"I am well," Teal'c lied. No purpose would be served by admitting a minor weakness. Not to her, not to any of his team. Whatever troubled him would surely pass. "It is you, or more specifically, your origins which are now the concern."

Weiyan Shi wrung her hands. "I have told you everything I know. I spoke with my father only once. A year ago. It was then he told me he must go away. Forever."

"Oh, he went away all right." O'Neill opened his eyes. "To a nice padded cell in China. He was spying for that god-damned slimy, snakeheaded — "

"Sir," warned Colonel Carter as another tremor threatened.

O'Neill sucked in a long breath. He expelled it noisily. "Fine, Carter. You tell her. Tell her how — " He turned away, shoving his hands in his pockets.

The tremor faded.

"Sir, there's a bigger question here," said Colonel Carter. "We know her father's a clone from Janet Fraiser's report."

"A clone?" Weiyan Shi laid her palm against her abdomen. "That is why he could not tell me the truth. That is why..." Her voice became inaudible.

"Weiyan," said Colonel Carter, "your father's genetic markers date back 4,000 years. Were you and your mother both tested by the IOA?"

"My mother," Weiyan Shi gulped, as if mention of the one who had born her was painful. "She doesn't have the necessary genetics to power the great chair."

"Then Ambassador Huang must carry the Ancient gene," Teal'c said. Weiyan Shi's small hand tightened within his own. Though her grasp should have felt as nothing, Teal'c hands ached. He released her grip and flexed his fingers. His elbows and shoulders ached as well.

"Is my father an alien like you?" asked Weiyan Shi.

Daniel Jackson knelt down beside her once more. "Your father's completely human."

"Cloned from a human," Colonel Carter emphasized. "A human who not only lived 4,000 years ago, but must have been a direct descendent of the Ancients, just like — "

"Like Jack." Daniel Jackson removed his glasses and gazed kindly into Weiyan Shi's eyes. "Look, I know this sounds crazy, but if Yu was telling the truth, your ancestor was Sun Tzu."

"When you think about it," Colonel Carter said, "it's amazing your mother even conceived. Four-thousand years of cloning would degrade the original DNA sample, no matter how much the Goa'uld used advanced Ancient technology."

Weiyan Shi's eyes widened. "If Lord Yu is a Goa'uld and he made my father, he cannot be bad."

Teal'c interjected, believing the record must be set straight. "Lord Yu is a parasitical creature, falsely claiming to have been your original emperor."

Daniel Jackson slid his glasses back on. "I'm not so sure his claims were false."

Clink. Snap.

O'Neill had retrieved his lighter from his pocket and was now flipping it open and shut mindlessly, his attention on the building.

"Perhaps we will find our answers in the one constant throughout these apparitions," Teal'c observed.

O'Neill twisted toward him, a half-smile upon his lips. "Now you're talking. I could give a rat's ass about clones and gene pools. If Yu's in there — "

Kawoosh.

The recognizable sound of the Stargate heralded its activation. Teal'c turned toward the cliff as the violent plunge of water settled into a stable event horizon.

"Carter? Any chance the gate's not a figment?"

Four figures emerged. Although they were too far away to ascertain their identities, Teal'c immediately recognized their khaki BDU pants, jackets and black tactical vests.

O'Neill stuck a forefinger and thumb in his mouth and whistled. "Over here!"

"Sir..."

"It's an SG team, Carter."

"I don't think so, Jack." Daniel Jackson slung a hand under Teal'c's arm and assisted him to rise.

As Weiyan joined them, they watched the four-man team descend along the side of the cliff and stride toward them. One of them had orange-red hair.

"What the hell's Balinsky doing here?" O'Neill growled. "I sent orders to Walter to kick his ass off of SG-13." He stormed toward the team. "Took you enough time, Dixon!"

Colonel Dixon walked directly through O'Neill.

"Great, more ghosts!"

SG-13 strode toward the crumbled walls of what had once been Yu's fortress. The team neared the ruins and their images dissolved.

The air rippled yet again, stirring up a great wave of dust that drifted toward them. The dust dissipated, revealing a more recognizable scene. SGC archaeologists dug trenches, others strung lines around several foot-deep holes. A tall, dark-skinned man with long plaits and a shovel jumped down into one such hole, shouting to an assistant who scurried in his direction.

"That's Kevin Hopkins." Daniel Jackson ran to the lead archaeologist. A college roommate, Teal'c recalled. Daniel Jackson waved a hand through the man's head, but Dr. Hopkins never flinched.

"And you wonder why instant replay was never approved in baseball." O'Neill pointed at the Stargate as another SG team — dressed in khaki uniforms and tactical vests — climbed down from the cliff. One carried a staff weapon.

Teal'c recognized the team member immediately. He was the man carrying the staff weapon. "This is indeed a faithful rendition of events."

"Yeah, super faithful," O'Neill's voice cracked.

The imagery sped up in a blur. The phantom version of SG-1 stopped by Kevin Hopkins, conferred, and then moved onward. Then Colonel O'Neill hefted a backpack toward the hill bearing the funerary statute. Daniel Jackson followed at a distance, his boonie-covered head turned toward the dig. Teal'c's doppelganger joined the then Major Carter and walked the camp's perimeter.

A moment passed and the images subtly changed. Teal'c's ghost-double conferred with Major Carter at the base of the far hill. A single rifle shot rang out. He glanced upwards toward the hill as a shower of red clay sprayed forth from the *Zhenmoushu's* claws.

Daniel Jackson's ghost descended from the hill, his face flushed with indignation. He stormed toward the ruined walls. Placing a hand against the building's doors, he tilted his head upwards and stepped back as if to obtain a better view. A great wash of light surrounded Daniel Jackson and he disappeared as a ring transporter took hold.

All that remained was his boonie cast upon the ground.

Teal'c turned his gaze upon the real O'Neill. His Tau'ri brother gripped the lighter, his eyes haunted with inner pain.

The need to assure O'Neill that these were merely specters of the past drove Teal'c to approach him. "We cannot change — "

Dizziness clouded Teal'c's vision. His body became numb.

"Teal'c!"

Fatigue overcame him and he collapsed to the ground.

"Come on, T." Jack shook Teal'c's arm. "Wake up!"

Nothing. Teal'c's face had taken on a definite gray tinge, almost like he was —

Nope, Jack wasn't even going to think it. He pressed two fingers against Teal'c's neck. There was pulse, barely. Jack glanced over his shoulder at that hellhole of a building, ready to take it apart brick-by-brick for answers.

Daniel dropped down on Teal'c's other side. "Does he need his tretonin?"

"If he does, he's outta luck." Jack slapped Teal'c face lightly. "Come on, buddy boy. Rise and shine."

"Wake up, Teal'c," Weiyan sobbed behind Jack. "I am trying, cannot you?"

What the hell did that mean?

Teal'c's eyes fluttered opened. "O'Neill, what has happened?"

Jack let himself breathe for the first time since Teal'c had passed out. "Okay, don't do that."

Teal'c harrumphed. "I did not do anything."

"Sorry, Teal'c." Carter knelt down beside Jack. "You did kinda pass out there. How are you feeling?"

"I am well." With a barely hidden grimace, Teal'c pushed himself up onto his elbows.

Putting a hand on Teal'c's chest, Jack stopped him. "Nice try, but stay put for the moment."

Teal'c sunk back, giving in way too easily.

Weiyan brushed by, wrapping her arms around the big guy's neck. "You will live?"

"He'll be his normal self in no time. That is," Jack gently pulled her away, "if you give him breathing room."

Carter shot him a look. A look that meant trouble.

He let go of Weiyan's arm. "What?"

Carter jerked her chin toward a spot a few feet off from Teal'c's position. Getting her message, Jack climbed to his feet and followed her out of earshot.

As Carter turned toward him, Jack noticed the bruises under her eyes. The kind she got when she'd been up for days straight. They'd been plopped down in this crap for a few hours, but days? Not even his internal clock was that messed up.

Or was it? His memory had played some nasty tricks on him when they'd first arrived.

He sighed. "A few real answers would be nice about now, Carter."

"Sir, if Teal'c continues to deteriorate…"

"You think he needs tretonin?"

"Maybe."

"Or maybe whatever hit those Dragon Guards got to Teal'c, too."

"Honestly? I think he was weakening even before those doors opened up." She slumped, a very un-Carter-like thing to do. "Once Yu's ships… I mean, those images —"

"I get it." Jack rubbed his face. "I'm pretty beat myself, but how come we're not hungry or thirsty?"

"Or why Weiyan's stomach bled out like that, and now — "

"She seems fine." Jack glanced toward Teal'c. Weiyan cradled his beefy hands while Daniel chattered on about god-knows-what. "Any chance her being here is just one big coincidence?"

Carter shook her head. "I doubt it, sir. What we just witnessed pretty much matches Daniel's account from when Lord Yu held him hostage last year."

She shifted her gaze toward the building, the one constant throughout this nightmare. "I barely remember that building from our visit a year ago. What is it about this place? Why the show and for who's benefit? Lord Yu captured Daniel as a sort of test, but — "

"Yeah, wasn't that a fun time?" He glanced down at a smooth, brown pebble he'd unearthed. If buildings and motherships could come and go, why were simple things like pebbles still around?

"The bigger question we should be asking is who's pulling the strings?" He knelt down to pick up the pebble. "You ever get the feeling that every time we've tied off a knot, the thread just unravels somewhere else?"

Carter sighed. "Pretty much."

He stood up. Out of the blue, a buzzing noise filled his ears. Carter said something, but he couldn't hear her.

He must have stood up too fast. He took a deep breath and his ears popped, like a rubber band smacking against a wall. The buzzing was gone. "What the hell?"

"Sir, are you all right?"

"Sam! Jack!" Daniel called. "Behind you!"

Jack whirled around.

And got a good, hard look at himself. Or rather, a khaki-clad phantom version. P90 in hand, favorite ball cap firmly in place, he — or rather, the phantom — stopped about twenty some-odd feet away and faced the building. Though his double shouted out soundlessly, Jack knew exactly what he'd said that day.

Daniel!

The phantom whirled toward the funky Unas-looking statue on the far-off hill. He raised a hand to his mouth and shouted. Soundless.

Daniel!

"Sir," Carter whispered, "none of this is real."

"No kidding." Though he believed her, the pebble in his hand said different.

Jack threw the pebble at his doppelganger. It sailed right through. He followed the pebble's trajectory as it skittered to the ground a few feet away and kicked up a puff of dust and sand.

"General!" Carter called out.

Still charging forward, his khaki-clad other stormed right through him without as much as a ripple. It was as if his current self had no impact on the bigger things at stake.

Yet another reminder of just how useless he felt. Here. At the SGC. Even at the Ancient outpost.

The buzzing returned with a vengeance. "Do you hear that?"

Carter raised an eyebrow. "Hear what?"

Another snap. The buzzing quit again. "It sounded like… I dunno, Carter, like bees, or a machine, or some — "

A shadow passed overhead. He glanced up, saw the source, and while he should've been surprised, he wasn't.

That was the problem with reruns. No surprises.

An Al'kesh dropped out of the sky, honing in on his departing double's six. Both the ship and his other self headed toward the cliff, an activated Stargate precariously perched on its edge. The saucer-shaped Goa'uld ship laid down round after rapid round of weapons fire as his other self scrambled up the cliff.

As he watched himself climb, Jack remembered how the chase had pumped his heart. The world had narrowed down to survival. Reach the gate. Stay alive.

Of course, last time this happened, he didn't have quite the same view. "Talk about an out-of-body experience."

Behind him, another set of footsteps pounded the dirt, headed his way.

"Jesus, Jack!" Daniel stopped beside him, eyes bulging. "What the hell were you thinking?"

"I wasn't." Another round of fire shattered the pathway leading from the cliff's topside to the active gate. His younger self rolled sideways as more enemy fire peppered the ground. Finally, in an act of bravado — or stupidity, Jack still couldn't say which it had been that day — he dived into the active gate and disappeared.

The Al'kesh did, too.

"Fun stuff, huh?" He missed that kind of action. No boring papers to sign. No casualty reports to read. No pandering to politicians.

Jack pulled out his old Zippo. Huang's kid, the crazy quakes, the lighter. It all added up to something. His thumb rubbed over the case, a pesky thought niggling at him.

Screw it. There was only one way to find out.

He eyed Weiyan. "She's got something to do with all this. Stay here."

"Jack, what are you doing?"

"A different approach." He marched toward the girl stuck by Teal'c's side like there was no tomorrow.

"You miss it, don't you?" Daniel called out. "The missions, the fight. You can't do it all, Jack."

"T-shirts, Daniel!"

"Excuse me?"

Jack didn't break his stride. "Make mine a double XL."

Daniel wasn't the only member of the 'if-only' club.

ANCIENT OUTPOST, ANTARCTICA
18 AUG 04/2100 HRS MCMURDO STATION

By the time Ambassador Zhu finished explaining the details of her short-term marriage to Lord Yu's spy, George wasn't sure whether to pity her or be outraged.

He'd yet to make up his mind when the bandage on her left cheek fell off, exposing a three-inch cut. Blood oozed from its edges. "Are you all right, Madame Ambassador?"

Zhu palmed her wound. "Compared to my daughter? This is nothing."

"General Hammond?" The click-clack of Lee's keyboard kept up for a few moments, and then, "If these numbers are right, the device sent out a significant blast of photonic energy during that last quake."

"In which direction, Doctor?" George braced himself, knowing he wouldn't like the answer.

"There were multiple epicenters this time." Lee squinted at the monitor. "From fifty miles away to a few hits several thousand miles off. Up near the Magallanes-Fagnano fault line." He looked up, frowning. "That fault line stretches almost 500 miles from the Pacific Ocean into Argentina."

"Doctor, I suggest you return your focus to shutting down the device." Noting Simmons' absence, George listened to the scurried footsteps and command barks emanating through the archway. What personnel were left proceeded with evacuations. The emergency exit door thudded shut.

The door!

Bolting up from Zhu's side, he joined Lee by the computers. "Could the Ancients have built an entryway of some type that might access the lower level?"

"If they did, we never found it." Lee switched the display to a schematic of the outpost's various chambers. A quick count told him there was six, but all on one floor.

George eyed the force field. "There has to be an entrance leading from this floor down to the next. We just didn't look hard enough. Airman?"

Lt. Gerling stuck her head in from just outside the archway. "Sir?"

"Take Lt. Brooks with you. I don't want one inch of this outpost left untouched. If there's another way down into that device, find it."

"Yes, sir." Gerling headed toward the main chamber.

George refocused on Ambassador Zhu and the 'Huang problem.' Her former marriage to an enemy spy put an entirely new spin on their situation.

He should be more surprised. For some reason, he wasn't. Standing two-hundred feet inside a glacier that could come down on his ears at any moment brought home the key lesson he'd learned in his eight years with the Stargate Program — crows always come home to roost.

In this particular situation, Huang was the crow and the Ancient weapons platform was the roost. A vital, but now dangerous, roost.

"You've put me in a difficult position," he told Zhu. "By your own admission, vital information that would've affected the IOA's selection of your daughter, and your post as ambassador — "

Zhu laughed, the sound bitter and empty. "If the Chinese government can see past a family member's crimes — "

"Ambassador, I don't blame you for Huang's actions, but the fact that Weiyan's overpowering ATA genetics are behind our predicament..."

"What do Huang's actions have to do with Weiyan's abilities?"

"There are security issues," he said half-heartedly. When the president had deemed the circumstances surrounding Huang's origins should be kept under wraps, current circumstances hadn't even been part of the picture.

"Security issues?" Zhu's eyes widened. "If she was your daughter, wouldn't you want to know?"

"It's getting colder in here." He tugged his parka's zipper up higher.

"General, I deserve the truth."

"It's not that simple, Madame Ambassador."

She gazed down at her daughter and sighed. "It never is."

Quit stalling, George.

He told her everything he knew.

CHAPTER EIGHTEEN

SHUNYI PSYCHIATRIC HOSPITAL
BEIJING, CHINA
2004 JULY 31, 9:00 PM

HUANG knelt within the four-walled garden and gazed upward. The city's polluted haze blanketed the night sky, but surely, tomorrow's sun would break its boundaries and reach this one spot. This one place he could succeed.

Satisfied, his hands plunged into the dense, black soil.

"You failed," a whisper murmured behind him. "At everything."

A woman's voice. A voice that belonged to another life.

He scooped back mound after mound of the dirt. Earthworms and bits of mica sparkled beneath the pale light of the night's full moon. Beside his burgeoning hole lay four bundled saplings. His reward for cooperation, for allowing himself to be placed in solitary confinement. For no longer saying those two words which revealed his burden. Two words which spoke of his ruin.

They cannot.

He would plant each sapling to honor Lord Yu's Dragons.

"Weiyan told me of your meeting," the woman said. "How you taunted her with a last goodbye before your American adventure." It was good soil. Rich soil. His trees would grow well here. Though the doctors refused him tools to do his planting, he would still succeed. They could not take away his mind.

Even though Jack O'Neill had taken his soul.

One moon. Not two.

Such a fool am I.

"Huang, please... Turn around. Talk to me."

The voice again. A time of trespass. One he must not remember. It was *bù zhǔn xǔ*. Forbidden. No Dragon Guard must take a wife or mate. Such had been Lord Yu's command.

One moon. Not two.

He picked up the nearest sapling. "For Kung Qiu," he whispered.

He removed its burlap cover. The small gather of roots and twigs smelled of cherry blossoms. Of promise. Placing the base gently in the hole he'd created, he began to swipe the soil in around its roots. Each stroke of dirt eased his heart, allowing his mind to wander. Though he begged his thoughts to travel further back in time, to a happier moment, all he saw was his ultimate failure to Lord Yu.

"At least do me the courtesy of explaining why you did this," the voice demanded.

He crawled to the next planting spot and thrust his hands into the dirt once more. He scooped back more soil. As he did so, the memories returned unasked, but demanding.

He remembered it all.

Lord Yu's capture of Dr. Jackson on Kunlun had given Huang the perfect opening to infiltrate Stargate Command. All it had taken was one call to the Americans' inept president with the threat of disclosing their secret program to the world. By forcing SG-1's team members who had the necessary naquadah to use the communications devices, he'd been given the opportunity to view his former home world once more.

He had sat within Stargate Command's conference room, so intent on contacting his master that he'd paid no intention to the trap closing in around him. The droning unimportance of words spilling from the porcine General Hammond had been inconsequential. Mindless banter that required little attention.

Huang had bided his time as SG-1 blundered through the outer defenses of Lord Yu's fortress, knowing that once Lord Yu captured them, he had only to announce his presence and his master would retrieve him.

"Former husband, I am being punished for your crimes!"

Huang turned his back on the voice and uncovered his second bundle. "For Qin Shi," he told the sapling.

A thrill ran through him upon remembering when the communications device had sent back images of his home world. Craggy mountain peaks enveloped in snow. Mist rising from the shores of *Zhēn Xiàng*. His amusement at SG-1's absurd struggles to traverse Lord Yu's maze, all the while hoping they'd fail, but needing them to succeed if his plan was to work.

He had ignored the signs of SG-1's ulterior motives. Perhaps it had been the delight at Colonel O'Neill's feigned demotion? The pleasure at witnessing his defeated stride past the communications device had been unquestionable. That accomplishment had made Huang disregard Jacob Carter's comments on the two moons of Lord Yu's home world.

There was only one moon on Lord Yu's home world.

Not two.

Huang shuffled further into the garden and dug a third hole. Only now could he admit to himself how arrogant had been his disregard for the Tok'ra's duplicitous words. He had been too caught up in O'Neill's downfall and the reunion yet to come with Lord Yu. He should have recognized the Tok'ra's lies for what they had been. A signal. A warning.

He picked up the third sapling. "For Lao Dan," he croaked, his voice thick with regret.

He should not have forgotten the words of his dead brother's ancestor. It shamed him now to remember.

The skillful man must be on his guard against being vain or boastful or arrogant in consequence of it.

Huang thrust the third sapling into the ground.

"I am being sent to Antarctica to oversee negotiations." The woman's voice once more. Another sin for which he could never atone.

The woman's voice dropped to a whisper. "I must conspire some way to bring Weiyan with me — "

"They cannot." Huang cringed as he spoke the banned words.

Heinous images of his failure to Lord Yu tumbled through his memory. *The fortress littered with the bodies of Lord Yu's Jaffa. A young warrior racing by the communications device, preparing to attack the pathetic Tau'ri. Electric blue arcs of zat'ni'katel fire decimating the brick-lined terrace.*

Through it all, he had sat in the SGC's conference room, a sense of panic seizing him. The device had rolled through the ensuing battle between Jaffa and Tau'ri, permitting Huang a moment's view of a young man bearing the First Prime's golden tattoo. *Green-flecked black eyes, square jaw. A high forehead that spoke of an aristocratic air born of intelligence, not blind faith.*

Another clone of Sun Tzu.

For Huang, it had been like looking in a mirror.

The device had rolled on. *Jaffa far too inept at battle erupted from the patio column's secret passageways. They became easy targets for SG-1. Stunned, he watched each warrior fall.*

The Jaffa had been pale imitations of those he'd known in his time as a Dragon Guard trainee. He had known then and there that Lord Yu needed him to return and set things aright. To take his place as Dragon Guard and become the true First Prime.

He picked up the fourth sapling, remembering how his dedication to returning to Lord Yu had been born anew upon seeing the Jaffa battle the Tau'ri.

A breeze blew against his neck. Another memory. One of desolation. Of his time in the frozen wasteland of Earth's southern pole. The being of light that helped him survive. He struggled to suppress the memory. Crushing the dirt between his fingers, a silent wail lodged in his throat, begging for escape.

"Huang, please..." A hand circled his wrist. Pulled his hand back from the soil.

The fourth sapling tumbled to the ground.

The words he must not utter tumbled from his mouth. "They cannot," he told the Tau'ri woman.

"Cannot what?" Quing Zhu whispered. "Tell me."

Memory of his failure pressed down on him. *The sound of rifle fire emitting from the communications device as it rolled by. A jumble of images. Bits of broken brick terrace. Collapsed Jaffa. A moment's glance of Major Carter and Bra'tac, the rebel Jaffa Master, racing toward O'Neill and the* Shol'vah *Teal'c.*

The device had continued rolling, heading toward a marble column near the center of the terrace.

"What have you done?" Huang shouted over the din of bullet and zat fire.

"What I should have done days ago," General Hammond had said, his pig-faced dense stupidity replaced with certitude.

The display stopped rolling, wedged up against the column. The view revealed the sacred statue commemorating the wife of Lord Yu's host. A memorial of the shared sacrifice of symbiote and man to save China from Anubis a thousand years ago. The green marble statue depicted the wife cradling a baby in her arms, a child at her feet. A glorious reminder of what mattered most.

Twin sets of Tau'ri standard-issue boots ran out of frame. O'Neill and the Jaffa rebel. Out of nowhere, P90 fire erupted from beside the statue. Lord Yu's Jaffa responded with a rapid succession of zat fire.

The statue disintegrated.

"No!" Huang cried out. "They cannot!"

Rough hands pulled him from his plantings. As the hospital guard dragged him from the garden, he permitted himself a final glance of Quing Zhu. The woman who had once been his wife. The mother of his child.

Cold realization hit him as they locked him in his cell. Had Quing said they would go to Antarctica?

"They cannot." He sank down on the thin pallet that was his bed. This was his punishment. To stay here and rot.

He deserved nothing more.

CHAPTER NINETEEN

ANCIENT OUTPOST, ANTARCTICA
18 AUG 04/2140 HRS MCMURDO STATION

"GENERAL Hammond?" Lt. Brooks poked his head through the archway.

George waved him in. "Report?"

"Major Davis radioed, sir." The airman pushed back his hood and wiped stray snow off his watch cap. "He's just rendezvoused with the SEALS over at Marble Point."

"Notify me the moment their chopper lands topside."

"Yes, sir." The airman hurried off.

George ran a hand over his eyes, fighting off fatigue that wouldn't end soon. In the past half hour, he'd provided Ambassador Zhu with as much detail as he dare regarding the Huang and Lord Yu. But he hadn't told her everything. Not yet.

Zhu's focus stayed fixed on her daughter's comatose form. "Please," she said as the airman left, "finish your story, General Hammond."

Now came the kicker.

"We have evidence to suggest Huang was cloned from one of Yu's original Dragon Guards," George said. "A direct descendent of Sun Tzu, I believe."

Zhu whirled toward him, her eyes widened in obvious disbelief.

"Lord Yu obtained the cloning technology from the ruins of an Ancient city," George explained. "The SGC's chief medical officer at the time was able to confirm that Huang's DNA contained unusual traits. Traits not seen for over 4,000 years."

Zhu chewed at her thumb as George detailed Lord Yu's odd revelations to Daniel Jackson. He found the nervous habit telling. While she'd exhibited genuine surprise at his revelation, there was something else going on in that mind of hers, something that may or may not have a direct relation to their current predicament.

"And the U.S. decided to keep this information from China because...?" She dropped her hand to her side. "Don't bother. The lack of trust between our two nations takes on many shapes, this being only one example."

"It goes both ways, Ambassador. We'd no idea that Huang had fathered a child."

Zhu shook her head. "A descendent of Sun Tzu. A viable, healthy clone. If this is the reason why Weiyan was always such a sickly child— "

"General Hammond!" Ambassador Duebel raced in. Not for the first time today, George wished Lt. Simmons could be in two places at once—helping evacuation efforts, and here, running interference with fifth wheel ambassadors who should have been long gone.

The Swiss ambassador came to a halt beside Zhu. "Any change?"

She snorted. "In a manner of speaking."

Duebel glanced at George. "I don't understand. The force field's still in place."

"Why haven't you evacuated yet, Ambassador? Where's Juarez?"

"He left. My God, it's cold in here." Duebel yanked his parka zipper up. "We were boarding the helicopter when a radio report came in... Ushuaia, Argentina suffered a powerful quake twenty minutes ago."

"Casualties?" George said a silent prayer.

"Several hundred wounded. No fatalities yet," Duebel replied. "General, this will only get worse."

"The Navy SEAL munitions team should be here shortly." He glanced at his watch. "Sunrise is in fifteen hours. In the meantime, I've given Dr. Lee the next twelve hours to find a way through that force field so we can retrieve our people. Once those twelve hours are up, the outpost will be destroyed as promised."

"Uh, General?" Lee hurried over. "If we know Weiyan's father could shut the device down, shouldn't we consider bringing him here? Four-thousand year-old genetics should be strong enough to — "

"A 4,000 year-old what?" Duebel asked loudly.

"Ambassador, keep your voice down, please." George shot Lee a silent warning. There was need to know and then there was need to *not* know. By now, the scientist should comprehend the difference.

"Sorry," Lee said more softly, "but Huang's ATA genetics could possibly shut down the drift device, and the force field. Then we won't have to blow up the outpost."

"Quing?" Duebel knelt down beside Zhu. "What does your ex-husband have to do with all this?"

"You'll have to ask the general," said Zhu, shifting her position with her legs tucked underneath.

George appreciated her discretion, but facts were facts. He urged Lee to get back to his work and then returned his attention to the ambassadors. "I'm sorry, but I can't allow an enemy spy access to this facility. We have no idea if he — "

"Now wait just a moment." Duebel shot up and glared right at him. "If Ambassador Huang — "

"Former Ambassador," George retorted. "As a member of the Security Council, you've read the official report. Huang's actions almost killed SG-1."

"And look at them now." Duebel flung a hand toward the hole. "Are you Americans so prideful that you're willing to punish the entire continent — possibly the world — just because an accused spy caught you with your… Oh, what's the American expression?"

"Caught with your pants down," Zhu muttered.

"Exactly."

"It's far more complicated than that," George explained.

Duebel crossed his arms. "If Huang's ATA genetics are even remotely as powerful as his daughter's, we need him here. Now."

Jack took one look at Teal'c's ashen face and knew exactly what he had to do. He grabbed Weiyan's arm and pulled her up from Teal'c's side. "Let's go have a nice little chat, shall we?

"I have done nothing wrong!"

"Yeah, yeah. You keep saying that." He mentally put a lid on any sympathy he might feel for the girl; he'd spent his life perfecting the act of being a bastard when needed.

That didn't make what he had to do next any easier.

Teal'c raised an eyebrow, but Jack gave him a short shake of his head. Stay out of this.

He dragged Weiyan a few feet closer to the building. No earth-shattering quakes started up, so that was a good start. He waved his lighter at Weiyan. "You're Chinese. You must know the *Art of War* inside and out."

"Sun Tzu?" Lifting her eyes, Weiyan mirrored Teal'c's eyebrow acrobatics. "Of course. It was my father's wish that I memorize his work."

Clink. Jack flipped the lighter open. "Yeah, I'll bet. How does the one part of old Tzu's writings go? Something about bait and lures?"

Snap. He flipped the lighter shut. "I'm a fishing fan."

"Ah…" She closed her eyes and recited, "'Offer the enemy a bait to lure him; feign disorder and strike him.'" Her eyes opened again and cocked her head. "There's another passage, General. One that speaks of pretending to be weak so that your enemy might grow arrogant."

"Been there, done that." Jack deliberately crossed his arms, the lighter still in one hand. "I gotta wonder… Your father nearly got us killed last year. By your own admission, you weren't even healthy enough to join the trainee program. And yet, somehow, you cleared the IOA's vetting process."

Weiyan's mouth shut tight. Not exactly what he expected.

He pushed it to the next level. "Now, I'm not that keen on the IOA. Frankly, there are times I think they're not much better than the Goa'uld, what with all their power-mongering, but those folks don't just let anyone in. Trust me, I know."

"I — I…"

"Go ahead," he said with as much patience as he could muster. "I'm all ears."

She bit her lip.

Clink. Jack flipped open the lighter again. "Well?"

"You will not yell and make the ground tremble?"

Snap. "Try me."

"My mother… She is Quing Zhu." She gulped. "She pre-approved my application for the trainee program."

"The Chinese ambassador?" Jack whistled. "Did she know about Huang's little affiliation with the Goa'uld?"

An itty-bitty trembler rumbled beneath his boots. A warning. Or in his case, progress.

"Answer the question, Weiyan." Jack threw back his shoulders, putting on the best mean-old brigadier general persona he could drum up. "Did your mother know or not?"

Weiyan nervously wet her lips. "I do not think so."

Jack went in for the kill. "But if Huang's name was on your application as next of kin — "

"My father's a good man," she muttered. "His reasons for doing what he did must have served some great purpose."

"Give me a break."

The ground shook. Harder this time. Louder.

"Jack, calm down!"

Apparently, not loud enough. Jack raised a hand, warning Daniel not to come any closer. The rumbling kept up. Carter hurried over to Teal'c and helped him to his feet.

Jack got in Weiyan's face. "So your mother snuck you in the backdoor. Faked your medical records — "

"Hemophilia is manageable."

"Your mom must've thought you'd be the prize student." He stared her down. "Was she gunning for you to be first in line to operate the weapons platform?"

"My mother thought I would fail!"

A loud crash. Jack didn't have to look to know the phantom Stargate had tumbled downward, all thirty-two tons demolishing the cliff. Still, there were no cracks in the ground around them. Jack opened his mouth, ready to push harder. An arm yanked him backwards.

Daniel stepped between them. "Stop it. Both of you!"

Weiyan turned away, her shoulders shaking.

"Back off, Daniel!" Jack shouted over the rumbling war of rock and dirt. "You certainly did fail, didn't you, Weiyan? When you sat in that chair, Ambassador Zhu — if that's really her name — shouted her lungs out at you, and bam! Those ATA genes spiked into overdrive."

"Enough!" Weiyan whirled toward him. "You have no right to treat me this way."

Boom. The ground shook. Hard. Jack managed to stay on his feet, but Weiyan stumbled forward. He stopped her fall and…

The rumbling stopped.

"Sir, we've got company." Carter nodded toward the building. A curtain of golden-white light streamed downward, washing out their view of the brick building. The curtain oscillated, forming three, then four glowing ribbons.

Jack pulled Weiyan upright. "You're right," he told her. No one should treat you like that."

"But — "

"I needed to get that thing's attention." He jerked his chin toward the building. "Nice backbone you're growing there, by the way."

"I have always had a backbone, General O'Neill."

"Having one and using it are two different things." He turned toward Daniel. "Let's see if Teal'c's up for a hike."

Daniel frowned. "You could've told me what you were planning."

"I wasn't sure it would work."

The ribbons contracted, losing their gold tint. Four white-hot ribbons merged into a solid pillar. A handful of glistening tendrils unfurled. It was a familiar image. One Jack had seen too often for one lifetime.

"Jack, if that's an ascended Ancient — "

"If it is, it can kiss my ass. Daniel, Carter, get Teal'c over here. Carry him if you have to!"

With Teal'c's arm slung across their shoulders, the two managed to half-drag, half-carry him over. As they reached Jack, the ascended being solidified into a hooded human shape dressed in a long, flowing white robe.

"You able to walk?" Jack asked Teal'c. His face was grayer than the SGC's walls.

"I will try, O'Neill."

Weiyan threw a supporting arm around Teal'c's torso. "You must not try, you must do!"

Teal'c managed a weak smile. Then he broke down coughing.

"Yeah, you're not going anywhere." Jack gestured for him to sit down. Teal'c complied, too readily which scared the crap out of Jack.

The ascended being — or whatever the hell was dicking with them — waved in their direction. "Look, I get that this could be some glowy Ascended what — "

"It could be Oma," Daniel said with far too much reverence for Jack's taste.

"Oma?" Weiyan bent down beside Teal'c.

"She is an ascended being," Teal'c explained between gasps. "A former Ancient."

Weiyan glanced up at Carter. "Did they not build the Antarctica chair?"

"Amongst other things," Carter replied with a bare sliver of a smile. "General, I recommend caution."

"No fooling." Jack eyed the alien. A breeze had kicked up. A light one, but enough to send the ascended being's robes flapping behind it. At least it had stopped waving.

Teal'c's breath grew more ragged. Jack considered marching right up to the alien and punching its lights out, but something told him that wouldn't be such a hot idea.

"I don't know about the rest of you," he said, turning back to the others, "but I'm getting pretty tired of being treated like a toy."

"Daniel, you knew Oma better than anyone." Carter tilted her head. "Would she really treat us like this?"

"Sam, I barely remember talking to her before I — "

"Died?" Jack offered.

Daniel shrugged. "She's always been fairly gentle. Helpful even."

"Tell that to the Jaffa she burnt to a crisp on Kheb."

"She was protecting Shifu," Daniel whispered. "This is... Different. I'm not sure how, but it is."

Teal'c started up another coughing fit.

"I don't care what's going on, Daniel, I've had enough." Jack raised a hand to the side of his mouth and shouted, "No more games! You wanna talk? Then get your butt over here!"

The buzzing came back, softer this time. He ignored it.

"Careful, Jack, don't — "

He shot Daniel a glare. "I'm not letting that thing kill Teal'c off." He turned back toward the alien, the buzzing intensified. Pressure crowded his eardrums.

The alien disappeared.

He shook his head. Tried to shake off the buzzing. "We're not moving!"

The breeze shifted to a full-on gust. A dry, bitter cold reminder of what they'd left behind in Antarctica. "Anyone feel that?"

Carter opened her mouth to speak, but Jack never heard her. Something slammed against his back. He stumbled and the wind seized him as if he was nothing more than a ragdoll. A sharp tug and he felt himself yanked forward.

Twisting sideways, he tried to squirm out of its grip. No luck. Dust and wind blew across his face. He glanced sideways, but all he could see was the dusty terrain speed by. The only upside was that he had company. Carter, Daniel, Teal'c, and even Weiyan were just as locked up as he was by whatever had them in its clutches. The distant horizon became even more distant as they were pulled forward.

Ignoring the wind's sting in his eyes and face, Jack refocused on the building up ahead. It was moving, too. Coming closer. A wave of vertigo hit him. If the yanking around didn't stop soon, he'd be a pancake in need of scraping off the building's walls. He threw up his arms, braced for impact.

The walls blurred. Jack squeezed his eyes shut, ready for what could only come next.

He jolted to a stop. Opening his eyes, the first thing he noticed was the warm air. The second thing was the blue light licking against bricked walls. They were inside a chamber of sorts, and though Jack couldn't see the ceiling, he was pretty damn sure they were inside that damned building.

The third thing, and probably the most important, was the hesitant smile of someone he never expected to meet again.

"It is good to see you, O'Neill." The robed alien pulled down his hood.

He looked exactly like Skaara.

Which was too good to be true.

ANCIENT OUTPOST, ANTARCTICA
18 AUG 04/2210 HRS MCMURDO STATION

George's latest argument with Ambassador Duebel was stopped short by the arrival of Major Davis and two Navy SEALS. The men wore bright orange coveralls and jackets with Byrd Station patches on their left sleeves. Blue wool watch caps affixed with the traditional eagle and trident logo of the Navy SEALS covered their heads. They each carried a yard-wide chrome-and-black box stamped with the recognizable 'explosives' label.

Colonel Ken Ferguson brought up the rear. George awarded Davis a grateful smile. "Glad you could make it. First time at the outpost? "

"Wish the circumstances were different, sir." Davis quickly introduced the SEALS — Lieutenants Kalsner and Mason. "With your permission, they should start laying charges — "

"Just one moment!" Zhu pointed at the chair. "If there's any chance my daughter can be saved by using Huang's — "

"Huang the spy?" Davis asked. "General, what's going on?"

"Have the SEALS lay their charges around the platform, Major," George ordered. "I'll be with you in moment."

"Yes, sir." Davis led the SEALS over to the other side of the platform. They put down their kits and flipped open the latches. Ferguson stood back, taking it all in.

George returned his attention to the ambassadors, his voice low. "Bringing Huang here is not going to happen."

"Because he claims to be a spy for the Goa'uld?" Duebel asked.

"Yes." George nodded. "And because sunrise happens just shortly after noon tomorrow. That's less than fourteen hours from now. There simply isn't enough time to retrieve him from Beijing. Do you understand?"

His lips pressed together, Duebel spun around and joined Zhu by the hole. He crouched down and took her hand.

"My last words," Zhu whispered. "They were — "

"Shhhh," Duebel said reassuringly.

George bowed his head, striving to fight back the remorse nipping at his heels. Though he'd bought Lee added time, George harbored doubts that the scientist could find a solution.

"General Hammond, we found something." Major Davis dashed around the hole, holding up a glass tube.

"That's Teal'c's tretonin," Dr. Lee said. "It must have fallen out of his pocket when the floor collapsed."

Davis handed the tube over to George. The force field's shimmering light reflected against the purple liquid inside. If Lee did succeed, Teal'c would need a dose immediately.

George thanked Davis. "Nice work out there today, Major."

"Thank you, sir."

"I trust McMurdo Sound is still in one piece?"

"Mostly, sir." Davis smiled. "When the 302s jumped into hyperspace, the ice broke up a bit."

"I suppose NSF Director Edmunds must be a little unhappy."

Davis glanced toward Ferguson. "Sir, in the grand scheme of things, I doubt that's high on Dr. Edmunds's list of concerns."

"In the meantime," George waved Teal'c's tretonin injector, "I'll ask Lt. Simmons to hold onto this. If we're lucky, Teal'c will need it as soon as we pry him out of that thing."

Lee stared at the injector. "Lt. Simmons, sir?"

"Yes, that's right." George turned back to the major. "And Davis? Ask the lieutenant to arrange for the ambassadors' immediate evacuation."

Davis' eyes narrowed. "Graham Simmons?"

"He's out by the com center. Probably trying to round up another pot of coffee if I know him."

Davis and Lee exchanged glances.

"Is there a problem?" George asked.

Lee scratched his head. "Lts. Gerling and Brooks are the only airmen who've been in the chamber since the accident."

George spun toward Davis. "Simmons has been here the whole time."

"Sir, I just talked with Graham Simmons a few days ago. He's in Colorado Springs at the SGC."

Ascension was one thing. Being human, another.

Daniel knew that and still he stared at Skaara, unsure of what to do, or even what to say. It was impossible to deny the wide gulf between them.

Even if his former brother-in-law didn't look a bit different since —

"Since my death?" Skaara asked warmly.

Daniel winced. "More like before my own…death." He'd

forgotten how perceptive Ascended Beings could be. Oma had certainly been that way.

It wasn't as if ascension had changed Skaara's appearance. Not by any means. He still wore the same long plaited black hair, olive fatigues, and cut-off chainmail vest taken from Ra's Jaffa. A loose bleached-white Abydonian-style robe hung from his shoulders, made all the whiter by the room's pervasive blue glow.

If it was a room. A blue mist hovered just below where the ceiling should be, obscuring Daniel's view. He shuddered. The room, or chamber — he wasn't quite sure which — was a good fifty degrees colder than outside. Though the ambient light had turned the bricks a mottled blue, he assumed they were inside the same building they'd seen outside. The same building that housed whatever had killed Lord Yu's original Dragon Guard.

Near the wall stood a row of squared columns, their bases wrapped with trellised panels reminiscent of the Ancient outpost on Earth. A glance over his shoulder told him he wouldn't be able to see further into the chamber. It was too dark.

As he turned back toward Skaara, Jack whispered, "This has gotta be some elaborate trick."

"No tricks." Skaara stepped toward them. "I promise."

"I don't know, Skaara." Jack shoved his hands in his pockets. "Planting your old Zippo..."

Skaara held out the lighter. "You mean this, O'Neill?"

"Ah, yeah. That." Jack's hands dropped to his sides. "See, I could've sworn I'd left it back at the SGC. In my locker."

The lighter disappeared. "Place and time have meaning only when the heart requires."

"You've been spending time with Oma," Daniel remarked.

"Before, after, during." Skaara shrugged. "Though the current carries the stream one way, the skilled oarsman can travel in both directions."

"Of course," Sam said. "Time wouldn't have any meaning if you're ascended, would it?"

"Carter?"

Sam turned toward Jack. "Quantum mechanics, sir. Theorists believe time is an artificial construct. Like Skaara said, the past, present and future can all — "

"Okay," Jack waved her off. "I get it."

Skaara cocked his head. "Are you not happy to see me, O'Neill?"

"Sure." Jack frowned. "I thought you ascended beings weren't supposed to interfere with us lowly folks."

Skaara matched Jack frown for frown. "I saw no other way."

"If you say so."

Daniel raised an eyebrow at Jack. While Abydos's destruction had been a painful discovery for Daniel upon his return to humanity, he'd known it had hit Jack just as hard. He wouldn't talk about it, though, no matter how much Daniel tried.

He understood why. Jack had grown close to Skaara during the very first Abydos mission nine years ago. That closeness had only deepened during the Stargate Program's early years. Whenever SG-1 visited, Jack went out of his way to bring something for Skaara, be it worn-out fatigues, comic books, even a baseball.

And fuel for Jack's old Zippo. Skaara would hurriedly fill his precious lighter and then ignite the fire for their evening meal of roasted lizard and yefetta flatbread.

Those memories made Daniel smile. That is, until he remembered their current predicament. "Skaara, what's this about? Why — ?"

"Carter, check on Teal'c," Jack ordered.

Daniel mentally kicked himself as he joined Sam in hurrying to Teal'c's side. Daniel had been so surprised by Skaara's appearance that he'd forgotten about everything else. Teal'c lay sprawled across the floor, a marble surface laced with thousands of thin silver lines etched into the stone. Weiyan crouched by his side, holding his hand. Kneeling down, Sam pressed two fingers against Teal'c's neck.

Skaara glided up beside Daniel and gazed down on the two. "Helping those in need is not an evil act."

He exchanged glances with Skaara. "You mean me."

Skaara bowed his head. "Though the Caledonians were blind, you are not, Daniel. None of you are. That is why I am here."

"Will he live?" asked Weiyan, her eyes darting back and forth between Teal'c and Skaara. She seemed fine. Actually, better than fine. She'd somehow managed to neatly pull back her disheveled hair, color had reappeared on her cheeks, and even the bloodstain on her shirt had disappeared.

"Pulse is erratic." Sam palmed Teal'c's forehead. "He's running a low-grade fever as best I can tell."

Teal'c's eyes fluttered open.

Relieved, Daniel refocused on Skaara. "Can you tell us — ?"

"Careful," Sam warned. "The general's right. We can't be sure that really is Skaara, ascended or not."

"Have we ascended?" Teal'c murmured. As Weiyan helped push him up to a sitting position, Jack bent down and clasped the Jaffa's shoulder.

"No, Teal'c." Skaara knelt beside him. "You are still very much alive." Though Skaara's voice sounded as light and friendly as ever, his face was solemn.

Jack dropped down on Teal'c's other side, the stress line between his eyes deepening.

Jack's stern visage. Skaara's grim frown. If anyone had told Daniel their reunion would be so dour, he'd have sworn they didn't known what they were talking about.

A convulsion hit Teal'c, reminding Daniel that this wasn't really a time for happy reunions.

Jack pressed Teal'c's shoulders back as the Jaffa's body shook. "If you really were Skaara, you'd help him!"

Sam stood up. "He needs tretonin."

"Then we must hurry." Skaara flattened his hand against Teal'c's chest.

A white glow blossomed across Teal'c's chest. He gasped as

the glow intensified, arching his back in another convulsion. Weiyan echoed his gasp with one of her own.

The glow dissipated and Teal'c sank back to the floor. His eyes closed, his breathing steadied.

Daniel sighed in relief. "He's going to be all right now, isn't he?"

"For a while." Skaara gave him a tentative smile. "As Colonel Carter said, Teal'c needs tretonin."

"For a while?" Jack rocked back on his heels and stared at Skaara. "I thought you said time didn't matter."

"To someone ascended, no." Skaara dropped his hand away from Teal'c's chest. "I am sorry, O'Neill. This was the only way to safely get your attention."

Jack climbed to his feet. "So says the ascended, all powerful, all knowing wizard."

Weiyan joined him. "Ascended?"

Sam explained. "It means transcending to a higher plane of existence. Most of the Ancients — the people who built the Antarctica chair and the Stargates are — "

"Not everyone who ascended was once an Ancient, Colonel Carter." Skaara returned Weiyan's gaze a moment longer and then rose with a grace beyond his young age.

Or what had been his age when he'd been alive.

Skaara stretched out his arms. "It is good to see all of you again."

"All of us… Do you know me?" Weiyan asked.

Skaara's smile broadened. "I know your father."

Taken aback, Daniel glanced at Weiyan. Her lips had formed a mute O. He couldn't blame her.

"Look, Skaara." Jack took a wary step closer. "I'm sorry if I'm having trouble believing you, but just what the hell is going on? And just how the hell do you know a Goa'uld spy?"

Skaara tilted his head. "I called to you, O'Neill."

"I guess I wasn't listening."

"Back up," Daniel said. "You knew Ambassador Huang?"

Anguish darkened Skaara's face. "By a confluence of circumstances which are deeply regretted."

"Circumstances which might kill Teal'c, you mean."

"Jack."

"No, Daniel." Jack spun toward him. "That man was working for those slimy, snakeheaded Goa'uld."

Skaara wrung his hands. "O'Neill, you must understand. Huang did not see Lord Yu as a demon. His loyalty was pure."

"Nope," Jack said. "Still not buying it."

"Sir, what about the earthquakes?" Sam offered. "When we first met Oma Desala on Kheb, she demonstrated the ability to pretty much affect all the elements."

Daniel turned back toward Skaara. "Were the earthquakes your way of getting our attention?"

Skaara's smile faded. "No. The environment caused the earthquakes, or rather, you did, O'Neill. You and Weiyan both inherited that ability. She awoke the device, but its function is fueled by your combined presence."

"The ATA gene." Sam chewed her lip in thought.

"Carter?"

"Sir, this entire 'environment' could be constructed of Ancient technology. It's possibly why you spoke in Ancient."

Skaara nodded. "I did call out to you, O'Neill."

"The buzzing?" Jack asked.

As Skaara gave Jack an apologetic shrug, Daniel reviewed what their ascended friend had just shared. Environment. Did that mean they weren't really here? Wherever 'here' is?

Or was 'here' on some ascended plain? Daniel mulled that possibility over. After everything they'd seen, all the random clues, was it possible that 'here' didn't even exist?

"Why the reruns?" Jack asked. "You know Huang so I have to assume Yu and his merry band of Dragon Guards has something to do with all this."

Skaara nodded. "It was important you understood Huang's origins... And how his devotion to Lord Yu resulted in the

Goa'uld's testing all of you when you rescued Daniel."

"Why couldn't you just tell us?"

"It is complicated. Daniel," pleaded Skaara, "surely you must understand. Some part of you must remember."

Not for the first time, Daniel wished he could. But for all his efforts, the only thing he'd managed to dredge up was a memory of seeing Bra'tac and Rya'c imprisoned. That small memory had made a difference, but there was so much more he could do. If he could only remember.

"Non-interference," Sam said. "Orlin was punished by the other Ascendeds when he tried to help the Velonians."

"We're not the Velonians, and we haven't asked you," Jack stabbed a finger toward Skaara, "to build us a weapon. Instead, we've been treated like rats in a maze."

"But you are using a weapon, O'Neill. One that has saved your planet from Anubis, but could now rip it apart if you do not take the necessary steps to stop it."

Everyone spoke at once. Sam wanted to know how to shut off the weapon. Weiyan wanted to know about Anubis. Jack insisted Skaara send them back to Earth immediately.

Everyone except Daniel.

Something Skaara had said nagged at him. Something about safely getting their attention.

That's when it hit him. Skaara's very existence could be in jeopardy. "The weapons chair. If that's what this is about, if Oma knows you're here, she could — "

Out of nowhere, Skaara's robes flapped outward as if a wind had blown through the chamber. He turned and pointed toward the room's darkened interior. "Who do you think sent me?"

A warm breeze blew across Daniel's face and he knew. "Oma."

The room lit up in a blaze of blue light.

Sam squeezed her eyes shut against the sudden brightness of the room. Her eyes adjusted, she opened them, and saw that the room was in fact a cavernous chamber reminiscent of the Antarctic outpost. Soft blue globes stuck out from trellised screens arranged along the walls. Squared-off columns surrounded a central platform — just like on Earth — but with one difference, the silver lines she'd noticed earlier in the floor also ran up the columns.

Squinting, she realized there were other differences, too. The central octagonal platform was much wider than the ones she'd seen at both Proclurash and on Earth. At least a good car-length in diameter and almost three, maybe four feet tall. Something else was missing, too.

"Where's the chair?" the general asked.

"This room served another purpose." Skaara gestured toward the platform. "Not as a weapon, but as a salvation."

"Will it save Earth?" Sam asked. "That's why we're here, right?"

"All in time, Colonel Carter."

Time. That had to have been the third, maybe fourth instance of Skaara bringing up the subject.

"Skaara, if Earth's in trouble..."

"Daniel. I promise, once you have seen and heard what has come before, you will be ready to face what comes next." Skaara headed toward the platform.

General O'Neill hesitated, glancing down at Teal'c. A thin sheen of sweat covered his face, but he wasn't shaking like earlier. Whether it was a lack of tretonin or something else, Teal'c needed medical attention. Soon.

Weiyan sank down beside him. "I will stay with him, General."

"Thanks," the general mumbled. He exchanged glances with Sam, the corners of his mouth twitching.

"Sir, you heard Skaara. Teal'c will be all right."

"Yeah, for the moment." He jerked his chin toward the platform. "Carter, you think you can figure out what that thing is all about and get us out of here?"

"Possibly, sir."

"Good. Whatever Skaara meant about Earth being ripped

apart… Maybe he thinks we have time, but I've had enough of the waiting game."

"Yes, sir." That made two of them. "Though, it would be easier if I had equipment to — "

"Eyes and ears, Colonel. That's your equipment." He grimaced. "And that brain of yours." With a swagger she knew the general wasn't feeling, he headed toward the platform.

With a nod from Weiyan, Sam joined the others. Curiosity mixed with wariness as she approached the octagonal platform. Shorter trellised panels lined its sides, each one back-lit by a soft blue glow. A plastic-like translucent substance covered the top, oscillating between phosphorescent blue and pale yellow. Dead center, a red control crystal jutted upwards, its base as wide as a basketball, its point honed to a viciously sharp point extending at least a foot in length.

"That's different." She pointed at two empty silver brackets on either side of the crystal. The right bracket was lined in blue, the left in white.

"Different, how?" Daniel asked.

"I've never seen this configuration before in Ancient technology." She turned toward Skaara. "That's what this is, right? We were in Antarctica one moment and now… Now we're where? I mean, I know we're inside the building on P3Y-702 — "

"In a sense. Before your letters and numbers, the System Lord Yu named the planet Kunlun." Skaara waved a hand over the platform. The air rippled, darkened, as if its mass was undergoing some sort of metamorphosis. "You've seen some images, now I will show you others."

The area above the platform coalesced, forming a miniature model of the Ancient city they'd found earlier. Complete with a central spire.

"Elysium Pedion," Daniel said.

"Elysium was the sister city of Vis Uban. The planet upon which Oma returned you to your former life, Daniel." Skaara cupped his palms over the virtual city and then pushed outward.

The spire rushed toward them. Its walls thinned and then disappeared, the view plummeting down through floors past various laboratory-like rooms.

"Vis Uban was the last city of the Ancients," Skaara said, "but Elysium had become home to many of their people's greatest scientists."

One floor showed Ancients working busily at pedestals not unlike the time-loop device on P4X-639. Another showed two men monitoring a polygonal vat, the viscous liquid inside churning like molten glass.

Sam gestured toward the image. "Is that how the Ancients made control crystals?"

"Many variations of crystals were made for many purposes."

The image tunneled downward until it stopped in the very room they were in, platform and all, with one difference.

Three crystals extended from the top. The traditional red control crystal nestled between a shorter indigo blue crystal and a flat, solid white one. The three crystals were connected by a series of transparent boards covered in thin lines — almost like circuit boards.

A glint of light beneath the crystals caught Sam's attention. She looked down through the platform's translucent top. Deep inside the base spun an incandescent sphere, the center white-hot. Pockets of gas rippled across its surface. She'd seen something similar once before. "Sir, look familiar?"

General O'Neill leaned in. After a moment, he shrugged. "Looks like a miniature sun to me. Wait a minute..." The general's head shot up. "Carter, am I nuts or does that look exactly like that photo-tonic thing Yu used to power his force field and clone his guards?"

"Photonic energy. Yes, sir. It's very similar to the Ancient technology we found in Yu's fortress. We didn't see anything like this on Vis Uban, but — "

"Lord Yu's acquisition of Ancient technology is only part of our problem," Skaara said. "The recent accident which brought you here has triggered far worse difficulties."

"Difficulties?" the general echoed.

Daniel raised an eyebrow. "Our problem?"

"These same mechanisms created the Ancient plague. On Vis Uban and Elysium Pedion."

The general yanked Daniel away from the pedestal. "Jack, what are you doing?"

"Saving your butt, Daniel. Thanks to thawing out an Ancient, the rest of us had the plague. Some of us got cured. Others — meaning me — got a snake in their head. Trust me, you don't want a piece of this."

"O'Neill, it is not real," Skaara said. "Even if it was, the crystal which caused the plague is long gone. The Ancients destroyed all the duplicating crystals when the plague began."

"All except the one Yu got ahold of." The general let go of Daniel. "So, not real? Okay, then why the show?"

"Wait a moment," Sam said. "What do you mean by duplicating?"

"You would call it DNA replication."

"Or cloning?" Daniel asked. "Like Lord Yu's Dragon Guards?"

"All powered by photonic energy." Skaara waved a hand over the platform. The circuit boards disappeared along with the blue and white crystals. Only the red crystal was left. "Three of these platforms were built. As time went on, each was modified for a different purpose. The two on Elysium and Vis Uban were meant for genetic formations."

"Uh, excuse me." General O'Neill raised his hand. "Does any of this have anything to do with Earth?"

"More than you can imagine. The crystal was installed in a device deep within Earth's outpost for geological transformations."

A sphere rose above the crystal, its blues and whites coalescing into the recognizable from of Earth. Or rather, Earth hundreds of millions of years ago when there had been a single land mass. A singular super continent.

"Pangaea," Daniel said. "But that was long before the Ancients lived on Earth, wasn't it?"

"Even then," Skaara said, "they anticipated that they might, someday, wish to colonize your homeworld."

A white-gold light flashed toward the southern tip. The super continent broke up, its individual landmasses drifting apart.

Sam reeled in astonishment. "The Ancients terra-formed Earth?"

"Carter?"

"I always thought continental drift was a natural part of our planet's development." She spun toward Skaara. "Is that what you meant by Earth ripping apart? We've somehow re-activated the outpost's terra-forming device. Can't we just shut if off by pulling the right crystal."

"It is more complex than that, Colonel Carter." Skaara pointed at the empty white bracket. "On Elysium, this crystal was used to generate photonic energy. Lord Yu took this crystal, as well as the encoding boards."

"The photon emitter and cloning technology. What about the red one?"

"The control crystal serves as a filter," Skaara said. "It can be turned on or off and uses the sun to extract photonic energy. That energy can then be sent into the Earth's crust to make mountains, oceans — "

The general whistled. "And rip the planet apart."

Skaara sighed. "If switched to its on position, yes, and while you have nothing to fear here on this plane...," he ran his hand through the platform, "the device on Earth is very real."

Sam copied Skaara's actions. Her hand went right through, as if nothing was there. She should be relieved, but she wasn't. Not if Earth was in trouble.

"Oma's methods of teaching take many forms," Skaara said.

Daniel frowned. "Oma isn't really here, is she?"

"No. But you must understand that 'here' is not where you believe it to be."

General O'Neill took a turn waving his hand through the platform. "If this control crystal got switched on back on Earth, how do we shut it off?"

"You are still on Earth, O'Neill." Skaara waved a hand over the platform. The air rippled, revealing five silhouettes stretched out across the countertop. The forms coalesced and the silhouettes became the bodies of five people.

Five very recognizable people.

Sam stared at her semi-transparent body sprawled across the platform's other edge. Her left arm covered Teal'c's waist, her right rested on Daniel's feet. The three of them — or rather, their bodies — formed a semi-circle around two other bodies, those of General O'Neill and Weiyan.

Daniel gasped. "When the outpost's floor collapsed — "

"Would someone please explain what's going on here?"

"My God, Jack. Look." Daniel pointed toward the platform. The bodies had solidified, and in Weiyan's case, a charred black version of the control crystal protruded from her stomach.

Daniel glanced over his shoulder toward Weiyan and Teal'c who still sat on the floor by the wall. He looked back at Skaara. "If we aren't — "

"Dead, Daniel." The anger in Jack's face stilled. "The word is dead."

"You remain very much alive." Skaara turned his gaze toward Weiyan.

"What about her?" Sam whispered.

Skaara dropped his gaze. "Her father's journey brought her to you, and now he must join you in saving Earth."

"Huang help us," the general sputtered. "Are you nuts?"

"What is happening?" Weiyan jumped up and ran over. Sam grabbed her before she could get too close.

"Uh, Jack?" Daniel pointed toward the ceiling. In unison, everyone gazed upward.

A ragged hole appeared in the ceiling above them. General Hammond peered down from its edge.

CHAPTER TWENTY

SHUNYI PSYCHIATRIC HOSPITAL
BEIJING, CHINA
2004 AUGUST 18, 9:00 PM

HUANG knelt beside his cot, his right forefinger sliding across the floor. Though he had no lamp, no mirror, or window, his eyes had long adjusted to the dark cell. Raising his hand, he judged the room's filth upon his fingertip. It would suffice.

A downward stroke. A lower dash across his brow. Higher up, an inverted bracket.

The *wénshēn* completed, he leaned back against his thin mattress. His daily devotion to Yu was a pale effort, but it was all he had to honor his lord.

A ragged sob escaped Huang's parched throat. The thought of never returning, of never seeing his lord and master was a bitter burden he would carry to his grave.

A burden of knowledge.

Knowledge of defeat. Of disaster. Of knowing his pride had allowed the Tau'ri to see through his plans to help his Lord Yu.

Huang's stomach gurgled, feeling a hunger his soul no longer possessed. Each day, food would be brought. Each day, he would refuse sustenance except a single sip of water and a crumb to salve his basic urges. He deserved nothing more. His prison cell served merely as a living tomb. He would die here, and for once, he found himself truly accepting that knowledge. It brought him peace.

Unbidden images swelled in his memory. Images of his life as a Dragon trainee with Lao Dan Shi. The steady thrum of Lord Yu's fortress barrier came to mind. As children, they would run along its perimeter, the pulsing barrier's hum an assurance much like the beat of one's own heart. The Jaffa would smile as they raced past, indulging in joyous freedom.

A whiff of dank air stuffed his nostrils, returning him to the present. The cell was warm, humid. For one brief moment, he decided it must be late summer in Beijing. The cherry blossoms long gone.

His face became wet, sticky. Ashamed at his tears, Huang shut his eyes again and allowed the dark its due.

A golden light warmed his eyelids. He welcomed its memory. Companion, savior, the light had saved him from Antarctica's treacheries. Huang thought back on his time in the Tau'ri's frozen wasteland with a newfound appreciation. Ice-blue glaciers. Crisp, fresh air. His Antarctic travails had been a time of ferocious landscapes testing his every move.

Though he also remembered the constant doubts, it was clear to Huang now that possibility had been in abundance. Each day a gift of life.

The light faded. A memory too far out of reach.

The darkness spoke. "The tree which fills the arms grew from the tiniest sprout."

A recollection? Perhaps. Though it did not sound like his teacher Lord Yu or even Shi, his brother.

"A quote of Lao Tzu?" He squeezed his eyes tighter, searching heart and mind for the voice's owner. "Many years have passed since I heard the words of the *Tao Te Ching*."

His voice cracked. It had been many months since he had muttered any word aloud. Quing's visit... Yes, he had last spoken aloud to his ex-wife. Was that a month ago?

A year ago?

The memory spoke again. "Lao Tzu also said, 'the journey of a thousand *li* commenced with a single step.'"

Huang opened his eyes, prepared to meet only the cell's black embrace. Instead, a young man stood before him. Swathed in a nimbus of golden-white light, his visitor could not be more than twenty, if that. Olive-skinned, with long plaits of jet-black hair, the youngster's wide brown eyes stood out in contrast to his bleached-white robes.

"Your journey nears its end, Huang Sun Tzu." The young man smiled broadly.

Huang returned the smile. "I am ready."

CHAPTER TWENTY-ONE

ANCIENT OUTPOST, ANTARCTICA
18 AUG 04/2230 HRS MCMURDO STATION

GEORGE peered down at Jack, SG-1, and Zhu's daughter, their condition unchanged. In his head, he replayed every moment of Lt. Graham Simmons' time at the outpost. From coffee to counsel, the visitor's actions had fitted the young man to a tee.

If it wasn't Graham, then who was it?

"I'm not imagining things," he told Dr. Lee.

"No one's saying you are, General, but…" Lee shrugged. "I never saw him. I gave you coffee the first couple of times, and then — "

"Brooks and Gerling. I realize that now." Beneath the force field, the rise and fall of his people's chests was the only sign they were still alive. "Is it possible we've had an alien visitor?"

Lee's voice lowered. "Maybe an Ascended Being?"

"If it was, then why the masquerade?"

"Well, this was their equipment." Lee pulled off his glasses and rubbed his eyes. "According to Dr. Jackson's reports, they were Ancients first, right? Maybe one of them wanted to see what we broke."

"By impersonating one of our own?" With a sigh, George turned his gaze back toward the force field. "I'd have appreciated the visit if they just gave us the instructions on how to fix this mess."

The frown on Jack's unconscious face deepened. He looked downright angry. Moving closer to the hole, George wondered what on Earth was going through his protégé's head. On the other side of the illuminated platform, Teal'c jerked from side-to-side, his broad chest shuddered once, and then his shoulders sagged.

As he quieted, George felt his own heart slow down in relief.

"General Hammond?" Major Davis called out.

"Report." George turned his attention away from the force field. The Navy SEALS had packed enough C-4 on the Ancient Weapons chair to blow up the entire installation.

"That's the last charge, sir." Davis beckoned Colonel Ferguson over. "Two Bell 212s are waiting topside to evacuate the last personnel over to Marble Point and then, McMurdo."

Ferguson hurried over and snapped to attention. He'd pretty much clammed up since his arrival. No surprise. The Ancient chair and the sight of SG-1 under that force field was enough to make anyone do the same. "At ease, son." George glanced over at the archway where Ambassadors Zhu and Duebel stood, each lost in their own thoughts. "How many can fit on one of those choppers?"

Ferguson slid a look toward Davis. Either the outpost spooked him or something else was going on.

Davis gave him a nod. "Colonel, how many?"

Ferguson returned his attention to George. "I can squeeze a good fifteen in, General, if there's no equipment to carry."

"That'll do it." He indicated the ambassadors. "Get them out of here. Leave me one chopper, but the remaining personnel should go now, including the SEALS and — "

"If you're staying," Dr. Lee chimed in from his computer, "I'd like to do so, too, General. There's still a good thirteen hours left. Who knows? Maybe that Ascended Being will come back, or I'll have a breakthrough with the device before we lose the western hemisphere." He smiled feebly, but George appreciated the sentiment.

And the reminder of what was at stake.

"Sir?" Davis turned to face him. "Permission to stay as well. I'd like to help, if you'll have me."

"Happily, Major."

An appreciative whistle came out of Ferguson's mouth. He

stuck a hand out toward the major. "You're serious as a heart attack. You know that, right?"

"Never more serious." Davis shook his hand with a smile.

George watched on as the two slapped each other's backs, fully aware of the difficulties the major had faced in dealing with the more 'by-the-book' colonel. Camaraderie came in all colors. Sometimes, they mixed. Sometimes, they clashed. Somehow, Davis had managed to persevere, do what was right, and win Ferguson's respect in the process.

With a final slap to the major's back, Ferguson stepped back and saluted George. "I was wrong, General. I thought all Davis did was tinker with budgets so those SG teams — What I mean to say is…" He dropped his hand. "True fact, sir. We never would've gotten those birds out of the ice if it wasn't for the major's smarts."

"Dismissed, Colonel. And thank you." George returned the salute. Ferguson gave Davis a nod and ran out.

No doubt about it, Davis was long overdue for a promotion.

Lieutenants Brooks and Gerling hurried in. George had sent them on what now seemed to have been a wild goose chase — searching for a 'back door' into the chamber below.

"Find anything?"

The airmen's matched frowns told him everything.

"All right. It was worth a try." He rubbed his eyes, contemplating how he'd manage to stay awake in the hours to come. Simmons' coffee would've come in handy right about now.

So would an explanation as to who — or what — had impersonated the lieutenant.

Gerling handed him a slip of paper. "This came in over the wire from McMurdo, sir."

George read the hurriedly scribbled note out loud. "Capetown, South Africa. 6.3 Richter along Antarctic Intercontinental plate. Emanating inland from shore. Aftershocks ongoing."

"We didn't feel anything, sir," said Brooks.

"That's Ancient technology for you." Lee took the note and

scanned it. "South Africa's thousands of miles away. If the device has that sort of reach, Europe can't be far behind."

In other words, it was time to move on to phase two. George turned back toward the airmen and ordered, "Assist Ferguson in escorting everyone topside."

Brooks dashed out, but Gerling stayed at attention. "Sir? Brooks and I would like to stay, too. I'm qualified to fly a Bell 212 chopper. General O'Neill deserves all the help we can give him, sir."

George sized the young woman up. "Permission granted. First escort our diplomats to the surface and then report back."

Gerling spun on her heels and strode over to the ambassadors. She spoke softly, presumably telling them, far more nicely than George, that they needed to get the hell out.

Duebel got the message, following Gerling out of the chamber. Zhu, on the other hand, stayed stock-still.

George girded himself for the inevitable confrontation. Of course she wouldn't want to leave her daughter — no parent in their right mind would.

He skirted the hole and approached her. "I'm sorry," he said, "but there isn't anything more you can do here except jeopardize your own safety."

Tears welled in Zhu's eyes. "She is my child. Any hope — "

"We won't stop trying until the very end. I promise." He nodded toward Gerling.

"This way, ma'am." The airman took Zhu's elbow.

George headed over to the SEALS as they packed up their kits. "You won't have room for those. Leave them here."

They exchanged glances, each as freckle-faced and wide-eyed as a pair of kids and George suddenly felt his age. It was high time he retired and he knew it. If Jack made it out of this alive —

"General Hammond?" The taller of the two SEALS — Lieutenant Kalsner — pulled a palm-sized green metal box from his parka's inner pocket. "Major Davis said we should leave the remote trigger with you. We set it to blow twelve hours from now. All you need to do is start the timer."

"Hang on a moment." Lieutenant Mason, the other and even younger of the pair, flipped open his case. He pulled out a bar of C4. A receiver tab stuck out of its side, its light gauge blinking yellow.

Mason jerked his chin toward the hole. "There's a small indent in the force field behind the chair. I'd like to try squeezing — "

"Get yourselves topside, Lieutenant. I'll place the final charge." Taking the C4 and remote, George dismissed the guards.

He circled the hole, searching for the right spot to plant the final C4. He found it, just behind the chair as Mason had said. While the rest of the force field lay flush with the floor, a hands-width-wide area dipped under the jagged edge. Unlike the rest of the force field, this particular patch appeared thicker, more opaque than the rest. George knelt down and wedged the C4 block into the gap, careful to not touch the force field.

Beneath that force field, Jack's frown became an outright scowl.

Forgive me.

George examined the remote's simple digital display and small keypad. At the bottom, a red start-up button blinked, its innocuous cadence a mock counter rhythm to the force field's thrum. The thing barely weighed half a pound.

A half-pound of wires, metal, and a simple transmitter that would blow up the Ancient outpost.

And everyone still trapped in its grasp.

"Sir?" Major Davis stepped up beside him and lowered his voice. "If you'd like, I can operate the remote."

"No, thank you." George dropped the remote to his side. He wasn't afraid to admit his protégé and flagship team had come to mean as much to him as his own grandchildren. Their dedication, their unwavering loyalty to him, the nation, and the planet made them the very definition of what it meant to serve.

"Integrity first. Service before self. Excellence in all we do."

If anyone was the inspiration for the U.S. Air Force's creed, it was Jack O'Neill, Samantha Carter, Teal'c, and Daniel Jackson.

"General?" Davis asked.

He stared at the remote. "If and when the time comes, Major, I think it's best that I be the one to pull the trigger." It was the least he could do to honor their last sacrifice. He thumbed the start button. The digital display changed from 12:00 to 11:59.

"Godspeed, SG-1."

If Jack had to pick the most surreal part of this experience, he wouldn't have chosen seeing Skaara. As much as he missed the kid, that wound had scabbed over, thank you very much. It only took a few bottles of scotch, an occasional bout of self-loathing, and the daily reminder that somewhere out there on the Oma Express, the boy was safe and out of harm's way.

A visit would've been nice, but who was he to complain?

Strolling through an Ancient ghost town wouldn't have been high on his list, either, and while Skaara's tale about Huang coming through the Antarctic gate some fifty-odd years ago raised an eyebrow, Jack really wasn't all that surprised. Actually, it explained a lot, though he didn't quite get why Skaara had interfered when Ascended Beings were supposed to be above that sort-of-thing.

Kid probably got lonely. Maybe that's why Daniel came back.

On the surreal meter, being told that he was in a funky dream-state, his body sprawled out on a platform in Antarctica, just underneath the weapons chair, came close to the top. But really, when it came down to it, the most surreal thing was…

"Please tell me Hammond didn't just plant a block of C4 feet away from his — I mean my — head!"

"If you do not act soon, General Hammond will have no choice but to destroy the entire outpost." Skaara pointed at the blackened crystal projecting out of Weiyan's gut. "You must fix things to be as they were."

Weiyan. The girl hadn't said a word since Skaara's little

parlor trick revealed their bodies lying on the platform. She just stared at her impaled image, chewing her lip like it was going out of style.

Jack reached out to take Skaara's elbow and then stopped himself, remembering that ascended folks weren't really there-there. They just looked that way. He stepped closer, lowering his voice. "What about her? Is Weiyan going to make it?"

"Her journey is on another path."

Jack bit back a reply. He'd spent enough time around Ascended beings and their cryptic language to know he wasn't going to get a straight answer. At least not on that front. He glanced over at Teal'c still passed out, still sweating like he was inside a furnace. "And Teal'c?"

"His tretonin is only an arm's reach away," Skaara said. "Once you have awakened, he will be fine. Then will you go."

"Go where?" Daniel had slid around the platform to stand beside his own comatose body. The doubled image wigged Jack out, but he'd seen worse.

"You want us to go back to P3Y-702," Carter said. "Kunlun."

Skaara nodded. "It is the only way to replace the damaged crystal in Antarctica. Huang will travel with you."

"That's never going to happen." Not as long as Jack could draw breath. "The man's a menace."

"Will the plague harm my father?" Weiyan touched the control crystal. Apparently, she wasn't listening.

For a father she'd only met once, she sure cares about the bastard more than herself.

Skaara stepped up beside her. "The plague has long faded. You should not fear this for your father."

"I don't." Weiyan pulled back from the crystal. "'The general who advances without coveting fame and retreats without fearing disgrace, whose only thought is to protect his country and do good service for his sovereign, is the jewel of the kingdom.'"

Jack grimaced, recognizing the words.

And the truth behind them.

"Sun Tzu," said Daniel.

Weiyan grinned. "When I met my father last year, his insistence that I read *The Art of War* seemed..."

"Irrelevant?"

She blushed. Jack found that rather amazing, considering the fact that she was basically staring at her soon-to-be very dead body, breathing her last breaths.

When he'd told her earlier that she'd grown a backbone, he wasn't kidding.

Still...

"Look, Skaara. I'm more than ready to go after this crystal if it'll save Earth, but Huang can't travel through the Stargate. No way. He's a security risk."

"He's also in a mental institution, sir." Carter glanced at Weiyan. "I'm sorry. I'm guessing your mother didn't tell you."

"No." The girl looked shocked. "She did not."

Skaara shook his head. "Two with the Ancient blood are required to open Kunlun's chamber. O'Neill is only one. The other must be Huang."

"Why can't Weiyan go?" Daniel asked. "She's certainly demonstrated she has the genetics."

Jack kept his face as neutral as possible. Maybe Daniel didn't get it, but she certainly did.

Weiyan touched the crystal protruding from her body. "If we wake up, I will die, won't I?"

"Wait a minute!" Daniel raced from behind the platform.

"There is no waiting, we must awaken at once. It is the only way to save Earth. Sun Tzu, and my father..." she gulped. "I understand now what matters most."

Daniel shook his head. "If they can save Teal'c when we wake up, they can save you — "

"Let it go, Daniel," Jack warned. "Let the girl have her dignity."

She's earned it.

He shared a glance with Carter who nodded. She understood.

Skaara turned toward him. "O'Neill, you must find it within

yourself to forgive Huang. Only by doing so, and permitting him to help, can you retrieve the crystal and save Earth."

"There's gotta be another way," Jack said. "One of the other ATA trainees — "

"Is it Huang you cannot trust, or is there someone else?" Skaara stared at him, hard. For a moment, it felt like Jack's clothes had been stripped and he was standing bare-assed naked while something older and wiser than his young Abydonian friend measured him up.

And found him wanting.

Jack shook off the feeling. "I don't know what you're talking about. I'd trust Carter, Teal'c, and Daniel to get me through anything. You know that."

"And yourself?" Skaara pressed. "Do you trust that you can use your abilities to retrieve the crystal? Using your genetics to operate the weapons chair will be a — " He grinned. "A cakewalk compared with how you must cooperate with the technology on Kunlun. Otherwise, the crystal will be lost."

"So I hate using Ancient technology," Jack retorted. "I'm a big boy. I can deal with it."

"Like the general who does not fear disgrace?"

He shrugged. "Something like that." It wasn't the first time he'd pretended a bravado he wasn't necessarily feeling. He hated using the ATA gene, hated giving himself up to something he could barely control. It didn't feel right, but neither did huddling like a coward while his planet got ripped to shreds.

A warm hand clasped his shoulder. Skaara's hand. "Unlike Huang whose path was set very long ago, your journey still has far to go, O'Neill."

"Thanks. I think." Jack cleared his throat. "You… You could visit sometime, you know. We could go fishing."

Skaara dropped his hand to his side. "In time all paths cross, O'Neill." He turned to face Carter, Daniel, and Weiyan. "Are you ready to return to Antarctica?"

"Wait!" Weiyan dashed across the room and knelt beside

Teal'c. "I am ready." She held his hand.

"What do we do?" Jack asked, keeping sight of Teal'c and Weiyan. "Click our heels together and say 'There's no place like home', or — "

The room disappeared in a flash of light. For a moment, all he could see was, well, basically nothing. Like staring at a white wall. Suddenly, he felt jittery, as if he'd had too much coffee before breakfast.

"Hello?" he called to the blank wall.

"I will not try."

Weiyan's voice. Somewhere far off.

A thumping filled Jack's ears. Rhythmic. Repeated.

"General! They're awake."

Thump. Thump-thump.

Unless he'd gone nuts, that was Major Davis' voice. Where the hell...?

The thumping became deafening. The white light, blinding.

"I will do, Teal'c," Weiyan whispered.

Thump. Thump-thump. Thump-thump.

"I will make you proud. All of you. Even you, General O'Neill. Even my moth — "

Jack's vision plunged into darkness.

Footsteps, yelling.

"The force field's receding below them!"

Though the thumping kept up, he felt his eyes open even though he could've sworn he'd never closed them.

Above a ragged hole in the ceiling, the Ancient outpost glared down at him. General Hammond's very round and very welcome face then slid into view.

"Almost thought I'd lost you there, son."

Every bone in Jack's body ached as he struggled to sit up. Daniel did the same, but Carter bolted to her feet. Davis reached down and gave her his hand to climb out.

Thump. Thump-thump.

She waved him off. "We need Teal'c's tretonin. Now!"

Davis opened his hand, a vial of the purple stuff stuck neatly in his palm. Grabbing the vial, Carter clambered over to Teal'c. She bent down and Jack heard a hiss.

Thump. Thump.

Beside him, Weiyan's eyes opened. She lowered her chin, glanced down at the crystal sticking out of her stomach, and closed her eyes.

The thumping subsided, but not before Jack recognized the sound.

It was the beating of his heart.

"Medic!"

ANCIENT OUTPOST, ANTARCTICA
18 AUG 04/2245 HRS MCMURDO STATION

Daniel sat on the weapons platform, processing everything Skaara had told them. Down below, Paul Davis and a female airman argued on how to best pull Weiyan out. If Skaara was right, all the efforts in the world couldn't save her.

Pulling off his glasses, he wiped his eyes with the back of his hand. She'd been so young. So innocent. She'd put her life in the hands of the IOA, of the Stargate Program, and all for what?

If he thought about it too much, he'd think about how Weiyan's life was never really meant to happen. Huang was never supposed to come to Earth, as a clone, he should've never been allowed to have children, and the mother —

Where was Ambassador Zhu?

Daniel scanned the chamber, but didn't see her. The other ambassadors were missing, too. Which wasn't necessarily a bad thing.

Jack and General Hammond stood by the back wall, their heads bent in discussion. A heated one from what Daniel could tell. Jack waved his hands around — probably trying to explain what they'd experienced — while Hammond's frown just deepened and deepened. The two generals occasionally glanced over at Daniel, then at Sam. She sat with Teal'c on the other side of the platform. The Jaffa's eyes were closed, but he already looked far better than he had for hours.

Daniel peered at the carnage below. Blood pooled on both sides of Weiyan's body. All backlit by the platform's self-illuminated top.

A low rumble filled the chamber. The room shook for a second and then settled down. A light dusting of ice wafted down from the ceiling, but no one seemed to pay attention. Apparently, a small aftershock was nothing compared to the quakes that had been hitting the southern hemisphere. Fatalities in the hundreds, thousands more homeless. It would get worse before it got better. He knew that.

He glanced at Robert Lee, focused on his monitor, studying quake reports from across the globe. All thanks to the Ancients' terra-forming device. Daniel believed in science. He believed in exploring the great unknown. If it wasn't for the Stargate, his life would've had little meaning.

But not at such a cost.

Someone put a canteen in his free hand. With a nod of thanks, he unscrewed the cap and gulped the cold water down. Once that was empty, he looked up to see Airman Brooks standing over him. "How long...?"

"Were you out?" Brooks stuffed the canteen in his parka. "Nine hours, give or take."

"Nine hours?" Impossible. Too much had happened.

"That force field had you locked up good and tight, sir. Not sure what made it finally drop low enough to get you out, but, well..." Brooks shrugged. "I guess alien technology can do anything."

Not anything, Daniel thought wistfully. *It can't save Weiyan*.

He stood up, his legs wobbly. Teal'c was still resting so he decided to take a short walk. Clear his head. A plank had been put over the hole between the platform and the rest of the chamber floor. He cautiously made his way across and headed through the archway and into the outpost's main room.

"Dr. Jackson, can you help me?"

Daniel turned toward the voice. It was Graham Simmons. The lieutenant stood by the stasis unit with a clearly distraught Ambassador Zhu.

"She was supposed to evacuate with the others," Graham explained.

Daniel raised an eyebrow. "Shouldn't you have done the same?" He didn't remember seeing the lieutenant there before the accident, but in all the confusion with the trainees and diplomats, he hadn't really been paying attention.

"Please," Zhu said. "Let me see my daughter."

He hesitated. Telling any woman their child was dying was hard enough. Breaking the bad news to Zhu could put the tenuous future of the Stargate Program in jeopardy.

"Of course," he decided out loud. With a nod to Graham, he ushered her through the archway and into the weapons chamber.

The two generals were still conferring.

"I'm sorry," Hammond said to Jack, "but request denied. Allowing Huang anywhere near the Stargate or the chair would be like handing over nuclear launch codes to the — "

The general's head jerked up as Daniel entered with Zhu by his side. Graham was just a step behind them.

"Weiyan!" With help from Teal'c, Zhu climbed down a ladder into the hole.

"Step away, Dr. Jackson," warned Hammond.

Soft sobs rose up from the hole, punctuated by Teal'c's murmured words of comfort.

"It's all right, sir." Daniel stopped beside the hole. Graham joined him in watching mother and daughter meet. Paul injected Weiyan with something. Hopefully, pain medication.

"Daniel."

"I know Zhu shouldn't be here, Jack, but the ambassador wanted to see her daughter, before — "

"Huang must accompany SG-1," Graham said. "The Ancient

blood runs stronger in his veins than anyone else's, even O'Neill's."

O'Neill's…

The exaggerated O. The soft double L's that almost sounded like R's. Daniel heard Sam gasp. He whirled toward Graham. Skaara gazed back.

"You must hurry, Daniel." Skaara stepped across the plank and stopped in front of Jack and Hammond. "The crystal must be replaced before your sun rises."

"Hello, Skaara," Hammond said, a tinge of awe in his voice. "So you're our mysterious visitor."

"I apologize," Skaara said sheepishly. "I had hoped to minimize my involvement, but time on this level has not allowed me to do so any longer. Not without risking the Others' attention."

Though Daniel privately wondered what Skaara meant by 'the Others,' there were more pressing matters at the moment. He hurried over to join Skaara and the generals. "What happens when the sun rises?"

Sam wasn't far behind. "The crystal's ruined, Skaara. There shouldn't be any threat from solar power."

Skaara frowned. "Each of you by now should know that what is seen is not always what is true. Yes, the crystal is damaged, but built within these walls are the conduits needed to bring new power from your sun."

Sam reminded them of the silver lines etched on the floors of both the Kunlun chamber and the one on Yu's planet.

"Excuse me, but," Lee waved toward the floor and ceiling, "there's no silver here."

"General Hammond?" Brooks raised his hand.

"Go ahead, Airman."

"Sir, when Gerling and I crawled through some of the outer hallways of this place, we did see some metallic carvings in the walls." Brooks shrugged. "We thought they were decorative."

"That's a problem, sir." Sam exchanged glances with Jack. "Silver works as a thermal-electrical conductor. If there's any circuitry left in the crystal, it'll super-charge whatever power's left and — "

"Rip the planet to shreds?"

"Huang must accompany you, O'Neill," said Skaara. "You must take him through the Stargate to Kunlun. Now."

"Even if I agreed to Huang's participation," said General Hammond, "there isn't enough time. Huang is in Beijing, the Stargate's in Colorado, and we're in Antarctica. I'm sorry, but we need to evacuate and go through with our original plan."

"Blowing up the outpost," Daniel mumbled, devastated at what the loss signified for Earth.

"Sir, wait!" Sam ran over to the hole. "Major Davis, are the F-302s still over at Observation Hill?"

Paul climbed halfway up the ladder. "Actually, Colonel, they're over at Marble Point. That's only a ten-minute chopper ride from here. Oh, wait!"

He scrambled off the ladder, landing on the outpost floor with a thud. "Use the 302s for hyperspace jumps! Hop over to Beijing, then — "

"Jumping in and around Antarctica is one thing," Hammond said, "but you can't go jumping in and out of populated areas with top secret equipment."

"But they could fly in," Sam said. "If final approach was handled at normal speeds."

"Carter, what do you have in mind?" Jack said.

"The 302s are capable of Mach 6, easily." Sam headed toward Robert's computer and tapped furiously on the keyboard. "There are two, right?"

Paul nodded. "I doubt Colonel Ferguson moved them back."

"You better hope you're right."

Another airman came in, holding a gurney. He went over to the hole and handed it down as Teal'c climbed up. He saw Skaara and bowed, surprisingly unconcerned.

"What will they do with Weiyan Shi?" he asked.

Daniel sighed. "I suppose they'll medi-vac her, maybe — "

"You must tell them to stop," Skaara said.

"I can't do that. What if there's a way to — "

"Daniel..." Skaara's brow furrowed, his eyes stern. "Her journey's end begins here. Tell them to stop."

A cold breeze blew across the back of Daniel's neck. He shuddered, remembering.

Please, Jack. Tell Jacob to stop.

"You're going to help her ascend," Daniel realized aloud.

Skaara nodded. "She deserves no less."

"I concur," Teal'c intoned. "If there are no objections, I will inform the airmen."

No one said a word. How could they? Death was one thing. What Skaara offered Weiyan?

General Hammond broke the silence. "Let them know, Teal'c."

Their Jaffa teammate hurried over to the hole and relayed Hammond's orders. Though Daniel couldn't see her, he didn't hear Zhu object.

"Generals," Sam announced from the computer, "I think this will work if General Hammond can get permission for a 302 to enter China's airspace."

"Easier said than done, Colonel."

Sam looked up from the screen. "Sir, their government already knows about the fighter-interceptors and the truth is — "

"Their butts are at risk as much ours." Jack scowled. "I get it, Carter. Do the math."

"Beijing has a military airstrip just outside the city. They're about 7,300 miles from here. At Mach 6, that'll take a bit less than two hours from Marble Point. I can fly out there, grab Huang while you take the other 302 and head directly for Petersen. I can meet you back at the SGC in," she ran another series of keystrokes, "another two hours. The trip from Beijing to Petersen is about 7,500 miles."

Jack folded his arms. "That leaves ten hours to go through the gate, grab the crystal, hop back in the 302s and fly back here before a whole bunch of C-4 goes off. What time is sunrise?"

"A little after twelve-noon," Lee said.

"Piece of cake except for one small change." Jack turned toward General Hammond. "Sir, I'd like to be the one to get Huang. I think I owe that much to his kid."

Hammond glanced over at the hole. "If you're willing to try it, then yes. There's a chopper waiting topside. I'll call the President and make arrangements."

With a nod toward Skaara, he headed toward the exit. "It's gonna be one heck of a phone call."

"Uh, General Hammond?" Jack raced after him. "Since we're short on time, can we request that Huang be waiting at the airstrip? I'm not exactly keen on the idea of going into a prison to sign him out."

"Sam said it was a psychiatric hospital," Daniel pointed out.

Jack's eyes darkened. "Same difference when it comes to the Chinese. Trust me."

"O'Neill," Teal'c said. "As there are only two seats on each Interceptor, I will remain here." Without waiting for an answer, he climbed back down.

Jack shared a look with Daniel, who could only shrug.

"Allow Teal'c this action, O'Neill," Skaara offered. "Daniel's path is with you and Colonel Carter."

"You'll take care of her after," Jack said. "Right?"

"Of course."

"And you'll take care of yourself? No more sticking your nose where it doesn't belong?"

Skaara grinned, reminding Daniel of how young he'd been before his untimely death.

"Daniel. O'Neill." Those soft Ls again.

Daniel's chest ached, thinking back on everything he'd lost in the fight against the Goa'uld. Skaara. Kasuf. Sha're.

Skaara met his gaze, his grin softening into a knowing smile. "So much lies ahead for you both. Find peace in your work, Daniel. Find peace in your life, O'Neill. Let go of the past and live for the future."

With that, Skaara faded away.

Daniel stared into the space where he'd been, wishing Skaara could have stayed longer. There were so many questions needing answers. Why had Oma sent him? How was Sha're's son, Shifu?

Why had he turned his back on ascension?

"Daniel?"

"Yeah, Jack."

"Let's go save the world."

ANCIENT OUTPOST, ANTARCTICA
18 AUG 04/2310 HRS MCMURDO STATION
18 AUG 04/0610 HRS STARGATE COMMAND

Teal'c sank down on the platform, eyeing the surrounding force field. Ambassador Zhu sat across, focused on her child. A blanket had been draped below the charred crystal protruding from Weiyan Shi's belly, covering her legs against the biting cold of the outpost.

While Teal'c's heart was glad that he and his team had wrested free of the platform's grip, Weiyan Shi was not as fortunate.

Was it ill fate, he wondered, or should he consider the path she would soon encounter to be fortunate?

"I have read Stargate Command's files concerning Dr. Jackson's ascension," Zhu whispered. "Will my daughter...? Will she — ?"

The woman broke down in a fit of tears. Teal'c waited patiently, knowing that the ambassador must summon the strength on her own to face what would happen next.

When her sobs subsided, Teal'c explained what he knew of both the legend, and the reality, of ascension. "Before learning the truth, I knew only of the tale told amongst my people."

Zhu returned to stroking her daughter's sweat-plastered hair. "If my former husband's origins are to be believed, all legends begin in truth. Tell me of the Jaffa's beliefs."

Teal'c bowed his head in assent. "When a Jaffa could no longer carry a prim'tah, they would make their journey to Kheb. There the Ko'lak would learn the path through the darkness, into the next life."

"I have read your file as well, Teal'c. If you no longer carry a symbiote, you cannot follow the ways of your people."

"On the contrary, Ambassador Zhu. When SG-1 first visited Kheb, an ascended being told my friend and mentor that only by losing our symbiotes would the path to ascension ever be possible."

"The tretonin." Zhu grunted. "Thanks to alliances made through Earth's Stargate, you might one day achieve what my daughter must now embrace."

Someone coughed from above. Major Davis appeared at the hole's edge.

"The F-302s are in the air," he reported. "Colonel Carter and Dr. Jackson are on their way to Petersen. General O'Neill's on track to land in Beijing in about 90 minutes."

"He will see my father," Weiyan Shi whispered. "Please, tell General O'Neill — "

A thunderous rumble shook beneath them. Another quake. Snow and ice tumbled down from the ceiling and though Teal'c did his best to shield Weiyan Shi, several small chunks of ice smashed against her legs. As the shaking subsided, he took note of the fact that her wound had cauterized around the crystal. Nonetheless, the pain would be significant and yet, she made no complaints. He was not certain whether this was a sign of bravery or the possibility that she could not feel her body.

In either case, Teal'c knew that the tremors would not stop. Not until O'Neill had returned with the crystal from Kunlun and shut down the device. A pang of guilt washed over him and he wondered once more at the possible hand he'd had in their current fate.

No. There was no way to truly know. What mattered now was Earth's future. He must face the present and do what was needed.

Weiyan's ravaged features told him how he must proceed. He stood up. "Major Davis?"

The major appeared again by the ladder. "What do you need, Teal'c?"

"An injection to blunt Weiyan Shi's pain. And another blanket."

A moment later, Major Davis returned and handed him a syringe and a plastic-wrapped blanket. Teal'c administered the shot to Weiyan's arm. He then tore the plastic off the blanket and shook it free.

Major Davis took the discarded plastic. "You've seen ascension happen twice, haven't you?"

"I have. First when Daniel Jackson departed, and then Skaara. The event is," he glanced down at Ambassador Zhu and frowned, "disquieting, but significant."

Balling up the plastic, Major Davis then glanced over his shoulder. "Airmen, withdraw to the outside chamber."

Muffled sounds of acknowledgement reached Teal'c's ears. He thanked Major Davis and unfurled the wool blanket and spread it over Weiyan's shoulders. She whimpered.

When Ambassador Zhu made no move to attend to Weiyan Shi, Teal'c slid over and cradled her head in his lap. "Your sacrifice will not be forgotten, Weiyan Shi."

She opened her eyes. "Please hold me."

"I will stay with you as long as you like." Ambassador Zhu crawled around the crystal and joined them at the platform's edge.

"Mother," Weiyan Shi cried out. "I am sorry I failed you."

"You have failed no one, child."

A gasp escaped Weiyan Shi and she squeezed her eyes shut.

Teal'c had seen and felt much physical pain in his hundred and six years of age, and yet watching Weiyan Shi, watching this young woman barely out of childhood, unsettled him greatly.

In her weakened state, her groans had become barely whispers. He knew she would not ascend until she was truly ready to do so, but surely, there must be something he could do to ease her final moments. Something beyond Tau'ri painkillers.

He began to sing. "*Kel ma kree. Sha'shan. Kel na t'ai. Or'intani. Kel han'dai.*"

Weiyan Shi's eyes fluttered open. "A song for Jaffa?"

"Indeed. My wife Drey'auc would sing this to our son Rya'c when he was very young."

"Rya'c." Pain shadowed across her face and she paused until it passed. "Will you see him soon?"

"When the time allows, yes." Rya'c had joined Master Bra'tac in assisting Ishta and the Hak'tyl women Jaffa in coordinating Fifth Column efforts. It had been many weeks since father and son had met. Teal'c silently promised to visit soon.

"Is he a warrior?" Weiyan Shi asked. "Like you?"

"Youth still has him in its grip, but yes, Rya'c is and shall always be a warrior." He gazed down upon her worried brow. "Just as you shall always be, Weiyan Shi."

With that, the pain left her and she fell asleep.

"This ascension," Ambassador Zhu whispered, "is it possible that my daughter might still exist, once she has died?"

"Believe it." Teal'c glanced at her. "You must. She sacrificed herself so that we might save your planet. That sacrifice must be remembered, not denied."

Ambassador Zhu brushed a wisp of hair from her daughter's forehead. "I will not dishonor her memory." She returned Teal'c's gaze. "Nor do I any longer believe that others who have served the program are fools."

"You remember our discussion."

"How can I forget your ardent speech about duty and honor?" She turned her gaze upwards toward the Ancient Weapons Chair. "Upon my return to China, I will devote my energies to convincing the upper leadership of the need to leave the chair here in Antarctica. Under the care of those who serve so that Earth may be protected."

"You honor your child's death," he said, relieved that some good would come of this day.

"What I wish to do, Teal'c, is honor her life."

CHAPTER TWENTY-TWO

20° 53' 10"N ~ 156° 40' 29W
INTERNATIONAL AIRSPACE
19 AUG 04/0105 HRS MCMURDO STATION
19 AUG 04/0805 HRS STARGATE COMMAND

ONCE THE bird was out over international waters with a half moon as its only companion, Jack loosened his grip on the flight stick and flipped his radio back on. While he supposedly had a secure channel, betting against Chinese Intelligence wasn't exactly a gamble he felt like taking.

"Mission Command," he said into the radio, "this is *Outpost One*. Package received. En route to disembarkation point."

A few hisses. A couple of pops. Then Davis' voice broke though. "*Roger, Outpost One. Standby for General Hammond.*"

"Standing by." Well, sort of. At their current altitude of 20 miles above sea level, Mach 6 meant flying along at... He hated math. Checking his airspeed gauge, he noted a cozy little 4,102 mph.

"*This is Hammond. Report,* Outpost One."

"Good to hear your voice, sir. I estimate arrival time in T minus 90 minutes and counting."

"*I trust you had no troubles obtaining your objective, General?*"

"Nothing I couldn't handle, sir." Jack winced. It was a bit of lie, but not by much. Landing at the Beijing airstrip had been a piece of cake. The thing rode the runway like a Cadillac. Getting out of the F-302 had been another matter entirely. Especially when several hundred of the Chinese Republic's million-man army and a slew of high-powered spotlights greeted him. Communism at its finest. All nicely lined up, their rifles trained right on him. Chairman Mao would've been proud.

An armored tank rolled up to the bird. The top hatch popped open and a middle-aged man poked his head out. "*Zhōng zhǐ*!"

The Chinese dropped their weapons. The guy looked familiar, but he knew it wasn't Huang. Wrong face shape and besides, the guy wouldn't go from being in a mental hospital to leading a battalion.

Dressed in a dark blue suit, the man climbed down from the tank and motioned for the two nearest soldiers to climb on up. As they did, another man came up the hatch. Though his hair had been shorn off to a shiny buzz cut, they'd let him keep the goatee, though it'd gone completely gray. It was a longer, more straggly mess than the last time Jack had seen him.

The two soldiers lifted Huang out of the hatch and that's when Jack noticed the cuffs on his wrists and ankles. He hated to admit it, but those restraints gave him peace of mind.

The soldiers lowered Huang to the tarmac. Besides a dark smudge on the guy's forehead, he seemed relatively cleaned up though Jack suspected it'd been a while since his last meal. He wore loose-fitting black pants and a matching collarless shirt.

Another soldier stuck his head out of the hatch and threw down a heavy winter parka. A soldier picked it up and shoved it over Huang's shoulders.

Obviously, they weren't fully informed on where Jack intended to take Huang. That was fine by him.

At the other man's lead, the soldiers escorted him toward the F-302. Between the soldier's open glares, the shuffling of Huang's cuffed ankles, and the oppressively hot Beijing weather, Jack had to muster up every discipline he knew not to shout at their idiocy. If they thought Huang was going anywhere near Antarctica, they were wrong. Dead wrong.

As they stopped a few feet short of the gantry, Jack took a long hard look at Huang's face. The man had single-handedly arranged for SG-1's demise while in Yu's clutches. Though he wasn't a Goa'uld, and not even a Jaffa, he was still the enemy.

And those pitch-black pupils edged with green flecks still

gave him an unearthly look.

"General O'Neill," said the leader, "your photos do not do you justice."

"Okay, and who might you be?"

The man bowed. "I am the people's true ambassador to the Security Council."

Jack snapped his fingers. "You're Ambassador Chen. I've seen your photo."

"And?"

What did the guy want, a compliment? Jack hated diplomacy. "Kinda hot for a winter coat, don't you think?" He jerked a thumb at Huang's parka.

Chen shrugged. "It is barely above room temperature."

"Yeah, right." And the sky's not blue, it's green. Jack just loved playing footsies with the Chinese.

He gestured at Huang. "If your goons wanna get Huang stowed on board, I'll be on my way."

"In a moment." Chen strode up to the F-302 and placed a hand on its belly. "We have long awaited — "

A low rumble followed by a good round of ground shaking stopped the ambassador from asking any questions about the fighter-interceptor. He flung out a few clipped orders to his men, they dragged Huang up the gantry and into the cockpit, and Jack hustled them down before they got a closer look.

After strapping in his silent passenger, Jack hopped in. Another trembler shook the tarmac, sending rippled waves of heat across the asphalt. With a quick salute to Chen — and no complaints — he got the bird out of there as fast as possible.

A half-hour out of Beijing, he finally let himself breathe, hence the radio-call to Hammond. "Ah, General? We felt a couple of quakes in Beijing before I left. How bad is it elsewhere?"

"Bad enough, Jack. Sydney's been hit, but we expected that. Australia's less than five thousand miles off the coast. However, there's been reports as far away as Russia."

Jack checked his watch. It was a cheap little Timex, courtesy of Airman Gerling. "We've got eleven hours left by my count."

"Affirmative. I've paused the explosives countdown to give you, Colonel Carter, and Dr. Jackson every spare moment I can, just—" The radio fell back into a bed of pops and hisses.

"General?"

"Hurry back, son."

"Uh, roger that." Jack signed off. He knew what Hammond really meant to say was, 'Don't screw it up.'

Jack could do that. Couldn't he? Even if he had to stick his hands inside a veritable funhouse of Ancient technology and let the machinery have a poke around his head? Sure, he'd do whatever it took to save Earth.

Screw Sun Tzu and his little book of war. Fame and disgrace had nothing to do with it.

An alarm chimed. He glanced down at a blinking red light over the proximity sensor. Probably a commercial plane heading toward Japan.

Switching his grip on the flight stick, he adjusted the navigational computer. Normally, the aft seat co-pilot charted their course, but that seat was taken so he'd slaved the nav-com up front.

He punched in a slightly tweaked setting. The computer beeped and a fat red error blinked across the screen. "Damn computer. Too many things to do."

"Lamentations will only hinder deeds." The clink of metal cuffs from the aft seat reminded Jack he had a passenger.

"So you do speak." He re-entered his course correction and the nav-com display switched from red to green.

"When words are necessary," Huang said.

"And was it necessary to get me and my team almost killed last year?"

Huang sighed. "My Lord Yu believed it so, yes. I did not expect you to survive the encounter."

"Surprise!" Jack snorted. "Your slimy, snake-in-the-head, boom-box leader didn't want to kill us. He just wanted see if we could kick Anubis's butt once and for all."

"Anubis?"

"Yeah, remember him? Cranky. Half-Goa'uld, half something else?" Jack held back on saying what. If Yu's spy didn't know Anubis had been half-ascended, there wasn't any reason to tell him. "Wore a long robe with a hood. Looked like something out of *Star Wars*."

"Wore," Huang repeated. "He no longer survives?"

Jack grinned. "That's right. We kicked his smarmy little ass. No thanks to your fearless leader, I might add."

The memory of how they'd stopped Anubis made the grin slide right off — sitting in that Ancient weapons chair, his brain so stuffed with data that he couldn't breathe. And this time… What was it Skaara had said?

Operating the chair would be a cakewalk compared to retrieving the crystal.

Oh, joy.

The F-302 sliced through a puffy bank of clouds backlit by the moon. Jack checked their position. Several hundred miles off the island of Maui.

"How is he?" Huang said.

"Anubis? Dead."

The cuffs clinked again. "No, I mean my master. Lord Yu."

"Your master." Jack twisted around in his seat harness and pushed back his helmet to get a good look at Huang. "I don't think he's missing you very much."

Huang averted his eyes. "I am a Dragon Guard."

"You're a clone. I've met your replacement." Jack settled back into his chair. "Actually, I met several generations. How does it feel, knowing you're just another in a long assembly line of carbon copies, not really meaning much in the grand scheme of things?"

"You would not understand," Huang whispered, his voice barely heard above the whine of the aero spike engines.

"Understand what?" *That every time I lose a man and write*

up another casualty report, that I feel like I'm chipping away at a piece of myself?

"How do you know about the Dragon clones?"

Maui went by. He altered course again, deciding to take the F-302 over Alaska and then straight down into Colorado.

"Yu told us all about them. In fact, when he did, your name never came up."

"By 'us' you mean SG-1? And yet, where is your team now? How is it you came for me alone?" Again, the cuffs clinked.

When Jack didn't answer, Huang added, "I know what it means to be alone, O'Neill."

"In case you haven't noticed, there are only two seats. Didn't Yu teach you how to count?" He tweaked the flight stick, pulling them up another five miles to avoid any commercial flights. "Besides, I like being alone."

"'It is impossible for the brave to advance alone, or for the cowardly to retreat alone.'" Clink. "So says Sun Tzu."

Jack rolled his eyes. "I know the quote. If it matters any, your kid spouted off all sorts of *Art of War* crap during our, uh..." Shared illusion? Yeah, that experience didn't need explaining.

"Weiyan. You saw my daughter?"

Off to the east, Jack saw the first hints of sunrise. Pink and yellow striated clouds hovered above the horizon. A reminder of what waited for them in Antarctica if they got back in time. "Where do you get off, leaving a kid like that? People like you should never be allowed to have children."

"I realize this. In ways you would never understand."

"Weiyan's a brave girl, Huang. Despite you abandoning her."

"I see."

"You should," Jack said, pointing out the starboard window. "You have the best seat in the house."

He nudged the nose north. At their current speed, they'd be over Alaska in about ten minutes.

"Tell me of my daughter, O'Neill."

And there it was, the real reason Jack had opted to do this

milk run solo. For Weiyan's sake.

"No thanks to you, she's got backbone." Jack told him everything. Including the fact that his daughter lay dying in a cold, frozen wasteland.

And if Huang didn't do his part in retrieving that crystal, pretty much everyone would follow soon after.

STARGATE COMMAND
19 AUG 04/0330 HRS MCMURDO STATION
19 AUG 04/1030 HRS STARGATE COMMAND

Daniel hurried out of the elevator and onto level 28, his backpack slung over one shoulder. He'd had two hours to nap, shower, dress in camo gear, and sling back enough coffee to keep him going for whatever came next. That, and ten minutes to stuff a few items in a pack. Not everything he packed was essential, but he'd had a last minute inspiration thanks to a side trip to the archives and a quick talk with Dr. Kevin Hopkins.

Daniel ran toward the armory, the precious item stowed in his pack. Huang. He was going to meet a direct descendent of Sun Tzu. If circumstances weren't so extreme, he'd have a million questions.

He knew he should trust Skaara, but he was half-terrified. The plan relied too heavily on Huang and Jack working together. Daniel just couldn't see that being a successful partnership.

At the armory, he grabbed a pistol and was halfway to the gate room, when the master-of-arms chased him down. "General's orders, sir." He handed Daniel a P90 along with a sling and two magazines.

Daniel shoved the magazines in a pant-leg pocket and took the rifle. He waved off the sling. He hated the idea of being strapped to a rifle. Shifting his pack to his left shoulder, he headed toward the blast doors, the P90 cradled in his right arm. The airman on guard slid his security card through the lock. The doors opened, revealing Sam over by the gantry, a P90 dangling from her chest.

Her wet bangs told him she'd rushed through their two-hour window just as fast. The real Graham Simmons — or at least, he hoped it was the real one — handed her a scanner. Daniel wondered if she'd told the lieutenant about Skaara's impersonation. Probably wasn't a good idea, all things considered.

Especially if it really wasn't the lieutenant. Could Skaara still be around, keeping an eye on things?

There was only one way to find out. Daniel headed over to join them. "Graham, how are you?"

The lieutenant grinned. "I'm doing pretty good, sir. You?"

It sounded like Graham.

"Good, good." Daniel looked closely at his face, his clothes, his hair —

"That'll be all, lieutenant." Sam grabbed Daniel's elbow and pulled him to the far wall. "That isn't Skaara."

"You're sure?"

"Too many contractions." She punched a few buttons on her scanner. A yellow light flashed on the display. She tapped in another series on the keypad and the light winked out.

"Sam?"

She flipped the scanner over. "Yeah?"

"Any word from the outpost?"

Sliding the battery case open and shut, she turned the scanner right side up and thumbed the 'on' button.

"Got your eyes and ears?" he asked, only half-teasingly.

"What?" She looked up from the scanner. "Oh, sorry, Daniel." She stuffed it inside her tactical vest pocket with a frown. "I spoke to General Hammond a few minutes ago."

"And?"

"Weiyan's still alive, but the general doesn't seem to think she'll last much longer. Teal'c's with her. Based on," she hesitated, "past observations, she won't ascend until she's ready to, um… What I mean to say, is…"

"Die?" He understood Sam's discomfort. While he couldn't

quite remember the last moments before his own ascension, he'd regained painful memories of the radiation sickness. Flashes of dialogue with Oma, with Sam, with Teal'c. His last moments with Jack.

I think I can do more this way. Please, Jack. Tell Jacob to stop.

Had he done more? Had he made a difference?

As if summoned by the memory, Jack strode in, dressed in camo, P90 hanging from his sling. Sergeant Walter Harriman followed him, waving a clipboard.

"General," said Walter, "the president left orders not to initiate evacuation to the Alpha Site. If I do this — "

"Last I checked, the president doesn't have a crystal ball." Jack yanked the clipboard from Walter, signed it, and handed it back. "Tell him I appreciate the vote of confidence, but I'd rather have him fire my ass afterwards than take any chances."

"But — "

"Come on, Walter." Jack tugged his cap's bill. "Nothing beats an old-fashioned 'I told you so.' On the other hand — "

"If President Hayes is wrong," Walter recited, "Earth will crack open."

"Like an egg." Jack turned toward Daniel and Sam. "You two ready to go?"

"Yes, sir." Sam glanced up at the operations room. "We removed the lock on P3Y-702 from the dialing computer."

"Where's Huang?" Daniel slipped his P90 between his legs so he could fasten his pack to his vest-back.

"The doc's making sure he eats a good meal before we leave." Jack jerked his chin toward Daniel's pack. "We're only going for four, maybe five hours. Whatcha got in there?"

"Nothing." Daniel kept his face impassive.

Jack waggled a finger at him. "You brought a copy of *The Art of War* for the guy to sign."

"Funny." Daniel picked up his P90. "Is this necessary?"

"Yes."

"I don't think Yu's going to bother us."

"You know the cliché, Daniel. Better safe than sorry." He turned toward Walter. "Dial it up, Sergeant."

"Yes, sir."

The blast doors slid open once again. Huang, his wrists and ankles in cuffs, shuffled into the room with SG-13 right behind him — everyone except Balinsky. They were also dressed up in camo gear, including Kevin Hopkins who'd been drafted in the past twenty-four hours to be their new team member. Unlike the others, Kevin didn't have a weapon out and drawn on the prisoner.

Colonel Dave Dixon kept his M-16 trained on Huang as they made their way over to the gantry. Though Daniel had never met Huang before, he couldn't help but notice how worn out the man seemed. Gaunt, hollow-eyed, his thin beard white and ragged. He didn't see any resemblance to Yu's current First Prime, Oshu until the man lifted his chin and stared up at the Stargate. Then the green flecks in Huang's dark eyes matched Oshu's exactly.

The gate began to spin. Steam rose from the bulky red capacitors. The inner ring ground along its track, the sound echoing against the gate room's cement walls. The ring slowed, stopped, and the first chevron lit up.

"*Chevron One encoded*," Walter announced over the PA system.

The ring circled back around. A half-sob escaped Huang's throat. "I never stopped believing."

"Quiet down," barked Dixon.

Daniel cringed. "Jack, is it really necessary to treat the man this way?"

"*Chevron Two encoded*."

"I never stopped hoping," Huang whispered.

Dixon raised his M16 directly into the old man's face. "I said, quiet down."

Daniel shared an uncomfortable look with Kevin.

Huang stepped around Dixon's rifle. "So long. I have — "

Ka-chink.

"Where's Siler?" asked Jack.

"I'm here!" Siler ran in, backpack in hand. He buckled it onto Jack's vest. "Sorry, sir. Took a moment to find — "

"I've got it from here." Jack handed his pack to Sam and turned around. Keeping her face neutral, she secured it to his vest-back.

"*Chevron Six encoded.*"

Startled, Daniel looked up at the gate. The first six chevrons were lit up. He'd been so caught up in the tension in the room, he hadn't heard Walter announce Chevrons four and five. A half-second later, the seventh one locked into place.

"*Chevron Seven locked.*"

The Stargate's brilliant blue kawoosh erupted and then settled into place. Huang's mouth dropped open, he took a step back, right into the butt end of Dixon's rifle.

"Don't move until we tell you." Dixon looked at Jack. "We're ready, General."

"Thank you, Colonel." Jack pushed down on his ball cap. "We'll take it from here."

"You're joking, right?" Dixon glanced at Huang and then back at Jack. "This guy's shenanigans almost got a whole bunch of our people killed. Since when do we play buddies with the enemy?"

The gate room shuddered, sending ripples across the event horizon. The quake didn't last long, but it was enough to make Dixon's eyes widen.

"Since we started monkeying with gadgets way out of our league." Jack raised two fingers toward gate. "Move out, SG-1."

"Daniel!" Kevin Hopkins called.

Daniel stopped and turned back toward his old roommate.

"Good luck," he mouthed.

With a nod of thanks, Daniel stepped through the gate, hoping that luck would be enough.

P3Y-702 AKA KUNLUN/ELYSIUM PEDION
19 AUG 04/0405 HRS MCMURDO STATION
19 AUG 04/1105 HRS STARGATE COMMAND

Sunrise greeted Daniel as he followed Sam through the gate and out the other side. A rose-colored wash of light blanketed the valley below, the planet's usual heat camouflaged by an early morning breeze. He climbed down the steps, scanning the valley for any signs of life, be it Lord Yu, his Jaffa, or even Skaara.

A sense of déjà vu teased him, and for a moment he wondered if they were still in the device's throes. Then he caught sight of the SGC's abandoned dig from a year ago. White flags flapped in the breeze, their ends attached to ropes surrounding the various trenches dug by team archaeologists. A few trees wilted in the barren dirt. On a hill off to the left loomed the three-story tall Zhenmushou statue.

At the valley's other end stood the chamber. Its high brown walls almost colorless against the rising sun.

A thwap from the event horizon. Jack stepped through, his hand on Huang's elbow. It didn't stop the old man from dropping to his knees in awe.

Jack gently pulled him back up. "Carter, my lower pocket."

"He's not going to be much help to us cuffed," Daniel said.

"I hope you're right," Jack said as Sam slipped behind him.

Huang's eyes never left the Zhenmushou. "My ancestors… I must pay my respects."

"Not going to happen," Jack said.

Huang dropped his head. "I understand."

"I hope that you do."

"Come on, Jack. I think the three of us are enough to keep him from causing any — "

"Got it, sir." Sam handed a key ring over to Jack.

He bent down and unlocked Huang's leg cuffs, then his hands. The cuffs clanked against the gate's stone platform as they dropped. "Happy now?"

By the time the sun had risen above the horizon, they'd

climbed down the hill and headed toward the chamber. Meter-high obelisks lined the half-dirt, half-paved walkway, their Ancient letters worn away by age. Daniel hoped one day to come back, to study the obelisks and figure out if they matched the ones he'd seen in their vision, dream, or whatever it had been. Though Skaara had shared what had caused the plague, he'd left out specifics. Daniel still had a lot of questions.

Huang never took his eyes off the *Zhenmushou* as they passed beneath its shadow. He grinned broadly until he noticed the four excavated graves beneath the statue's base. The grin dropped away.

"I would ask why you chose to disturb my ancestors' remains, but the answer would have little meaning." He looked at Daniel, his eyes as dark and hard as the paved stone beneath their feet.

Jack kept up the pace with Sam at his side. They had at least another ten minute hike ahead of them and by Daniel's watch, that left them less than four hours to open the chamber, retrieve the crystal, and gate back to the waiting F-302s to go back to Antarctica.

Daniel glanced at Huang. "If your ancestors were originally from Earth, how did you get back there, by ship?"

"Through the Chappa'ai, of course." The old man gazed again at the statue. "The one in Antarctica. It was long ago, fifty years in fact. I fought past many Serpent Guards to reach it — they fought bravely, their marksmanship superlative. Particularly one, I remember — a tall, dark powerful Jaffa. I escaped, following two others to your land."

"Tall and dark, you say?" commented Jack. "Carter, sound like anyone we know?"

"I doubt it, sir. If Teal'c knew about the Antarctic gate, wouldn't he have told us when he joined SG-1?" Sam looked at Huang over her shoulder. "A few years ago, we found two Jaffa frozen in the ice by the gate. We'd always assumed they'd been there for two, maybe three hundred years."

Huang's eyes took on a distant look. "Ice and snow can age

a man in ways you cannot understand."

"And from Antarctica to China?" Daniel asked.

"At first, I was guided by a strange light. Golden-white."

"Daniel, could that've been Skaara?"

"Possibly." Though Skaara had never really explained how he'd managed to skip back and forth in time, it certainly sounded like him.

"Friend or foe, I cannot say."

Sam slowed down to match Huang's pace. "There wasn't anyone else down in Antarctica fifty years ago. How did you survive?"

"Seal meat."

"Okay, that's just gross." Jack shook his head. "Those creatures deserved better."

"I am not proud of what I did, O'Neill. I did it to survive."

"Still doesn't explain how the hell you got out of there."

"Sir Edmund Hilary found me." Huang went on to detail how he'd met the explorer. He had just begun to share how he rose through the ranks during China's Cultural Revolution when they arrived at the chamber. He froze. "I cannot. It is *bù zhŭn xŭ*."

"You're going in," said Jack. "Whether you like it or not." He pointed at the transporter rings. "Keep a good five feet away. Daniel, if you don't mind?"

Approaching the wall, Daniel took in the intricately carved stone surface covered in Chinese pictograms and Ancient glyphs. A circle with a dash in the middle represented the sun. Beside it, a half circle with a vertical line meant the moon. Three apexes crowded together upside down — like a series of mountains.

"Kunlun," whispered Huang. "Behind those walls lies death."

"Not according to our mutual friend," Jack said.

Daniel found the crack running down the wall's midsection. He tried pushing on either side, but the doors wouldn't give.

Sam took a turn with no luck. "Sir, I'm willing to bet the door is keyed to the ATA gene."

Jack motioned for Huang to join him at the wall.

Wild-eyed, the old man backed away. "No, no!"

"You can," Jack said, stomping toward him, "and you're gonna. Think of it this way. Yu would want you to save Earth, wouldn't he? That overdressed snake likes Earth."

"I cannot." Huang trembled so violently that Daniel became worried that he might have a heart attack.

Then he remembered the item in his pack. "Wait a minute." Opening it, he pulled out the three-pronged bronze wine vessel unearthed near the chamber just a year ago.

"I have something to show you. Something that I'm pretty sure comes from Earth, but… Well, take a look."

Huang's shaking subsided, but he still didn't move.

Holding the cup by its fluted bowl, Daniel showed it to him. "We found it right over there," he pointed toward the dig area. "There's writing inside. Xian. That's one of China's dynasties, from before — "

"It is the language we are first taught as children." Huang choked back a half-sob and took the cup. "You found this here?"

"Daniel…"

"Jack, give him a moment. It's a lot to take in."

Huang traced the long thin lines with his forefinger.

"Do you know what it says?"

"It is a hero's cup. It says…" Huang's lip quivered. "It is a quote of Sun Tzu. From before *The Art of War.*" He dropped the cup to his side, his shoulders shaking. "It says, 'Great is the hero who would die for their country, but would much rather live.'"

Huang dropped to his knees and held out the cup.

"You keep it." Daniel waved him off. He re-zipped his pack and joined Jack by the wall. "He'll cooperate. Just go easy."

Jack tilted his head back, looking up toward the Ancient writing at the top of the wall. "Nice quote, by the way."

"Sun Tzu at his finest."

"If you say so." Jack slapped the wall. "How about we get this thing open? Then maybe everyone can get back to living." He turned toward Huang. "What the hell?"

The old man, still kneeling on the ground, lowered a dirt-covered finger. Smeared on his forehead was a roughly drawn replica of Lord Yu's sigil.

"I am ready." Huang stood up.

"I don't think so," Jack replied.

"You do not approve of my *wénshēn*?"

"Not really."

"Then I pity you." Huang strode to the wall, his step lighter, a faint smile on his lips.

In a sense, Daniel mused, the old man had re-found his purpose.

Sam checked her watch. "Oh-five-hundred outpost time, sir."

Jack stared at Huang. "How much time does that leave us?"

"Three hours to get to the gate and make our window."

"Jack, just..." Daniel stepped up to his other side and whispered, "Whatever it takes, right? We need to get this chamber open, get the crystal, and — "

"I know what we need to do, Daniel. Thank you." He rubbed his palms together and then raised them in front of the wall. "You ready, Huang?"

The old man bowed. "I have always been, O'Neill. Are you?"

"On the count of three then." Jack gave the countdown.

The two men pressed their palms against the wall.

A low rumble. Dirt showered down.

And then, the wall opened.

ANCIENT OUTPOST, ANTARCTICA
19 AUG 04/0530 HRS MCMURDO STATION
19 AUG 04/1230 HRS STARGATE COMMAND

Paul Davis found General Hammond by the archway, staring at the stasis unit. "Sir, there's no reason you need to stay.

When Gerling gets back from McMurdo, she could take — "

"Major, as much as I appreciate your concern, I'm staying." Hammond raised a hand over the stasis controls. "I think you'll find Dr. Lee determined to see this out as well."

"Yes, sir." He wasn't surprised.

"These Ancients," the general dropped his hand to his side, "the technologies they built. Takes a pretty wild imagination to come up with ways to reform a planet, keep a man frozen in time."

"Don't forget the Stargate, sir."

Hammond chuckled. "How could I?"

They walked back into the weapons chair room. Dr. Lee was tinkering with one of the Mark IIs. Low murmurs came from the hole — Teal'c and Ambassador Zhu. Paul followed Hammond over to the ladder. Down below, Teal'c cradled Weiyan's head in his lap. The ambassador sat beside him, stroking her daughter's hair. An IV bag ran to the young woman's pale arm, hopefully providing her some small measure of pain relief.

All because of the Ancients and their wild imaginations.

For a moment, Paul wondered if it had all been worth it.

"How's she doing, Teal'c?" Hammond whispered.

He looked up. "She is sleeping, General Hammond. The fight to live remains strong. Any word from O'Neill and the others?"

"They've gated to P3Y-702," Hammond replied. "No other word yet, but we're hopeful they'll meet with success."

Teal'c laid his hand back down on the blanket. "Skaara assured us they will succeed. Have faith, General Hammond."

"Ambassador Zhu, is there anything we can do?"

"Nothing." The ambassador managed a brief smile. The effort lasted less than a second.

Hammond headed for the rear of the platform. Paul followed him and they sank down on the one edge still connected to the main section of floor.

"Paul, I meant what I said earlier." Hammond turned toward

him. "We get through this and it's time for a promotion. More than time. Put in the paperwork, son. You've earned it."

Another rumble ran through the room. Paul glanced over at Lee. The scientist squinted at his monitor, ignoring the sound. The tremors died off.

"If we get through this," Paul said.

"Sure," the general said. "Think of it as a reprieve. No more trips to the frozen south. No more last minute dashes to Colorado Springs. Just a warm desk in D.C. at Homeworld Security." He shrugged. "Of course, it snows in Washington, too, but not always."

"Sir," Paul swept a stray chunk of ice off the weapons platform. "What if I didn't take a promotion? I know the Air Force requires promotion or retirement by a certain point."

"Homeworld Security's a special situation." General Hammond shrugged. "Don't you want the promotion?"

"What about the SGC, sir?"

"We can find another liaison, Lt. Colonel Paul Davis."

Another liaison. "Has a nice ring, sir."

"General Hammond!" Gerling ran in, her parka dusted with snow. "I've brought provisions from McMurdo, sir. Not much, but some coffee, water, some Power Bars to eat."

"Let's get some coffee for the ambassador and some water for Teal'c. They must be hungry, too."

"Yes, sir." She unzipped her parka and pulled out a folded-up piece of paper. "McMurdo's latest casualty reports. I thought you might want to see them."

Hammond unfolded the report. As he scanned it, his face stilled. He handed the paper to Paul and closed his eyes.

Paul held off reading it. "Bad, sir?"

The general stood up. "Bad enough. Dr. Lee? Care to join me for some well-earned, though probably terrible, coffee?"

Lee raised his head from the monitor. "Did I hear something about food?"

"Power Bars, if you'll have them." Hammond strode out,

tailed closely by Dr. Lee and Lt. Gerling.

Paul read the report. Ten more deaths. All civilians. Building 155 had collapsed, but not before a few people had managed to chase everyone out of the facility. He scanned the list of names, not recognizing any until the last one.

He rose to his feet, not looking forward to sharing the name with Teal'c. Crossing over the plank, he looked down into the hole. Eyes rolled back, sweat dripping from her forehead, Weiyan turned her head back and forth.

"*Ni shi shui*?" she mumbled. "*Wo meng*?"

"What is she saying?" Paul asked.

Weiyan's mother wiped her eyes with her parka sleeve. "She says, 'Who are you? Am I dreaming?'"

"*Wo jiang xie zia wo bao fu*."

"I will release my burdens," Zhu translated. Her hand grabbed Teal'c's arm. "What does that mean? She is an innocent. What burdens could she possibly need to release?"

"You must ask her." Teal'c gently raised Weiyan's head and shifted over, allowing Zhu to take his position. "You are her mother. Tell her she is free to move on." He stood up. "Then, allow her to do so."

Zhu's eyes widened. "You are leaving?"

"Do not regret these moments, Ambassador Zhu." He began climbing the ladder. "I will not be far."

"*Wo jiang xie zia wo bao fu*," Weiyan whispered. "*Wo jiang bu hai pa*."

Zhu bent over her daughter and broke into sobs. Paul's throat constricted at the sight of a mother saying goodbye to her child. He backed off the plank, giving them more privacy.

Teal'c joined him by the back wall, purple bruises under his eyes told Paul all he needed to know. He hesitated, unsure if he should share the report from McMurdo. Weiyan had spoken about releasing her burdens. Telling Teal'c would just add to his, no doubt.

"You have something to tell me, Major Davis." Not a question, just a fact. Teal'c was like that. He could see the truth in anything.

Paul held up the report. "Another building collapsed at McMurdo. The personnel director, Hannah Presley… She died, Teal'c. Trying to save everyone else. I'm sorry. I know you two got along well."

"I see." He crossed the back of the weapons chair and climbed onto its platform, his back to Paul. "Her red-leaf tea…" He gripped the chair's headrest. "Major Davis, I believe I have a confession to make."

"A confession? What could you possibly need to confess?"

"I believe my actions many years ago have brought this disaster to pass."

Taken aback, Paul stepped around the chair to face Teal'c. "How could you have anything to do with — "

"Many years ago, while a lieutenant in Apophis's ranks, I, along with many others, escorted three Serpent Guards who had been tasked with a secret gate address. An address I was not permitted to know."

"What's that got to do with anything?"

The ground rumbled. Not as bad as before, but it served as a reminder that time was running out. Paul glanced at his watch. "Six more hours until sunrise."

"Major Davis, I believe that I witnessed Huang escape through the Stargate to Earth." Teal'c went on to describe how two men, disguised as Serpent Guards, attacked the Jaffa. One made it through. The other died.

Paul was stunned. It was a lot to take in. The idea that Teal'c might have known about the Antarctic Stargate from the start being just the tip of the proverbial iceberg.

Listening to the murmured sounds of a mother soothing her dying daughter, Paul surveyed the damage done to the outpost. It would take weeks for the Army Engineers to shore everything back up.

But it wouldn't bring back the dead. Or make it easier on the dying.

"Did you get a look at the body?" he asked Teal'c. "Or the Jaffa who got through?"

Teal'c frowned. "I did not."

"Was that the only time Apophis sent troops through to try and reach Earth?"

"No. Apophis made many attempts over the years. He did so for several planets, Earth was only one."

Paul scratched his chin. "And that was the only time enemy Jaffa infiltrated the Serpent Guard?"

"*Bie li wo. Bie li.*"

Whispered shushes emanated from the hole, followed soon after by humming. Paul listened for a moment, unable to make out the song. It was soothing. Quiet. A simple melody. He supposed it must be some sort of Chinese lullaby.

"Infiltrations were frequent." Teal'c let go of the chair. "Ra, Heru'er, Cronus. They all sent spies. Try to — "

"So you don't know," Paul said. "Look, Teal'c, you can't blame yourself for everything. That's not how it works."

"O'Neill would say as much." Teal'c bent his head. "Master Bra'tac would also agree."

"I'm with Master Bra'tac," Paul said, "and General O'Neill, of course."

Ambassador Zhu continued humming. The tune changed, a speedier tempo with almost a playful quality.

The corner of Teal'c's mouth tugged up in a faint smile. "When I was very young, my father told me the burden of wrongful blame was a falsehood to oneself. One that places distance between what we believe to be true and who we really are, setting our soul adrift from its true purpose."

"True purpose." Paul reflected on General Hammond's offer. It meant safety. Security. A pay raise.

If they survived the next few hours, he would be a fool to turn it down.

P3Y-702/KUNLUN/ELYSIUM PEDION
19 AUG 04/0615 HRS MCMURDO STATION
19 AUG 04/1315 HRS STARGATE COMMAND

Sam flicked on her P90's tactical flashlight, raking the light across the dark chamber. Silver curlicues were etched into the marble floor. A row of columns lined the far wall. "This looks familiar."

She stepped inside, aiming her light toward the center of the room. There it was, an exact duplicate of the Antarctica terraforming platform.

And the one in their shared vision.

Using her free hand, Sam pulled out her scanner.

Daniel joined her. "Anything?"

She thumbed on the display. The meter barely budged. "Less than 0.3 micro-Sieverts. Most likely, from background radiation." She turned toward the general and held up her scanner. "No considerable photonic radiation, sir."

"Good thing, too. I forgot my sunscreen," the general said from the doorway. "Come on, Huang. Get ahead of me."

Huang clasped Daniel's cup to his chest. "You do not trust me at your back, O'Neill?"

"Not really." The general waved his P90 toward the chamber's interior. "Step in, nice and easy."

As the two men entered the chamber a blue light flashed brightly and then settled down into a soft glow. A low pulse thrummed through the chamber, amplified by the marble floor and stone walls.

"Shouldn't that be glowing red?" Daniel pointed toward the control crystal.

"It's dormant." Sam approached, her scanner still unable to pick up any unusual radiation. Intact, the crystal was a darker red because it wasn't active, but it was right where it should be. Smack in the middle, with an empty bracket on either side.

"Dormant's a good thing, right?" General O'Neill came up on her left with Huang beside him. "We just need to grab the crystal, get back to the gate, and take this puppy to the outpost."

The general secured his P90 under his right arm and reached out a hand toward the crystal. He motioned for Huang to do the same. "On my count."

She glanced down at the meter. "Sir, wait!" The needle was off the scale.

General O'Neill pulled his hand away. "What?"

The needle dropped to normal levels. "That doesn't make sense, unless... General, Mr. Huang, I need the two of you to touch the crystal, but don't grab hold of it."

With a nod from General O'Neill, the two men touched the crystal with their fingertips. The needle pinged again.

"Don't make any moves." Adjusting the amplitude, she ran another scan. The needle stayed off the chart.

"How much longer, Colonel? Not that I'm complaining, but we're under a bit of a time crunch— "

The ground shook, a low rumble reverberating through the chamber.

"Sam," Daniel warned.

Suddenly, an ear-splitting crack resounded from somewhere outside.

"Hands off, hands off!" She pulled both men back from the platform. The tremor immediately stopped.

"Carter?" Dust trickled down on the general's head. He yanked off his ball cap. "Skaara didn't say anything about there being a problem."

"No, sir. He didn't." She held out the scanner. "I'm getting inconsistent readings. It's almost as if— "

"Forget that meter thing." The general checked his watch.

"I need to run more tests."

"We've got two-and-a-half hours left before we're outta time. Use your head and if that fails, use your gut."

"What's wrong?" Daniel peered down at the scanner and its near-zero reading.

She aimed the scanner at the crystal. Nothing. The needle didn't move. "Daniel, touch the crystal."

He did. Again, nothing happened.

Of course not. Neither she nor Daniel had the necessary gene.

The general had said use her head. Fine, but not without double-checking the theory forming in it. A theory no one was going to like.

"General, just one more time." She gestured for him to touch the control crystal. "Mr. Huang, you too."

As soon as they touched the crystal, the needle slammed to the meter's far right. The ground shook. More dust fell.

"Satisfied, Carter?" shouted General O'Neill over the noise.

She shoved the scanner in her vest pocket. What was the point? It was useless. "Sir, I'm pretty sure that the moment you pull the crystal, the device will initiate a sizeable eruption similar to what happened in Antarctica."

"How sizeable?"

She pointed toward the opened doorway. "Sizeable enough that, if the gate sits on a fault line, it'll get buried."

"Just like it did in our vision," Daniel said.

"We've come this far." General O'Neill shooed Huang from the platform. "There's gotta be something we can do."

"It doesn't matter to the device if the crystal is damaged — like on Earth — or pulled." She pointed at the silver lines on the floor. "In fact, here it could be worse because the sun's already up."

"I could dial the gate in advance," Daniel offered.

Sam shook her head. "That won't work. The gate's almost a mile off. The quake could be instantaneous. We need some sort of buffer. Something to at least temporarily block any stored up energy from reaching the platform."

"Like a dam," Huang said.

Sam raised an eyebrow at Huang's sudden contribution. He'd kept so silent since they'd entered the chamber. Still, he had a point. "A dam is exactly what we need. Something to hold back any energy from reaching the planet's tectonic plates long enough to gate out of here."

"With the crystal," Daniel added.

"Kinda like sticking a finger in a dike," the general said.

"You may be on to something, sir." She leaned over the platform and examined the two empty brackets. Each one was about five inches long, maybe an inch wide. She eyeballed the bracket beneath the control crystal. It was both longer and wider. "Not a finger, a hand."

"What do you have in mind?"

"The general figured it out, really." She backed away from the platform. "We need a finger in the dike, or in this case, a hand. Something to trick the bracket into thinking there's still a crystal attached."

"Would a jacket work?" Daniel started to unbuckle his vest, but Sam stopped him.

"It needs to be carbon-based," she said. "Like the crystal."

"Or a diamond," Daniel said. "That's carbon-based, right?"

General O'Neill snorted. "Oh, sure. Let's just run back to the SGC and see if Siler's got one lying around."

"Actually, sir, there's one other option for a carbon-based form." She retrieved her scanner and ran it over her hand. "Us."

The needle wobbled, then settled back to normal. "On the quantum level," she explained, "we're made up of tiny particles of light, and these particles of light have an energy frequency. One that could block the emissions long enough for everyone else to gate out with the crystal."

"And then what?" asked Daniel.

She didn't know. "We don't have time for me to run simulations. I couldn't even guess — "

"Forget it, Carter. What fun would it be without a surprise or two tucked inside the cereal box?" The general dumped his pack on the ground. "Daniel, head to the gate. Start dialing."

"Wait," Daniel said. "What?"

"But, sir!" She tried to catch his gaze, but he turned away, his focus on the dormant crystal.

"Not another word, Colonel. I'm going to do this."

No one moved. How could they? Leaving General O'Neill

behind just wasn't an option.

"Do I need to remind you both of why we're here?"

"There has to be another option."

"We don't have time for options, Carter."

In her eight years serving with SG-1, there'd always been time for options. "What if we — ?"

"Forget it, Carter." The general kept his back turned. "Daniel, get your ass in gear."

"Jack..."

"Just follow my orders, Daniel."

"I could do it, you know. I could stay behind. Even without the ATA gene, I should be able to... I mean, if the gate collapses, you could send word to the Tok'ra. Maybe the Asgard could pick me — "

"Get it through your skull, Daniel. I don't want your help."

Daniel jerked his head back, obviously stung by the general's words. "Fine." Swooping up his pack, he stormed toward the doorway.

"Dr. Jackson!" cried Huang.

Daniel stopped.

Huang held out the cup. "You will want this back."

"Keep it." He looked over at the general who still refused to turn around.

"See you on the other side," Sam said.

"Right." With a final nod, Daniel ran from the chamber.

Sam refused to give up as easily. "General, what if I — ?"

"Negative, Colonel." He shoved up his jacket sleeves and motioned for Huang to step up to the platform. At first, the old man didn't move, glancing back and forth between her and the general. She understood his confusion. She was pretty much feeling that way herself.

Huang looked down at the cup. "I am ready." He stepped up beside the general.

"This will be a snap." General O'Neill turned back toward the platform. "We're gonna pull this sucker out, Carter. Then the two of you will run like mad."

CHAPTER TWENTY-THREE

P3Y-702/KUNLUN/ELYSIUM PEDION
19 AUG 04/0700 HRS MCMURDO STATION
19 AUG 04/1400 HRS STARGATE COMMAND

"*I'M AT the gate*," Daniel radioed in. "*Dialing... Now.*"

The *kawoosh* sounded distorted, tinny. From Jack's position beside the platform, he could barely see the Stargate. It was too damn bright out there. A glint of sunlight off the distant hill had to serve as confirmation that the gate was active.

He thumbed his vest pocket radio. "Roger that. Carter will give you the head's up when they head for the gate. Standby."

"*Good luck, Jack.*"

"Yeah. You, too." He signed off.

Carter was staring at her watch again. "Five hours till sunrise at the outpost, sir."

For all of Skaara's fancy quantum talk about time, down here in the real world the clock kept ticking.

"Thank you, Colonel." He glanced at Huang. "Think you can double-time it out of here, old man?"

Huang placed his precious cup on the platform's edge. "I will do what is necessary."

He raised his chin with just a wee bit of indignation. Enough for Jack to be convinced they had a shot at doing what they'd come here to do.

"Carter, got your pack ready?"

"Ready." She held up her pack, unzipped and ready to go.

He flashed her a smile, until it occurred to him that it could be the last time he'd get to do that.

Which sucked.

You're stalling, O'Neill.

Huang bellied up to the platform. Jack couldn't help looking at the smudged sigil on his forehead — Lord Yu's stamp at its finest. Part of him wanted to ask why the old man had done it, why he'd almost gotten them all killed. Why it was so important to bother with that asinine mark.

Still stalling.

Huang lifted his hands. "I am ready."

Jack cleared his throat. Reached out toward the crystal. Skaara said this would be worse than the chair. Okay, fine. He could handle it.

"On my count," he told Huang. "One. Two — "

Huang jerked his hands back.

"Damnit, Huang. What is it now?"

"My Lord Yu." Huang turned his head toward the doorway. At first Jack thought he was looking at the active Stargate, but then he realized that wasn't it.

Huang was looking at the statue up on the hill. "He will never forgive me for helping you. He will hunt me down. He will murder my ex-wife."

For a moment, just one short moment, Jack found himself pitying the guy. "I told you, he won't do anything of the sort."

Huang turned toward him, stark desperation on his face. "You do not know that."

Jack snorted. "Actually, I do. Your buddy Yu and I had a nice chat after your little setup. Turns out he likes Earth, especially China. Go figure."

Huang's gaze slid down to the cup. "I did not know."

"Well, now you do." Jack rolled his shoulders. This hands-raised-in-the-air stuff was getting tiring. "Can we get on with it?"

Huang nodded and raised his hands. "To honor my crèche-brother, Lao Dan Shi."

Jack reached out toward the crystal. "One. Two. Three. Pull!" He grabbed hold and —

The city of Elysium Pedion flashed through his mind. Ancients gliding across walkways. Rooms filled with more of them, wearing long, beige lab coats. They tossed numbers and symbols through the air, as if playing catch with a baseball.

Jack shook the images from his head. Huang was tugging at the crystal right along with him. It wouldn't budge.

"Pull harder!"

A buzzing filled his ears.

"It will not come free!" Huang shouted back.

Jack slid a palm around the back of the crystal. Shoved it toward him. Pulled it upwards. Nothing.

He placed his other palm across the base.

Sunlight sucked out of the room in the blink of an eye. An electric shock sizzled his muscles, burned through his bones. Ate at his insides.

The world went dark.

Thump. Thump-thump.

ANCIENT OUTPOST, ANTARCTICA
19 AUG 04/0715 HRS MCMURDO STATION
19 AUG 04/1415 HRS STARGATE COMMAND

"*Wo jiang xie zia wo bao fu. Wo jiang bu hai pa.*"

Weiyan Shi rolled her head from side-to-side, her face contorted in pain despite the Tau'ri's narcotics. She mumbled the same words again and again, and while Teal'c knew ascension would free her from her current agony, the waiting was difficult to witness.

"*Wo jiang... Wo jiang.*"

"What is wrong with her?" asked Ambassador Zhu, her weariness shrouded in an implacable mask.

"I cannot say." He crouched beside mother and daughter, his legs cramped, his muscles weary.

"Cannot or will not?" Ambassador Zhu demanded. A half-choked sob escaped her lips.

He had asked the other SGC personnel to vacate the weapons chamber in respect. The ambassador's confrontational manner made him wish he'd done otherwise.

"*Bàbà*," Weiyan whispered. "*Wo jiang.*"

Ambassador Zhu's shoulders slumped.

"What is it she says?"

"She calls for her father." The ambassador frowned. "I am the one who is here. Why call for him? He has done nothing for her, nothing."

"*Wo jiang, Bàbà. Wo jiang.*" A great shudder ran through her. "*Wo jiang.*"

"What have I done?" Ambassador Zhu whispered.

A rattling reached Teal'c's ears from above. He glanced at the ladder permitting access to the outpost's main floor. The rungs shook.

Yet another tremor.

Fortunately, the vibrations subsided soon after they'd begun. The replacement of the control crystal could not come soon enough. Teal'c spared a moment to silently wish his comrades a quick success. For both their sake and that of Earth.

"*Wo jiang, Bàbà. Wo jiang.*"

"I have failed."

Teal'c returned his gaze to Ambassador Zhu, an eyebrow raised in question."Ambassador Zhu, you cannot fail as Weiyan Shi's mother. She is your child by birth, is that not so?"

"Of course she is." A defensive response, but Teal'c heard the truth in the woman's words.

"*Ni shi shui*?" Weiyan mumbled. "*Wo meng*?"

"Have you told her she is loved?"

"I—I have not." Sniffling, she raised her head and looked back at him. "Not for many years. When the doctors discovered she had hemophilia, that her needs would outstrip her abilities, I could not hide my disappointment."

A strained laugh erupted from her mouth. "Huang abandoned us before she was born, before the doctors presented their diagnosis. He left me alone to care for her. Alone to..."

She pressed her daughter's head to her chest.

It was then Teal'c understood. How could Weiyan Shi move

on if her mother would not allow her to do so? It had been Ambassador Zhu's harsh words that had caused her child to lose control in the weapons chair. Now, it was the mother's need to love her daughter that kept Weiyan Shi here.

"Tell her of your love," Teal'c commanded.

"I do not know how."

He thought of Rya'c, of the anger in his son's eyes upon the death of Drey'auc, his mother. The road to redemption between father and son had been difficult, but it had begun with one simple truth.

"Ask for forgiveness," he told Ambassador Zhu.

"*Muqin*?" Weiyan Shi's eyes opened. "Mother, don't leave me. I am sorry. I — Please, do not be angry."

"Shhhh, little one." Ambassador Zhu stroked her daughter's brow. "Of course I am here. There is no place I would rather be than with my child."

"...taken you from your duties. Ahhh," Weiyan Shi moaned, "Forgive me my fears."

Teal'c took her hand. "You need not fear, Weiyan Shi. A great journey awaits you."

"I will try, Teal'c."

"No, Weiyan Shi. You will not try. You will do."

"I will do." She squeezed his hand in return. "Mama?"

"I am here," replied Ambassador Zhu.

"Forgive us both," Weiyan rasped.

"Both?" The ambassador's eyes widened. "Weiyan, it is I who must seek your — "

"Father... Please forgive him, too."

Ambassador Zhu nodded. "*Duì bù qǐ. Yuánliàng.*"

A brief smile passed over Weiyan Shi's face. She released Teal'c's hand and raised it to touch her mother's face. "I love you, too, Mama."

Her eyes rolled back and she sagged. "*Wo jiang bu hai pa*," she whispered.

The ambassador translated. "I will not fear."

"*Wo jiang xie zia wo bao fu.*"

"I will release my burden."

"Now, Quing Zhu. You must let her go."

The ambassador began to back away, but he stopped her. "Not like that." He reached out and touched her shoulder. "Within you. Grant her what it is she needs to depart."

Ambassador Zhu bent down and whispered into Weiyan Shi's ear, "I will always love you, child of my heart."

A great sigh escaped Weiyan's lips. For a moment, she lay still, and then said, "*Wo jiang xie xia wo de bao fu.*"

"I will release my burden," Ambassador Zhu repeated.

"*Wo jiang bu hai pa. Wo jing zou jin guang mang.*"

"I will not fear. I will go into the light."

Weiyan's hands dropped to her sides, her death apparent.

"Is that it?" Ambassador Zhu demanded. "You promised— "

"Wait."

A pure white radiant blaze of light rushed upwards from Weiyan Shi's body. Though Teal'c had seen the process of ascension twice before, he could not help but bow his head in reverence.

"She is beautiful!" exclaimed Ambassador Zhu.

Teal'c lifted his head to gaze upon the light. The glowing form hovered above them, energy surging within its nebulous mass. Two tendrils unfurled from within its center, one extending to the ambassador, the other toward him.

"Goodbye, Weiyan Shi," he whispered.

The tendrils pulled back. "Live well, Teal'c."

She shot upwards through the ceiling and disappeared.

PLANET DESIGNATION: UNKNOWN
STATUS: UNKNOWN
TIME: UNKNOWN...UNKNOWN...UNKNOWN...

He stumbled across darkness, through a rippling pool, and out into a pool of white light.

Where the hell was he, for crying out loud?

He squeezed his eyes shut. That begged a larger question.

Who the hell was he? For the life of him, he couldn't remember his name.

Thump. Thump-thump.

Eyes closed, he felt warmth. Clean air. Complete stillness. No sounds of animals or civilization, just lapping water. Directly behind him. He opened his eyes. It was too bright to see much of anything.

He whirled around, coming face-to-face with a vertical stone ring at least three times his height. The ring loomed over him, its center filled with a bluish puddle of water.

He found the massive thing familiar. Almost comforting in an odd sort of way.

As if he and the ring were old friends.

Thump. Thump-thump.

He'd been here before.

Thump. Thump-thump.

He knew that sound.

Thump.

He knew his name. He remembered what had happened.

Jack turned his back on the Stargate. Peered into the overbright white world around him.

The crystal. He'd pulled it and now…

Thump. Thump-thump. Thump-thump.

His heart pounded in his chest. He got it. Why did it have to be so frigging loud?

He raised an arm, expecting to find the crystal in his hand. Instead, a glowing-white strand wavered into view. He raised his other arm. Another shimmering strand floated up.

He glanced down at his body. No boots. No legs.

Thump-thump.

No nothing.

"Crap." Something must've gone wrong. When he'd pulled the crystal, he must've gotten himself killed.

He groaned. "Please don't tell me I've ascended."

Waving his hands in front of his face did squat. More strands slithered back and forth. Like a bunch of ribbons blowing in the breeze.

Bright, shiny ribbons. Almost mesmerizing.

Almost peaceful.

Thump. Thump-thump.

Would ascension be so bad?

No more casualty reports. No more sending good men and women to their deaths. No more sitting back and feeling useless while those same men and women became nothing more than a line on a piece of paper.

If he'd ascended, maybe he could finish what Daniel had set out to do. Maybe he could go kick some Goa'uld butt. Wipe them out before Oma and her gang caught up with him.

Keep Earth safe.

Thump. Thump-thump.

Hell, maybe he'd give himself that peace of mind he always wanted.

"Is this what you truly wish, O'Neill? To ascend?"

Jack recognized the voice. "Skaara?"

Another cluster of ribbony strands blossomed from out of nowhere. The strands darkened. Solidified.

Skaara gazed at him, patiently. Calm. For all the kid's youth before he'd taken a walk on the Oma-side, it was Jack who suddenly felt very young. And very foolish.

Thump. Thump-thump.

Skaara's white robes flapped in a breeze Jack couldn't feel.

Wait a moment.

Jack glanced down at where his body should've been. With relief, he took in the sight of his green BDUs, his black t-shirt, his black boots.

"That's funny," he said. "I could've sworn I wore camo when I got here."

Skaara raised an eyebrow.

Jack explained. "You know, beige and tan camouflage. Nice

way to blend in with the sand and all that."

"Blend in." Skaara gestured toward Jack's green BDUs. "This is how you see yourself."

Jack shrugged. "I always said they'd bury me in my BDUs."

"You are not dead, O'Neill."

"Yeah, I didn't think as much." His eyes rested on the Stargate, its event horizon thwaping against the ring's stony sides. "But this is it, right? I'm gonna ascend?"

"If that is your wish. What about Earth?"

That was the first thing he'd take care of. Quick jaunt to Antarctica. Shut down that device before it ripped his favorite planet in two, then onward and upward.

Watch out, you slimy Goa'uld bastards, I'm coming.

"How about an orientation tour?" he asked Skaara.

"Ascended, you will see the universe, but, O'Neill," Skaara stepped closer, "you cannot interfere. You can do nothing." He tilted his head. "But that is not who you are."

Thump. Thump-thump.

"I don't know, Skaara. Maybe..." He sighed. "Maybe I— "

Thwap.

A human strode through the gate. It was Huang— Sorta. The old man looked younger, more like when Jack first met him. His black hair had grown back in. His beard was neat, trimmed. Barely gray. He wore classic Jaffa armor, a gray cloak hanging from his left shoulder. A jade pin shaped like a dragon held the cloak in place.

And on his forehead was Lord Yu's sigil etched in gold. Just like a First Prime.

Thump. Thump-thump.

Huang glanced at Skaara. "You. I recognize you."

Skaara dipped his head in greeting. "It is good to see you again, Huang Sun Tzu."

Sun Tzu? It took a moment for Jack to remember this guy was a clone. A copy. A several thousand year-old Xerox of the real McCoy.

Huang peered into the void. He inhaled deeply. "There is a tranquility here. A solace I have not felt for many years. Not since…"

"Antarctica?" Skaara stepped up beside Jack.

Huang turned to face them. As he did, the lines on his face smoothed out. Within moments, Jack realized he was looking at a younger, maybe twenty year-old version of Huang.

"I was not happy in Antarctica, but, I came to understand its power. Nature unbridled. Free from expectation. Hope. The land's nature was relentless. Unforgiving, and yet, it was honest. Truthful."

Thump. Thump-thump.

Huang ran a finger along the gold brand on his forehead. "At the time, I did not recognize that truth."

Jack scowled. "What would you know about truth? Your lies almost got my people killed — "

"O'Neill," warned Skaara. "To ascend requires giving up one's burdens. Make peace with your past. Let it go."

Let it go. Jack dropped his head. Could he do that? For the first time in a long while, he didn't know what to do. Usually, he'd just go by his gut. Do the right thing. But now? Could he let Daniel, Carter, and Teal'c just die? Let Earth suffer?

Thump. Thump-thump.

A hand squeezed his shoulder. Huang. "'Great is the hero who would die for their country, but would much rather live.'"

Jack sighed. He was tired of all the quotes, all the brouhaha of burdens. Of letting go.

Thump. Thump-thump.

He was worn out, period.

"Can we bypass the speeches and just move things along?" He needed to get to Earth. Try and stop that device before things got any worse.

"Sun Tzu's quote was meant for you, O'Neill." Huang dropped his hand from Jack's shoulder. "It is you who must promise to heed his words. You must live. Lead. If not for yourself, then for others.

"I was never meant to do so." Huang bowed toward the waiting Skaara. "I was never really meant to be."

Calm settled over the man's face. A calm Jack envied.

"So that's it," Jack said, surprised at how bitter his words sounded. "I'm supposed to go back there, grab the crystal and then just leave you behind? Well, what if I want to be the one left behind? What if—?" He turned away, disgusted. Not with them. With himself. He was so tired. Tired of losing. Tired of winning.

Tired of fighting.

Clink. Snap. Clink. Snap.

"Still playing with the Zippo, Skaara?"

"Do you want it back, O'Neill?"

"No." Jack kept his gaze on the void ahead of him. "I told you years ago, keep it. It's yours."

"And yet, you were drawn to retrieve the lighter when I left." Clink. Snap.

"I don't know, Skaara. Maybe... Maybe I just hated to see it go to waste."

"Do you know why?"

Jack turned back around to face his old friend. Huang was gone. "Because I couldn't let go."

Skaara held out the lighter. "Hold on to your life, O'Neill. I promise, it will be worth living. For you, and the many you will touch."

"If you say so." Jack had heard the same rhetoric from Skaara before, mere hours after Abydos and everyone on it had ascended.

"You do not believe me?" Skaara held out the lighter.

Thump. Thump-thump.

"Then believe in yourself."

Jack took the lighter. In the white light of the void, it felt solid. Real. A bit of metal and flint that had become an anchor in his upside-down life.

He wrapped his fingers around the metal casing.

The void went black.

P3Y-702/KUNLUN/ELYSIUM PEDION
19 AUG 04/0720 HRS MCMURDO STATION
19 AUG 04/1420 HRS STARGATE COMMAND

There was no sound. No movement. No change.

The platform's translucent panels stayed fixed in a constant blue. If it wasn't for the breeze blowing across Sam's neck, she'd swear she was looking at a photograph. General O'Neill and Huang appeared frozen, their hands wrapped around the control crystal, their knuckles white as if in some sort of death grip.

In the past five minutes, neither man had moved. From where she stood by the doorway, it didn't even look like they were breathing. In between their hands, she could see the control crystal emit a steady red glow.

That could be a good or bad. She had no way of knowing. Her scanner wasn't of any use, the needle unmoving from its basically neutral position.

The breeze picked up. Hot air blew through the chamber, sending sand and dirt in a swirl across the silver and marble floor. She checked her watch again. Ten minutes.

"Sir?"

General O'Neill didn't even blink.

"General!"

Nothing.

The crystal was active. Their job was done.

Why wasn't there any seismic activity, and more importantly, why weren't they moving?

She waved a hand in front of the general's face. He didn't flinch.

The needle wobbled.

"General?"

The needle pinged. Hard and to the right.

"Huang?"

Beneath Sam's boots, she felt a low rumble. Getting louder and stronger by the moment.

A column crashed behind the platform.

The men remained frozen. Almost as if they were in the grips of some sort of stasis.

Another column crashed. Pulverized stone and a millennium of dust sprayed across the chamber.

Should she pull them off the crystal? Shake them awake?

Sam hesitated, knowing she had to do something and do it fast, but the question was what? The wrong move could crack the ground open, swallow the gate, and leave them stranded.

And Earth still in trouble.

The tremor grew stronger. Debris and stone dust rained down from the ceiling.

She could leave now, bug out before the gate was lost. Maybe find another way to stop the terra-forming device in Antarctica. She looked at General O'Neill and wondered, could she do that? Could she leave him behind?

"You said to trust my gut." She grabbed his arm and pulled.

Nothing.

"Jack!"

His elbow jerked. She stumbled backwards from the sudden movement.

"Carter?" He turned toward her, the crystal in his hands.

"Sir! The bracket." She climbed to her feet and ran around the platform to face him.

Huang shoved the general aside. "Hurry, O'Neill." He plunged his left hand into the bracket.

The shaking subsided. While she could still feel it beneath her, the earlier roar had lessened to a sound like distant thunder.

"I don't understand," she told the general. "I thought — "

"Leave!" Huang insisted.

"Sir?"

General O'Neill kept his gaze on Huang. "It's what he wants."

"Do not lie, O'Neill. It is what we both want." He bent over the platform, his face twisted in pain.

A thin stream of light erupted from his back. Huang shot back up and Sam gasped.

The man's face was covered in dozens of light particles swimming across his skin. The particles expanded. Moved down through his arms, his chest, his legs.

"His body's de-molecularizing," she said in awe. "Breaking down to the quantum level right before our eyes."

"We have to go, Carter." General O'Neill grabbed his pack from the ground and stuffed the crystal inside.

Sam looked again at Huang — or what was left of him. Most of his body was covered in agitated light particles, swarming around each other in a state of flux. All she could see was his left arm shoved down in the bracket, a corner of his mouth, a bit of forehead still covered in dirt. His brown eyes widened, not in fear, but in astonishment.

The general slung the pack over his shoulder and swooped up his P90. He ran for the doorway. "Now, Carter!"

Sam broke eye contact and raced after the general.

"O'Neill!" Huang shouted.

He stopped at the doorway.

"Do not break your promise!"

Sam whirled toward General O'Neill, his haggard face giving her no clue as to what Huang meant. He glanced at Huang and then back at Sam.

"Sir?"

"Come on, Carter. Let's go home."

Within the darkness sparked a single flame. A candle's light never meant to shine upon the shores of man.

Between one moment and the next, another current winnowed across the ever-present stream. He had returned, his youthful energy sending ripples across dimensions she'd yet to share.

And share she would. She knew now that his yearning for companionship had nearly caused yet another tear in the fabric.

An unanchored boat will only drift.

His return meant yet another repair accomplished beyond

the Others' view. If they discovered what had been done, she would be banished, having broken their highest law. Interference in the lower planes was forbidden.

Even if much of what occurred had been their doing.

Or lack thereof.

"Are things as they should be?" she asked.

"See for yourself," Skaara answered.

Galaxies were born. Suns imploded. Black holes plunged into nothing.

A new flame burst into being. "Weiyan?"

And then another. "Father?"

Joy. Rapture. Twin comets streaked beyond a nebula. They became one. Broke apart and spiraled beyond a moon.

Soon she must teach them both what it meant to be ascended, but for now… For now she would allow father and daughter this moment of reunion.

"And the device?" she asked Skaara. "You are certain?"

"He will do the right thing, Oma. He always does."

MARBLE POINT AIRSTRIP, ANTARCTICA
19 AUG 04/1130 HRS MCMURDO STATION

Daniel sat in the rear of the chopper with Jack and Sam, fighting back a yawn. They took off from Marble Point and headed for the outpost. A golden-yellow smudge appeared on the horizon, the first signs of sunrise's imminent approach. Jack and Sam looked equally worn out. Especially Jack. He kept his eyes front, his mouth shut, the pack containing the crystal secured to his lap.

Whatever had happened on P3Y-702, Jack wasn't talking about it. Not even to Sam. Once they'd returned through the gate, and ridden to Petersen, Daniel had offered to fly back with Jack so he'd have someone to talk to. Someone to help him work through why Huang had stayed behind instead.

Jack had insisted Daniel fly with Sam. As the F-302 flew south, she'd explained to Daniel what she'd seen, but even she had no idea why Huang had stayed. And while her description of Huang's de-molecularization sounded extraordinary, Daniel had no way to know what it meant.

The smudge on the horizon spread, becoming a thin line of yellow against the gray predawn. He checked his watch. Thirty-five minutes till sunrise. "We're sure this is going to work?"

"If Skaara says it will," Jack said, "then it will."

"Okay." Daniel knew Jack could be blunt when the need arose. "I'd like to stay for a few weeks, see if there are any inscriptions around the device."

Sam grinned. "I'd like to as well, sir. The technology might come in handy in — "

"Will it help us fight the Goa'uld?"

"I don't how, sir, but I'd like to think we could figure out a way to harness its abilities for use on Earth."

"Can you copy the Ancients' doohickeys on your own?"

Sam's eyes widened. "No, sir. That would require a level of skill that — "

"Daniel, don't you have a treaty to sort out?"

"Paul Davis can work that out." Daniel gestured toward the bag in Jack's lap. "What you're carrying there, and how that platform fits into what happened to the Ancients, don't you think it's worth — ?"

"I'm tired of thinking." Jack closed his eyes.

ANCIENT OUTPOST, ANTARCTICA
19 AUG 04/1140 HRS MCMURDO STATION

Daniel groaned when he heard they'd have to take the emergency stairs down to the outpost. It made sense, given the ongoing tremors, but still…

Halfway down the spiral staircase, Daniel quit complaining. Another tremor hit. The steps shook, chunks of ice plummeting down on their heads. He stopped, gripped the railing, and prayed it would be over soon.

Jack didn't say a word, he just kept going. Jumping over

fallen ice, taking two steps at a time. One hand on the railing, Daniel followed with Sam bringing up the rear. Jack's single-mindedness had its advantages, Daniel knew that, but it had gotten them into as much trouble as out of it in the past. He wasn't sure his friend's determination would be enough to command the SGC for the long haul. Especially if Jack seemed so miserable doing it.

The quake ceased as they hit the bottom floor. Jack kicked open the door. General Hammond stood beside the stasis unit that had once held Jack in its grip. Ancient repositories, Goa'uld sarcophagi, stasis units… For all the insight gained from these unimaginable technologies, Daniel couldn't deny the cost.

Especially for Jack.

"Welcome back, SG-1." General Hammond turned toward Jack with a wary smile. "You ready, son?"

Jack unzipped the pack and pulled out the crystal. "Ready isn't quite the word, sir." He tossed the pack at Sam and bolted through the archway. She raced in after him.

Daniel hurried over to Hammond. "Weiyan?"

"She's gone, son." The general gestured for him to follow. "And I can't say if it's a good thing or a bad one."

Another tremor shook the room.

Sam had gotten to the ladder first. Teal'c joined her in holding the rungs as Jack swung on, one hand holding the crystal against his side.

"Daniel! Get your ass over here and help me out."

Running into the chamber, Daniel got a glimpse of Paul Davis and Bill Lee off to one side. Ambassador Zhu stood between them, a fleece pullover pressed to her chest.

Weiyan's pullover.

Knowing there wasn't time for condolences, Daniel gave Zhu a quick nod and slid down the ladder to the terra-forming platform below. The force field hugged the walls, undulating as if it were welcoming them back. The crystal cradled under one arm, Jack swept away a good foot of snow piled over the brackets. Daniel joined him, clearing the central red bracket of any debris.

"Fifteen minutes, sir," came Sam's warning from up top.

"Right." Jack stepped in front of the red bracket, his face screwed up in concentration. He raised the crystal and—

The ground shook, sending a spray of ice and dirt down from the hole's edges. A chunk fell on Daniel, hard. He pressed a hand to his head.

"You all right?" Jack asked.

"Am I all right?" Daniel pulled away his hand. "Shouldn't you, you know...?"

Jack glanced at the crystal. "Yeah. I should." He lowered the crystal into the bracket.

The platform lit up, its blue panels thrumming loudly. Like the sound of a heartbeat, Daniel realized.

The quake stopped.

Daniel blew out a long breath. "Well, that's— "

Jack's hands were still on the crystal.

"The tremor's stopped. You can let go now."

"Exactly." Jack closed his eyes, his hands splayed across the crystal's top-most facet.

"Jack?"

The crystal lit up, its glow casting a red light across Jack's face. The thrum became louder, quicker. A racing thump loud enough to echo through the room.

"That's enough," Jack mumbled. He slid his hands down the sides of the crystal and sparks flew from the platform. Daniel jumped back, but Jack held on, his brow creased, his eyes squeezed shut. The light within the crystal turned darker red.

"What are you doing?"

The thrumming stopped. The illuminated panels dimmed and then went dark. The only light left was from above.

Jack stepped away from the platform, sweat running down his forehead. "It's dead, Daniel. Finished. No more threats to Earth."

"What? It's not that simple. You heard Sam." The charred crystal remains collapsed into dust. Stunned, he whirled around. "We could've learned how to harness its energy. We could've learned how to — "

"And risk ending up just like those dead and gone Ancients?" Jack ran a forearm across his wet forehead. "If you don't mind, I'd like to live a little longer."

CODA

FERRAR GLACIER, ANTARCTICA
19 AUG 04/1335 HRS MCMURDO STATION

SUNLIGHT peeked out from behind a patch of clouds as Jack hiked past the waiting chopper. Though he'd donned a wool cap along with the rest of his cold-weather gear, his parka hood was down. The cold air felt good nicking at his skin, keeping him from feeling completely numb and worn out.

He reached the rocky promontory beyond the chopper pad and looked out over the valley below. The crunch of footsteps behind him was no surprise. No doubt his former teammates had decided to come along for the show, short as it might be.

Looking out over the Ferrar Glacier, he took in the rugged white valley, surrounding cliffs, the deep crevasses that looked like someone had squeezed blue gel toothpaste onto the snow. Somehow, Huang had survived all this. Maybe Skaara had helped, but Jack suspected the clone's basic cussedness had more to do with it than anything else. Cussedness and maybe something else. Something everyone needed.

Faith.

In Huang's case, that faith had been sorely misplaced.

In Jack's case, it was about finding that faith in himself.

He grinned. He could do that.

"O'Neill." Teal'c's parka hood was zipped up tight enough that Jack couldn't see half his face.

"I thought you hated cold weather."

Teal'c turned toward the sun, its zenith past and gone. "Upon our return to the SGC, I would like to visit my son. He is with Ishta and the Hak'tyl."

"Warmer climate on that planet, I suppose?"

"Indeed."

"Wow." Daniel stopped beside him with Carter.

"Bring back memories, Carter?" He knew this had been her first view of Antarctica years ago when they'd been flung from the previously unknown gate into what they thought was an ice planet.

"Lots of memories, sir. Not all of them bad." Her eyes crinkled. Underneath all that fleece and polyester, Jack was sure she was grinning. That was Carter. Always up for a challenge.

"...Zhu's agreed to revisit the treaty," Davis said, matching strides with Hammond as they headed over.

"Considering all she's been through," Hammond said, "I'd take that as a win, Major."

"I think so, too, sir."

The two came up on Jack's other side. He gave them each a nod and turned his attention back to watching the sun peek in and out of the clouds.

"First day of sun for the year," Carter said. "It's supposed to last an hour and thirty-nine minutes. Should set in another eight — "

"Ack!" Jack said, waving a glove-covered hand. "Don't ruin it. Just watch. Enjoy."

"Sir?"

"When's the last time we just watched the sun set, Carter?"

The group settled down and Jack let the peace and quiet wash over him. That was the best part about so much snow. It made everything quieter. Newer.

Simpler.

"General Hammond?" Davis asked.

Jack stopped himself from groaning out loud. If he wanted peace and quiet, there was always the cabin.

"Sir," Davis said, "About that promotion — "

"Promotion?" Jack congratulated the major. "About time, Davis. We were starting to — "

"Actually, General — Generals, I mean — " Davis shoved

his gloved hands in his pockets. "I think I can do more good at my present rank. I know I'm not critical to the SGC, but I'd like to think I've done my part. Both with the treaty, and, well..." He shrugged.

Jack had heard about Davis' little brainstorm getting the F-302s out of the ice. "If I may, General, I'm with Davis. If he's happy, how about letting those forced promotion regulations slide for once?"

Hammond nodded. "Happy and helpful. Can't ask for more than that, I suppose. I'll notify the Secretary of the Air Force. I'm sure special dispensation can be granted. For now."

The world back on its keel, Jack turned toward the glacier. "Out of curiosity, General, how'd you get China to release Huang into our custody?"

A muffled sigh escaped Hammond's extra-extra large parka. "The president promised to consider giving them the plans to the F-302."

"Great." Jack remembered Ambassador Chen's admiring the bird during his brief visit. There'd definitely been something downright paternalistic about the way the guy had stroked its underbelly. "Good luck with that."

Carter frowned. "What about the 303, sir?"

"They want the plans to that as well."

"They're gonna build their own 303?" Jack watched the sun dip lower in the sky. "With what resources?"

Hammond grunted. "Remember, the president hasn't agreed yet. He's just said he'll consider their request. As far as resources are concerned, I'll leave that problem up to my successor."

Successor? Jack felt his eyebrows shoot up into his scalp. "General, is there something you've neglected to tell us?"

"I hear tell that there's a great fishing spot in Maryland, just some forty minutes from the Pentagon." Hammond slapped him on the back. "If you'll excuse me, I'm going to head over to McMurdo and help coordinate the relief effort. Davis?"

Jack did a double take as Hammond trudged off toward the

chopper with Davis in tow.

Fishing. In Maryland.

He turned back toward the valley, the darkening sky turning the white snow to a soft gray. A sparse slice of the sun hung just above a mountain off in the distance. A moment later, a bit of smoke wafted upwards. Jack realized it wasn't just any mountain he was looking at, it was Mt. Erebus.

"If the Chinese do build a 303," Carter said, "I wonder what they'll call it."

"The *Sun Tzu*'s a good name."

As the sun dropped behind the volcano, a breeze picked up. Cold. Bracing.

Jack pulled up his hood.

Yep. It was good to be alive.

THANKS TO

The Polar Star's fine crew & expedition team for opening my eyes to the wonders of Antarctica. Special thanks to Danny Edmunds, Hannah Lawson, and Pierre & Wendy Malan--all who went beyond the call of duty to answer even my most outrageous of questions about the fragile continent's magnificence.

Carey Adams, Mark Biggs, and all of Missouri State University. Their encouragement allowed me to help the reader experience the coldest, driest, and yet most powerful place on Earth.

Jen Brooks, Laura Gerling, Rhonda Mason, and Susannah Sinard whose support and feedback kept my hand securely on the tiller.

Sally Malcolm and Tom Reeve for their belief in this project.

David Read, Lindsey Allen, Marian Trupiano, Kristin Muzina, and Maureen Bensa for sharing my exuberance for this much loved franchise.

Capt. Angela Webb and the United States Air Force for their technical advice and steadfast dedication to our country.

Joy Anne Baker whose Stargate Glyph font set came in super handy in completing this project. And a special thanks to the real-world Weiyan who provided the Chinese translations.

Gateworld.net for providing the ultimate guide to all

things Stargate and for their continued friendship.

The cast & crew of SG-1 — especially Joel Goldsmith whose music lives on in the hearts of all Stargate fans.

To my family, for their patience with my obsessive need to explore the bottom of the world.

The great polar explorers Roald Amundsen, Robert F. Scott, and Ernest Shackleton whose Herculean efforts to reach the 'the end of the axis upon which this great round ball turns' continue to inform and inspire humanity at every turn.

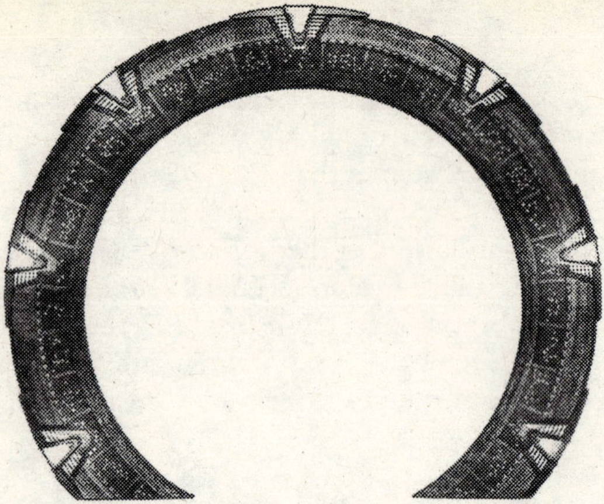